NICK SNAPE

A DRAGON OF THE VEIL

WARRIORS OF SPIRIT AND BONE BOOK ONE

For Dad
I hope I made you proud
Miss you

BRANDSHOLD

HANDREN MOUNTAINS

ANVIL

PARTERA PLAIN

JENSE

RUSHOLME

DENT

FARNFORD

ERSTENBURGH

MAKALENA

RIDTH

SOUTHERN REACHES

MERES PORT

VALLEY OF THE UNSPOKEN

KHUND

Karak

PANTSIL

ISLES OF TEES

ISLE OF MERES

SHELBY

PROLOGUE

A Time Before Dying

Handren Mountains

The pebble rolled and fear gripped. Laoch's green eyes catching its slow momentum along the mountain path. The tiny stone picked up pace, bouncing from protruding rocks to clumps of sprouting grass. Heart in mouth, and kneeling lower, he pressed one leg against the narrow path, the other into the bitterly cold rock face. Laoch then shifted his neck, straining to peer around the curved corner where the path disappeared.

Nothing. But it's never bloody nothing with these bastards.

A dark green Ranger's cloak shrouded his leading shoulder. Holding a bow in his weaker left hand and with his back to the ledge, he sensed the rest of his Spear rise behind him as he signalled. With arrow nocked, taking slow breaths to calm the mild shake in his shoulders, he stepped out from under the angled ledge. The guide walking behind him was a Handren, with Laoch convinced she was part sure-footed mountain goat. The path was treacherous, and of all the ways to the forest plateau, he was beginning to regret her choice, casting one nervous eye towards the windswept edge as they rounded the curve.

She probably regards it as being as wide as the Queen's Road.

Green-laden branches wafted in the breeze, their tips bending in response to the billowing gusts. Laoch's inner voice reminded him they were perched a few hundred yards above a rock-strewn ravine with nothing but the valley's mist between him and a shattered corpse. As he edged closer, a sliver of the moon peeked out from the clouds. In the pale moonlight, he could see that the rocky ledge widened out ahead of him, ending in a tumble of scree that led up to the forest edge.

"See," Delish whispered, pointing to the base of the small scree pile, her other hand upon his cloaked shoulder. "Many don't know this way. The path is unseen from above. Only the Handren."

"Aye, but the Unbelievers are devious bastards as your people already know. Stay sharp and pass the word down the line." Laoch, cheeks smothered in green moss residue, hands gloved and with equipment swaddled in soft cloth and leather, signalled her back, turning to search the slope for the quietest route.

Delish got us here, but I can't let her lead us in—we need her safe if we have to run.

A gentle tap let him know they were ready. His Spear of six plus Delish—a raiding party by nature—were fully aware of what came next. Usually, they were skirmishers, primed to harass an army's supply routes, often hitting the Unbelievers' reserves and command posts before melting back into the woods or mountains. Therefore, the perfect choice for a rescue mission.

But they'll know we're coming, just not this soon.

Laoch chose his route, and with a last glance to the top of the scree, scuttled across the grass and shingle marking the start of the slope. His first step up greeted by a gentle patter of rolling scree, he risked another, soon winding a path back and forth to minimise the chance of starting a full cascade. He paused halfway, signalling Delish to send the first of the Spear. Grimacing as his brother, Láidir, started upwards, he carried on to reach the apex of the slope, gently kneeling before laying flat, staring out into the murk of the forest edge. Despite the wind, the inner trees merely rippled, shielded from its gusts by a protruding ledge. Still and quiet. Just the odd hoot and response of owls echoing through. Laoch, relieved, doubted much of the moon's light would penetrate the dense forest as it rose.

Láidir dropped to the floor next to him, his Ranger's cloak covering a silenced sheath. With his bow laid flat and an arrow nocked, he nodded towards the trees. Laoch shook his head and signalled all-clear, glancing back to check the rest were making near silent progress. He eased up his scarf to cover nose and mouth, then knelt, indicating Láidir to guard. His brother tugged at his own scarf before rising to one knee with eyes intent on the forest. Moving from tree to tree, crouched and edging his way deeper into the woods, Laoch caught the gentle scent of smoke and cooking meat. He checked the air's drift between the leaf-filled branches, and judging the aroma's direction, slid a mottled boot knife out to scrape a Ranger's mark low on the nearest trunk. Pointing towards his first marker, he looked back to ensure Láidir had seen it. Only then did he move on, a keen nose and the tang upon his tongue guiding him.

With soft-soled boots treading lightly amid the twigs an unease crept over him as he went deeper, a shift in mood that hung over the forest. Laoch's skin tingled with a familiar warning of wrongness, one that had kept him alive this long during the Crusade. He paused, scanning the woods, a flicker of distant orange and yellow backlit the trees as the branches shifted. Amid the streams of occasional light, he picked out the curve of a furred hat with its ear flaps drooped low.

Good. Shame he has the sense to be looking away from the fire behind.

Notching another mark, Laoch then crept to his right, eyes on the guard until a tree masked his position, and waited. Within a few minutes, Láidir reached his second mark, glancing his way, before sidling over, crab-like in the strange way he'd adopted since taking a quarrel to his thigh four months back. Hunkering down, the Ranger knew what came next.

"I'll skirt around. Stay here, only engage if you're spotted." Laoch's kept his muffled words as low and distinct as he could, adding well-practised hand signals.

"And the Captain?"

Laoch sighed, admonishing himself as the warm air pushed through the scarf, coalescing into a small cloud. "If you feel he is threatened—and only if. Otherwise wait for my return." He tapped his brother's leg. "No heroics, you daft bastard."

"If I'm a bastard ..." Láidir left it hanging, Laoch knowing there'd be a beaming smile behind that moss-streaked scarf.

"Hah," Laoch clapped him on the leg again and headed around the assumed edge of the Unbelievers' camp. Peering ahead, seeking the next guard, dragon's breath rose unheeded, and Laoch traced it back to a head and nose poking out from beneath a tree. The man's gloved hands clamped together as he exhaled another rasping plume. Keeping his distance, he moved each time the guard stomped his feet and squeezed cold fingers. Laoch soon reached the far side of the encampment, the breeze carrying no scent of me—

Eh?

Laoch dropped, feeling a tug at his mind. A familiar scent lay on the wind, one he couldn't initially place. Sweet, yet retaining a soured tang. Not fruit, nor the musk of a wood.

Rum.

The wrongness set his mind reeling. He looked over his shoulder, back out into the dark of the forest.

A second ring of guards? Did I miss them?

His stomach churned, with his bow hand pulsing as he pushed down his frustration. Laoch kept the composite weapon ahead of him, the arrow tip as dulled as the rest of their equipment. Three slow paces brought the sweetness wafting, and he eased his head low around the base of a tree trunk. A clump of bushes partially masked a pile of furs strewn with leaves and twigs ten yards away. A hand protruding from the lump shook an unstoppered bottle, the gentle splash of a heavy liquid forcing more of its scent into the air.

"Bloody 'ell." The words were slurred, and the pile shifted, a face sliding from beneath a skin to peer into the bottle before moving it to his mouth. Drunk or not, the man's glance caught Laoch's eye, the bottle pressed against lips shaking as the arrow slammed through one side to ram deep into his throat. Laoch ran. Soft boots whispering across the divide, driving the boot knife into the guard's neck, his other hand pressed upon the rum-tainted mouth. Blood spurted, the Ranger ripping the knife clear to silence the Unbeliever forever.

Dropping, he scanned the woods before heading back to collect his bow when a low moan rose from the earth behind him. Laoch spun and took a defensive stance, his bloodied knife in hand, only for the groan to rumble once again. Blinking, he stepped closer, the soft sound choked by a half-sob. Dread ran up Laoch's spine, joining a churning stomach as he approached the mound, expecting to find a guard or lover deep within the warming fur. With knife ready, he pulled at each skin, exposing the next one by one until only a metal grate remained. A yard across, the struts were bonded in a way he'd never seen before. The stones beneath formed a circle and from the void in the ring's centre a stink rose—pungent with human sweat, blood and faeces.

No.

Laoch's dread rose, caught between going back or releasing those below. Was it a trap? Perhaps leading them in while the prize was elsewhere? Or standard practice for a people with such little regard for the Seven?

Halfway between each thought, he dropped the furs around the edge of the pit, using them to muffle any sound as he slid the two retaining bolts back to release the grate. Lifting it clear and placing it aside, he prayed to Hope before speaking.

"Captain," he whispered, the sound hardly penetrating the dark. "Rakslin?"

A moan, high-pitched, half-panicked, arose, Laoch repeating the name. A hand appeared from the black. Bloodied and mud-caked fingers gripped the stone's side, soon followed by a pained face. The Captain's dried tongue failed to form words, Laoch taking the ache in the man's eyes as agreement. He took the hand in his, ignoring the winces, and pulled the man up and free of the hole. The smell hit him hard. A waft of cold, burned meat and shit striking at his senses. Laoch lowered him to the floor, raising a finger for quiet when a second hand emerged from the pit, beseeching.

"How many?" asked Laoch, fearing the answer.

Rakslin held up his other hand, four fingers raised. Swallowing, the Ranger turned back, grasping the filthy arm and lifting. An agonised moan echoed back, piercing the night, bouncing from tree to tree—and a shout arose from the camp's direction.

"No." Drawing the tortured man up, Laoch eased him to the floor, heart surging as the noise from the camp heightened. Knowing full well how Láidir would respond, his brother likely assuming Laoch had been caught or spotted, wouldn't hold back. "Seven bloody hells." Angry, he reached for the next, a dirty arm grasping his leg from behind.

"Let me." The captain's dry words scraped Laoch's nerves, but he nodded back to Rakslin, helping him to kneel next to the hole and dropping a thin rope in case it might help. Spinning, he ran, and grabbed his bow from the tree where he'd dropped it, nocking an arrow on the move. Closing in on the screams and shouts, a fearful smell emanated from the maelstrom of light and shadow of a supposedly panicked camp. He heard Láidir's bellowed signal, a second round of arrows slamming into the melee. An Unbeliever guard, half-turned towards the camp, came into view. Laoch's arrow on the run struck his shoulder, blunting against the metal plate sewn in there. The woman turned with sword half-drawn when his second arrow drove into her cheek, smashing bone and penetrating nose cartilage. Falling, she screamed, only for Laoch's boot knife to put it to an end. And then it hit. A wave of heat, flames rising. The tang of alchemical fire washing over Laoch in a rush, knocking him from his feet. With cloak smoking amid the acrid ash, he pulled himself up using a low branch, to be greeted by a wall of orange fire pulsating where the camp had been. Delish ran towards him, eyes wild and hair alight, her exposed skin along one arm bubbling. Unseeing—fear and pain written upon her body—she careered past only for Laoch to grab her leg, pulling the mountain woman to the ground. He clambered over her, rolling Delish onto her back and wrapped his cloak about her arm. Her eyes began to focus, though pain warped her twisted lips. Seeing Laoch, she raised her other hand, touching his cheek. "Láidir," was all she said.

Laoch dragged her up, hating himself but grabbing the woman's face in his hands. "The Captain is back there, understand? Yes? Answer!"

Delish nodded, blinking back ash-stained tears.

"Get him out, yes? Take him and go. Whatever happens, he is your priority. Are you with me, Delish?"

"Yes. The Captain. Laoch ..."

"No." He pushed her in the direction of their priority, the mission. Whatever was back in the camp was a price already paid. With a last glance, he nocked an arrow, holding three more between his fingers as he spun and ran into the fury of flame and smoke.

Emerging into the ash-covered clearing, tents roared with chemical flame. Laoch winced as horses screamed. Banefire stuck to their flanks, cooking flesh and burrowing deeper. Choking back a sob, Laoch stepped into the madness, eyes roaming, ears hurting as seared throats released their agony upon the world. And there, half twisted on the ground, hair ash on a red raw skull, lay Láidir. Laoch spun the body over, expecting death, to be greeted by an agonised screech from absent lips. Raw flesh still burning as the banefire clung to the last threads of skin and muscle. Rearing back, Laoch's stomach lurched, acid searing his throat when laughter echoed from behind. Slowly turning, he saw ten of the Unbelievers watching him, bows raised, each arrow tip glinting in the flames. Laoch spat, awaiting the end, but ignoring them all as he drew back his arrow and loosed. It crashed into Láidir's skull, cracking the eye socket, driving into his brain. No responding arrows flew. No shafts to penetrate a shrivelled heart. Laoch strode out, finding each of his Spear one by one. A leader's duty.

...He screamed. Fire burning into peeled, flayed skin. Eyes filled with the memory of his brother as laughter spilled within his ears. The aroma of cooked meat forcing his mouth to salivate. Whispers of where it had come from bringing tears to a Ranger's eyes ... he rolled, legs trapped, mouth wide with unrestrained pain. Crashing into the darkness, desperate.

Pain pierced the void. A wetness that belied the heat and flame, the tang of blood upon not so dry lips. Laoch's eyes flickered open, hands running down his legs. Old scars bubbled yet healed, greeting his fingertips. Bringing one hand to touch his moist lips, he dabbed at the blood, before spinning over on his mattress and reaching out for the cloth he knew lay at its side. A ting of metal greeted his fingers, and a sigh escaped his bloody lips. His hand ignored the rustle of cloth and grasped the flask. Laoch lifted it to his lips, the sweet smell of leaf-green rum masking the memory of smoke-filled nostrils. He poured in the last mouthful, sighing as his parched throat congratulated him on surviving another night. Laoch ran his finger around the flask's opening, dabbing the recovered liquid onto his newly cracked lip. Memories threatened to roll in, and he pushed them away, driving fingers deep into his eyes before remembering the rum and swearing when the stinging alcohol brought him completely awake.

"Shit on the Seven bloody hells. Another bloody morning in my world of joy." Dropping the flask on the sweat-stained bed, he reached for the stoppered bottle, shaking it and sighing with relief at the answering splosh. "To you, Captain Rakslin." And he knocked it back.

I

OF PATHWAYS AND VEILS

Outer Veil

The Wyrm Ship Captain glanced at the bone compass once again. The needle confirming what he already knew, that they were approaching the outer veil in the manner best suited for piercing the spiritfire curtain. Experience hard won by the Wyrm upon whom he sailed, having learned to adapt to protect its charges. After all, they had followed the pathway with senses honed from years of searching the void, the deft nuance of each veil, a taste the Wyrm Ship had refined. But the spirit captain was obsessive, the years taking its toll on his once unfettered mind. Insanity barely kept in check by the rigour of compulsion to quell his impulses. Such rituals soothed his deranged thoughts, allayed his fears. Enabling the connection with the Wyrm that swam the edges of the known, and more importantly, the unknown realms. He felt the Ship respond to the first caress of the curtain, a pulse of agreement pounding through the bone beneath his bare feet.

The Captain instinctively fretted over the Sealgair, sending his thoughts cascading through the living deck, hoping the pupating and cushioning sacs may soon be needed. Three times his mind slid through the veined pods, lightly touching each body held within, finding little had changed. Twenty life preserving sacs still lived, rooted to the Wyrm Ship by white-streaked tendrils that drove into the living flesh of its hull. Yet he sensed loss, with six more of the Sealgair—the preserved hunters—suffering death after their flight from Repanti. His spirit senses glided through their pods, finding only corpses rotting inside. There would be more soon, their time short, the ship upon the last dregs of its long life. How long had he slept?

'Cut those Sealgair loose, Wyrm,' he thought. And the Wyrm Ship responded, the white tendrils sliding out and shoving the dead sacs towards the deck's edge.

At first, the Captain couldn't recall why they were here. Racking his spirit-preserved mind, only to be rewarded with expectant *duty* and nothing more. Traces of memories lingered that were tantalisingly close to the surface—but in that way lay danger, though *how* he could not recall. He knew the Sealgair were key to a future, and his addled mind took an age to extract fact from hallucination. Fires burned, souls torn and shredded. A people consumed so others may live. Somewhere in that maelstrom, a truth lay, a purpose. But ritual imprisoned those thoughts, keeping him on track to complete a task he couldn't remember.

And then he knew why he was there. Recalling the Wyrm's touch upon his spirit mind. The creature's discovery of an outer veil of an uncharted realm. The trigger to wake him once again from his slumber.

'How long has it been? How far have we come?' he wondered.

Eight of your years, and you have slept for two of those since Repanti. And distance is meaningless.

The Wyrm Ship drew within touching distance of the wavering curtain of the outer veil that flowed in and out, like the world breathed beneath it. Each pulse shined with a deep purple that rose in intensity as it sucked inwards, fading on the outward ripple. The Captain felt, rather than heard, the Wyrm speak. Its strange mind unable to grasp human words. Only thoughts and images passed between them.

Sighting of a potential pathway ahead, my Captain.

'Aye,' thought the Captain.

Preparing the façade, hull skin imbued, alive and intact.
'Good, but keep it steady, Wyrm.'
Realm veil contact. The spiritfire curtain has not responded to my touch. My fin-sails have been stowed.
'Keep them tight inwards, can't let them catch.'
Captain, we're about to pass into the outer curtain. You need to go below, or you'll dissipate.

'*Aye, you can't let me go yet,*' thought the Captain, descending the first rib bone step.

The facade has formed ... we are penetrating the curtain.

The deck hatch slammed shut, the scrape of bone-on-bone shuddering through the Captain as it arced with laces of purple fire. A shimmer of light from the hatch lock shrouded the energy, drawing it in upon itself. The living bone absorbing the spiritfire as was the Wyrm's want, for it fed upon the wisps of power emanating from each realm. Except, of course, many of those realms had wrapped themselves in curtains. Veiling the life within from the spirit sight of their predators. The Wyrms, mere grazers, fenced away from their food source and forced to learn new tricks or die, or worse, fall prey to the predators themselves—the Constructors. The Captain sensed the ship's weight shift. Its store of spiritfire reaching out like paired, taloned hands, ripping a hole within the curtain. The Wyrm named it a gate to ease his mind. To the Captain it was a wound, one that suppurated, leaking the very thing it was designed to hide. A danger that signalled to their hunters of what may lie beneath. The ship baulked, before pushing onward, speeding up as the curtain laced itself together, desperate to heal itself before it was too late.

Such guilt.

We are in Captain; we have slipped into the outer veil.

The Wyrm Ship Captain walked back up the ribbed steps, white eyes darting about the purple-hued heavens surrounding the ship. He felt spiritfire pulse against the hull, probing, querying for something that was not quite right. But the façade held—though he'd check again, the unceasing ritual holding his mind together.

2

WHERE RANGERS FAIL

ERSTEN FOREST, NEAR ERSTENBURGH, BRANDSHOLD

Laoch knelt against the rotten tree trunk, knee squashing the brown, mottled fungi as he peered into the night. The mist had risen, shrouding the lower half of the twisted tree trunks of the forest's edge, the bark damp, pungent and heady.

I bloody hate fog.

Laoch drew in a long breath, mindful to keep it low and quiet, thoughts wandering to the bottle under his arm. Dismissing it, he glanced back, Tapin and Kerund both kneeling behind, composite bows in hand and waiting on his orders. They'd been his Ranger Spear for the last six months, patrolling the farmland and woods east of the city. Thus, keeping the local villages assured that the Prince Consort did care, as rumours of the Unbelievers travelled the trading roads between them.

It's bullshit. They ain't here, I'd know. But the villagers, those who have turned their heads from the bloody Seven—now they may well be.

Rain began to fall, the drizzle light but unwelcome, scratching at his mood.

Laoch gave the signal for his Spear to proceed, their way unlit, with torches next to useless in the damp. Besides, they only served to highlight you as an easy target. In his mind, only sound, the attuned human eye, and instinct bred from the Ranger training—or a life in the woods—could be relied on.

And a drink. You can always rely on that. Not Gowan's crap about honed senses, hardened muscle and bloody drills. A drink and a night on the town work just as well.

Tappin and Kerund separated, using the cut timber left to dry in piles as cover. A hint of pride flickered in his mind as they dodged between the undergrowth to reach the first of the pine trees, though he kept the grin well away from his face. Raw as unbroken colts—he had at least shaped them a little, got them listening. The hours spent around the tavern table discussing tactics and old incursions making an impact. He would never know if they were presented to him by Captain Rakslin as a joke or a redemption, but looking at them now, he allowed a sliver of pride to slip through.

He shifted his bow against his forearm, arrow nocked, feeling the comfort of the familiar weapon while watching them enter the forest. They reached their designated cover positions, allowing their eyes to adjust to the gloom as the canopy thickened, masking out any remaining residual light. On their signal, he rose, keeping low as he mirrored their movements until he once again took position at the point of the spear. Ahead, the darkness gnawed at his nerves, mind flicking back to the agonies of the northeastern borders, and a raid into the forests that demarked the Unbelievers' lands. Laoch pushed it down, the tinge of smoke and burning flesh assailing his nostrils, a memory he didn't need right now. Unbidden, his right hand checked the metal flask resting under his left armpit. The subconscious squeeze calmed his mind.

Movement?

The soft snap of a wet twig played at the edge of his hearing, the deadening atmosphere preventing any hint of direction. He signalled Tappin out to the east, the female Ranger responding, initially trusting her evolving instincts. Laoch sensed the shift, her nerves kicking in. Tappin's movements becoming rigid and losing fluidity, her confidence dipping as she moved away from him. They had learned to work together—to trust and have each other's back. In combat, survival and success relied on your Spear. But Rangers were more than that. Often operating alone, surviving on wit and instinct against enemies that enjoyed flaying the skin from whoever they caught. Laoch glanced down at his left hand. The scars and the blackened fingernails were too much of a reminder. The darkness pressed in, cooked flesh wafting in his mind.

Piss off. Still work to do.

Waiting, Laoch racked his memory of what lay ahead. They'd patrolled the area a month ago, with a stream around five hundred yards ahead. By its side, one of the timber shacks the woodsmen used during the autumn and winter months as they selected and felled the prime trees for the city. This area also grew the flexible ash and hardwoods for the University Meisters, much of which ended up in the heavier weapons that were gaining traction in the Prince Consort's preparation for the next Crusade into the Unbelievers' lands.

Laoch let out a sigh as Tappin returned, her blue eyes a little wild looking with the pupils wide. He noted her breathing, an edge to her movements, and assumed she had something more than errant rabbits to report.

She bent low next to him, her breath steaming. "Disturbed someone, they ran along a deer trail to the north," Tappin indicated the direction with her hand, "in a hurry, too."

"Armed?"

"Couldn't swear to it, but they were carrying something." Tappin spat on the floor. "Local, I reckon. Or been here a while, knew their way."

Laoch nodded, mulling over his orders. With the Consort's rising paranoia, he would be expected to check it out despite his misgivings. And he assumed this pair would report to any superior who asked whatever he chose to do.

"Okay. This isn't Unbelievers, right? Unless they're local, and this close to the village, I'd have my doubts. They'll be poachers, stealing meat from the Queen's lands. You take Kerund and follow their trail. I'm betting an ale they're holed up in the woodcutter's hut near Taverner's Stream, but assumptions cost lives. I'll follow and take the rear, provide cover."

"Lead?" Tappin bit at her lip, shifting her feet.

"Yeah. 'Bout time." Laoch gave his best smile. Tappin looked far from convinced. Ignoring it, he signalled her out, and she swung behind, collecting Kerund on the way after a brief, whispered conversation. Laoch enjoyed the glance his way. Kerund wasn't much younger than him and had been in the City Militia before the captain sent him his way after one too many brutal alleyway beatings. It would do him good to follow the village girl for a change.

Laoch watched them disappear into the dark, slipping a hand under his armour and flipping the stopper off his rum. Taking a swig, he eyed the direction they'd left in, feeling the warmth slip down his throat, and waiting for the raw alcohol to bite home. As it did, he lifted the bottle for a second time, hesitating, pursing his lips.

"Bloody poachers." He took another swig and rammed the flask back into its holster before taking up his bow. Laoch, bent low, followed the broken trail, discerning the footprints in the mud regardless of the darkness and the rum. Despite his training, Kerund's heavy footsteps announced his presence to all who would care to listen. He had gotten away with it near the city, but that lack of care would see the man dead anywhere close to the borderlands. His throat slit and likely the charred body left as a warning. Tappin had a lighter touch, more aware of the telltales she left, though there was always more to learn. Potential, if she could only see it herself.

Within a few minutes, he'd caught up. The hut lay in complete darkness, but the mist held the smell of candle wax and a fire—either recently doused or covered with the lack of ambient light. Tappin had taken position thirty yards from the eastern side. Kerund was creeping forward from the west, moving in a low crouch towards the outer edge of the hut's cleared yard where the cutters worked. Laoch dropped behind a tree stump, its top notched with a thousand axe strokes, woodchips piled around it. With his arrow nocked, he waited to see whether Kerund had learned a little subtlety—or would this be another hot-tempered alleyway charge?

The ex-militia man reached the edge of the clearing, ducking behind an open-sided roof covering drying logs. He swept to the left, ensuring he could use his composite bow in the easiest position for his right-hand dominance. With the hut door just ten yards distant, and no movement, Laoch sensed the change in the man's mood.

No bloody patience in this one. Just go up, slow, listen first. Like we talked about.

Nearly choking, Laoch watched him swap out to the Ranger short sword, a weapon suited to close quarter fighting amid tight spaces. If he stepped in now, would Kerund learn, or would the embarrassment kill any chance of ever getting through how poor his independent thinking was?

Wait.

Kerund barrelled forward, short of shouting, "City Militia, hold fast," he couldn't have been more brazen. His shoulder hit the hut door, well-built and inward swinging to stave off the worst of the winter. It gave. The iron latch bending, snapping as his weight carried him on through. Laoch glanced over to Tappin, expecting her to follow in, only to see the Ranger freeze, eyes desperately seeking his.

Yes, he's bloody useless—but he's still your responsibility. Shit.

Decision made, he drew his sword, charging forwards. His own bow left behind in the need for haste after Tappin's hesitation. The wooden walls shook as he took his first stride, and a short, sharp exhalation of air followed after a hard blow landed. Laoch reached the door as somebody barrelled out, a wicked and blood-ied knife in their hand, lashing out towards his stomach. Laoch struck, chopping the keen-edged sword down into the assailant's neck and biting through the sack cloth collar, smashing bone and parting the shoulder. Blood spurted, washing over his cloak, and the figure clattered into his chest. Laoch felt himself topple, angry he'd let himself be caught out with the rum blunting his reactions, knowing he'd acted on alcohol induced instinct.

He slammed into the ground. The tang of fresh blood reaching the air, his mind panicking at the fear Kerund might have fallen under his blade. Shoving the inert body away, he rolled to his feet, the scarlet edged sword out in front, waiting to defend himself. When nothing emerged from the hut, he angrily signalled Tappin over, and approached the doorway, eyes adjusting to the dark. Heat rose in the fireplace, ash fluttering in the warm breeze from a shrouded fire. Placing his back to the wall, Laoch eased in, swapping hands to grasp a poker and lift the rough metal covering, enabling its light to sweep the room. Rabbits swung from a line in one corner. A broken stool lay underneath, Kerund's head resting against one of its splintered legs that had clearly knocked him out. On the ash-covered table, a half-skinned rabbit lay spread out, and by its side the snare that had been its demise.

"Rabbits. Not even against the Queen's Law. In the name of the bloody Seven, Kerund." Laoch stalked out of the door, pointing to Tappin and back into the hut. "See to him." With one hand gripping his sword tight, the other pulsing, he strode over to the corpse. Sucking in a breath, he knelt, sweeping the woollen cap from his assailant's head. A ragged tuft of hair slipped out, brown, roughly cut above a young face. Far too young.

"Shit." Laoch placed his hand against the boy's neck, knowing the answer, but an inner hope drove him. The heartbeat was absent. He'd taken the life of a lad of no more than eleven summers old. In his mind, the image of Lord Justice arose, the head of his House and bearer of his sins. The man who'd nurtured him back from the brink of madness after Captain Rakslin returned a favour hard won, releasing him from the clutches of the Unspoken's Elite.

With his chest aching, he stood, hands flexing, as the sword dropped to the floor. Laoch spun on his heel, driving into the hut, the first boot to Kerund's prone body met by Tappin's squeal. The second by her slamming into him, dragging him away.

"No, Laoch. It's too much."

3
THE QUEEN'S GAMBIT

THE WHITE PALACE, ERSTENBURGH, BRANDSHOLD

"Queen Erin, and Prince Consort Adama."

The Queen sighed, appearing to care nothing for those waiting. The Prince Consort, however, sat eagerly on his simple wooden throne, eyes darting over the object covered in sack cloth in the middle of the room.

"Yes, Jacka, proceed with the show. But you really do need to get on with it. I have other, more pressing matters to deal with and a hunger to sate." The Queen placed her hands in her lap, palms upturned, back straight and eyes lively as she peered at Jacka. The Prime, his usual jacket resplendent with his office insignia, stood next to a middle-aged academic fluffing her robe sleeves.

Prime Jacka Vardrin delivered an accepting smile in response and gave the Meister Alchemist Kinst the nod to begin. Three years as Prime and not once had the Queen outwardly shown a modicum of enthusiasm for the potential of alchemy. Jacka knew it was deliberate, a play for the Seven Gods' Houses and the Palace Court, a mummery to throw them off the scent of her pursuits. Yes, she played her role as decreed. Fawning when it came to coins in the pocket or the political influence it may have. Then she was keen to have her say, making sure everyone kept within the bounds of scripture as the Houses dictated. That's why Jacka had to avoid the Queen's Court for now, because what he was about to show would reach the Houses on the wave of gossip. That, and he knew the Consort would enthuse over the potential, setting the Court once again on edge as the man espoused about the next Crusade. Jacka needed the Queen's full, outwardly unenthusiastic backing to get this approved—without it, the potential mining costs would be severely delayed by the religious expediency of the Court Treasurer, and thus fall under the gaze of the Seven Houses. But the secrets of the Unspoken and her Unbeliever army's weapons were slowly being cracked. Meister Kinst learned something new every day as the Queen risked the wrath of the Houses in her pursuits.

I can hear her now, whispering to herself. Make this powerful, a sign to the Seven that such learning will be effective. That science, as well as religion, should lead the Crusade against those who refuse the faith. Ah, my Queen, such potential. If only we can see it through the issues of short-term coinage, and of course, High Lord Penance and his accusations about scripture.

"So, as you know, Your Majesty," began Meister Kinst, "the flash powder has been in production at the University for three years now. We have developed a simple, easily reproducible procedure that any fool could follow. We've started to make the explosive powder in greater quantities and the use of ceramic flash pots has improved Your Majesty's Ranger's capabilities. No one would dare contemplate attacking Erstenburgh with the firepower you have to hand. Not even the Unspoken at the head of her Unbelievers would make such an attempt."

Jacka sighed internally as the Queen eyed the academic, trying to deduce where the Meister was leading. The exaggeration wasn't overly welcome, the Rangers too few and the flash powder useful only in small-scale combat. Foot soldiers were the mainstay of the army and the most in need of such new developments. The Rangers withdrawn by the Consort from their usual role providing

scouting and skirmish support along the borderlands, the failure
of the Crusade feeding a depression that dragged his Queen down
with him.

*But—may the Seven Gods forbid—an attack on Erstenburgh?
The Prince Consort was paranoid enough already without you
mentioning it, Kinst.*

The academic, more socially adept than most of the Learned,
caught the Queen's angled head and thoughtful gaze.

"I mean to say: *once* we have continued to increase the speed
with which we make the powder. The mining of the saltpetre
has, at least, started to improve. What I offer has great potential.
Ecne, if you please." The academic clicked her fingers, eyeing
the acolyte standing next to her who reached towards the cover
at her side, sliding back the grey material to reveal a long shaft
from a large ballista. Attached to its end was a ceramic bulb, four
times the size of the ones the Rangers had access to. The Queen's
Consort sat up straighter, eyes sparkling. "We have managed to
use an inner layer of thin iron alloy to line the ceramic. Inside, a
slightly more concentrated form of the flash powder mixed with
shards of metal discarded from the smithy. This we would name
Erin's Wrath, if we may?"

The Queen hid a smile, enjoying the moment, her eyes distant.
But Jacka knew she was calculating the potential before catching
herself and returning to the usual dour expression. Adama rose
from his chair, pulling down his brocaded uniform jacket while
striding down the steps to examine the weapon.

*Wave the potential in the Seven Houses' eyes, and just maybe
they'll push past scripture for the chance of overcoming the Unspoken. If they wish another Crusade, they will have to allow more
'science' to flourish.*

"We also think," said the grey-haired academic looking straight
at the Queen, "we could adapt beyond the ballista. Perhaps widen
the use of the trebuchet with larger pots, even build carts laden
with Erin's Wrath for ramming an advancing army. The potential
is endless, and in the long term, may mean we can transport such
powerful weaponry a good distance, say to the borderlands."

"The Unbelievers? That far—on wheels," stated Adama. "If we
could manage such a thing with the trebuchet too, we could knock

down their walls, end their blasphemy. How long are we talking, Meister?"

"I think about three months before Erin's Wrath is ready for production on a larger scale. But we'd need the mines at full capacity, the potters under our wing as well as our own forge. But we could have Erstenburgh's walls fully equipped in six months, the Union's Battalion in a year."

"Cost?" asked the Queen, her tone indicating she knew what was coming. Jacka remembered the original Flash Powder had put a half penny on each citizen's taxes, the people willing after the failed Crusade though the merchants grumbled. Knowing the Queen, she'd already guessed this would be at least that again, maybe a little more. A thousand Brand Rounds.

She will see the potential. And I have primed Kinst with a sweetener for the treasury.

"The University's projections are based on current funding levels and mineral availability. If you bring on board some of the affluent merchants and mine operators for a *share* in the developments, we can significantly drop the initial two thousand Brand Round outlay," said Jacka Vardrin, holding his nerve. Among some of the outlay upon the Gods' Houses recently, this was a drop in the ocean, and he knew he'd have to come back for more should the merchants baulk at their percentage and not honour the verbal agreements he had already pocketed.

"A share? Of what?" said the Queen.

"Of the mines, Queen Erin and my powders. Prime Vardrin indicates they worry over their trade routes into the southern lands, and west towards Jense and Makelna. Allowing the merchants access, at a price, could significantly spread the burden, even negate it."

Jacka smiled to himself, hands behind his back as he watched the Queen nodding to herself.

Still wondering about the quality of your Prime, my Queen? Can you see me? How I shine for you? Only the Seven Houses can prevent where this is going.

4

A DESERVED TIRADE

SMERRAL RANGER ENCAMPMENT,
ERSTEN FOREST

Laoch rubbed the dirt from his eyes and released a ragged sigh. His horse mirrored the Ranger's mood, head down, slightly to the side as the rain finally gave up playing with them and began to pour. His sodden cloak dripped but, thanks to the Consort insisting the Meisters help with equipment design, it functioned well and kept the rain at bay. The University's impact had surprised him and, despite the Queen's constant concerns over costs, word was it would continue. Only the Prince Consort's demands for the study of the Unbelievers' alchemical weaponry might scupper it, the man's thirst for another Crusade worrying. That, and his monopolisation of the Elite.

Laoch led Kerund's horse, the Spearman tied tight across the sparse saddle and a rag stuffed in his mouth, keeping him quiet. With Tappin at the rear, he walked the horse into camp, eyeing the central command tent with trepidation, wondering if he'd still be in the Rangers in a few hours' time. He dismissed the subconscious squeeze of his arm—rum would be the final nail in his coffin right now.

Tempted, it'd get the misery over with.

He pulled the horse up in front of the tent, the awning drooping under the weight of water. Laoch lifted one leg over the horse's withers and slid off, hitting the mud with little care before cutting Kerund free. The Spearman hit the watery sludge hard and Laoch walked past, eyes cast downward, bile in his throat. He so desperately wanted to let fly, vent his frustration again on the *failure* looking angrily back up at him. But no.

Why give Gowan the pleasure?

Gowan waited there, the First Ranger clearly composing the shit she was going to lay on him. The scrape of leather knees upon the mud announced the ex-militia's rise from the floor, and Tappin, having helped him up, placed herself between him and Laoch.

Just as guilty, Tappin. You froze on me. Forced me to act when I shouldn't have to. The lad would be alive. Now that bastard Gowan will take yet another chance to embarrass me.

Laoch spoke without turning around, his head aching. "Yer ready for this? If she's loud, yer done. And so am bloody I. Do yer hear me, Kerund? I'll not be able to hold my tongue if she starts. And if they drum me out, I'll be mistaking a practice arrow for one of those armour-punching specials Meister Arknold designed. One I intend to release up your bloody arse. Of course, you won't feel it after I've kicked yer to bloody death first."

I need another bloody drink.

Gowan waited, boot pressing against the mud outside the tent amid the roots of a sodden bush. She wore the usual annoying smile, and Laoch sensed the expectant pleasure coursing through her—he was in no doubt that his Spear felt it too. The First Ranger motioned them over, Laoch leading them with shoulders back and bloodshot eyes on his nemesis. Under his left arm he could feel the bottle pressing, the leaf-green rum calling his addiction out.

"So, what's this pig's arse? Why have you trussed up one of your own, Laoch?" Gowan looked into each of his Spear's eyes, her voice low and menacing, blue eyes glinting hard-edged steel.

"It's so I don't beat the rest of the shit out of him, Gowan. The man's fine until he has to bloody think, only to find he has nothing but muscles for brains." Laoch glared at Kerund over his shoulder, fire in his eyes, daring the man to challenge his words.

Only silence answered, and the squelch of mud. He knew he was
focusing on the ex-militia man, trying to bite down on what he
wanted to spew on Tappin's shoulders. The woman had stood by,
leaving Laoch hanging. But then it would fully come back to him,
his incompetence in bringing them up to standard.

*Here's your chance, Gowan. Don't miss it, 'cos if you do, I'm on
yer like a bloody rash.*

"I'll have to report this, Laoch. You can't tie your own bloody
soldiers up." Gowan's quiet voice cut through the gathering crowd,
the three other Spear's patrolling the area coming over to watch
Laoch laid low. He felt their presence, the target for Gowan's ire
having brought many of them down in the past during his drunken
hazes. Whether by words or fists, they cared not. Laoch knew he
deserved the kicking his ego was about to take, and more besides.
If he was out on his arse, it'd mean choosing a new drinking
den—as those watching on would be gunning for him if he lost
the protection of the Rangers—and he hated change, especially
with a tab to pay. He held back the shame as best he could, but
his ragged nerves were raw, and patience low.

"He cocked up, cost a lad's life. Reckless."

Gowan had remained motionless as she spoke, but now walked
forward, sniffing the air with that goading smile on her face. "That
the leaf-green grog I can smell, Duckard's crap from the Five
Bells? You're swaying, Laoch. Need a crutch?"

"With all respect, Ranger, piss off." Laoch nodded Gowan's way,
smiling, while forcing the bile back down his throat, unable to say
any more as the venom leaked into his mind. Turning on his heel,
he led the Spear away. Each step hammered into the mud. He
could feel the other Rangers' eyes on him—they knew. They'd
heard what Gowan had chosen. But everyone would clam up,
each keeping their counsel until they had the opportunity to find
him in a back alley. One without a Kerund to save him.

*Don't let them show she gets to you. Don't look the bastards in
the eye.*

"Captain Rakslin's on his way," shouted Gowan at his back. "We
will discuss the outcome an hour after we break our fast in the
morning. Be there, *Ranger* Laoch," Gowan practically spat his
name out, the disdain and poison flowing among her words.

Laoch picked up the reins of his horse, sympathising with the mournful look he received in return. Yet now he had the second stage of the debacle to face—Sura. The one sliver of sunlight in his life that he'd been slowly drowning out in case it overwhelmed him. Hope was a bitter mistress to the lost, especially to those whose souls still roasted over a firepit in some far-distant forest.

On reaching the camp stables, the lean-to shelter pressed tight with sheltering horses, the look from Ranger Henti sent him spiralling. He staggered, just catching himself. His wearied and frayed spirit denying that final embarrassment. She had the Meisters' waxed material held high, examining the heavy crossbows underneath for any water ingress. On hearing the familiar nicker from Laoch's horse, she had turned, empathy shining in her eyes, her elven skin glowing in the lamplight. In his irrational state, Laoch couldn't see beyond the pain he deserved; couldn't believe that he was anything else but a failure after the mission's debacle. Bad news travelled faster than a horse with its tail alight in the Rangers.

Laoch tried to push down the anger into the pit of his stomach, knowing his mind sought an excuse, a reason for it not to be his failure, but it wasn't working. In his heart, he had killed a child, cut him down with no thought but for his own skin. The rum, the nightmares, all adding to the pain rather than forming the shield he sought. His fists clenched, fingers pressing into already raw skin. He was on the precipice, and a push from Gowan, or the pull from Sura Henti, may topple him into an abyss he would never climb out of.

"Laoch," Sura called. He didn't look—in truth he couldn't face it. Those cat-like eyes would pierce his own, driving inward to shame his spirit. She would read his black-heart and end any vestige of the old Laoch that still crawled inside. He needed her, needed the belief she had in him, the balm to ease his ravaged soul. Yet feared what it would expose, and that he'd drag her down with him. "Ranger Laoch, of the Queen's Rangers, I'm talking to you. *Don't* ignore me."

The directive in her voice pulled at him, the need to look her in the eye far too compelling. The slitted black pupils drew him in, her soft features framed by the shock of spiked, grey hair.

"You need to let the anger out."

Laoch couldn't hold back, slamming his hand onto the hay cart's wooden side, trying to mask the shame with physical pain.

Sura continued, undeterred. "Let it go before it eats your soul and takes Tappin and Kerund with you. They cocked up—as if you never have, or I."

It struck him then. She didn't know, not about the boy's death and the added shame it brought.

"Gowan," was all he could let out, lips tight against his teeth, the need to lose himself in the drink pulsing in his mind. Laoch squeezed his eyes together, feeling his blood keen for the rum under his armpit. Instead, he began a beat on the cart with his palm, taking a breath as he pushed the boy's face from his mind, slowing a pained heartbeat. Regaining control, he nodded towards Sura, feeling the anger settle. Releasing it now would only lead to the loss of his commission and violence in the taverns later. Gowan would win. Gowan always won.

"You know why she's like this. You always have."

"It was one bloody night. I was drunk."

"You led her on. Everyone knew she had a thing for you. You drank the city dry together and then humiliated her in front of everyone. In front of the Rangers."

Laoch squeezed his eyes shut, two fingers pressed in, hazy memories of her attempted kiss and his subsequent shoving of Gowan in the horse trough. Harsh, but he hardly remembered it. Unlike Gowan.

How long can she hold a bloody grudge for?

Sura moved across, her smile tight, taking his horse's reins and encouraging the bedraggled animal beneath the shelter. Elven hands smoothed its flank, before she ran her fingers over the neck, the horse dropping its head as she whispered into its ear. After a responding whicker, Sura glanced at Laoch, and they both proceeded to strip down the saddle and worked together to dry the horse. All the while, they spoke. Words flowing despite his pulsing head as he explained what had happened.

5

THE MEISTER'S OPTIMISM

THE MEISTER STUDY ROOMS, ERSTENBURGH UNIVERSITY

"Her Majesty has agreed, Meister Arknold. I have an official mandate to move Erin's Wrath forward—to plan for larger scale production," said Meister Kinst, her fingers steepled in front of her as she lounged in the huge, intricately patterned, chair. She felt the weight of its age against her back, and perhaps for the first time, worthy of its ancient significance.

Arknold let that sink in as she poured an amber spirit into a glass, the sweet smell of maple bringing a flush to her cheeks. She handed the glass to her friend, happy to revel in Kinst's success.

"What do you need me to do?" asked Ecne. The acolyte sat on a stool opposite, rubbing a recent burn mark on her hand. "You are including me in your plans, I assume? I haven't hurried and scurried at your command for these last five years for nothing?"

"No, my dear girl. Your studies have gone as well as can be expected with someone of your ... breeding. And now we are being taken seriously, well your place in the world may well be

fortuitous. Yes? Not only first-hand experience of the flash powder, but my work on Erin's Wrath may lead to significant status for
us both. Way above your current station, and my perilous financial
position. I even have the ear of the Prime right now. My star is
rising, as they say."

Ecne coughed, hacking up the unpleasant taste that sat at the
back of her throat. The daily purge had not gone so well, her
lungs reticent after the damp night air. She rose from the stool,
bidding her Meister a fair day and headed for the door, and the
afternoon session that would decide her fate. Though proud of
her Meister's rising status, and her minor role within it, Ecne's
mind railed at the possibility of missing the archery training she'd
paid for. Her father before her, and grandmother before that,
had served in the Rangers, though the training had been less
rigorous in the days before the Union and the steady growth of
Brandshold's leadership in the alignment of small city states. But
still her weapons training meant something. Skills that she could
hold up to her family, a salve to their worries over her acolyte
status. So, she'd paid for personal training by an ex-Ranger named
Jessen, who had shown great patience over her stamina with the
sword, and now a wandering eye with the bow.

*Money talks, eh? There's little coinage in being educated. Hah,
father. Wait and see.*

"Ecne, hold," called Kinst, waiting for the acolyte to turn
around. "Meister Arknold and I will be needing to set another trial
session with the ballista and Erin's Wrath. Somewhere away from
the city as we scale up the range."

"Yes," replied Arknold, a smile reaching her eyes, realisation
striking that Kinst's rise may drag her along too. "But where?"

"Any ideas where would be best, Ecne? We spend far too much
time cosseted in the University."

"There's a clearing in Ersten Forest, Smerral I think it's called.
The Rangers use it as a camp on rotation with two others, but it's a
mere stone's throw to the Queen's Road. It would be much easier
to use that, even with a larger ballista's weight."

"Good," said Meister Arknold. "I will make the arrange-
ments—Smerral. Yes? I can get the Consort's Guard to supervise
its movement."

Ecne let out a relieved sigh, thinking Arknold may well have dropped the role on her after previous experiences. The Meister had lost her acolyte recently to a pox and had called on Ecne a few times in the last few weeks. She turned to leave again.

"You'll need to supervise its preparation on arrival though, Ecne. And the Erin's Wrath will need your presence during transportation. One burning set of carts, and the Queen will be changing her mind. You're going to be busy, so put an end to this weapons training business today. We have vital work to do for the Queen." Meister Kinst gave her a tight smile, forcing agreement from Ecne with a nod.

6

A RANGER'S LAST CHANCE

SMERRAL RANGER ENCAMPMENT

Captain Rakslin's voice remained steady, measured. The praise slipping from his lips sincere and well-considered as he let the three new Ranger Spears know they made him proud. The man was well-loved in the city, a veteran and to some a hero. One of the reasons the Ranger's local patrols had become more popular among the Queen's Court than he'd first feared. With the Queen's favour, these new Rangers would be the flesh upon which the skeleton of Erstenburgh's Guard could defend the city surroundings from the fear of Unbeliever infiltration. Freeing, he hoped, the remaining Rangers to return to their true role along the Union's borders.

But not all agreed with his philosophy, or the softly-softly methods he used. Some took advantage, some pushed as far as they could. Rakslin let his eyes roam over the remaining Spear, with Gowan, shoulders back, as proud to be standing there as the captain himself. And by his side, the slovenly excuse for a Ranger that Rakslin's detachment owed their lives to. Failing to hide the heavy sigh, he dismissed the other Spears, holding his hand palm out to signal Laoch's to remain.

"At rest," he said, the gently spoken words commanding respect with his usual air of controlled confidence.

Laoch knew the voice well. It had put him in his place often enough since the captain took him in. On the verge of a painful loss of commission—drunk, disorderly and insubordinate in any order you chose—he'd dragged Laoch back to work with the Consort's new demands. The forging of the Rangers into patrol units for the city giving the tortured Ranger a last chance to prevent his descent into whatever hell he'd chosen. Laoch had tried, he really had. Going at least a week at one point without a single barracks ruck or tavern fight. Why had Rakslin not thrown him out?

I only saved his bloody soldiers once. Only for him to rescue me in return when I'd rather have died. I must have screwed his life up a hundred times since.

Sura had talked him through the twisted mental mess he'd made of the patrol. She'd stripped the events down one by one, berating him when he finally admitted to the rum, but not giving up. He'd half-expected Gowan to make an appearance in the stable, rile him some more before the meeting, get his ire up so he'd be a ragged mess when the captain arrived. Sura, however, had the sense to keep him busy with the horses—though in silence after his admission—possibly worse than the beating Laoch sensed she wanted to dish out. But she knew how to wheedle her way into his anger, smooth words calming him enough to face the impending consequences. Words that eased his spirit, welcomed inside despite the fear they rose in him—tearing down the walls around his darkness and exposing the pain that flared at its centre.

Immolation they call it. Death by fire. If she breaks my walls, will my spirit burn with them?

Can I risk that?

The captain's voice cut through Laoch's thoughts, the hairs on his neck rising as he awaited his fate. "I have heard Ranger Gowan's initial report. I haven't written it down; I'd likely have to burn it on the pyre of a few Ranger commissions." He didn't look at Laoch, but he knew who he meant. "Tell me what I don't know, Gowan."

Laoch felt Kerund's eyes boring into the back of his head, the man's livid bruise on his cheek a result of an eleven-year-old lad getting the jump on him. The ones around his ribs bore Laoch's boot mark and were a few less than the frustrated Ranger felt he deserved.

Waste of bloody time and effort.

"Sir. Laoch's Spear report they came across someone in the forest near Taverner's Stream. He assigned Kerund to lead, Tappin to support, building on their training as he surmised it was likely a poacher, not an Unbeliever coven or incursion."

"And, Ranger?"

"According to Kerund, they approached a woodcutter's hut, suspecting their quarry was in there. Kerund entered and was knocked out. Laoch then followed in, concerned for his Spear-man, only to be attacked by the poacher." Gowan stared directly at Laoch, eyes steeled, barely containing his emotions—yet her voice remained flat.

"You didn't act in this situation, Tappin?"

"No sir, I was on cover in case there were others in the trees." Tappin held the captain's gaze briefly before she let them drop to the floor. Laoch side-eyed her, more than a little disbelief running through him at the lies being spoken on his behalf.

"You believe a bloody word of this, Gowan?"

"In all my time with Ranger Laoch, sir, his respect for procedure has been shite, sir. His methods sloppy, his attitude in the gutter." Gowan finally let the emotion hit her voice.

Rakslin choked, bringing his hand up to smother the sound, feigning a cough while eyeing his First Ranger. Gowan had finally said in the open what everyone else thought, even Sura, and he struggled to understand how she saw anything good left in the man. The elf was an enigma to him, patient. But then she had her own grief.

Laoch spared Gowan a flickered glance, a moment of clarity flashing before his eyes. The image of him being thrown out of the camp played out, probably dumped in whatever crap filled pond she could find on the way. Forcing a grin as he imagined dragging the First Ranger in with him. A second dunking.

Didn't see that coming, did yer?

"Not holding back, First Ranger, eh? Well, Ranger Laoch, anything to add before I decide what in the Seven Hells I do next?"

"No, sir. The First Ranger has it right." Laoch looked back towards Kerund, one eyebrow raised, but he was staring at the floor, face screwed up and trying to hold himself back for whatever reason. Laoch made a guess he was fighting himself, unsure of where this was going.

Gowan and Rakslin stared his way, surprise playing out between them at his reply. Laoch cracked a grin, unable to hold back as he embellished the lie. "Kerund acted within procedure but still has the City Militia mentality of going it alone. He should have called for Tappin, or if concerned about others, me." Laoch threw Gowan a huge grin before turning back to his captain. "As for being shite, well, she's probably right there, too. Because she's always bloody right—never lost a soldier in battle nor failed a mission. Oh, hang on, that's right, she was at the bloody back giving out the bastard orders while the rest of us bled. Or burned."

Rakslin winced at the last words, briefly distant, before the glaze passed, his eyes damp in the corners. Gowan had likely stiffened, probably her face wearing a scowl. Laoch didn't look, nor care.

Score one for the shitty Ranger.

"Marvellous. Just great, and as usual, your attitude has a little green spirit and tobacco leaf dripping over it. What do you suggest I do with Kerund?" The captain glared towards Laoch, twisting his head to the side—the affectation caused by the Unbeliever burn mark that tightened the skin around his eye socket.

"I'll be honest, sir. I don't think he's ready for working independently. As part of a Spear, led by experience, he does fine. Thinking on his own, he reverts to what he knows. Militia bully tactics, no ... discipline." Laoch smiled as Gowan spluttered.

"I'd suggest he works with another experienced Ranger, someone else who he might listen to. Perhaps Ranger Gowan. Kerund can bask in the sun shining out of her arse." Laoch kept his face stern, eyes on the captain, ignoring the exasperation the officer had given up hiding.

It's my head Gowan wants, may as well serve it up.

Rakslin shook his head, staring directly at him, sparing no sideways glances towards Kerund nor Gowan. Laoch knew better than to react. He'd pushed the goading and self-destruction as far as he dared. He couldn't help it. An inner path laid bare in his mind, struggling with the hope Sura potentially offered against the abyss he deserved. There was a long, long pause before Rakslin moved to stand in front of the ex-militia, breaking his gaze from Laoch—barely contained fury in his eyes.

"You can recite the Ranger's code word for word, but you do not believe it, man. You have taken little on board since I assigned you to Laoch, though I fear I am partially to blame for that."

"Yes. Clear, sir." Kerund swallowed, wincing as his painful jaw complained, keeping his eyes forward.

"I'll reassign you to Ranger Gowan. But you need to calm that head rush of yours down. It'll get you killed, or worse, someone in your Spear. As for you, Ranger Laoch, you are to remain behind. Spear dismissed."

Gowan stood waiting, expectant, until the glare from Rakslin directed her towards the command tent's exit. Laoch eyed Gowan as she made to leave, eyes locking with the woman. He let a smile slip out, not the hate the First Ranger expected, raising her eyebrows.

Little victories before they set me free to drink myself to death.

He looked back to his captain. His mind overlaying the officer with images of his past Spear, their skin sloughing from their bodies, the charred meat acrid as he sucked in the hot air. Eyes boiling in their sockets as they screamed, arms beseeching, while melting muscle slid from bone. Laoch pressed his fingers deep into his eyes, screwing them up. Willing his friends and brother back into the abyss.

Rakslin's scarred, burnt hand slid onto his shoulder, squeezing as Laoch forced the memories down. "Last chance, Laoch. I can do no more." He tapped at the man's ribs, the flask ringing under his knuckles. "This'll be the death of you before Gowan."

Laoch could only nod as the man turned away, tears building, watching his captain's back as he left for whatever the Consort had set out next.

I would save you again, old man.

He walked to the doorway, praying to the Seven that Gowan was not there waiting. One word, the wrong look—or that smile—and he'd blow. The final nail. Laoch paused, blinking away the tears, before bending under the awning, striding out to see Sura and

Gowan in animated conversation. Well, more of a one-way tirade, the First Ranger's eyes sliding over her shoulder to look his way. The elf and the Ranger, friends from their time in the Unbeliever Crusade, and at odds. It'd be almost funny if it weren't his future at stake.

Sura left with a final, fierce glance towards Gowan, then back to him. He couldn't read it. The elf's anger closing her off. He made to turn away, wanting to avoid the woman who'd marked him, but Gowan strode over, grabbing his shoulder.

Oh shit.

Laoch spun, fingers pulsing in and out.

"You're a bloody mess. I don't know what in the Seven Hells she sees in you, what kernel of hope lies dormant in there. I'll make sure you're swallowed up in that pit you're so bloody determined to throw yourself in, before I allow it to germinate. And as for Kerund, I'll turn him around. He'll be leading the bloody Rangers by the time I'm done."

Laoch shrugged, letting the anger ease a little, watching Gowan's back as she strode away through the mud. His thoughts whirled as Sura's fierce but blank eyes slipped into his mind.

Despite what I did to deserve this, you're still an arsehole, Gowan.

7

A VEILED HOPE

THE INNER VEILS

The spirit captain sensed the Wyrm's concern, the bones and flesh rippling with a worry borne by the fear of detection. Memories were sliding back in, disjointed, out of order. But he knew in their previous experiences the most powerful veils featured at least one glyph on the pathways. Subtle, hidden, but triggering a powerful rejection from a secondary glyph woven within it, forged by the realm's most capable Magi. Though the encounters were rare—humanity's spread countered by the Constructors who sought them—they had experienced strong veils as they rode the pathways in search of their goal. Their fear was double-edged, with each penetration potentially exposing the realm to the predators, the Constructors, like a flamed torch in a deep void, drawing the hunters in. His mind rejected those thoughts. Unable to face what his cause may have created in its wake. He—they—were seeking salvation for all humans, though ritual and obsession hid how it was to be achieved from his mind.

'We have failed so many times—ah, a memory—before.'

The Wyrm Ship maintained its outer façade, with scaled wings stowed tight to the skin and bone hull. Minimising its profile in the hope of slipping by any glyphs—the avoidance of detection key to arriving unannounced and in one piece. It too could feel the Captain's worry through his feet, the pulse of his spirit heightening as they closed in on the final veil. They had slipped by six, a number unknown on their mission—the three veils of Repanti being the most they had encountered up to now. Hope had blossomed, this realm's spiritfire so well contained by the veils that only the strongest Magi could have formed them—invisible to all but the most attuned. No Constructor would find it. Their prime hunters lost to them, in fact these were the very beasts the Captain and her sought under the veils.

Not knowing what lay beneath each curtain was new to the Wyrm. Its life in the void and pathways one of aeons of solitude, feeding upon the wisps of energy that leaked between worlds. It could taste the taint of humanity, had swam amid their ripples, and when brave enough, feasted until the Constructors rose and hunted its kind. Now human and Wyrm rode together, a bond forged from desperation, seeking a tool they could wield.

The Wyrm knew its time was short, age taking a toll upon sinew and bone. This would be the last ride into a realm, sailing the veils to an end it wished would bring hope to the few that remained of its kind. Not so much a sacrifice, but an ending worthy of its duty. The Captain knew this, though he walled it in within the creeping maelstrom of his failing mind. He also knew their time was short, and soon their bond, and her physical form, would die as the binding broke upon the last boundary. Maybe they'd have a last day together, if the wisps of his soul retained any latent strength. Or maybe not.

The Wyrm's skin prickled. The spiritfire immersing the veil overwhelming its senses and leaving the creature as prey to happenstance. The final, inner curtain's apparent strength was disconcerting. The seep of spiritfire so weak, it was almost non-existent. Knowing it diminished, the Wyrm called for a veil gate to form, those its kind used to slip in and out of a realm unseen when brave enough to feast upon the energy within. With the skill born from aeons spent in the void, a final thin stream of power split the veil, widening into a splintered crack. The Wyrm Ship began the journey through, the energy used to hold the gate sapping at the last vestiges of its reserved strength. It knew finality—this realm was to be a resting place for eternity.

The Wyrm deployed bony wings on the Captain's order, slowing the ship's bulk as they brushed against the tears of the failing gate. The Wyrm felt the rush of its own spiritfire, the force of *will* splitting the veil, struggling to hold back the curtain that railed against the hull. It wanted to be closed, to shut the realm off, to *contain.*

But what is there to contain? Even with the gate wide, there is so little taste of spiritfire on the wind. Either humanity has left or been drained—the spiritfire is so weak under the veil, feeble. The creatures we seek cannot be present my Captain—there is nothing here for them to feed upon. We have failed.

Two more Sealgair died as it spoke in the Captain's mind; the seed pods unable to maintain life as the last energy reserves diverted to the gate transition. The ship rallied, desperate to survive. The journey had to be completed, or any hope they could save the Captain's realm, Mondrein, or the last of the Wyrms, would end. Condemned to a drained, pitiless death.

The veil's curtain pressed inwards. The gate squeezing against skin and bone, a feeling of denial coursing through the Wyrm Ship, laced with fear and dread. Then the façade fell, the natural camouflage the Wyrms used to hide their presence. A glyph fired, the first enchantment to reject them on recognising their intent. A force hammered against the skeletal structure, anger and fear powering the glyph—a giant hammer to smash into its side.

Hull ruptures forming in the skin, stress fractures within bone cage, Captain. But we are through.

It knew their time was short now ... after so long on the search, it had all happened so very quickly. But for what?

'*This is wrong,*' thought the Captain and the Wyrm together.

A second glyph broke, power surging into the Ship's ribs, the nearest bone turning to dust.

8

THE FRUSTRATION OF KNOWING

THE ALCHEMICAL MEISTER'S WORKROOM, ERSTENBURGH UNIVERSITY

Meister Kinst placed both hands against the wooden box. With her green robes stained by powder, mud and an unhealthy level of her own sweat, the last thing she wanted to be doing was having this conversation.

"This is the safe box for Erin's Wrath," she said, eyes glazing over as the Priest-in-Waiting twisted his lips into his fourth grimace of the last few minutes. "It'll be stored in the cart for transport to the clearing. Smerral, yes. That's where we're going."

"Yes," said the Priest, pushing his cowl back with ink-stained hands. He rubbed his bald pate, before returning to the bound notebook he'd been scratching away in. The hooked nose twitched as the sneer rose in intensity, and then he wandered over, lifting the cart's lid to peer inside.

"There's nothing special about it, other than the padding to cushion the bolt heads. The quarrel pots are lined with an inner core that cracks on impact, mixing the two elixirs."

"The pots," he replied, dropping the lid and writing something down in his book. Kinst was convinced he was deliberately trying to set her paranoia flying. Over officious as all clerks and administrators seemed to be. Especially the Keepers of the Scripture, those from House of Wisdom assigned to monitor the 'science' going on in the University with a predilection for making Kinst and Arknold's life as much of a misery as possible. "I understand you have lined these with an iron alloy, yes?"

Kinst sighed, annoyed. She'd been through all this with the last Keeper when she'd first presented her ideas to Lord Wisdom. But they sent a different Priest each time, forcing her to tediously repeat her explanations each time.

"Yes." To save time, and more of her rapidly depleting patience, she grabbed the scroll Ecne had recovered for her from the workshop stores. Bearing the Lord's stamp, she hoped to deflect yet another explanation of the process. "Here."

"Ah. Good to see you are prepared, Meister Kinst. I like that. I like that very much." The Keeper grasped the scroll, and to Kinst's instant misery, proceeded to read through.

"Surely that is enough proof that I am within scripture? It bears Lord Wisdom's seal, your House's sigil."

"Normally, yes. But the Lord was very insistent I was thorough. It appears the High Lord Penance wishes a careful examination of what you and the Grand Meister are doing. The Overseer, yes? Takes those words very seriously does Lord Wisdom, especially when he is *also* being overseen. So," the man handed over the scroll, "that seems to be in order. Now the elixirs, those that combine to make this Erin's Wrath. You have the Lord's scrolls for those?"

—

"I must protest, Lord Wisdom." Grand Meister Arknold paced from side to side, hands clasped behind her back, thumbs digging into her palms.

"Protest away, Grand Meister," replied Lord Wisdom, bending over his writing desk, the sides piled high with numerous books and scrolls on each side. He had one rolled open before him, a finger scanning across the line he was reading. "But it won't make any difference."

Arknold stopped pacing, her heart thudding. As the Grand Meister, she was the liaison between the House of Wisdom and her charges—the Meisters and acolytes of the University. "You are deliberately antagonising Meister Kinst."

"Me? I think you have that wrong. I am simply following scripture, as laid down by the Seven a thousand years ago. Meister Kinst pushes every sacred word she can, as do you. There are boundaries to your studies, rules laid down so we don't repeat the mistakes of the past. If it was not for the failed Crusade, I believe that I, and the rest of the Gods' Council, would already have put a stop to this Erin's Wrath nonsense." The Lord sighed, wrapping the scroll he'd been reading with a ribbon and placing it aside.

"I ... we have the Prince Consort's requests to meet."

"Within the bounds of *scripture*," The Lord's emerald robe rippled as he slammed his hand down. "And *we*, Grand Meister, the seven who make up the Gods' Council, will not have that line crossed. Am I clear?"

"Perfectly," replied Arknold, shoulders bowing under the Lord's stare. These meetings were just one of the reasons she regretted taking on the mantle of Grand Meister. The other being the squeeze on her personal time for research. "But all we have done, you have already approved. Why are we subject to more checks?"

"Because there is a matter of trust." He picked up the scroll he'd bound, waving it towards her. "We need to ensure what you present, and what you create, match. It is the will of this House, the foundation upon which this University is built. Knowledge, as we know, is sacred. And the sanctity of that needs to be *verified*. You, yourself, have remodelled your siege engines without permission. Pushed the boundaries."

"Those are tests. Not creations. How can I know something is worth making if I can not change or adapt to—to experiment." Arknold knew she had slipped into a pleading tone, annoyed with herself. But Lord Wisdom had that effect on most.

"Aha. You see. That is the very word Lord Penance says leads to trouble. Especially, I might add, when you do so *with* Meister Kinst. Checks and boundaries have kept academics such as you from leading us astray since the first sacred word was written by the Seven. Now that is enough. My Keeper will be visiting your workshop within the hour. I do hope you are prepared, Grand Meister."

"Of course. Everything already has your seal, as you know."

"I am sure that is the case. But even so, it needs to be verified." The Lord's smug smile grated on Arknold's nerves, and she dug her thumbs harder into her palms to stop the retort.

How did Kinst describe him? A bloated bag of swamp gas. Not far wrong.

9

A QUEEN'S WRATH

THE ALCHEMICAL MEISTER'S WORKROOM, ERSTENBURGH UNIVERSITY

"Okay, we have Meister Arknold's new ballista with us today, so the Queen's deer may take a beating, eh? Took them a year to recover last time she tried it out. We are returning to Smerral, with another extra duty to perform. We're also running guard on one of Meister Kinst's experiments, something we need to handle with a lot of bloody care, understand?" Rakslin smiled briefly, enjoying his own humour, and the bonds it helped forge. Kinst was well known for her production of the flash powder, already incorporated into the hand thrown pot bombs that were now standard issue in each Spear since the last Crusade. One or two early versions had gone awry, lost hands and arms more than common than they would have liked. But now regarded as having potential and a useful tool in the defence of the Union. Whatever they were babysitting had to involve something explosive.

"We'll be using Arknold's battlecarts, with Gowan on oversight. Ranger Lewis' Spear will bring the extra horses. Understood? You have your orders. Tread lightly and follow instructions … all of them." Captain Rakslin emphasised the last few words as he glared at Laoch's Spear.

"Dismissed."

The four Spears filed out, aiming towards the barrack's exercise yard to meet with their transport battlecarts. Their steel shod wooden wheels sunk into the mud, steam rising from the waiting pairs of powerfully built horses harnessed at the front, their muscles rippling. Sura ambled towards her position, thoughts on the Erin's Wrath that would soon be hitched to the rear of the cart.

"Hey, all good?" Laoch shouted, careful to catch her eye as Sura turned his way. Elves always appreciated eye contact, finding the human need to stare anywhere else an excuse for an argument, or a fight. Sura was good at both, but Laoch had always been the one to understand the need and could hold her gaze.

"Yeah, I'm good. And you smell like you avoided the bottle last night. Have you shaved, really? My, I think you might even have had a wash." She reached out, grabbing his chin and moving it from side to side. Her sly grin sucked him in as her soft, smooth skin shone and humour lit her eyes. The smile lifted the pointed ears that had earned her race the elven label, their own, Schenterenta, simply unpronounceable with a human tongue.

"Very funny, and all true. Listen, you talked to Gowan after the meeting. You can't defend me forever. I ... I need to ..." Sura's smile faded, face-to-face with Laoch, eye to cat-like eye. The mood instantly shifted.

"Yes, I spoke to her, and she wanted your arse thrown out, and whatever remained of your reputation with it. And I can't say I blame her anymore—where have you been for the last few days, eh? Not a word. Everyone's assumed you disappeared down to the bottom of yet another bottle. Tappin depends on your example, your methods and bloody support—especially after they went out on a limb for you. I am not your counsel, Laoch. I can't carry on talking you through the crap you put yourself in all the time. The anger, the drink." Fire lit her eyes; all traces of humour wiped away. "It's time to make a choice. Stop the drinking, stop pissing about winding everyone up. By your Gods, Laoch, deal with it. Elnega had half his face burnt off by these barbarians you fight, and he doesn't get in half the shit you do."

"And you think he sleeps better than I? And he drinks the Khundish under the table," replied Laoch, looking to the floor before remembering not to. His clear, drink free mind not agreeing with him right now as it whirled. "They–." He stopped; Sura's face told him to shut up and listen.

"It will help. Your Spear won't bang on the Captain's door with tales to tell. But I will, Laoch. I can't keep this up. I am your friend. But I have enough of my own crap to deal with ... with the new recruits." Sura's eyes dropped, the elven dismissal, and she spun, following the rest of the Spear towards the battlecart.

"They giving you trouble about being an elf? Which ones, Sura. I'll ..."

"You'll do nothing. It's my shit to sift, no one but me fights my battles. Understand that, and you might ... ahhh who am I kidding." Sura spun back round to face him, eyes piercing through his soul. "I need certainty. Understand? We're done, Laoch. I can't take any more of your crap. I can't trust you."

Laoch could feel the darkness and pain boiling in the back of his mind as Sura walked away. It began to press on his senses as it had so many times in the past—the slash of the knife, the flames caressing his flesh. He pushed back, forcing it deep down. But all that slipped in unbidden was the image of a boy, no more than eleven, eyes empty as the blood drained away. Hands rung with the vibration as his blade hit bone, skin tingling with the warm gush of blood and a life taken.

Looking down to his disfigured hand, it remained barely a scratch compared to the pain he'd dealt a family somewhere. The last two days spent moving from village to village, seeking the lad's home and the parents missing their child. But none arose, his conclusion the boy was a runaway, or had lost his kin somewhere in the chaos of life. Either way, he'd paid for the lad to be transported and laid to rest in Justice's House in Farnford, the next town along the Queen's Road.

I thought a new beginning. Wrong once again.

—

Feeling Laoch's eyes upon her, Sura bit at her lip, anger and a depth of sadness grating at her thoughts. Lost in both worlds and needing to fight everyone and no one—her past, her heritage and most of all those that felt they had a right to judge.

Enough self-pity.

Peering ahead, one of the newer intake from the city guard sat in the doorway of the battlecart, picking at his teeth with a splinter of wood. Bloodshot eyes looked her up and down as if she was mud on his shoe. Pausing, Sura waited for whatever asinine rubbish the man would spew. He'd chosen exactly the wrong moment to piss her off.

"Out of the way," she said, half an order, eyes locked on his. The ex-city guard looked her up and down again, mumbling under his breath.

"You know much about my kind? We don't do that."

"Those pointy bastard ears heard me? Who'd have guessed. Heathen bitch. What in the Seven hells are your kind doing here. The Houses should flay you as an example to the Unbelievers."

"I fought the Unbelievers, and lost good Rangers, friends. You don't get to besmirch their memories." Sura stepped back, marking the new Ranger's body language, sensing the challenge to come. Eyes peered over the cart's edge, a mix of veterans and trainees anticipating what was to come for very different reasons.

Maybe it is time.

Standing with his hands balling in and out, she smelt the anger on his foul breath.

"Fuck you. You don't get to judge my people as good or bad. You and your bloody weird ancestor shit. How many have you got stuffed in those caves?"

One less than there should be.

"This is insubordination, Ranger ...?"

"Topsun. Don't forget it."

"I won't." Sura let the Patterning in. Physicality and mind unifying at the expectation of combat, forging in a body honed by the rhythm of the fight. The man twitched, a decision made, the merest flicker of eye movement and nerve response as he chose to back his words with actions. The elbow pulled back, and she moved, stepping aside from the blow, weaving back in to grasp the man's throat, her other hand wrapped around his balls. "Topsun, right? See, I *never* forget a name. Which do I rip out first—your balls or your throat? You have three, no two, ah maybe one second ..."

"Ne-neither." The words were choked and barely audible, making her grimace.

"Sorry, they didn't hear you in the cart and they are curious to see which body part this heathen bitch chooses." Squeezing harder, she let the anger into her eyes, the cat-like slits narrowing further. "Say it again. Louder."

"Neither," he choked out.

"Eh? Was that sorry you heathen bitch for every word and thought I just had?"

The man nodded, Sura squeezing harder.

"Yes. By the Seven I'm sorry."

"Not good enough," Sura twitched both hands, feeling the ex-city guard's fear response. "Latrine duty, you righteous bastard. For a month. Understand. You get to clean this heathen bitch's crap up for a whole tour of duty."

Topsun nodded, Sura's smile greeting the reddening cheeks as she released. The laughter behind enough to drive the Ranger back towards the barracks. She looked up to those waiting on the cart, catching the nods of approval from the vets, and an agreeable amount of respect from the newer recruits who'd not witnessed her in action before. Shaking her head, Laoch back on her mind despite the release of pent-up anger, she climbed the battlecart ladder and took her position beside Rogin - her posture tight, frustrated. The switch from humour to the warrior inside a true reflection of her Schenterenta heritage. She desperately tried not to look at Laoch as he approached, but the compulsion was too great and she risked a glance upwards, eyes laced with pain for the man, but quashing the longing he sought. She knew, in that instant, the root he'd nurtured within her needed to wither away—to rot along with the self-inflicted mess of his pain that so reflected her own. A loss she had to face, before he exposed the rawness inside.

In her mind, she persuaded herself Laoch would never be ready. The anger and daymares engulfing him on the darkest days and ruining his life—unable to commit to something that crossed boundaries. She knew it now, despising the voices of her Elders in the back of her mind that railed against the taint of the humans.

Sura looked over, Laoch meeting her eyes, and where he'd expected need, she gave him anger. She shook her head, forcing the tears down.

"Okay." Laoch tapped under his arm, only the sound of his cloak's rustle coming back, the flask absent. "But I'm trying."

Sura nodded back, sliding her eyes to the side, trying to let the tension slip away.

"What did he say?"

"Huh?" replied Sura, before realising Rogin had spoken to her.

"Topsun. What did he say about your kind?"

"No idea. We may have pointy ears, but we don't hear any better."

"You're kidding me." Rogin nudged her shoulder. "Really?"

Sura shook her head, noting Gowan's approach. "Didn't hear a bloody word."

Gowan eased her horse in next to the battlecart, "Rogin, you have the reins. Laoch's probably feeling a little worse for wear this morning—it's a shame as I have to ask you to keep it steady seeing as you're carrying enough Erin's Wrath to blow me to the Seven Veils. Maintain your discipline, Spears, even you Laoch." Gowan glowered over to him, and Laoch tensed in response, waiting for whatever was coming his way. There had to be a price to pay for Sura's intervention, and the failed attempt to get rid of him.

The glare, however, slid by. Gowan's eyes roaming to the second, smaller cart hitched to the rear. Laoch felt the tension pass, the First Ranger's instinct to follow *procedure* overcoming her desire to kick him some more. As Rogin eased the horses forward, and the heavy battlecart jolted from the muddy courtyard, he found himself agreeing with Gowan's decision. Erin's Wrath, by all accounts, was not something to be mishandled in the middle of an argument—it'd end up giving them a damn fine view of the Gods' Seven Veils.

10

A PASSING

THE INNER VEIL

*V*eil penetrated. The veil is ... strange, my Captain. It almost lives, one second strong and powerful, the next lost and lonely. It tastes of humanity's gains, and the Schenterenta's pained loss. You feel it?

'*Yes,*' thought the Captain.

We will end soon. You and I. Be no more.

'*I know,*' thought the Captain.

I do not wish it to end for nothing. More Sealgair have passed, my spirit is low, I have little left to give them. Some might be ... damaged.

'*Yes,*' thought the Captain. '*They knew the risk, as did their families. As did I.*'

You had the choice, I as a Wyrm, had none.

'*It is you and your kind we are also here to help. Though, as you say, the spiritfire is so weak here ... it will end soon, I fear. As will our hopes.*'

Yes, the time is passing. Even your veil does not compare to that we just slipped through.

'*Prepare the pods and make your first selection quickly. I can feel your bones part, your skin stretch.*'

It is ... unpleasant. I think you call this fear.

'*They ripped my spirit from my body, Wyrm. And bonded it to you. What have I left to fear?*'

I thought I would miss you, but I was mistaken. You think nothing but for yourself.

'*A Wyrm Ship? With feelings? Now that would be something to truly fear.*'

You are mistaken, Captain. There is one more thing you should fear. But the Wyrm Ship chose not to send that thought.

II
WHEN A SOUL CRIES

QUEEN'S ROAD, ERSTEN FOREST

E cne shifted on the battlecart's wooden bench, hankering after a cushion, but knowing it would only embarrass her in
front of the hardened men and women she could smell in the enclosed space. The tall, lanky acolyte eased her legs out, attempting
to ignore each bump that railed up her spine. Pushing hands together and resting them on her thighs, she let her eyes drift around
the inside of the cart. The Ranger Spear pointedly ignored her, the
acolyte's light green robes singling her out amid their patchwork
cloaks in hues of browns chosen for the winter camouflage. It
was a proud moment—despite the awkwardness—a moment her
family would celebrate. Though not a Ranger herself, she noted
the bag of cushioned pot bombs carried by every third soldier.
Her work, or at least under Kinst's direction, had led to the second
version. A little less volatile, though they needed more force on
impact to crack the internal sections.

*And now Erin's Wrath. Another step, perhaps, towards the sci-
ence being accepted by the Seven Houses.*

At the rear of the battlecart, the wheeled ballista bounced along,
its hitch less than perfect but secure enough. Grand Meister Ar-

knold had fussed over it so much and ended up over-complicating it with her worries about the experimental weapon. Ecne had despaired, nearly pushing the Grand Meister aside, just catching herself in time when the glint of the gold-trimmed green robe reminded her of Arknold's status. Ecne used to wonder just how she managed to come up with the adapted designs to match Meister Kinst's creations. But the time spent supporting Arknold since her acolyte passed had opened up her workshop to Ecne—like a cave of wonders. Among the jumble of burned or broken Unbeliever weaponry, she had cobbled and built a multitude of designs that had sparked Ecne's own imagination. For a while, she had toyed with suggesting a change of role to support Arknold, which would allow Kinst to train a new acolyte, until her Meister mentioned Lord Penance and quoted the Seven's scripture. The mixing of the sciences remained forbidden; an act that could lead to Ecne being forced to join Penance's House. Possibly, as word would have it, even a Meister's fate should they push their supposed heresy too far.

As the thoughts streamed unbidden, Ecne's world turned sideways.

Gowan grabbed the saddle's pommel, hands gripping tightly as she felt her spirit wrench from her body, the embodiment of the soul scraping across her mind, ghost-like fingers digging deep to hold on. She stared down at her own back, her physical body stock still as the spiritual one gripped hard, anchoring itself tight in her own will. Her horse reared, front hooves bouncing onto the stone road, scattering insects right and left. On the battlecart, Rogin stared ahead, his body still, eyes empty. Behind him a shimmer rode the air—and Gowan knew, her fear pulsing, that her body was just as empty.

The external force stopped, her spirit slamming back into the waiting body. Her mind fogged for a moment before the world made sense once again. Gowan veered the skittish horse over, grabbing Rogin as she pitched forward, pushing her back onto the bench. With the pair of heavy horses neighing wildly, bucking against the harness, she wheeled alongside to take a bridle in hand. The battle-trained horses calmed under her presence, and she trotted alongside until able to bring the whole cart gently to a stop.

"Fuck me," she said, whispering to herself.

What in the Seven Gods' names?

Gowan quickly surveyed the battlecart with Sura gripping the bench next to Rogin, staring at those around her, eyes fearful. The rest had succumbed to a brain fog. A few slumped, others dazed but standing and checking on their colleagues. Laoch held onto Kerund, the soldier conscious but eyes rolling, with Tappin leaning against the cart sides.

"A Soul Tear," whispered Sura, her eyes flicking towards Gowan as she finally let go of the bench. "My spirit, Gowan. It hurts, and I could sense everyone's pain. I have heard of it, but it is a myth amongst my people. One rarely spoken of. If it is true, the Spear will be alright, mostly. All except those whose hearts fail." Sura stepped down the ladder, grabbing Laoch by the arm for balance. "The story is not ours any longer, though. It speaks only of the shamans from the past. From a time before your people arrived."

Gowan nodded, not understanding a word her friend spoke. Such things were not of interest to her, only Fate and her House. She cared for Sura like a sister, but the person she embodied, not the elf she was—something that gnawed at her sense of belief.

Duty.

"No mind. It's done. We have a job to do. See to Rogin and I'll check the other battlecart." Gowan spurred her horse away, briefly glancing at the hitched cart of Erin's Wrath and concluding that as she still lived, it would be fine.

———

Meister Kinst settled down into the chair, easing her back into the cushions, aiming for one of her favoured naps at this time of day. As her eyelids sank, hairs along her wrists and arms rose, standing on end as her body quivered. The tingling spread over her shoulders, and up the back of her neck. The Meister's eyes popped open, a queer feeling washing through her brain, wiping the thoughts of sleep away with a wave of separation. For a moment, she felt herself slip from her body, a disconnect. Sliding outwards with arms outstretched, desperately trying to hold on to her body.

She snapped back, her spiritual self instantly melding with the body she'd left behind. Kinst stood, mouth wide, staring at her hands and then into the mirror only to be greeted by her own reflection.

Was I asleep? Dreaming? But the time? I must have slept for an hour.

Shouts echoed from outside the door, the Meister stepping out to find the servants in disarray as luncheon plates spun, and cutlery lay strewn upon the wooden boards. The Meister strode in, helping the University retainers to their feet, their eyes distant until they focused in on the Meister's face.

By the Gods, what just happened?

12

AN END'S BEGINNING

HOUSE OF PENANCE, ERSTENBURGH

The rupture washed over the roof, fluttering tiles, sending the flocks roosting skyward in squawks announcing a new danger to any that would listen. Lord Penance, mind rooted in his self-belief, cane pressed into the purple streaked marble before his House's entranceway stared upwards as the birds circled. His heart pounded as his spirit held fast against the invisible storm breaking along his soul. A pained hip railed against the stiffness he demanded, begging for release. With a firm grip upon the bond between body and soul, Lord Penance refused the call. Withered, blackened fingers holding tight upon the cane top. His purple-dyed tongue searching amid his ruined teeth, drawing out the tang of the junip fruit. Lord Penance let the taste enthuse his body with the memories of its effect, emboldening his inner strength. The wave passed, his spirit holding firm, and he released the tension within his body. An unfortunate, but dampened scream, slipped from his lips as his pained hip shuddered. Needles driving into the bone joint as a reminder of his burdens.

The High Lord felt the world shift, his place within it moving ever so slightly to the left before it pulled back into place—as if riding a wave when it plummets. Stomach lurching, he adjusted the cane, desperate to prevent the embarrassment of a fall. With caws echoing above, the fluttering of wings still declaring the crows remained on the wing, a Priest leapt the steps, hands wet, eyes wide to brace his High Lord. Briefly accepting the damp embrace, Penance let out a sigh as his hip popped, the pain a sharp reminder of who he represented. He pushed the priest away.

"No need, Stent. Leave me be," the words spilled gruffly from his stained lips, though the young priest caught her Lord's grateful eyes as she stepped away. The Lord demanded a different message for those that watched, however, and the priest moved back further, a small bow accepting the stern response.

"Sorry my Lord, my mistake."

"Never mind. Go see to the others, check on them." Lord Penance glanced back up at the sky, ears now picking out voices on the wind. Wails. Fear. "Wait. Fetch the Priests-in-Waiting, girl. Now."

"Which ones?" Stern asked, the duty one she had not performed before.

Penance cocked his ear to the right, his face set grim as voiced fear rolled down the surrounding streets about the House of Penance. "All of them. We're going to need everyone with what's coming."

The priest sped off, her thin purple robe flying in the wind as she took two marbled steps at a time in her haste. Lord Penance followed, taking each of the seven steps to his House's entrance with care. His hip complained, a sore back joining in, before he turned back as the first of his flock came into view. The noise rolled over him, beseeching, eyes rolling or wide-eyed and wild. Hoarse voices calling on Penance to scourge them, punish their bodies for whatever act had caused the flutter of their souls, the threat of its parting.

The sea of words crashed over him, causing the High Lord to flinch before he lifted his cane high, waiting a second before bringing it down for the tip to clatter into the waiting bell at his side. The brass shook, the ring piercing the hubbub, and a silence fell. All eyes upon the purple-robed Lord who'd rung the Prayer Bell.

Penance did not speak. He simply waited, eyes bouncing from person to person, each greeted with a gentle, stern-faced nod. A single finger raised from a blackened hand; a reminder of his role far more than the purple robes wrapped about his person. The first footfalls echoed behind him, stiff shoes upon smooth stone, and he finally chose to speak as his priests emerged.

"Yes," he said, the firmness to his words pulling his flock's attention. "We felt it too. Calm. This is not your punishment, nor your burden. It is ours. Share your fears." He looked either side, steering the priests out into the people, knowing that more city folk would come soon to seek whatever Penance his priests bestowed.

Be kind?

Hah, if only we could.

He let his mind wander, thinking on the other Houses, and how many of their flocks would be seeking solace within their walls.

We must dampen the fear, before it overtakes the city and wherever else the Soul Tear was felt. And then ... then we must find out the cause.

He glanced inside the House entrance, seeing that Amarnta waited there, the leader of today's scheduled service. She dealt in pain and sufferance with a zeal, an ideal priest for today's Mass. Lord Penance turned back, walking down amid his flock, singling out those with a greater need to suffer and sending a steady stream inside to await their punishment.

My burden.

After an hour, the crowd thinned, most responding to quiet words or a touch from Penance's priests. Each leaving with a small rite of atonement as they returned to whatever job or home awaited them. The High Lord refused to show his exhaustion, letting his priests see a leader bearing his pains, and strode up the steps as they streamed back inside. Standing at the top of the seven marbled steps, Lord Penance's eyes scanned upwards.

"Do they settle?"

"No, Sneed, they do not," he answered, pursing his lips, letting his head drop. "Did you feel it?"

"Without the purple junip fruit to fortify, yes. It took me, I fear to say. Swept my spirit near out from its root." The old priest stepped from the shadow of the doorway, eyes roaming his High Lord for the tiredness he undoubtedly expected.

Lord Penance nodded, raising his blackened hand to pick at his teeth subconsciously, "A Soul Tear, Sneed. I thought my time would have passed before this. And now ..."

"It is your burden. Yes. And ours."

"Let them rest, the priests. But not long. Then send them out onto the streets. We need to know who it affected, and how far it spread."

"Yes, I shall see to it."

13
SOUL SEARCHING

The White Palace, Erstenburgh

Grand Meister Arknold picked at her nails behind her back. The thumb nail digging under each one at a time, hoping and praying to the Seven Gods in turn that the Prime would do her the courtesy of ignoring the uncouth habit. Once she stopped, the nerves would overwhelm her, and the Queen's questioning would lead to a sobbing heap on the floor begging forgiveness for anything and everything.

Again.

She stepped closer to Kinst, the Meister Alchemist, confidante and—only when drunk—a hero of hers despite the reversal of status. In her mind, Kinst should be wearing the heavy robes of the University leadership, and the burden it imparts.

The woman has, forgive the expression, balls of steel.

"Yes, Your Majesty. All within the University, except the Elvish contingent who remain close-lipped, expressed the same response. If they were awake, they experienced the spirit separation. Only a few, mind, stated that they had a lesser experience, and one barely any at all. Each of those, on my research, was either washing or immersed in water. Wouldn't you agree, Meister

Kinst?" Arknold threw her friend a longing look, aching for the woman to weigh in and support her response.

"Yes, Your Majesty," said Kinst, stepping forward and letting her eyes meet the Queen's. The glance enough for her to ascertain the Queen's opinion on Arknold's credibility, knowing from the Prime's frequent briefings that she had little respect for those that could not hold her gaze. "The Grand Meister has it right. Our acolytes were quick to ascertain the information. May we ask, was it the same in the Palace?"

Arknold squirmed inside, recognising what Kinst was doing, and the risks she seemed to revel in.

So, she's not asking you directly, my Queen. Especially in front of your subjects. But you know the information is important. If this was an attack ...

The Queen took a second before replying, not looking towards her Consort nor the Prime before responding but taking her own counsel with a considered answer. Her eyes narrowed, a gentle curl to her lips as she spoke, "There are reports across the Palace. From the stables to the Court. Prime Vardrin, have we any news on the water contact the Meisters have alerted us to?"

"No, Queen Erin. But I will investigate. Many were still in shock, and well, with the servants they can panic. Possibly choose the answer everyone else gives, as a precaution." Vardrin snapped his fingers, the footman quickly reaching his side before the Prime's arms returned to their usual position behind his back. He whispered into the trusted servant's ear as the Queen's heavy gaze fell once again upon the Grand Meister.

"I feel the University has a huge role in finding out what happened, Grand Meister. Don't you? High Lord Penance will be here soon, and I will set him the same task. Surely between the Gods and the University we can find answers, yes?"

Arknold swiftly nodded, not trusting her voice as the saliva in her throat rapidly evaporated. She felt a nudge in her arm, Kinst bowing and keeping her eyes low before turning to leave, the audience over. She mirrored her friend, and hustled out the door as the court servants opened the white, carved filigree doors. The ones that gave the illusion that all within the audience chamber could be seen and heard, though the Grand Meister knew better. After all, they were her design, and the nuanced disruption of sight and sound a craft she was proud of. Among others, a little more deadly.

"Jacka," cut in Adama, the Prince Consort clearly out of sorts. He'd remained silent throughout, hands gripped together firmly, as if in prayer on the throne. "This threat ... I can sense its evil." The Queen nervously glanced at her Consort, Jacka half-expecting a bejewelled hand to reach across and calm the man until he remembered the recent coldness that lay between them. "Recall our soldiers in the outlying villages. Set the Rangers around our walls. I need to feel ... protected."

14

WHEN HOPE FADES

EMERGING FROM THE FINAL VEIL

This realm should be strong, powerful like its veils. Yet inside ... nothing.

'It is too late, the end of me Wyrm. Can you ...?'

You fade, Captain.

'I ... am ... leaving ...'

I will release the remaining hunters, the Sealgair.

'Yessss...'

The Wyrm Ship felt the wrench, the roots of the Captain's spirit parting from its deck. The bone and skin burned as the Captain's form dissipated into the ether, his smile of release, immersed in pain and joy, the last of him to fade.

Goodbye, Captain. Our journey was long, our quest agony upon our souls. But there remains no rest for you, no meeting with your family amid the Well. Your journey is not complete, your task not done. Our people need you still, to see if one last sliver of hope remains for us all.

The ship felt the first joint slide apart. The bone-white skin stretching and tearing as the pressure from within, and the glyph releasing spiritfire without, twisted and yawed the Wyrm out of shape. It sent its *self* along the bones of the deck, seeking the remaining pods, desperate to release their hope upon the final realm they had travelled so long to find. It drove its *will* up through the white-laced veins rooted to the deck, the last of the Wyrm's spiritfire rushing to engulf the Sealgair pods. The bow snapped, bone and marrow splintering, and uncontained wild power roared inwards from the veil itself. The ship screamed, the immense energy too much for it to contain as the marrow in its bones boiled, cooking the Wyrm from within.

My last gift ... save us.

The pods cracked, releasing opaque crystalline balls to roll across the bone splintered deck. Four tumbled off the stern side as the ship gave one final twist before wrenching apart. The last glyph's assault pausing briefly, as if waiting, before ramming together the remains of the ship into a tightening ball of bone and skin that swirled among the whirling, wild energy. Until—with a final pop of bone—it disappeared. The glyph's power and the Wyrm within, at one with the realm it hoped would save their kind.

And there, wavering, a final, larger silvered ball spun, hanging amid the starlit sky above the clouds—a faded spirit inside trapped and fated. It did not fall. Held fast by the orange-laced curtain that lashed out from above, sensing the creature within. Spiritfire wreathed its outer skin. The arcs of power battering at the crystalline metal—crashing against it, desperate to gain entry and destroy the abomination. Yet the sphere held fast, resisting the power. Waiting as the Wyrm had required while four shimmering Sealgair plummeted towards the swirling clouds below. The last vestige of the Wyrm's façade smothered the remaining sphere, freeing it from the grip of the spiritfire, for no more glyphs or curtains remained to defend the realm.

Three silvered spheres emerged above a green and rain-covered forest, plummeting to crash through branches and deep into the mud. Twigs and leaves fell after them, covering the glowing balls—each reflecting back on itself as the light receded to leave a mirror-like surface. As the last bent leaf whirled to rest upon the ground, and animal life screeched in panic and fear, a crack broke through the cacophony. An eerie silence washed over the forest. A sudden pause, waiting for the next. Another fracturing sent shivers through the leaves and the wolves finally took up their howl with a mix of fear and challenge.

The third sphere neither cracked nor fractured—instantly flying apart as the warrior unfurled from its embryonic position. A crystalline helmet dripped a green jelly-like substance as it pierced the air with arms outstretched, mirrored like the helm, embracing the sky as it welcomed the rain washing it clean. The creature let out a roar. Shouting a guttural defiance to the sky, quelling the wolves and reigniting the maelstrom of noise and movement that burst outward through the forest.

Reaching down, gauntlets roamed amid the shattered remains of the sphere, emerging with a sheathed sword that it pulled halfway from the scabbard before slamming it back. Probing hands then recovered more equipment—a holster, with crossbow and quarrels following. Each checked and stowed before the helm turned towards the other spheres, their outer covering finally cracking as gloved fingers emerged. Rasping, harsh words flew, with a pommel crashing down to fracture the remaining shells, stepping back to allow the other armoured forms to rise and greet the rain.

And above the cloud, unseen to the eyes of all, the largest sphere dropped. It spun furiously, pushing on through the cloud, sending ripples like a pebble crashing into the surface of a pond, to emerge into the realm below. Free to do as it will.

15
WHEN FEAR RIDES IN

SMERRAL RANGER ENCAMPMENT (ONE DAY LATER)

C aptain Rakslin entered the camp, one hand animated, talking rapidly to the Queen's messenger at his side. The woman's yellow and green livery matched that of the sweating horse she led, the Erstenburgh Royal colours. Rakslin looked to the Veils, everyone recognising his display of controlled temper, before beckoning them over. Clearly he, and his guard, had been caught on the way to the clearing and was far from being in a good mood.

"We have been recalled," yelled Rakslin, the usually soft-spoken Ranger Captain hitting the vocal level of a murder of crows. "Everyone to their battlecarts now. Get the Meister's ballista stowed and ready. Show me some discipline."

Rangers and their Spears scattered to their designated roles, dodging the Queen's messenger as she set off, her lathered horse carrying her back towards Erstenburgh. For the older Rangers, the captain's urgency and instant demands dragged them back to days gone by, when Rakslin had overseen the Queen's Rangers on the Crusade. Word was he'd calmed somewhat since returning to devise the Consort's localised patrols, and the new recruits had seen nothing of his famous temper. As the veterans moved at speed, the rumours of its might flew thick and fast.

"Get the carts' ballistae loaded, I want them cocked and ready. We've not been recalled as a bloody exercise. Something's cooking, Rangers. Something bad. I can smell it on the wind," bellowed the captain, before turning to his second-in-command, eyes watching the encampment as everyone hurried. "And we better not bloody need them. What in the Seven Hells is this? First this bloody Soul Tear, according to our elf and now word of an unknown threat. We're in Ersten Forest, not the bloody borderlands."

The captain let a brief smile flicker as the Ranger's discipline shone, the vets of the Crusades and border skirmishes quick to keep their Spears in line. Up north, you dallied, you died. Soldiers and equipment dropped into ready positions, two Spears in the horse-drawn battlecarts, the rest on horseback—only Laoch and Kerund remained out of position as they carefully hitched the Erin's Wrath.

"Don't hurry that, lads," he half-whispered, his second-in-command nodding along.

Gowan barked orders at drivers and the Spears, hurrying them up as her horse stomped next to the metal shod and toughened wood of the battlecarts. Eventually each driver signalled their readiness to move out, reins in hand and calming words whispered to the horses.

Rakslin eyed the vets, each astride an experienced horse, eyes scanning the area.

"They feel it," Rakslin said, pulling his horse round. "The quiet."

"Captain," whispered his second-in-command, a spyglass to her eye. She scanned the silent trees along the forest's edge as the battlecarts finished forming up, the waiting horses skittish. "There's something to the east, amid the trees. Movement." The Ranger handed over the long thin tube, Rakslin reaching out from astride his old war horse. He turned, surveying the area he'd been directed to. Amid the trees, branches warped and moved, their shapes briefly misshapen. Unusual until they bounced back. He sucked in a breath, holding it as he steadied the eyeglass, trying to reduce the tremor of his old hands. The image cleared a little, and the pine trees and scrub bush swayed naturally in the gentle wind.

"Nothing. Got me seeing things. Bloody panic," he said to no one but himself.

Sura's hands gripped her Schenterenta bow lightly, the Patterning of her warrior's heritage indelibly marked in her mind. Her aptitude with the short Schenterenta bow and spear forged by the elven combat exercises that honed their skills and could be practised anywhere. Sitting in the cart felt so wrong, against her instincts to be open, free to move in response to threat. She had seen much of war during her time on the Unspoken's borders that lay north of her beloved Partera Plains. But even that felt right compared to this.

Tension washed through the cramped soldiers, words falling to a whisper. The usual dark, Fate-laden jokes absent.

I can feel it. The silence out there.

Tension coiled around Sura's heart. She eased a breath out, and taking a slow one in, checked her quiver, then adjusted her sword. The harnessed horses stopped their nickering, hooves no longer pawing at the ground. With trepidation, she rose, easing her head past Rogin to peer out the hatched window at his side. Behind her, the cart suddenly weighed down, leaning sideways, with Kerund's grunt piercing the silence as he climbed heavily aboard. She made to turn, to look for Laoch.

A roar ripped through the encampment—a rush of turbulent wind that tore at the cart's covers, whipping by and thrashing the trees' branches beyond the clearing. Debris swirled and clattered against the battlecarts, the experienced warhorses rearing at their sides, throwing their Rangers as panic set in.

The sky cracked. Lightning racking the grey clouds, the thunder rumbling heavily across the trees and deep into the clearing. A bolt struck the outer trees, splintering branches; a white fire burning briefly before the pine sap caught and orange flame took over. A second boom tore through the air as something crashed, spinning furiously, dropping from the sky to slam into the rear battlecart. Wood and splinters showered the powerful, harnessed horses, peppering their bodies, splitting limbs. Soldiers screamed, bodies broken and afire. The air suddenly rife with burnt flesh and cooked blood.

Sura dragged herself from the floor of the cart, rubbing her eyes clear of dust and debris blown in by the wind. The air filled with a deathly whistle, and something flashed across her eyeline as she forced them open, smashing into the ground nearby. Mud and grass sprayed across the battlecart, forcing her to duck, only for her to rise and catch sight of three bejewelled figures standing at the wood's edge. Twenty yards distant, and highlighted against the burning trees, their entire bodies were encased in a strange crystalline armour. Sura blinked, stunned, as they flickered in the light. The polished surfaces reflecting flame and smoke. Impulse made her raise her bow, nocking an arrow despite the cramped space and the madness overtaking her cart.

Breathe, keep on breathing. Wait.

Captain Rakslin stared at the glowing metallic sphere that spun and pulsed in the centre of the wrecked battlecart, blood smoking on its surface. His mind reeled, lost to the oddness that had killed his soldiers within, and near destroyed the mounted Spear under his command. Everywhere horses and soldiers screamed, splintered wood and metal armour piercing human and beast alike. Rakslin worshipped the Seven Gods as they all did, with particular devotion to the House of Penance, the Overseer. A veteran of the crusades, he'd seen much. But nothing prepared you for this.

He swore, shouting at his second-in-command to send a signal arrow before turning to whoever remained, "Unbelievers, worshippers of the Unspoken God, the Eighth. Take the blasphemous bastards dow—"

The shout died in his throat—a crystal-clad soldier raising a hand, and whatever lay within its fingers exploding with a white, pulsing power. A seething bolt of lightning had sped across the intervening space, and Captain Rakslin's last, choked command never reached the ears of his waiting soldiers. He reached for his throat, fingers digging into an open wound before collapsing, eyes to the Veil as life left him behind. A revered hero sprawled across the mud and blood, his faithful warhorse spinning wildly as madness struck.

Sura tracked across the mirror-armoured soldiers and chose her target. The arrow flew, the Schenterenta ignoring its path as she searched her quiver for the next, distracted by the explosion of noise and movement in the cart. Eyes flickering up, relief coursed through her on seeing Laoch alive and backing out of the door, heading for the rear of the cart. Then the ballista launched, Rogin releasing a heavy bolt, briefly watching the quarrel power towards the targets. The driver let the weapon hang as the cart jolted, turning to Sura as she nocked her next arrow.

"Sura," Rogin shouted over the noise of the clamouring soldiers and the cart's rearing horses. He reached over from the front, tapping Sura's hip, bringing her back as tension flowed in her shoulders. "Can you take the reins; they're going to run if I don't calm them."

Sura nodded, standing and clambering over the intervening bench, mind reeling at where Laoch had gone until realisation struck.

The Erin's Wrath. That's where Laoch went.

She crawled through the hatchway, grabbing the reins as Rogin dropped off the cart, and a scarlet rivulet filtered into her vision amid the hoofprints rammed into the muddied ground.

Rakslin.

Sura stared down from the box seat. A blood pool around his leather cap leeched into the mud, surrounding the deathly face of the human she'd followed since joining the Rangers—one of the few to accept her race, no questions asked.

And her world burst in a churning mass of wood, metal and earth—the rear of the battlecart rising from the ground, the noise of the explosion ringing through her brain, battering at her consciousness. The huge cart spun, with the metal-shod wheels squealing and splitting around her, slashing at the screaming horses as they were wrenched upwards.

Laoch.

16

AS SCRIPTURE DEFINES

ANTECHAMBER, THE WHITE PALACE, ERSTENBURGH

"**M**y Lord Penance, it has been a while since you graced my palace with your presence." Queen Erin glanced over the silver goblet pressed to her lips, sharp eyes assessing the most powerful leader in the city, probably the whole Union. She was no fool. She may hold the purse strings and the attention of the court, even the nobles. But this short, hard looking old man held sway she could only dream of. The walking stick clutched in his withered right hand testament to the man's hold over the Godly Houses, and therefore every man and woman of the Union, with each of the Seven having a House of their God in every town and city.

The cold, green eyes slipped up from the chair the servant placed nearby, his look to the young boy one of disdain and implied threat. The lad, ruffles around his throat and ornate palace slippers upon his feet, swallowed hard before lifting the chair closer to the highest religious leader in the land. Wordlessly, he hooked the cane around the intricately carved chair before easing himself downwards one vertebra at a time with a sigh. Pulling the deep purple trouser up at the knees, he placed his equally purple cloak over the top, before easing back into the chair.

The Queen knew this was all for her, defining when and how this conversation would start, marking him as the one to lead. Practical to the core, she waited—this man held her fate in the palm of his hand every day. With his favour, she reigned. Without it, she and the Union would fall into chaos until he spoke, and the Gods' Council chose. Forever at their mercy. Yet once chosen, they—he—rarely interfered.

Until now.

"Yes, my Queen. Sometime, not since that debacle of a Coronation."

"I believe," the Queen steeled herself before carrying on, needing to make some mark, "that was more to do with the Council's choice of Prince Consort, Lord Penance."

"For that, you can blame Lady Fate, my Queen. And the, erm, political will of her following. I only acquiesced when he presented as *malleable*."

Queen Erin winced as the Lord smiled, the lips tight against the purple teeth caused by the Lord's fabled diet. Each of the Houses' Lords and Ladies bore the mark, and to a lesser extent the Priests-in-Waiting who were their successors. It was one of many secrets the Houses of God held tightly onto, and one sought by her predecessor before his speedy fall from grace. His ex-communication, and that of his family and according to her sources, those of his spymaster had been one of those tightly kept, but widely known secrets that kept the walls of faith in the Houses solid, and in control of the masses. Where King Panset was now was a true unknown, one Erin had chosen not to pursue.

"Yes. That's a good word. Bastard and drunkard are another two. How much longer before I can have him ... replaced?"

"Is that why I'm here? Surely the Soul Tear is more, shall we say, pressing?" The Lord turned his head slightly to one side, his smile sending shivers down her spine, eyes unable to slide away from the purple lips even if it was within etiquette.

"No, sorry my Lord. And Soul Tear? You use those words as if this phenomenon is within your knowledge."

"It is an elven shamanistic term. Part of the Penance of being on this land is to know from whom we stole it. At least in their eyes. A Soul Tear they name it, and it feels ... apt."

The Queen steeled herself, raising her eyes to the Lord before she spoke. "Then you experienced this too? Within Penance's House?"

"By Penance's protection, no. But the masses did, which you would know if you had cared to ask more widely than your decadent palace. All those that were not touching water, as I believe you already know, were affected to some degree. My priests are out in Erstenburgh now, and as I assume you have, we are sending birds to our other cities' Houses to see how far this phenomenon spread."

"Lord Penance, I have Jacka engaging with this," she paused as the most powerful man in the Union snorted, "he will gather what I need. The ... the fate of my predecessor has left some sections of the court bereft."

Lord Penance sat forward, hand on his cane, chin hovering above. "I'm not in the mood to dance with words, my Queen. My gaze will not fall upon you, nor your court if you build back that network of snakes and liars. I believe history shows it is *necessary*. Just keep them out of the Houses of God, yes? Jacka already has fingers in many pies, he just believes he has kept it quiet.

"Now, to the matter at hand. When I get word of the spread and *depth* of the Tear, I will be needing your Meister's help to identify the centre, the source. One who is good with numbers and maps, yes? Meister Yanpet perhaps. Have him informed; he'll enjoy the suspense." Lord Penance placed a hand on the chair arm, pushing himself up with his cane as the servant approached. One glance sent the boy scurrying away as he rose. "And, my Queen, a word to the wise. The Grand Meister Arknold and Meister Kinst. Yes? They are sailing close to the wind. Much of which is forbidden started with such experimentation and led to the need for our people to move here. They must be watched with more rigour, and, my Queen, they must not work *together*. Our scripture is clear, our path chosen by the Seven because of the mistakes of the past. They dabble and I *do* hate that word, so."

17

A COWARD'S RETREAT

SMERRAL RANGER ENCAMPMENT

G owan walked between the fires, eyes scanning the corpses of friends and comrades. Their bodies split and broken upon the floor, metal shards and wooden splinters peppering their torsos. She signalled Millian, Topsun and Dunst to stand guard, the only survivors from the Rangers she'd found so far. They took position while Gowan knelt beside Laoch, checking the Ranger for injury, noting the rise and fall of his chest in a steady rhythm.

"Bloody typical you'd live through it." Satisfied the cuts were mild, she spared a glance for Laoch's scarred hand, clicking her tongue against her teeth as she imagined the pain inflicted. "No more than the rest of these poor bastards have suffered."

A white bolt seared over her shoulder, heat washing her cheek as it slammed into Millian's chest. The man's scream choked off, leather burning, the flesh below sizzling as the bolt bore its way inwards. Dunst collapsed next to him, his neck afire with white lightning. Sparks streaked down his shoulder and wrapped themselves around his right arm. Gowan dived forward, body smothering Laoch as another bolt slammed into the ground nearby. A harsh bark broke through the air, like a fox's grunt, followed by rasping shouts that set her teeth on edge.

The First Ranger rolled to the side, gathering her bow and coming up onto her knees to find Tappin and Kerund hiding beneath the shattered cart. Both were unscathed, shaking as a mirror-clad enemy appeared amid the smoke and flame. The fluctuating shimmer belied Gowan's attempts to focus on what was in its hands, but the twang was familiar—a bolt flying that flared into a white flame similar to that still burning along Dunst's chest. The bolt pierced Topsun's arm, driving on through to sear into his ribs. The man grunted. His sword wavering before his grip failed, and the weapon tumbled to the floor. Topsun dropped to his knees, mouth wide in a silent scream when a second bolt rammed into his chin.

Gowan loosed. The arrow cracking against the polished armour, shattering on impact—no dent or scratch to show for it. She notched a second, eyes on the enemy who drew a white-edged sword from a sheath at its side. The armour flickered, responding to the movement and the surrounding flames. With the outline clear, Gowan released, the arrow darting to strike against the armour's helm. It flinched, turning to face her as Tappin charged towards it, sword out, eyes wide and fear filled.

"No," Gowan shouted, but too late. The young Ranger slashing down with a strength spurred by dread, only to strike the enemy's weapon, the slide and riposte driving its edge deep into her neck.

And Gowan ran.

———

A buzz hummed in Sura's ears—a low-pitched sound, hollow, dulling the senses. She shifted her head, and pain seethed down her spine as it announced it was still attached. The grind of splintered wood against her neck brought back the last few seconds before the world had gone black. She reached behind, shoulders arguing but moving to pull away the piece of cart smouldering against her cloak. Eyes stinging, moving in and out of focus, she eventually brought Meister Kinst's stamp upon the wood into view.

"Crap," Sura rolled onto her front, drawing knees underneath before remembering the enemy. Panicking, she rose too quickly, head spinning with vertigo and stumbling to the floor. She vomited as a hand dropped onto her back, catching her between embarrassment and fear when she looked into the eyes of the acolyte. Her addled mind searched for the woman's name, scanning the light green and blood smeared robes for injury before realising she hadn't checked her own yet.

"Shh," the acolyte whispered, finger to lips, pulling her close and pointing.

With pained ears, she knelt down, eyes following where she gestured. Two of the three armoured figures from the forest's edge stood near Ecne's shattered battlecart. Splintered bones and the twisted remains of its horses poked up between them and their shimmering armour. One held a sword out, pommel up, the other a crossbow, as fires burned around them. They were human-sized, and their movements, to her eyes, definitely not of her kind. The sword's pommel smashed downwards, striking the now static crystal-metal ball with a loud ring. A small fracture appeared on its surface. A second strike widened the cracks, and a gauntleted hand broke through from inside, showering the air with a green mucus. Ecne let out a whimper, bringing her own hand up to smother the sound, while Sura stared. The sword-wielding figure tore away the last of the outer shell, stepping back to allow whoever was inside to pull themselves clear. They emerged bracing a blackened, withered hand, causing guttural barks of conversation between the two waiting armoured figures. Sura had seen such a hand only once before, when Lord Justice had inspected the Rangers on their first arrival back at the city. With a flash of white light along its edge, the sword wielder raised their weapon, slashing down to severe the offending limb at the wrist. Sura bit down on her own tongue, using the pain to stop the urge to cry out as she waited for the blood to flow. But none did. Instead, blackened smoke arose from the wound. The smell of burning flesh mingling with that brought on the wind.

The three strode out of the shattered cart, marching through the smoke and flame, heading back out into the forest as Ecne grabbed hold of her arm, pulling her close. Fear-filled eyes drew her in, and Sura clasped her near, muffling the few sobs the acolyte allowed herself, holding on until their new enemy disappeared from view.

"I'm Ecne," stated the voice against her shoulder before pulling away. The young human slipped her arm underneath Sura's, lifting the elf to her feet. This time she stayed standing, blinking as the young woman took both her cheeks in her raw hands. "I don't know elven sensitivity as well as human, but how are your ears?"

The hum had already dropped, nearer a low drone, and she told her so before pushing the hands away. Contact with an elf worked one way, on their terms. "Laoch," she said, staggering towards the smoking battlecart. "We need to find Laoch, and anyone else alive."

———

Darkness whirled through Laoch's brain. He could smell the acrid fire, feel the heat and taste soot upon the hot wind. Past soldiers' screams battered at his mind, but as he awoke, new ones greeted his bewildered mind.

Breathe ...

But he couldn't breathe, with choking fumes catching in his throat. He coughed, rolling to his side, phlegm spat across the grass.

"Laoch!" the forced whisper hit his ears; the voice pained but recognisable. He coughed again, expelling the ash.

"Laoch, you hurt?"

Laoch opened his eyes; but they were tear-filled and blurry, refusing to focus. Yet the voice called, and his soul lifted.

"Laoch,"

He felt warm, slick hands wrap around his cheeks. Blinking away the last of his tears he wrapped his hands around them and ran his thumbs along the back of the grimy hands. Just for a second, in that brief instant, the world could have ended for all he cared. All that mattered was the elf he held.

Sura?

Blinking again, his eyes fell on a strange face. Soot streaked, with a green robe wrapped about the neck and shoulders.

"Shit! Sura?" he tried to push the hands away, but still disorientated, was forced to hold still while the fingers probed the back of his head.

"She's here, but I need to check your neck." Ecne threw what she hoped was a reassuring smile. "You've landed awkwardly. I just need to be sure it's not injured before you move again." The acolyte eased her hands around the top of his shoulders, gently pressing, waiting for the Ranger's response. When she got none, she sat back, nodding to Sura who appeared over her shoulder.

"Laoch, we need to move. I found Tappin, she's ... somebody killed her after the Erin's Wrath blew. And you need to see Dunst and Millian, their injuries ..."

Laoch stared over Ecne's shoulder, looking towards the elf who offered her hand to pull him up. Laoch clasped it, rising to his knees and checking himself over before fully standing up. His eyes drank her in, taking a long look as death lay around them.

"It's just minor cuts, I'm okay. I'm okay." Sura reached out her hand, before pulling it back, folding her arms tight. "I need ..." Sura paused, "we need you back with us, Laoch. Focused. Things have gone to shit."

"You don't say," said the acolyte.

Laoch looked from her to Ecne, noting the acolyte's hands were red and seared, her nails bloodied. Laoch knew those injuries well; the vestiges of his nightmare jabbing at the back of his mind would never let him forget. His querying look met with a nod from Ecne.

"I tried to get some out, but ..." The acolyte's eyes dropped to the floor, red-rimmed from the heat and smoke.

Laoch grabbed the woman's forearm, grasping the smeared robes.

I have to get my head together, for Sura will not lead knowing many would refuse her word. Save who's left. Save me.

"That you tried is enough." Releasing, he looked around, spotting Tappin and wincing as he caught sight of her face locked in a silent scream. He strode over, crouching down to close her eyes, touching her cheek with the back of her hand. "Kerund? Rogin?"

"Not seen Kerund. We found Rogin beneath the horses. Laoch ..." Sura dropped next to Dunst, the seared neck still hot, bubbling. She removed the half-burnt quarrel, lifting it towards the approaching Ranger who took it from her, examining the feathered rear.

"It's not any Unbeliever fletching I've seen, but they change so quickly." He took a sniff, wrinkling his nose as the acrid tang hit his nostril. "And not their banefire, either. Did you see them?"

"Three figures and they glimmered, you know, like their armour was made from polished metal or jewels. They killed Captain Rakslin, his neck—it just burned through. They were so fast. Next thing I knew, the battlecart was spinning with me in it. When I woke, two were in the rear battlecart, breaking open whatever had smashed into it. It was like an egg, but so much bigger, with another one of those Unbelievers inside."

"Polished armour, you mean like mirrors? Why would you?"

"They were hard to hold in your eye, it kind of reflected everything around them." Sura ducked her head, staring at the ground as she visualised their movements. "I have little idea who they are, except they didn't move like my kind."

Laoch rubbed the back of his head, feeling an ache in his shoulder. "My memory's sketchy, but something took a shot at me and hit the rear cart carrying Erin's Wrath. How in the Seven Hells I'm alive, I don't know."

"Nor me," said Ecne. "You should be shredded meat, strung on the trees over there." Ecne pointed behind him, a grim smile flickering until she looked around again—the sudden pain behind her eyes caught by Laoch. For all the acolyte's bravado and seeming calm, the woman would crumble if she wasn't directed.

"Ecne," Laoch reached out, taking the acolyte's head in both hands. "Look at me. Yes? We are alive, and we stay alive so we can inform the Queen and the city. That is our duty. By the Ranger's code."

The young woman nodded back, blinking away the unbidden tears, wiping her nose before spitting on the floor. "Yes, Ranger."

"We need to look for weapons, Sura. Then we move. We must let the city know."

Laoch grabbed Dunst's bow, pulling the quiver from the Ranger's belt and attaching it next to his own. Giving his sword

and hunting knife a quick check, he stood, scanning the area towards the guttering pine trees as Sura gathered her own weapons.

18

IF ONLY THEY COULD SEE

THE HOUSE OF PENANCE, ERSTENBURGH

"Sneed," whispered Lord Penance, cold eyes watering while candles guttered around the chamber. He waited, withered hand twitching impulsively against the cane top as he pressed his central palm down in an attempt to stave off the cramp pulsing through it. The pain ran up his wrist and he felt the fire spreading along his forearm, reaching for his elbow. Should it pass the joint, it would be an end to the whole arm and the decision on the new Lord would have to be rushed forwards.

Perhaps not the best time for that.

"Sneed," he repeated through gritted teeth.

A purple stone pulsed sickeningly on a plinth in the centre of the chamber, responding to the Lord's breathing, mimicking each breath in unison. The connection between it and his mind had been severed, dropped as he'd finally let go of the Wyrding stone—but it always did this, almost as if it wanted to taste the life it had been so swiftly separated from. Lord Penance saw the severance as a guillotine; husk-like fingers mentally chopped off, releasing his hand as the Wyrding attempted to take control. Visualising the tips spiralling to the floor and tricking the stone into thinking it had been released.

Like it is a thinking, breathing, living stone. Rather than one that is simply ... inhabited.

The old wooden door flew open. Its ancient oak clattering against the stone wall of the Veil Chamber, leaving a scraped mark in the soot and dust. Sneed drove through. A silvered platter in his hand, reaching out towards his Lord with black-stained hands. The platter shook a little, and the large brass metal needle on top clattered as he approached. Lord Penance reached out with his hale left hand, gloved finger wrapping around the plunger, before lifting it clear of the tray. He brought the contraption up to his eyes, pressing the plunger and forcing a little air out of the capsule inside before black liquid spurted from the top.

"Sneed, please," he said, sending a brief glance over to the old priest who stood by him, hooked nose running with his usual mix of blood-flecked snot. The priest slid Lord Penance's sleeve past the elbow, wincing at the knotted veins glowing with purple fire. He pulled at the metal tube melded just below the elbow, tapping it before removing the cork stopper. A watery blood dripped from the opening, ignored by the Lord as he slid in the needle's tip, activating the plunger as it entered the vein. A slow sigh escaped his lips, eyes involuntarily flickering upwards as the cold black concoction eased the fire in his arm. After a few seconds, he slumped back into the chair, Sneed removing the hypodermic from his arm and hand to place it on the platter. The remaining liquor bled onto the silver-plating, laced with a glimmer of spirit-fire Sneed ignored in the hope it would fade into the air.

"Sneed," croaked Lord Penance. "You must send word to the other Houses. We must meet, and soon. A quill if you please and paper. Then fetch the Priests-in-Waiting, whether they like it or not their slumber is at an end this night."

"Yes, my Lord." Sneed walked to the door, before pressing his hands against its frame, pausing to grip hold with both hands, one withered the other hale. "I felt it, Lord Penance. I felt the wound, and then your calling. Your pain was ... unexpected."

"The Wyrding was the worst I've experienced since you re-linquished the Lordship, Sneed. Worse than my first taste as a

Priest-in-Waiting. The Veils may well have been penetrated—it is the only way to explain the Tear and the ruptures I felt rippling between the Veils."

"They will heal," said Sneed, turning to face his Lord. "You know this, it is written."

"And we must call Mass, I know. This I will do. But first we must know what penetrated the Veils, and more importantly why. And if I am right, Penance did not take its due at the outset. Why did the glyphs not fire? So many questions, Sneed and I have no answers but one."

"Yes?"

"Where. Whatever it was has arrived in the direction of Ersten Forest. Send for Meister Yanpet, Sneed."

19
A RANGER'S DUTY

Smerral Ranger Encampment

E cne strained to see through the black smoke, watching for danger as instructed. With the wood-fed fumes and damp air catching at her chest, she wrapped a strip of cloth around her nose and mouth. As an acolyte of the University, she was Learned—much to her father's chagrin—but not weak nor without sense. She professed an inner strength that belied her appearance—coupled with her family's tenacity. The minor burns on her fingers testimony to her determination.

Remaining on guard, Ecne glanced over as Sura scoured the death and destruction for anyone alive, her cuts drying in the heat of the fire. The red streaks caked her elven ears, neck and arms, enhancing the inner warrior Ecne visualised as she walked, bow in hand. She had the easy confidence of a natural soldier; always ready to step up and invariably be unpredictable when they did. Her presence strengthened Ecne's resolve, despite her heritage. The whole of her race labelled with an ancient name from human history, a time before the Landing when the Gods had seen fit to re-home their wayward children. But these were no elves of their past, not gentle folk. Harsh, brutal in their treatment of those that went against their tribal traditions, and despite a thousand years of living side by side, a sullen intolerance of humanity.

"As my father would say, between Sura and Laoch, my arse may make it out of this," she said to herself, focusing back on the trees as ordered.

"Any sign of anyone alive, Ecne?" asked Laoch as he approached.

Ecne kept her eyes forward, scanning the woods while answering, "None, nor whatever was releasing that ... that banefire. What's happening? Is this an attack on the city? The Unbelievers?" She'd held back her natural urge to question everything for as long as she could.

"All I know is that it's an enemy in bloody weird armour, and their weapons are things I didn't think possible—beyond what the Unbelievers used during the Crusade. You make the bloody stuff; you know of anything that can do that? Whatever hit the rear battlecart blew it completely apart. Not even Erin's Wrath managed that. There's not much of anyone left." Laoch took a breath.

"No, Ranger. I haven't. That white fire? I have never seen anything able to control elixirs of that magnitude." Ecne breathed in heavily, trawling over the possibilities. Meister Kinst had talked of controlling explosions, and often tempered her elixirs to reduce the heat and impact. But not to this level of control, and certainly not contained in something so small as a quarrel tip. "Never mind focus it in such a way."

Shaking his head, Laoch's eyes roamed from Sura to Ecne and back again, taking in their current physical condition, their posture, the aura they gave off. Before the drink, before the anxiety had consumed him, Laoch could assess a soldier like the Learned studied their books and parchment. He'd know just how far to push, what state of mind they were in, when to knock them down and when to rise them up. Was he capable of that anymore?

"I know what you're thinking, Laoch. I can feel you looking," Sura said, her eyes red with smoke as she rejoined them. "We need out of here and if that means a fight, so be it. The three of us survive this and get to the city." Sura turned her head and raised an eyebrow at Laoch. "We stand together. Not all hunters have teeth and claws."

Laoch nodded back, Sura's determination hitting home, the elven saying aimed towards the acolyte who had already surprised them both.

"Damn, you been reading my thoughts? Ecne's an acolyte, all books and words, however hardheaded she maybe." Laoch caught himself, saying words aloud that may have been better kept quiet. "No offence meant."

"None taken," replied the acolyte, though her cheeks reddened beneath the ash.

"Okay, as Gowan would have it, we go by the Ranger's code. Let's see what's out there first."

Laoch moved between Sura and Ecne, placing his hand on Ecne's shoulder, and squeezing as he moved past. He crouched low as he glanced at a stricken warhorse, its eyes empty, kicking something at his feet. Looking down, the captain's leather helmet lay trampled in the mud, his command insignia splattered with blood. Laoch kneeled, moving the cap aside and collecting the spyglass beneath it, saying a silent prayer of thanks to Justice before pocketing the old man's insignia.

"Couldn't save you this time," he whispered, stuffing the spyglass into a pouch on his belt. He dragged the captain's cloak from around his cold shoulders, turning to face the acolyte. "Here, get rid of the robes. They'll drag you down in this weather. Useless in the mud and rain."

Ecne stared at the cloak, half-thanking Wisdom it was blood-free, and half-sick at the thought of wearing a dead man's clothes. Seeing that Laoch was brooking no argument, she shrugged off the now heavy robe, slipping on the lined cloak. She eased it around the short sword and quiver Sura had found her once she had explained her limited ability.

Laoch indicated he was moving out and could hear Sura adjusting her position to watch from behind. His eyes constantly scanned the tree line; there was no movement—experience and instinct telling him they'd gone—but you take no chances.

He signalled them both to wait, then kept low, making the smallest target he could as he moved towards the body he could make out ahead, fearing the worst. It felt like every step took an age, waiting for that fatal arrow or the fire quarrels the enemy was using. But nothing came. On reaching the decapitated corpse, Kerund's distant eyes stared back a few yards away. Biting down at yet another loss, he moved on, picking out a trail of boot prints that didn't match any he knew. Underneath, however, were the standard issue prints of the Rangers. And he only knew one Ranger that refused to wear anything else. To confirm his thoughts, Gowan's knife, the edge still glinting in the orange glow of the pine tree flames, lay trampled in the dirt nearby. It bore the First Ranger mark, her name etched beneath.

Forever by the code. Eh, Gowan.

With no sign of the enemy, Laoch waved Sura and Ecne on, hands clasping and unclasping as a focus for his spiralling mind. He needed a second, a pause, though the adrenaline drop allowed the abyss to press back in. Beyond the trees, the encampment burned, with the armoured battlecarts shattered and their horses lying broken and torn. A battle they hadn't been prepared for.

Breathe.

Loach needed to look, to remember. In the maelstrom of fire and smoke his Spear lay dead, those he'd sworn by the code and his Queen to protect—to be their leader—and act as a Ranger should. They had been his responsibility, and he'd abandoned them in drink and insubordination. And now, when he had taken the first step away from the brink, they'd fallen. Laoch took one more forced glance towards the camp.

My fault, mine and mine alone. Here lies my folly. Another Spear lost.

Laoch pressed fingers into his eyes, pushing back the hot tears that threatened to come—desperate to squeeze away the darkness and the stink of his own burning flesh upon the Unbelievers' firepit.

Laoch spun as Ecne and Sura joined him, their eyes also on the ravaged command camp.

"No more," Laoch said, his tone grim. Trying to hold back the despair that coursed through him. The ghost image of Tappin lying prone on the encampment flickering in his mind's eye. Sura glanced over, taking in the sombre shake of his head before he looked up, locking tear-filled eyes with hers. She flicked her head towards Ecne.

Laoch coughed, nodding back. "If we head due west from here, we will hit the Queen's Road. About three miles. We can take that towards the city, perhaps commandeer horses if we can. We need to make sure the city knows what's happening out here." Laoch cast his eyes to the ground as he thought through the possibilities. "Then there's the Queen's Elite. The Prince Consort has them camping a few miles away. Unlikely, but they may have heard the explosions. We could stand and wait here for them as an alternative. See if any of the Ranger's horses return." Laoch glanced at them both. The tension in Sura's body posture told him all he needed to know. Gowan was a friend, and her loyalty would expunge the sensible options—at least in his view. Duty required he pushed on through.

Here it comes.

"Laoch, we don't abandon our own. It was Gowan's knife, you know that. She's possibly alive, or the enemy have her." Out of the corner of his eye Laoch saw Ecne's head nodding, eyes still on camp. "No one else knows she's out there, and if we leave her to her fate, what are we? We are minutes behind, armed and pissed off. Besides, if they've taken her to find out about our numbers and positions—they could be chopping off her fingers as we speak."

Laoch held that thought, pushing a cruel riposte away despite the temptation.

"She's a Ranger. If she's alive out there, then she knows how to survive, and it'll give us double the chance someone gets back to warn the Queen. We don't know they have her, but if they do, she should be able to hold out long enough to be found." Laoch locked eyes with Sura, knowing this was about to get heated. "I did."

Sura flinched, Laoch suspecting the pain in his eyes had taken her aback. She knew most of his past.

Though not all.

No one needs to know that.

"I could remain here," said Ecne, her voice unsteady, but eyes hard. "Watch for any rescue, show them the path you take."

"We should survive this together, Ecne." Sura flared towards Laoch. "And we are the Queen's Rangers. Gowan needs us. I can't believe you'd let—"

Laoch tensed, sensing Sura about to bristle, emotions rising to fight for the rescue of her friend. "Nothing to do with who it is, but what we are. You said it, *Queen's* Rangers. That duty comes first."

Angry, Sura forced herself to stop, biting back words her honour demanded she speak. She knew what Laoch had to do, and it went against her loyalty, the need to find her friend. But the Queen, her city and the acolyte were the priorities. And if the enemy was near, the acolyte stood little chance alone.

Laoch rubbed his sore eyes, "You want to lead? We're the same rank, Sura."

"No," she kicked at the ground, clicking her tongue, before keeping her voice low. "You know these woods better than I, and you were ..."

"I was a First, yes. *Before*. I seem to have lost a good many things I used to have." Ignoring the flash in Sura's eyes, he carried on, kicking himself for angering her. "It's clear these hostiles, whatever they are, have moved on. But they could be back. So no, Ecne. Sura is right, you come with us. Perhaps they were after the Erin's Wrath, checking on our capability and the explosion spooked them. And that makes you, an alchemist, a prime target too. And if Gowan is still alive, then she'll be heading for the city, anyway." He paused, waiting for Sura to acknowledge his words before carrying on. A reluctant nod sent his way in response. "Okay, we head west. Sura at the rear. Ecne, eyes on everything to the left. This is an experienced enemy, and they may leave a few surprises if they think they are being followed." Laoch let out a sigh as he finished; he couldn't lose any more people. His heart ached as another vision of Tappin's contorted face slipped through his mind's eye.

The last one. I can't let any more of us die today.

———

Gowan ran. Legs pumping, leaping roots and branches with a pounding heartbeat resounding in her ears, the drumbeat spurring her on. Driving deeper into the forest, her sense of direction lost amid the adrenaline and fear coursing through her body. She had waited at the trees' edge at first, watching the encampment, waiting to see where the Unbelievers headed. But they had emerged her side, smoke billowing around them as the glimmer of their armour took up the pine-fuelled flames. An orange, flickering nemesis that near froze her to the spot. It had been the raised hand, the fist pointing her way that had spurred her feet, breaking the paralysis and she'd ran.

Now she crashed through the undergrowth, driven by a primal instinct to survive as the strange bolts flew either side, streaking past. Detonations echoed amid the trees as they hit the trunks and branches ahead, her mind unable to process how or what they were as fear forced her onwards. She didn't know if she ran for herself, or her Queen. She just knew she had to live, to tell someone of the monstrous acts committed against her Spear detachment, of the death the Unbelievers heralded. If it meant she lived, so be it.

Someone has to.

Heat exploded in the small of her back, sending her sprawling, her prized bow flying from her grasp as she hit the mud. Gowan rose back up, chest constricted as dread took hold, scrabbling for the weapon. Grabbing it, she rolled behind a tree, hand dropping to the quiver at her side. She expected it to be empty, that life would play last one foul trick. She knew this fear, how it constrict-ed her heart, tore at her sense of duty. Able to organise, follow procedure, even devise a battle plan—be a soldier. But come the fight doubts rose—was she ever strong enough? Laoch had teased at the edges of those memories. Goading her in front of Captain Rakslin, daring her to deny what he knew to be true. It was why she hated the man—not because of his rejection of her—but because she confided in him and spoken of her desperation. And Laoch had laughed. The Ranger who *had been* what Gowan so wanted to be, belittling her honesty, while trampling on her heart. A man who'd drowned his own heroism in drink and self-pity.

Her hand felt the feathered nock, pulling the arrow clear and sliding it across her thumb. Drawing back the string, she let out a long steady breath.

Training. Procedure.

Sighting the four Unbelievers as they broke through the under-growth, she whispered a prayer to Fate—for who else's House should she worship at? The arrow flew, driving into the armoured thigh of the left-hand pursuer. She expected it to scrape across the plate, or shatter and fall. Instead, Fate held her hand, and the arrowhead drove inwards, biting deep into the flesh beyond.

Gowan bit back the whoop, eyeing the three who dived for cover before turning and running. This time when her heart hammered; each beat was interspersed with a little joy. She pushed away an errant thought pressing into her mind, the abandonment of Laoch back at the clearing. Leaving him to his death amid her own fear.

See Laoch. I am not a coward.

20

WHEN HAPPENSTANCE INTERVENES

WEST ERSTEN FOREST

T he horse, lathered, steam rising as the rain fell, pulled up
sharply alongside Ranger Elite Oisin's own temperamental
horse, its eyes rolling at the smell of the messenger's ride. Oisin
had been expecting the green and purple colours of the Queen,
or the gold crest of the Prince Consort, perhaps. But the rider was
all in purple, the House symbol upon the shield at his back that
of the kneeling man in prayer, the red-lined scourge underneath.

The House of Penance. Just what I need right now.

The messenger priest eyed him warily, knowing full well his
House would not be sought by one such as Oisin. The man's
mountain heritage, and the whispers of their past allegiance with
the Unspoken, had marked him for some time as an anomaly amid
the Queen's Elite, yet held in high regard for his skill and clear
loyalty to the Queen and the Union. On his word, his tribe had

supposedly turned from their ancient, foul rites and as one joined the House of Fate five years before.

As for not being welcome, no messenger in purple could ever expect that.

"I am the Queen's soldier, priest. What would Lord Penance want with such as me?"

"My Lord has the Queen's boon, Ranger." The priest handed over the sealed letter, a dual stamp on the rear confirming his response. Oisin steered his horse to the side, avoiding his troop who were busy striking camp after the last set of orders to return to the city.

He cracked the seal and scanned the scratched hand, letters painfully formed. Pulling over his cloak's hood to prevent the rain ruining the message, he peered back at the priest, expectant. Already in his hand was a rolled oilcloth, one he handed over to Oisin while ensuring that Meister Yanpet's mark could be seen sewn into the cloth. Oisin collected the roll, gracing the messenger priest with a nod and a word of thanks that took him by surprise.

Grace to those who have asked for service; a sword to those that demand it.

As the messenger steered his horse away to leave, Oisin summoned over his weary troop. They'd been in various parts of the forest over the past few weeks, each task carried out with a growing awareness that the Prince Consort was preparing for yet another bout of religious paranoia. Oisin had no doubt they were going in deep, without military sanction nor identification. Under the guise of woodsmen perhaps, trappers, by what the mad Prince had them doing—in reality a protection squad rehearsing an escape and evade retreat. But the Queen had sanctioned it, and therefore he was duty bound and quashed the rumours within his own Elite Spear about how long it'd be before he 'disappeared' up his own arse. Or just disappeared.

Oisin slid off his horse, dismounting to be greeted by tired frowns and half-smiles.

He kneaded his shoulder, arching his back, thanking Fate that at least he could ditch the horse. "Tanka, Fenecia, settle down."

"We're not doing Penance's bidding, are we?" said Conch, her deft hands working at the weft and weave of yet another basket-container likely damaged by Tanka's lack of care.

"Bidding? No. He has the Queen's mark, and Yanpet's."

"A Meister and a Lord? Sounds better than practising to be bloody babysitters." Tanka spat on the ground, not having to open his mouth as the spittle flew through the gap at the front of his teeth—a gap Oisin had readily provided when the man had questioned his tribe's loyalty. Just the once.

"Not babysitting, no. More like actually being a Ranger, searching the forest." Oisin unrolled the oilskin to reveal the map underneath, mindful to keep it covered under his cloak hood as the rain fell and his troop pressed in. "We're going here," he said, pointing to an area deep within the forest, six miles to the northeast and directly through the wildest section. His finger rested at the start of the foothills. "A seek and report, unknown what's there but we're to be ready for anything. This is at the double, no slacking, no tents, nothing. We run in, we run out. Tanka, you get to stay with the horses.

"Piss off, Oisin. In enemy territory, I'm with ye. But out here you could slap their arses and they'd return home themselves. I know what you're doing, I'll keep bloody up. Need to run off this lazy man's belly, anyhow." Tanka grabbed a layer of fat under his leather armour.

Oisin let a half-a-smile reach his lips as he nodded, knowing Tanka would react as he did, and letting the decision be his, ready for when he started his moaning and groaning. Oisin estimated maybe five, ten seconds in, but it could be his lucky day.

"Finish the stowing, grab light packs and equipment. Tie the horses with feed and cover. You have five—want it done in four."

21

THE FIRST BLOOD OF REVENGE

ERSTEN FOREST

S ura kept on the half turn, her eyes constantly seeking anything out of the ordinary, bow relaxed but arrow nocked. She kept her finger flexible, ready to draw against whatever hostiles they were facing. Her mind railed at what she'd seen in the camp—the strange egg, the glint of the edged weapon cracking it open, and the way their armour moved with its background. And that which emerged, a withered hand chopped and seared.

What are we facing? The Unbelievers? We must hold on and get Ecne through this—get us through this.

She flexed her body as she walked, keeping the muscles and tendons free of any tension and rigidity as her kind taught. A habit now with her place in the tribe lost, life leading her to use those skills for the Queen—the Usurper to some of her kin. But most were simply indifferent. Her people so set in their rituals tuned to the natural rhythm of seasons and weather, the arrival of the humans a thousand years ago was just another turning. A change like the shift of the wind, or the drop of a leaf, and nothing more.

Laoch crouched and signalled a stop. Their pace had been good though Sura worried constantly about any breaks. Speed mattered, for Gowan as much as them. The sooner they returned, the swifter her rescue could be. She knew Laoch had to work hard to keep them heading in the right direction, any deviation costing them time. He was using all the craft he knew, the experienced Ranger explaining a compass was near useless in these woods, the rock outcrops somehow affecting the needles.

Holding back the worry, she scanned the forest. Her innate sense of the plains and its shifting light not so much use in the dreary woods, with a canopy that swayed with the rain and wind. Trees were okay on their own, or in a copse for shelter—but a thick forest gave her a constant itch at the back of her neck. A sense of being pressed in upon, with someone or something always watching. Another reason to work through her relaxation routine.

Laoch signalled her forward and, squatting by his side, Sura peered uphill as the forest sloped into the murk. With her eyes adjusting, she caught the tiniest glint of light blinking in and out from behind a nest of tree roots where they drove into the ground.

"Mirror," whispered Laoch, Sura agreeing with his assessment. Turning, he signalled Ecne to wait, and indicated silence before sending Sura out to the left into the denser undergrowth. Checking her arrow remained correctly nocked, and sliding a second into her hand, she crept low, looking to flank the potential enemy and get a better viewpoint.

She knew Laoch would wait. Half a mind on keeping Ecne safe behind him, the other half that should she be spotted, any shift in position may expose the target to his aim. With feet light, each step measured and between the noisiest ground litter, Sura ducked beneath a leafy bush, its leaves wet, to spy the extending leg of the mirror-clad enemy. They were waiting, clearly injured as a thick blood-like substance leaked from the knee, the head bobbing occasionally. With Laoch out of sight, she made her own decision, drawing back the bow to take aim. Slowing her breathing, she took her time, thoughts on the likely strength of such a strange armour. Watching, she caught the merest hint of cloth underneath every time the head drooped, Sura assuming the blood loss was taking its toll. She let fly, the helical fletched arrow spinning in flight to drive into the join. It dug deep. The hoarse cry emanating from the helm bringing a little joy into her heart. Sura rose, nocking the second arrow, but approaching with caution as the soldier slumped to the floor. A glance towards Laoch's position took in the Ranger's movements, his bow drawn, moving out to the right with as much caution as she.

The armour flashed, white fire racing along the surface, causing Sura to flinch away when a vision spot formed. The twang of a bow string spurred her instincts, the elf dropping to the floor, expecting something to fly her way as a crossbow released. A roar tore through the woods, followed swiftly by the crackle of flame as wet bark and pine needles heated. Sura risked a look, beseeching her ancestors that Laoch still stood. He was running, the flame burning through a tree to his right, bow still drawn and she caught the moment of release. The arrow drove into the prone soldier from a mere yard away, striking deep into the wide gap after her shaft kept the neck exposed. Purple laced blood spurted and a spluttering gurgle cut off as Laoch drove his boot knife into the same crack and sliced sideways.

A single arc of white fire sparked, catching the Ranger's hand and running down the blade's edge before fading away. By the time Laoch drove the blade in a second time, Sura had joined him, a third arrow nocked and drawn.

"Dead?" she asked, Laoch kneeled back at her words, breathing hard. His knife purple and red stained.

"I'd say so. Seems the bastards can die."

Sura stepped back to sweep the forest. Elven eyes scanning deeper into the murk and up towards the mountain near its centre. "There could be more."

"I doubt it but keep watch anyway. This one was injured. I think they dumped them to slow us down." Laoch rolled the corpse over, noting the mirror-plate armour from shoulder to foot and the solid helmet that they had both found a gap under. The surface reflected the light streaming through the tree canopy yet seemed to be fading. He ran a gloved finger along its sheen.

"It's not metal," Laoch rapped it with his dagger hilt, the sound dull, like stone. He looked back from where he'd come, Ecne's head popping out from behind a fallen tree, eyes locked on the corpse. "Might as well use some of that learning. Ecne!" He waved the acolyte over, the woman practically running to reach his side. By the time she arrived, the armour's exterior had dulled, now reflecting little from above.

The Ranger rolled the corpse on its side, finding an area yet to lose the shine, and showed the acolyte who immediately ran her hands along it.

"Warm," she said, then placed her fingers on a dulled section. "And that's cold. I've never seen anything like this, even in the Grand Meister's workroom and she had all sorts of Unbeliever equipment."

"Nor me," said Sura, kneeling, focused on the woods. "But there was a crossbow—I heard it. Just before the explosion."

"Only just missed me, too." Laoch stood, eyes on the ground, scuffing the leaves and pine needles aside until he spotted the crossbow's handle. A small one, low range. The string burnt through, and limbs bent. "Broken."

Ecne raised the soldier's arm where the left hand was missing, and the stump seared. "We were there, Laoch. This was the one who crashed into the battlecart." She dropped the blackened limb, glancing down at the injured leg. An arrow shaft penetrated through, snapped off both sides. Its splintered, wooden edges protruding from the thigh.

"Aye, Ecne. A wounded soldier. One that would hold them back and they paid for it. Ruthless, like we know the Unbelievers are." Laoch's foot kicked against something else on the floor, and bending, he uncovered a small quiver containing two quarrels. Drawing them out, the tips appeared strange, not sharp nor metal. A choke from his side was swiftly followed by Ecne's hand wrapping around one shaft. Laoch let it go, shaking his head at the acolyte. "They not teach you any patience at the University, nor manners?"

"Neither," replied Ecne, sitting down cross-legged on the edge of her cloak and holding the quarrel up. "You think these are what explode," she said, though Laoch doubted it was to anyone but herself.

"Have you checked under the helm," asked Sura, risking a look back. "The armour has no insignia. No mark of the Unspoken. Every soldier we fought bore the dragon mark."

"No," he replied, bending down.

"Laoch," said Sura, eyes expectant and getting a return glance. "Be careful. There was a white light, like lightning, on the armour before it fired."

"You saw that too? Thought I was going a little mad, or it was a weird reflection." Laoch tapped under his arm. "Perhaps my blood thinning out. It ran along my dagger too." Unnerved, he reached for a pair of gloves from his belt pouch before searching for some form of clasp. Eventually, his fingers slid into the bloodied gap under the chin and released a clip.

He lifted it away, Sura catching his startled reaction from the corner of her eye. Laoch now stood holding the helmet, completely exposed to any archers.

"Down, Laoch," she whispered. He turned to look at her, shock written all over his face. "Down," she repeated forcefully.

Laoch blinked and looked back at the corpse before finally crouching. Sura backed towards him, eyes swapping between the trees and Laoch before peering over his shoulder. Large, pure white eyes stared back, set over a pronounced nose. The mouth tight with exposed and rotten, purple-stained teeth. The skin, however, was completely dry—rippled and flaking like the husk of a peanut. Laoch pressed a hand against one cheek, gloved fingers peeling away layers that broke apart in his hands to float away on the breeze, exposing more translucent skin underneath through to the bone.

"What?" he said, head turning to Sura. "You seen anything like this before?"

"No, not on others. Only the skin of our dead after they are long exposed to the sun. Before they are wrapped," Sura and Laoch looked at each other; what was there to say?

"Or alchemical fire," said Ecne, now on her hands and knees, the quarrel forgotten as she stared at the haggard face. "But the eyes ..."

Laoch threw a questioning glance towards the acolyte, only for Ecne to lean in, ignoring the query, curiosity continuing to overcome any discipline she'd been trying to hold on to.

Sura automatically returned her gaze upon the woods, her mind reeling. The Unbelievers had looked as human as any other, and definitely not like this corpse. But there was a familiarity in its appearance, something nagging at her mind. Yes, the skin had dried and looked much like how the shaman prepared their dead. But ...

"The teeth," she blurted. "They chew the junip fruit. Like our shamans, and your Lords and Ladies of the Houses."

Ecne knelt down next to the corpse, smudging some boot marks Laoch had carefully avoided so far and much to his annoyance. She lifted the corpse's lips, examining the teeth and a little dread trickled down her spine, remembering where she'd seen teeth like that once before—when faced by Lord Wisdom at his investiture. And his blackened hand.

She carried on, unable to hold the Learned within her back. Carrying out a concise examination, she took in the eyes, skin and especially the purple-stained blood around the neck. Eventually, she reached out, touching the husked skin with the back of her hand before gently feeling around the top of the eye, dismissing the tattoos across the eyelids.

Laoch's posture shifted, the acolyte sensing the Ranger's need for urgency—a trait he shared with Meister Kinst.

"Is there something you can tell us?" Laoch whispered. "Something from all those bloody books you've read. The face, it could well be an Unbeliever. They are just like us, all colours of skin, shapes and sizes. But that skin, those eyes."

"I'm an alchemist, not one of the anatomists. But Meister Kinst has had me ... err ... experiment with some of our elixirs on body parts ..." Ecne stopped herself, stiffening.

"You know what's happened? Who this might be?" Laoch asked. "Then I need to know, understand? We're facing an enemy we know nothing about and this ... this seems barely human. Those eyes."

Ecne nodded, turning to look at the Ranger, before pressing her hands against her knees and continuing, "I would say it looks human, certainly not Schenterenta." Sura winced, the pronunciation of her kind's true name twisted and painful to hear. "And the wound to the arm has similar burns to those Kinst achieved with some of her work for the ..." Ecne winced. "But the face? I have seen some of Kinst's work cause small parts to dry out like that but accompanied by burn and scorch marks. This seems ... different." Ecne reached inside the neckline, pulling back the crystal plate and grey cloth to expose part of the upper chest and the husk-like skin beneath. "Its all over, I'd say if we stripped him down, we'd see it was all like that."

"This is not helping; we need to move on. Get back to the city." Laoch sighed, turning to survey the area, thinking. "They were in a hurry, but all this Unbeliever's equipment has gone. They stripped anything useful except the crossbow. We keep going."

"But the armour, the body?" said Ecne, standing with a lingering look at the body. "The Meisters—"

"—can wait. It's not going anywhere, is it? The armour should keep the wolves off until we get back." Laoch stood, keeping low, eyes scanning the ground looking for any trail left after Ecne's disregard for it. He soon caught the broken trail the Unbelievers had left, their heavy prints sitting deep in the ground where they pounded into muddier patches further out. And there, beneath them, a standard print.

Shit. No.

He glanced over to Sura, her eyes elsewhere. Following the prints, he spotted they soon crossed his intended direction, before moving further up the slope to the northwest. Biting the tip of his tongue, he looked back to find her eyes on him, daring him to look away.

Ah, the Seven bloody Hells.

Holding his first thoughts back, he motioned Sura over, pointing out the trail. She had little real tracking sense, the elves specialising in roles much as humans did. But she knew enough for him not to take the risk.

"Gowan?"

"Or someone else in standard boots. So yes, it has to be her. And she's heading more northwest. By the look of it, she's on the run." He twisted his mouth, trying to keep the emotions from reaching it. They should be heading west, to the city.

"We wouldn't lose much time if we followed a while." Her hand reached out grasping Laoch's arm. A touch on her terms that she knew was unfair. "A quick look."

He sighed, knowing if it was anyone else asking, he'd not back down. Angry with himself but bowing to the inevitable, he pointed down the original trail. "If we have to backtrack, that's your direction. Right Ecne? Go that way to the Queens' Road." Dragging his knife from his boot, he notched a mark upon the tree the

Unbeliever had hidden behind. "Now move out, acolyte. Get your focus back on keeping yourself safe, or all this new stuff you've learnt will be for nothing."

Sura let a brief smile grace her lips, realising he'd bowed to her will rather than choose what he thought best. But no mind, despite the fire and death around them, her resolve about him had to remain unbroken. She couldn't risk anything taking root again, and there was an emotional scab to pick at. "You're still not forgiven."

"Forgiven?"

"For leaving me without a word for two days. Did you think I wouldn't worry?"

"I was ... doing the right thing."

Sura nodded, letting her eyes drop to the floor, dismissing him. Laoch waited, clearly hoping to continue explaining, but the elf turned away.

Ecne collected her bow, shaking her head at them both before checking the arrow was properly nocked. The acolyte dropped the two crystal-tipped quarrels into her quiver, then waited until Laoch stirred and headed out, following the tracks up the slope.

"You really do things to dead bodies?" Sura asked as she took the rear, an edge to her voice.

"Yes. Sorry, I know your rites and how it makes you feel. But the only way to *know* things is to try them out. Like your people when they first found out which foods were edible—that knowledge, passed down from generation to generation, will have come from someone experimenting in your past. Some may well have died in the process, you see?"

"Sometimes, you don't *need* to know things, Ecne. Some knowledge is ... unwarranted, nor does it make our land a better place."

"You sound like the Gods' Houses—can't do this or that. Quoting scripture, setting our limits. We could do so much more."

"Always wanting more is a human thing. Isn't that why you came here?"

"The Houses speak of a cataclysm, an ending to our own land if you like, brought on by our actions. Hiding from knowledge and science isn't going to change the past, but it could change the future." Ecne took a quick glance back. "Stop it from happening again."

"I do not understand your Gods and Houses, all these human things. But I do know what you speak is heresy to them. You need to be careful, don't get caught up in what you just saw, or you will get *that* knock on your cell door. I do know that no one leaves the House of Penance the same afterwards. I heard of one, and she is now mute."

Ecne stared ahead, suddenly choosing silence.

22
A TORTURED MIND

THE HOUSE OF PENANCE, ERSTENBURGH

L ord Penance walked down the central aisle, withered hand pressed to the cane as he placed it ahead of him on each second step, clicking out a rhythm through the silent chamber. Each pained stride reminded him of who he was, the protector of the faith. The guardian of not only those silently praying for forgiveness, but of all of humanity. This was the role he had sacrificed his hand and his health for, a gift freely given for a heavy burden in return. But one he relished. Refusing to give in to the temptations that beset the powerful—marking the knowledge scripture said he should know, and no more. Unless, of course, it meant the fall of the Houses and subsequently the Seven. Some knowledge the Gods hadn't decreed upon because it appeared so unwarranted in their time. But people did not always realise that they needed to repent, and had to be shown, led, beaten and yes, sometimes, tortured into *understanding*. Now that learning had not been forbidden, and so his House had knowledge about anatomy that the Meisters would have sold their soul for.

And some already had.

The click reached the end of the aisle, Lord Penance taking his place at the altar, turning to his congregation massed before him. A brief, purple-laden smile crossed his lips as he lifted the scourge whip on high, a bead of blood still present on its steel-edged tip.

"We hold Penance together, my children. You give so your God understands your heart, that you are true to his word, that you understand what is right ... and what is not." He felt the surge rush through him as all eyes turned his way. That little peep at his true power he allowed himself when his people shone with fortitude and love at his words. "You serve him well."

His cold eyes fell upon the priest at his side, the young woman's wrists lashed with cuts and bruises beyond the norm. A zealot.

I so like zealots. As does Penance.

"Priest Amarnta will lead you in your worship today. Come forward, give of your self to our God and receive your penance from his House." His smile returned as the murmurs grew, many kneeled at the foot of their benches, hands clasped, eyes upwards to the ceiling. Some, he knew, had chosen a single line of the painting upon it. Maybe a dragon scale, or the edge of Penance's mighty whip. They would focus on that one line and trace it over and over. Their prayers and pleas for forgiveness sent to Penance's Veil, beseeching. Others would choose to trace the whole image line by line, often choosing their God's armoured form as he brought down his weapon to smite the blue-scaled dragon wrapped around his body. Whichever was their choice, they would enter with that in mind. Arriving at their allotted time and always choosing the same place, stood by the same people as they begged and pleaded.

Ordered, regular. Just how it should be.

He glanced at the ceiling, remembering his choice—the hated dragon's tongue. Forked, a deep red and wholly evil—he had traced that line a thousand times and more before he finally joined the House. And now, he could not bear to look at it.

If they only knew.

The click of his cane now lost amid the murmurs, Lord Penance headed for the altar doorway, sparing a glance back to ensure Amaranta was as *controlled* as she should be. Kneeling in front of her upon the thick, crystalline plinth, was an old man with vivid blue eyes and a look of fervour upon his face. Lord Penance sensed the change. That moment when the crystal leeched the man, draining that fervour—in the man's mind he would be thanking Penance for taking his sins and wrongs upon himself. The reality was so much more.

After a few seconds, the priest helped the man up, the fervour in his eyes gone. A crooked man once again, reaching out to take his penance. The mottled green food block, just a few inches square, that he placed under his tongue. A scene repeated in every House of the Seven—for whatever their worship each ended the same. The plinth, the gift and the Veils endure.

Lord Penance let the internal smile flicker across his lips but pushed it down. Refusing to allow others to see anything but the stern, inhuman head of the faith and scripture. He must forever be held in fear, be seen as the wielder of the scourge. The one to keep humanity in line with the rules set down by the Seven.

For if we do not, it will be our end.

He slowly turned away, dragging himself from the next rapturous scene as a young farm girl took her place upon the plinth. She had likely just blood-flowered, and this her first time upon the stone. Her giving would be painful, the pathways raw and unset. For all the dread he should cause upon the world, he could not bring himself to revel in that moment. Memories of his own daughter—one he'd cast aside to take on the church—haunted him still. Hers was the only one he'd ever watched. Watching from on high in the galleries, unseen and unheard as he wept.

My penance.

The cane tapped its rhythm. His stride taking him away from the People's Chamber and towards the worn steps that led ever downwards. He sucked in an expectant breath, wincing as he took the first step, feeling Sneed step in behind him. Older than he, the relinquisher of the burden he now wore. His body had mended, his soul maybe not. Twenty years his elder, yet likely he could take each step with far more ease than when he wore the purple cloak.

Will I recover? Will I go on to serve the next Lord? But I feel so old.

Twenty steps down—each one a penance of its own—he branched off from the stairway, heading down the lit corridor of priests' cells. At least, that's what the masses thought they were. The second Lord had reworked them, moving the priests into the depths below the building. Not for penance, nor as punishment, but because he couldn't face the hundred steps needed to reach the knowledge they sometimes required. These were the quarters of the repentant, at least they would be once each occupier realised that's what they *should* be doing.

Lord Penance rapped on the door of the fifth cell, a muffled cry from within mixed with a faint sob signifying he had the correct cell. Sneed moved in front of his Lord, removing the bundle of keys tied inside his cloak. With the scrape of key in lock echoing, he pushed open the door.

Inside, Meister Yanpet lay stretched out on the wooden table. Hands and feet were hooked into blood-stained chains. The man's eyes weeping as they flitted from the tools of torture aligned along the wall to the Lord's cold, green eyes.

Penance squirmed inside, hating the mummery and the fear it created. Knowing that a slip now would lose the mood he was striving to create. Yanpet was close to breaking point; a smile or grimace at the wrong time, and he'd never recover. But it was hard. The man clearly already fully repentant despite no one actually touching him. The mocked-up room had a high success rate, stretching back decades according to his predecessors.

Lord Penance sat at the chair Sneed proffered, wiping it down before resting his weary body with hands crossed over his ever-present cane.

"So, Meister. As you were saying, all knowledge should be shared, yes? That is the purpose of the University."

"No, no Lord Penance. I was mistaken. You were right, some things should be for the Gods' eyes only. Just the Seven. I can't even remember what we discussed, or calculated, or whatever we did. No. Penance has taken his due."

Lord Penance raised an eyebrow, and Yanpet dissolved into a quivering wreck.

23
AN ENEMY'S
TONGUE

NORTHWEST ERSTEN FOREST

T he going was getting tougher, the trees tangled in wild pat-
terns as they intertwined across the increasing number of
rocks. Underfoot the vegetation was thickening, hiding the knot
of roots and fallen branches, slowing Gowan due to the care
required. One twisted ankle, or a moment of misplacement, could
lead to her suddenly being a burden they didn't want—and an
ending to any hope of surviving what was to come. The ache in
Gowan's legs and back increased with every step, bound hands
making movement awkward. A gauntleted hand pressed into her
back, shoving her forward.

Gowan stumbled, pulling herself up at the last second, memories of the second quarrel that had bounced off her shoulder plate
coursing through her mind. It had sent her into a tangled pile of
branches, legs and arms caught amid the tangle of clawing wood.
By the time she'd freed one hand, the crossbow had dropped
into sight, its crystal-tipped end glowing with menace. Behind it

a helm reflected the glow back, equally fear-inducing and angry. So angry. But no killing blow as of yet.

How can I get through this? What would they want from me? Apart from troop movements, and our weaponry, and the wall defences. Shit, I'm going to die.

Another push to the back urged her on. Gowan attempted to bat away the self-doubt, the real enemy of survival. She was a Ranger, and duty and discipline could see her through. Not the despair creeping up her throat, the nausea rising to envelop her thoughts. But training couldn't mask the pain and she needed to hang on—to match their pace for as long as she could. Gowan half suspected that if she stumbled again that keen-edged sword would be out, and this time it wouldn't be sheathed until bits of her lay on the forest floor.

By the code, Gowan. Stay alive.

A little relief spread through her as the apparent leader brought them to a stop. Hand signals sent both the other soldiers left and right as the commander moved behind Gowan. Armoured hands pressed her to her knees, followed by the scraping of a sword sliding out its sheath. The keen tip dug menacingly into the soil to her right. Gowan took the hint, remaining deathly still. Rasping words filled her ears, the desperation in the tone cutting through her lack of understanding. The crystal helmet appeared in her view. The leader on their haunches facing Gowan and yet more words flew. She shook her head in response.

"I can't understand your words. Please. I don't know anything."

More words rumbled from behind the helmet, and a gauntlet reached out, flipping the seamless visor of the helmet, lifting it up. Gowan choked, eyes watering as the dry dust wafted into her mouth and nose. The eyes staring back were deathly white, pupil-less, one misted and weeping, the other insistent. The woman's thin lips rode over broken, purple-stained teeth—her skin dried to a husk, flaking, and the cause of the dust filling her lungs. Gowan caught her breath, chest heavy with dread before the dry dust forced a cough. All she could do was watch the lips move, the sweet breath washing over her as words rumbled out. She tried not to look, she really did, but once her eyes roamed to the tongue, she couldn't drag them away. It flickered into view between the rotten teeth, split at the tip and a metal staple where the cut ended. It wasn't natural, the internal edges of each section had been cauterised.

Gowan shook her head, unsure whether it was at the words or the sight. The female soldier's hand reached out, grasping her head and cupping the Ranger behind her neck. Gowan swore, heart hammering at the expectation of a killing blow. Instead, a warmth spread from that hand, wheedling into her skull and flooding her mind. She saw the woman upon a stone table, her eyes blue, the skin whole. Upon her eyelids tattoos burned red—the depictions akin to the elven writing Sura had once explained were carved upon their tombs. The warrior's hand grasped another, and Gowan realised she lay side by side with a near identical person, the features so similar yet clearly male. The man's eyes shone bright, but faded slowly, a rivulet of purple sliding from his lips. His smile drifted as the muscles relaxed and blue eyes rolled upwards, their whites startling but lined with the same purple hue. Gowan watched the moment of death, could see and feel the spirit detach. In that moment she knew what came next and struggled against the pressure in her mind, but the warmth gripped her tight, made her watch as the two souls merged. The woman's eyes rolled up, whites that bore into Gowan's mind in a warm but strong embrace, as the muscles spasmed and the body kicked. Hands dropped onto shoulders and pressed the woman back, their skin softly mottled like an elf's, though older than any she'd seen. The soldier's mouth opened, and a split tongue emerged—its ends newly charred—and the scream washed through Gowan's soul.

"Come back to me." The words were dry, still harsh. A rasp she now knew caused by the split tongue. "To me. You understand me now, yes? Yes?"

The warmth slipped away, releasing Gowan's mind, and she stared at the moving lips. The sound remained the same, but yes, she understood.

Do I lie?

The soldier read her face, the other hand sliding the glowing sword beneath her chin. "Yes, you do. Where is Leront? We know he is here; the heart responds to our call. Where?"

"Leront? I do not know anyone by that name."

The woman blinked. The effect sickening her stomach. Eyes catching the purple rot at the edges of the misted eye.

"I don't," said Gowan, looking up and seeing a small hill rising from the woodland, Mt Scian looming behind, for the first time. "You think he waits up there, on that hill for you?"

The woman pushed herself up, turning to face the hillock. "On? No. But maybe in," she said, more to herself, dismissing Gowan in that moment. The sword whipped back, the tip against her chin, snicking the skin. No words passed, but Gowan got the message.

Through the rough vegetation growing under the thinning canopy, the rocky hill appeared almost placed on the forest floor. The whole forest was littered with smaller ones, all composed of the same grey rock, though of varied size and shape. Gowan had heard one of her old Spear talk of the great ice in the south. The glaciers that scraped the southern mountains near Makelna, dragging the shattered boulders along with them. Around the southern reaches, he'd explained, there lay much bigger outcrops. All dropped by the receding ice and witnessed by the elves long before the Landing.

Bullshit. Just like all this.

What in the Seven Hells is happening?

The pair of Unbelievers waited as the leader approached. Words passed, Gowan unable to hear, but the two others seemed to agree and started walking around the hill's base, helmets facing the outcropping rock. Gowan blinked away the rain seeping into her eyes, desperate to press them together, to change what she was seeing. The two armoured soldiers held their hands out, palm forwards as they swept around the rocks. And their hands—and Gowan had to check herself again—glowed.

Lamps? Where?

The white light seemed to fill the air around the palms, glinting off their wet armour. And as the intensity grew, Gowan was forced to drop her eyes to the floor, spots forming in her vision. She heard an unfamiliar noise, like an amplified ripping of parchment or paper. Unable to resist, she looked back and the two glowing forms stood only a few yards apart with legs planted wide. Something passed between them, an unheard signal or a twitch of the head, for as one the palms became fists and the intense white light shot from their hands like a fire arrow—but brighter—and with no substance. The four lights merged at the back of a small overhang, focused on one spot. The mud and grass inside bubbled, sloughing away to leave exposed rock. The stone appeared to absorb the four streams, unmoved. Gowan sucked in a breath, eyes locked on that position—mind reeling at what she was witnessing and unable to link the pieces together.

What? How?

And nothing happened. No glow or reflection. Dead, inert stone remained. Soldiers throwing pot bombs would have had more effect. There'd be a mark, singed rock or flaking stone. But nothing. He looked back to the armoured hands, mind assuming she was seeing two humans like the leader, encased in the polished armour. But now, doubts were creeping in.

Unless it was alchemical, like Meister Kinst and that acolyte of hers. Perhaps the armoured suits and gloves protect them against the elixir burns?

Guttural barks emanated from their commander, striding towards the overhang as one of the others dropped in beside their prisoner. Gowan swallowed, her mind translating the sounds. Whoever Leront was, she was convinced they'd found him. Now standing and facing the same spot their white light had hit, the leader's hand seemed to reach inside her armour, emerging with a crystal—one that pulsed with a similar light to that thrown by the soldiers. It reminded Gowan of festival lights, flickering candles lit inside coloured glass jars. Fingers rolled around it, forming a fist, with the other hand wrapped over the top, squeezing. Light erupted between the gauntlets, blinding Gowan, her brain filling in the gaps as she visualised the light surging from the combined hands to slam into the rock. She shut her eyes, squeezing them beneath the lids in the hope she could clear the flashing spots overwhelming her vision. Forcing them open again, the world seemed a blur. Everything appearing as if layered on top of each other and not quite synchronised with how it should be.

My bloody eyes, you bastard.

The rock face bulged outwards, pulsing. Moving swiftly in and out of focus. It rung like metal under a smithy's hammer, or a bell when struck. Another thirty seconds passed before a squeal emanated from the lead Unbeliever, and the stone shattered, collapsing forwards and onto the ground. Gowan blinked the dust from her eyes and gazed at the long metal snout and jagged teeth that protruded from where the rock had been, matched by a similar jaw below. Dust swirled, dulled by the grey light as dusk began to fall and the rain poured. Yet the metal sang. A high-pitched keening that cut through her mind, a tug that wrapped around her belief.

What in the name of Fate?

Her eyes fell to the jagged teeth encasing a grey stone entrance—the perfectly smooth door inlaid with an intricate image, causing Gowan to choke. With heart pounding, she chose her spot as she had every few weeks for so many years hen kneeling in Fate's House. Her sight moved to the dragon's eye and began to trace.

24
WHEN VENGEANCE CALLS

NORTHWEST ERSTEN FOREST

The Unbelievers were close. He could feel it, instincts setting his nerves on edge. Duty demanded someone got back to the city, yet loyalty to Sura had called him to the rescue of Gowan. Not that it seemed to have made any difference in her demeanour. She remained spiky, pushing him emotionally away.

What am I doing?

Laoch signalled for eyes up, Sura acknowledging and whispering to Ecne. He kept the pace steady; they needed to prepare themselves if there was to be a fight ahead, though with an untrained acolyte at his back he desperately wanted to avoid one. He needed to slow their breathing, calm their hearts. They'd had a tortuous few hours since the initial attack, and their readiness would be key if they were to face Unbelievers, if that was what they were. Their trek should have been more demanding, stamina drained as they forged a path through the undergrowth. And though he hadn't checked the weight of that armour, he suspected it would be heavy and limiting. The Unbelievers he'd fought on the Crusade had been professional soldiers, the choice to leave one of their own behind to delay any pursuit reflecting the ruthless efficiency he'd encountered there. And you never send your weakest behind enemy lines.

Over his years of military service, before Captain Rakslin had rescued him from the pit he'd dug himself, Laoch had seen far too much of the evil men and women could do to each other. The border skirmishes meant little, power plays and counter strikes designed to keep the other side unbalanced, on edge. Wear them down. But the actual war with the Unbelievers, the followers of the Eighth and Unspoken, had been something else entirely. The Prince Consort declared them heretics, and the Unbeliever moniker became a label to whip up the masses, to ensure the Queen and the Houses were on the side of the righteous. He knew this, and nothing made you more honourable than pitching your enemy as a violent and demonic horde. He was a Queen's Ranger, doing the Union's bidding, and Hope, his House at the time, decreed it righteous, and that the Unbelievers were flouting scripture. Laoch had expected the truth to be very different. The Unbelievers small in number but made up of those that embraced Ecne's 'science', and disparaged the Houses of God as if they were the real evil. They were, after all, not the ones seeking change, and the religious war was not of their making. But his mind soon changed, finding the maimed and tortured in their wake and the apparent glee they took in the death of others. The Crusade battles were like any other, until it ended, and the screaming started. Banefire they called it, and the Unbelievers watched on as soldiers melted in the flames—his own memories raw as each of his arrows had pierced his own heart, as much as those of his Spear and brother.

Laoch glanced down at his hand, a shiver running down his spine. The darkness pressing in, just a little. He forced an image of Sura forward in his mind, one filled with the joy of finding him alive amid the battlecart, as he fought back from the abyss. A light in the void, despite the rejection.

Need those dangerous thoughts out of my head.

A moment of stillness set Laoch on edge. Something had changed. A difference in the atmosphere—a quiet hush leaving only the gentle drumming of rain on leaves. He crouched, signalled and brought Rakslin's spyglass to his eye. There was movement—a glimpse through the thicker trees that drew his eye. A small, rocky hill rose ahead, and though he couldn't be certain, there appeared to be a Ranger kneeling before it. Beside them, an Unbeliever, their armour partially mirroring the forest and reflecting both stone and tree.

Is it deliberate? In battle, would seeing yourself reflected back be off-putting, the corner of your eye filling your head full of misinformation? Every edge in combat has a price.

Or perhaps a different purpose?

Another appeared in the spy glasses' field, sword in hand, clearly in command. Laoch was convinced the chaotic charge to the small, rocky hill smacked of urgent desperation. Perhaps the madness post battle the Unbelievers had shown in the past. But the armour and weaponry spoke of professional, well-equipped soldiers—and the 'science' in Laoch's mind that corresponded to the Unbelievers. Yet, as he looked on, it dawned on him why he had caved in to Sura. It stood there in the eye of his spyglass—a need for revenge. Payback. Justice for what they had made him do.

Bloody revenge, with no rum to quell the need.

A keening rose, piercing the air which filled with light, emanating from the hill. Something dropped behind him to the forest floor, Laoch turning to find Sura curled into a tight ball, hands pressed to the side of her head. Ecne fell to her knees by the elf's side, hands wide, seemingly searching for a way to help. Laoch ran over, heart pounding just as the keening came to an end. Motioning for the acolyte to watch behind, he sought Sura's eyes, seeking permission. Her pain was evident, but he took the squeeze of the lids as a 'yes', pulling her head onto his knees, soothing her forehead.

"It's passing," she said. "That hurt, like my ears were boiling inside. The sound was full of pain." After a few seconds, she pushed his hand away, rising to her knees while locking eyes on his. Laoch felt his heart lurch before standing and offering his hand, which she duly ignored, getting herself up. Laoch shrugged, making sure she didn't see.

It seems I still have a lot to learn.

"It came from the hill," said Ecne, pointing towards the rising dust cloud. "There. They've caused that, maybe with some alchemy I don't know."

"There's three out there," Laoch whispered in response, "and one Ranger—probably Gowan. No archers on high as far as I can see."

Sura's eyes narrowed in surprise, her look questioning as she peered back at the hill.

Laoch shrugged. "They seem so focused on what they're doing that their discipline is all over the place. We take no risks—incompetence doesn't mean they aren't bloody tough. Or have a trick up their sleeve."

"We're going in?" asked Sura. "I thought ..."

"They seem preoccupied. Let's take the chance while we can. You take the left flank, Sura, and I'll go right. A hundred count, eyes up and on the Unbelievers, then we return and report back. If we have any doubts that we can't take them out, or rescue that Ranger, we leave. No argument. Ecne, I need you to keep track of their movements. If any move towards Sura or I, or even point a weapon in our direction, you have my permission to release—and remember to call out a warning and move when you do. Understand? Make sure if you miss, it's bloody close enough to put them off." Loach took a step back, eyeing them both. "If it goes to the Seven Hells out there, one of us needs to make it to the city. Understand? If it's a choice, the city comes first."

"Yes, Ranger." Ecne checked her quiver, looking around for a decent position and settling for a rotten tree, half-slumped onto the muddy floor. Laoch gave a nod of approval and he and Sura moved out, nice and low, keeping leafy bushes between them and the outcrop.

25

THE SCIENCE OF SPIRITFIRE

Northwest Ersten Forest

"Someone's nearby," barked the commander.

Gowan watched wide-eyed as a sphere of light grew slowly from her armoured hand. She knew of the Unbelievers interest in 'science', their war machines and banefire holding back the Crusade. That was until the Consort recognised the futility as his army starved. But this was no lamp, nor the flame of banefire. After all she had already witnessed, this smacked of a power she couldn't grasp. The sphere had an end, the ball of light having a substance that defied how fire and light should behave. Within it she saw a familiar face, elven ears and a softly dappled skin, rolling in pain with hands clamped to her ears.

Sura.

"Take cover," the leader uttered, signalling across to his captors, each now sparkling with a gentle white glow before their armour shimmered, heightening its reflectivity. She expected the pair to disappear, for what other purpose was there for the mirrors? But instead, they stood out even more, bright against the rock, before the whole effect faded. The lustre of the crystal now pulsed, and the two dropped behind the rockfall they had caused. A few moments ago, she would have baulked, and likely run seeing two soldiers in such armour. Now it was just another event in a very weird day, and a dangerous one.

Where are you, Sura? Nearby? And was that vision real and happening now?

The Unbeliever's sphere pulsed, the white light splitting into three smaller balls floating like dandelion heads. And then they unfurled, wings spreading wide, two glowing white eyes in each, staring at Gowan. The impossibility hammered a dagger into her mind. The owls beat against the breeze, silent—rising into the falling night.

Ecne concentrated on the scene ahead, marking the two most likely to react if Sura and Laoch were spotted. Having nocked an arrow, she placed another two ready at her side - trying hard not to think of the Ranger who'd carried the weapon before her, the mess his body had been left in after the Unbelievers attack. Ahead were those responsible and, as strange as it seemed, it was her duty to make them pay.

Can you see me from the Veil, father?

Keep to your training he would say, slow your breathing. Steady your heart. Breathe.

Ecne knew there were far better archers than her, and that knowing the feel of your weapon was half the skill required. Where did the balance lie in the bowstring? What was the perfect pull point for each distance? And did that cause you to have a slight sway to the left or right on release? She had no chance to learn about the weapon she carried, so was reliant on Jessen's training and the knowledge gained on the archery range.

I will not let them down.

Ecne blinked, and the commander lit up. A glow that swathed the Unbeliever in a light that refused to reflect back from the mirrored armour, remaining around the hand. She could see it, but it did not extend, no shafts reaching outwards as a flame would. A perfect sphere. Gawping, the ball split, three smaller versions floating towards the darkening canopy. Ecne pressed her fingers into her eyes, trying to come to terms with the alchemy, if that was what it was. As she looked back, the spheres had left, the Unbeliever now staring in her direction, the sword pointing.

Realisation of her vulnerability struck home. She was knelt in a wood, bearing a bow, having never used one in anger. Could she kill? The alchemical weapons she helped make certainly had and would again in their hundreds. With mind reeling, flashing back to the destruction of the camp, she smelt the tang of Erin's Wrath on the air—of cooked human and horse flesh. Her hands went to the pouch at her hip, gently squeezing the three pots Sura had recovered back at the clearing.

Is that what I am now? A killer?

The small hairs on the back of her neck prickled, her mind suddenly shouting about something behind her.

Am I just on edge?

A white flash of movement behind disturbed the stillness, and she simply knew. Ecne rolled, trying to pull the composite bow around, seeking a target. The arrow flew involuntarily, the acolyte lost in what fluttered there—a white, ephemeral owl that hovered with piercing eyes cast upon her. Appearing to pulse gently, she could see straight through it to the trees beyond. Fear gripped her, knowing she should be reaching for the short sword at her side but paralysed by the dread. A ghost, an owl that should not be, something beyond her science—and it erupted, her brain on fire as the intensity of light overwhelmed her mind.

⸺

Sura dropped, a creeping sense of fear spreading through her thoughts. Something was wrong and out of place, beyond her usual dislike of the forest. Akin to the instinct Laoch showed whenever danger was near. Where that wrongness lay, however, was swamped by her ill ease with the trees and the ever-changing light—unable to discern a source for the strangeness prickling at her.

Sura's first instinct was to protect, to get to the acolyte, the most vulnerable.

I need to move.

On her elbows, Sura pushed herself backwards, aiming for deeper cover before standing. An eerie silence crept in on her senses, suddenly aware that the low chatter of woodland life had stopped. A fluttering behind brought her up short, nagging at her senses—something imagined or at the very edge of her hearing. Pivoting on her left forearm as if to look over her shoulder, she exploded in a roll to her right. A flash and flicker of intense light washed over her head as she spun. Sura's abdominal muscles surged, sculpted by her dedication to perfecting the Patterning. She rose at the waist and let loose, her mind expecting an Unbeliever wielding their crossbow and those searing white bolts. Instinctively, she released into the space at waist height. Immediately dropping the bow, she exploded into a twist and roll, spinning to a crouch with the drawn elven sword guarding her front, expectant of the danger. Sura blinked briefly, seeking whatever had caused the light to flash over her, but no one returned arrows or stood ready to engage. There was nothing there.

Am I hearing and seeing things now? I hate trees.

Laoch paused. He'd been following his own orders, eyes on and above the hill, tracking for any movement. Insubordination had brought him close to losing his commission and time again, the war hero tag his only saviour from disgrace. It was the constant battle with the memories that drove his temper and shortened his patience, deepening a malaise that loomed large over his day-to-day life until Rakslin had stepped in. One day he was on the verge of discharge, the next he stood in Erstenburgh Barracks, quill in hand. The captain had saved him from a life on the streets and likely a dagger in the back, or that of a mercenary in the southern borderlands—given him some purpose again. A favour owed and returned, though he had reminded him every day for the last two years.

Now he was once again at war, his skills and instinct back in play. And intuition had told him about the attack, that something had his mark, and he needed to move. Maybe the young Laoch would have chosen differently. Maybe ran or dived and dodged first. This older Laoch, world-weary with a body more honed by drink than was good for it, chose to stand and fight.

The Unbeliever emerged from the bushes, armour glimmering—a pulse that caught his eye but no longer reflected the light. It held one hand ahead of itself, palm out, as if showing Laoch it was empty. The other held a curved sword on high, its blade angled upwards behind his head. Ignoring the unusual stance, Laoch dropped into his own well-practised version. His slightly sideways stance designed to put others off guard, the sword out front, eyes roaming as he feared the rest may soon appear.

The Unbeliever took one step forward, the sword slicing the air to clash against his own as Laoch twisted into the parry. The metal on his sword sang, the ring joined by sparks as the white-edged blade bit into his. Ignoring the bile rising in his throat, Laoch recognised the blow, and the switch in stance that accompanied it. He was being tested, his opponent confident in their own ability and seeking a weakness in his.

The backswing crashed against his sword, the speed of his low parry just enough to keep the tip clear of his leg. Laoch dropped low, sword kept high as he kicked out at the Unbeliever's feet, ready for the downward strike that whipped out, aiming for his head. His boot connected, but the impact was too low, met by a spark from the armour that sent a strange light running along his toe guard.

Oh crap.

Laoch threw himself back, avoiding the slash as the Unbeliever stepped away and then in to follow. Moving forward to meet the blow, a flutter behind sent his instincts screaming—fearing an attack from the rear. Laoch's mind raced, seeking options against an opponent that was almost playing with him.

26

TO COUNSEL FEAR

THE HOUSE OF PENANCE, ERSTENBURGH

T he Lord tapped out his rhythm, stepping through the door and nodding to Sneed as he reached the meeting chamber. Pushing the door wide, he entered with stick high and demeanour exhibiting the strength and confidence required when dealing with the six Lords and Ladies that awaited him. They rose as one around the circular table, bowing their heads as he took his place. Once returned to their seats, they placed hands palm down, pointing inwards towards the golden, glowing glyph inlaid into the centre.

"Penance," said the Lord, and each in turn placed their withered hand upon the glyph, and six streams of thick, viscous energy sped into the gold metal of the symbol. On contact, the metal shone, absorbing the power. Its heat briefly filled the room; faces lit by the now white light gleaming from the centre of the table. "Thank you. Now for the matter at hand. Lady Fate, if you will."

Lady Fate pushed her hands against the oak tabletop, pressing her palms down flat, wincing against the pain in her right hand before speaking, ill at ease. "Lord Penance and fellow Houses, I have scried the Fate Stone, as I believe you all have by the pallor of your skin and the blackness bruising your hands. My Veil was whole, resealed but weakened. I have never seen this before, nor do the records show an occasion where the Veil has been so thin. Perhaps not since the Houses were first formed. My glyphs fired, their strength from the residue was near total. I can't believe anything could have survived that, yet Lord Penance tells us something likely did. My priests search, but Fate has chosen not to reveal anything more than the Soul Tear felt by our congregations." Lady Fate lifted her hands, the truth saying done, and pushed back her red hair from the brilliant blue cloak she wore as the mark of her House.

"You have all let me know your Wyrding, and no other glyphs but Fate and Honour's have fired. Not mine, nor the other four. Whatever came through must have been hidden or shielded from the spiritfire. I can think of naught but the Constructors." He felt the dread release having spoken the words that set their future in stone and pain. Each of the Lords unable to vocalise it, paralysed by the fear twisting in their stomachs, and washing through their minds. "We must prepare for what is coming. If we have been found, then our only recourse is to strengthen the Veils, power the glyphs and then prepare the people."

"Prepare them? For what? For slavery? To be drained and fed to those ... vile creatures. There is no future if they get through. Nothing but the black of the abyss." Lord Justice slammed his hands upon the table, palms down, ready to speak the truth. "We are lost, my Lord. Whatever we do now will only delay and anger those coming. My people will be bound and chained, giving succour to the beast."

"Maybe," said Lord Penance, green eyes lighting with a fire beyond just a reflection of the central crystal. "But we cannot abandon our charges. The Gods gave their lives so we may live. Sacrificed themselves to ensure our safety and entrusted the human world to us. They gave us the scripture to live by so Constructors' eyes would slide by, uninterested. I for one am not going to let a thousand years of sacrifice be a mere smear on humanity's time in this realm. We make a stand, Lord Justice. This is our purpose." As he spat the last words, the Lord rose from his chair, turning to stare at the white, curved wall nearest the door, head bowed.

Penance seethed. Acid rising in his throat as he mulled over Justice's outburst amid his own fear of what was to come. For a millennium, generation by generation, the seven heads of the Houses had kept their flock hidden. The burden heavy, the personal toll painful on body and soul, and more than a few had to be culled as they lost their minds. A misspoken word, a lapse in faith, and the foundation they'd built for survival would come tumbling down. And with it, the Veils, exposing them to the wrath of a race that hungered for their very souls.

And the war, the religious Crusade against the unfaithful who had turned their back on scripture one by one. How many had died trying to bring them to heel? Only for more to slip by and join their ranks as their faith wavered, the scripture ashes upon their lips. They thought the rules would never end, their lives bound and constricted by faith.

If only they knew.

"You talk of a stand, but by whom?" cut in Lady Honour, her eyes wreathed by her greying, wild hair. On her shoulders her orange cloak sat heavy, as if she bore the weight of the world on there. "Us? Or do you mean ..."

"The scripture is clear," said Lord Justice, the youngest in the room by some ten years. "You can't mean to go against it?"

"The words were written to hide behind," replied Lord Penance, turning to face the room and gripping the top of his chair. "But if we have been found—if—then its purpose will have come to an end. We are not strong enough on our own, and though I doubt spears and swords will keep us safe, it may come to that, or we bow down and give fealty to our enemy. Naught but slaves and spirit-dolls for eternity. If this *is* the Constructors, we must tell the world about our lies and deceit."

"All of it?" asked Lady Fate, her skin losing more of its colour as it drained away. "I fear that we would be festooned on a spike should we reveal all. Not all, Lord Penance. It would be abominable."

27

THE FIRST
COINCIDENCE

With Tanka on point guard and probably throwing up his guts, Oisin circled the dead enemy. Newer boot marks and scrapes had been carefully placed to the side of the unknown prints, except in one place. The boots of a villager maybe, or a poacher?

"This tracker knows his job," whispered Oisin to himself, but then speaking out. "Do we know anyone in the Rangers who has this skill?"

"Only Laoch. At least he did until the drink and the night sweats took him. War hero, Oisin—led a rescue of his captain and the battalion messengers. They had riddled the clearing with bane-fire. Lost his younger brother with the rest of his Spear to that shit," Fenecia replied. "Can't see it being him. Last I heard he'd been barred from every drinking den in the city."

"I know the name and who he rides with." Oisin ran a hand over his face, scrubbing his day-old stubble. "Damn."

I could do without that confrontation.

Oisin bent down, running his eye along the line of the mirrored armour. His first thought was of an Unbeliever, but doubts were creeping in as he glanced at the ruined skin.

"You saw the face, Oisin?" asked Conch. Having taken point, she had come across the body the first.

"Yes. Yes, I did. Make sure you all look. Whatever the shit this is, we have a new enemy. And that bloody armour ... any ideas?" The First Ranger glanced around his troop. None seemed willing to give a view as they pointedly looked the other way.

"No," piped up Conch eventually. "But it gives me the shits. And it ain't no coincidence that we've been sent this way."

Oisin snorted, half in agreement and half in despair they'd been the ones chosen. "Okay, we are done here. We are losing light and according to my crappy memory it's about to get tougher going. Hold off on the torches for as long as we can. Conch up front."

"Again?" Conch let a brief grin slip out, before checking her equipment was tightly stowed and heading towards the broken trail cutting through the woods. She checked the ground and broken vegetation, and satisfied, broke into a trot.

Oisin fell in behind her. Tracking was going to get horrendously difficult as they lost the light, especially under the trees. Nothing compared to the mountains around his home village, but bad enough. The bearing had been northwest throughout, straight for where Lord Penance had sent them.

Not a coincidence. What is this?

28
WHEN REALISATION STRIKES

NORTHWEST ERSTEN FOREST

A strangled cry cut through the silence somewhere to her right, Sura turning her head to catch the exact direction. It hadn't been Laoch, she knew that, and it was no death cry. She trod lightly and sideways into the vegetation, plotting a line around the back of Ecne's position, with her elven eyes cutting through the ever-darkening dusk. She held the bow with an arrow nocked and half-drawn in front of her, crouched, scanning the trees. Each step took her nearer to a confrontation, to conflict—a time to live or die.

It has to be done.

Ecne came into view, her chest rising as she lay on her back. Her face red, awash with sweat. Sura moved on by, eyes still on the trees to her left where the Unbelievers waited. Somebody had attacked Ecne, though she remained alive, and she suspected they were close. A ring of metal upon metal cut through the undergrowth, leading her in the direction Laoch had taken. She upped the pace, still wary, but urgency taking her feet on a path the beat

of her heart required. A grunt broke through the next bush, and
she crouched to see an Unbeliever lift their sword, striking down
upon Laoch. He rode the blow, his parry forcing the sword to slide
down to his right in a manner that was far too awkward.

Fear gnawed at her, coupled with the feeling of being watched.
A flutter in the last of the day's streaming light set her senses on
edge and she drew back the bow, aiming for the Unbeliever. Laoch
took another unnatural movement to the side, this time receiving
a flat blow to his thigh.

He's deliberately not looking behind. Why?

Sura crashed through the bush, bringing the bow up and aiming
behind Laoch, fingers twitching as she searched for a target. The
owl hovered. Its white eyes focused on the Ranger's back; the
bird's movements as strange as Laoch's. But Sura's mind was
quick, the strangely raised left hand of Laoch's opponent mirroring the creature's movements. She pivoted, letting the arrow fly to
strike the gauntlet, rewarded by a yowl and a spark of white light
that splintered the shaft. Sura reached for another arrow, ignoring
the flash of burning light high to her right as Laoch's opponent
roared in anger. The Unbeliever wrapped both hands around
their sword grip, slamming the blade downwards, smashing into
Laoch's desperate parry. His sword shattered, the edges glowing
as they thumped into the surrounding trees and Sura let fly. The
arrow striking between helm and chest plate, biting deep into
where she hoped the throat lay exposed.

Laoch, down on his knees from the last blow, punched out.
His open hand blow ramming the stomach plate. The Unbeliever
twisted, the blow landing on his hip but forcing him further round.
On the turn, its boot lashed out, the armoured toe catching Laoch
under the chin to send him flying.

Sura, calm despite the mirrored figure that turned her way,
drew swiftly and let loose a third arrow. It cracked into chest
plate, sparks rising that soon guttered out though fractures formed
underneath. The Unbeliever strode out to her right to bring the
white-edged sword swinging down towards her shoulder. Using
the grace of the elven Patterning, Sura pulled her shoulder back,
her hip and leg swiftly following. The enemy's body slammed into
her as it followed through on the sword stroke, and Sura rode the
hit. Taking the blow on her right side, she allowed her body to

bend against the impact as she spun backwards. Now facing the enemy's back as they stumbled forward, she swiftly nocked and released a shaft at point blank range. The arrow pierced the grey cloth between the back plates, and blood spurted. Its purple tinge startling Sura as it laced the shaft.

Stay down.

The soldier's hip and shoulders twisted, and the sword streaked across Sura's vision—a backwards left-handed blow sweeping towards her waist. The Patterning kicked in, and intuitively Sura raised her bow to block, again spinning left to reduce the impact. The sword bit into the wood, smoke rising as it sliced along the limb towards her fingers. Sura's whirl reduced the momentum of the blow, and she wrenched the bow through the last of its arc, pulling away from the blade with little to spare. Momentum carried her apart from the enemy, briefly back-to-back, and Sura ran, legs and heart pumping. Her mind raced, hoping the enemy would see her as the major threat, to leave Laoch and follow her. Mind searching for options, she found few and drove on, hearing the pursuit despite the blood rushing in her ears.

She reached Ecne, sliding to a stop and ripping the acolyte's bag from her belt. With her chest pounding, fingers grasped the acolyte's pride and joy, wrapping around a ceramic pot cushioned in the pouch. Three of Kinst's concoctions lay within the pot. One liquid, the other powder. Sura had no clue what they were, nor cared, but she knew what they did. On impact the internal seal should crack, the two elixirs combine, and boom. If the hit wasn't strong enough, or at times, the elixir had hardened, it was no more use than a stone. One in ten failed—or as Gowan called it, *one in dead*.

Sura rose to stand sideways on with arm back. A tingle of fear ran through her as her eyes took in the white light wreathing the enemy's armour. Like a ghost of the forest, it powered towards her. Wisps of white fading behind the apparition as it charged, sword held high. She threw, the sideways action intended to maximise the pace of the ceramic explosive as it closed in. Sura then dived towards Ecne, the explosion roaring in her ears. The inner metal lining and shards of pot glanced off her back as she rolled to protect the acolyte. Bushes and trees strummed with the shrapnel until silence fell once again.

29
DO THE BRAVE ACT ALONE?

NORTHWEST ERSTEN FOREST

The explosion roared from the forest, echoing off the rock wall. Gowan's two remaining captors moved in response. They both lifted their dulled helmet visors and Gowan took in their eyes and mottled, husked skin. A moment of panic swept through her. Past denials squashed as the deeply shadowed, white eyes gathered in the minimal light, their tattooed eyelids glowing in a shade of red as they blinked. Their words went unheard, but she sensed the despair lacing the tone.

Gowan was a woman of training and discipline, a soldier through and through. She needed everything in its place, readily accepting how the Gods' Houses dictated their lives. But those eyes did not belong, nor the tattoo or diseased skin. Least of all the carved doorway with metal-forged jaws. She took a step back—the urge to run strong and immediate. Yet fear held her in place even in the face of the unknown. If she ran, they would cut her down.

I need to live.

An anxious and clearly male enemy soldier approached her, lifting Gowan to her feet, careful to keep her between him and any potential attack. He pulled her towards the carved door, the soldier slipping a handbow from his belt along the way. Roughly, he turned Gowan to face the doorway, and she heard the scrape of a knife against the leather band binding her wrists. Blood rushed into her dead hands. Flexing fingers to relieve the numbness, she used the time to steal a glance at the man's tormented face.

A now familiar series of harsh words emanated from his mouth full of rotten, purple-stained teeth—the soldier punctuating with gestures towards the door.

"Open it. Use your spiritfire, I cannot."

"I have no idea what you mean," she replied.

"Now."

When Gowan didn't move, the white-eyed man grabbed her left hand, pressing it against the scales of the beautifully rendered dragon on the door. A strange warmth spread through the top of her hand from his palm. It triggered something within her, a connection she never knew was there. Mind, and that which was *her*, her *self*, caressing each other—a kiss of two disparate parts. The warmth spread into her own palm and the surface layer of skin tingled, soon followed by a pulsing white light. Gowan was too shocked to react. Almost glued to the door in that instant. She was in the middle of a real-life ghost story, though this tale was not being told by the fire with a warmed jug of rum.

I must have died, and the Veil is testing me. Lady Fate decreeing me not worthy. I will be cast before Penance, to bathe in his ire for eternity.

Gowan felt her skin calm, almost numb again as the tingling faded. It didn't hurt, but as the husk-skinned man released her, she left a palm-shaped glow upon the dragon's scales. Horrified, Gowan looked at her reddening hand and back at the wall.

Can this get any stranger? What has Fate in store?

The man's armoured hand reached out to stroke the glowing door, the light pulsing in a steady rhythm in response as his white-tinged fingers touched the carved scales. Withdrawing the hand, he twisted it around, palm flat and a weak light seeped outwards towards the door.

Gowan glanced over, realising that the soldier was focused on his own actions and not her, despite the weapon in his other hand. Whatever their goal was, it was centred on that door and not her. It was almost as if she'd served a purpose and was now once again irrelevant. She glanced at his hand. The light remained weak, the stream intermittent, guttering, and she could see pain etched upon the man's face. His skin flaked as it wrinkled, aging before her eyes.

Is Fate tempting me? Do I act now?

Gowan stole a look towards the other guard watching the woods. His deep white eyes were stretched wide; his appearance gnawing at Gowan's already frayed nerves. The menacing crossbow moved in his hands, tracking something in the trees. The notched quarrels were dull in the poor light, and their ends crystal tipped instead of the metal the Rangers used.

Light washed Gowan's face, drawing her attention back to the door. Its glow had spread, nearly completing the dragon engraved into the stone. As the pulsing white crept along the intricate carving, a head began to form on the door—appearing to Gowan as not one but seven human faces interposed on top of each other, each spilling a different shade upon the stone. Seven colours for the Seven Houses of the Gods. A sense of dread washed over her, and the door opened slowly, exposing the void behind. Ancient air blew across her face. The smell was musty, cold and damp—the way she imagined a burial chamber to be. Every hair on Gowan's body stood on end.

Forgive me Lady Fate.

30
NO QUARTER GIVEN

NORTHWEST ERSTEN FOREST

S ura stooped low and hurried across to the sword-wielding Unbeliever lying still on the forest floor. As she neared, the chest heaved, laboured movements fighting for a breath. A flutter from thumb and forefinger confirmed her suspicions and she kicked the sword away; its edge having lost much of the white lustre. There was a deep hole in one side of the crystal chest plate, punched through to the body's cavity lined with purple-tinged gore and shards of the mirrored plating.

The visor had cracked open, exposing the wide-eyed woman within. One pure white eye was clouded, the other full of hate. Sura watched as the eyelids flickered, thoughts spinning as the previously unseen tattoos shimmered with a low luminescence. Schenterenta symbols. Death rites. But not one—a pair linked together. Those of a twin.

But you are not Schenterenta. What is going on here?

A bubble of blood slipped from the woman's thin lips and seeped from the malformed eye. A gasping, wheezing set of garbled words emanated from her mouth, buzzing with anger. Sura ignored them, placing a hand over the woman's mouth and slashing through what remained of the exposed neck.

The enemy of my people, whether you wear our symbols or not.

Despite the impact of the symbols, Sura understood that the shock of such things, and close combat could engulf a mind if she let it in. Even some of the lesser elves had fallen prey to such creeping doubts. But not her, not now. This enemy had struck one of her own and killed many more. You put a wall around that. Move on. Laoch had suffered for years as the distress of conflict battered at his mind, and Sura was sure if he could understand this simple concept, it would give him peace.

Such a contrast to her fear of loss, however. Something far more likely to incapacitate her than the trauma of taking an enemy's life. That way lay a darkness of spirit. She had been there before, and more than likely remained in its grip. The grief for her twin removing all that she was in one swoop, the pain too much to bear. Her attempts at taking her own life a huge taboo to a people with so few children. Now she was dead to them, a banishment from the tribe that felt deserved.

And she needed Laoch—*now*.

Need?

I need to know Laoch is safe, that is all.

Sura reached for the handbow at the woman's side, sliding it off the belt and checking over the mechanism. It seemed light and fitted her hand well. Satisfied, she removed the belt and quiver, adding them to her own. Swiftly looking over to the dulled sword, she came to a different conclusion. Rasping the bloodied ritual knife along the grass, Sura slipped it back into its sheath, returning her sword too as she chose the handbow. Setting it, she placed one of the crystal-tipped quarrels in place. It was likely to be short range, but her preference, nevertheless.

Sura reached Ecne as the acolyte unsteadily regained her feet, crouching low with her bow loose in her right hand, eyes on the small hill in the deepening murk of the forest dusk. Sura gently squeezed her on the right shoulder on the way past, urging the acolyte to follow. They tracked along the broken path, heading towards Laoch.

On reaching the bush where she'd first spied Laoch in combat, Sura spotted him laid in the same place. He remained still. She couldn't see the rise of his chest, nor any flicker of movement. Ecne attempted to pass her, pulling the elf back as she made to check on Laoch. Sura sucked in a breath, releasing her full glare upon the acolyte. Those eyes, that look, had stood down Captain Rakslin. Just the once, but he'd never forgotten or forgiven—and now he never would. Ecne's resolve wilted under the full glower of Sura's will. This was for her to do, Sura's decision to make.

With an eye towards the rocky hill, she crouched low, speeding across to Laoch's side. Placing a hand upon the small of his back and the other on his shoulder, she turned him over. Laoch grasped her arm, pulling Sura off balance as he rolled on top and astride her waist. She slapped out, the force of the blow sending the man sprawling with a yelp.

A quarrel writhing with white fire crashed through the under-growth on her left side, fizzing in from the rock outcrop. It was wild, but the powerful bolt smashed into the thick branches above Sura's head. Fire erupted where it hit, Ecne horrified as it seared inwards, shearing off the whole heavy branch. Unthinking, the acolyte sprung forward, shouting, while taking one step and leaping with arms outstretched, catching Sura as she spun towards the perceived threat. The heavy wood crashed into the mud behind them, a pained shout from Laoch echoing through the bushes. On landing, Ecne felt Sura squirm. Realisation soon hit and Ecne bellowed her name before she ended up on the end of something sharp. The elf glared at her until the acolyte stood, spotting the branch straddling Laoch.

A second bolt thudded into the ground behind Ecne, the grass and ivy igniting as it buried deep. Sura rolled to her feet, sprinting for Laoch's prone body and slid to a halt just beside him. She dropped, checking for his breath with some relief as Ecne drove her shoulder into the branch. The acolyte felt it give, shoving it away while Sura pulled the complaining Ranger from underneath.

Another flaming quarrel came crashing in, missing them by inches, again digging itself into the ground near Ecne as she threw herself backwards, stone and soil flying by. Sura scrabbled in her acquired pouch, removing a pot bomb, and with hardly a second glance, hurled it towards the source of the bolts. She doubted it would have much impact even if it landed close; the tattooed enemy had taken a real beating before her armour failed. The distraction, however, may buy them some time. By the time the ceramic pot had flown between the trees she had dragged Laoch to his feet and they were running for the bushes.

"Run," shouted Sura.

"What do we do now?" asked Ecne, following behind.

"We move!" hissed Sura. "And we keep moving until we reach cover."

31
A PARTING GIFT

WEST ERSTEN FOREST

"Noooo. No. No. No."

The silvered metal cracked slowly under the pummelling assault from inside. Dents ruptured outwards, the fractures widening, erupting as the creature within unfurled in a rush of power and spite. Anger flared—white and boiling—searing the surrounding air. Insects fell as the heat spread, wings charred, legs cindered. Steam rose from the leaves and branches and hot fury rammed into the bark, burning it clear of the heartwood underneath.

"You bastard, Wyrm. I will see you in hell. I will tear your spirit from the heavens and cast it amongst the demon Constructs. I will feed you to them morsel by morsel, each piece torn from your soul." The Captain screamed into the sky, back arched, spirit mouth stretched across the construct's visage he inhabited. "You vile, betraying bastard. I died for you and your people, and you will not let me rest!"

The metal leg kicked out—jointed and hinged at knee and ankle—a surge of white spiritfire lacing across it as the kick punished the metal shell around it. Shards smashed into the steaming undergrowth, the forest life scattering as a fist pummelled into the trunk of a young pine tree, snapping it in half. The Construct gathered the pieces, thrashing them against the next tree before hurling it sideways out of his sight.

"Bastard betrayer." The armour bent at the hip, hands splayed upon its knees, almost as if it was panting though no sound nor mouth could be seen to confirm it. The Captain rose, helmeted head giving the impression that it looked down upon armoured hands, squeezing each digit in turn with the off-hand poking in between. He then manoeuvred his elbow and shoulder. Feeling the joints shift and move as if he was human, though he knew he was far from that anymore. To his left, ghostly eyes picked out a puddle upon a raised stone, and he strode over, metal feet crushing the vegetation and sinking deep in the mud beneath. Staring down, the true horror hit him. He recognised the helmet, though buffed and glinting with an oiliness in the rain. With a shaking hand, he reached for the visor, fear and dread roiling where he perceived his gut to be.

Will it be me? Or the demon that inhabited this Construct's Suit? What choices will they have made to shred the last vestiges of my mind? Yet I feel more alive than in that hated ship, my mind my own again.

But he knew the answer. The rites were as old as their time in Mondrein's Realm. Time spent hiding from the Construct Horde, time spent preparing for the day they would be found. There was no hiding place for the likes of him and his people, nor the servants they had stolen then freed in their escape. Just delay and preparation. He'd been a fool to himself thinking the journey would end with the Sealgairs' release. Their own sacrifice of time and life stretched out as they gave of themselves to complete their task. Eight years of hibernation, only to burn out in mere hours.

The Captain should have known the Elder Council would have another way. Refusing to put all hope on the Sealgair but retaining a second opportunity to gain Mondrein's last hope.

And it is my fate to inhabit the Inhibitor Construct. The guard they had captured as the original Elders made their escape.

He let the visor drop, refusing to look. It would achieve nothing but more pain.

They know I would not let it be for nothing. Trusting a thousand years of hiding, with the histories of our past and fate woven into all we do and are, to compel me. But a lesser human might crumble. Curl up within their possessed form and give in to the agony. So they chose me.

He stood back from the water, spiritfire infusing his joints, before striding over to the shattered shell. The Captain reached down, emerging with a falchion and its sheath, belting it to one side before collecting a bastard sword—the hand-and-a-half weapon the Inhibitor Constructs favoured. This he shouldered, pommel above his left side with the scabbard hanging down across the baldric, keeping the sword out of the way. Finally, he lifted the dual crossbow. The hated weapon of the Constructs who could pull the foul thing back by a single hand, filling the quarrel with stolen spiritfire. A few of his adapted quarrels carried the crystals the Elders imbued with their personal store of power, but not all. The rest would require him to learn, and if he met resistance, learn quickly.

As here I am, a harbinger for these people we once called friends. What will we bring down upon them as we attempt our own survival?

Therefore, I must act with haste and take no quarter. Before I lose myself in the choices I must make. Blood will be spilled, but less than if our hope remains unfulfilled.

A rhythm beat in his atrophied heart. A *calling*. A sign he had prayed for since he first gave up his life to save his realm. The Captain felt it draw him on, a beacon, not like those his people used to warn of dangers beneath the waves. No—one to lead its masters to a resting place. He strode out, letting the *calling* decide his fate.

And behind, unseen, white fire glowed. A glimmer upon a metal shell that beat to the same rhythm.

32
WHEN FATE
INTERVENES

NORTHWEST ERSTEN FOREST

The pot bomb struck the stone-covered ground, bouncing once to strike the pillar at the side of the doorway and rolling to a stop at Gowan's feet. She stared at the explosive, eyes wide, counting the seconds she had left to live. It wobbled once, the Ranger wincing, waiting for her innards to be sprayed all over the metal teeth that menaced either side of her. On five, amazing herself, she reached down and grasped the pot unnoticed as the male Unbeliever stepped into the void.

Fate?

Gowan followed him in with her thoughts spinning, almost numb as she walked by the dragon's door. The Seven looked on as she passed, eyes seemingly following as she entered the murk of the metal-ribbed passage—Fate's gaze burning into the nape of her neck. Demanding. The compulsion was overwhelming, and her hands throbbed, a fatalism washing through her being. Gowan reacted, unthinking. She dove forward, her shoulder ramming into the back of the male soldier's upper thighs, driving them both deeper to crash onto slime-covered steps. They tumbled down in a mix of armour, legs and the buzz of angry words, coming to rest with Gowan laid across the soldier's legs. Scrabbling up the mirror-armoured back, Gowan reached for the large cross-bow strapped there. The Unbeliever bucked, muscled arms and legs heaving, attempting to fend her off, yet Gowan's hands still reached the weapon's stock. She yanked it upwards, pushing her knees into his back, trying to angle the weapon down and engage the unfamiliar mechanism. Then she saw the snapped bowstring. Heart yammering and out of time, she let go, deciding to pummel the Unbeliever's head into the mould covering the metal-lined floor. The soldier's knee and hip surged upwards, and Gowan found herself thrown forward to land on her back. A moment of fear coursed through her, the pouched pot bomb a hard lump against her lower spine. Immediately she twisted over, placing hands on the floor, with knees bent underneath and head up, eyes on the enemy who lay between her and freedom. Amid the slime lay the handbow, cocked and enticing.

Oh shit, what have I done?

Gowan feinted to the right, then went low on her left as the soldier reacted. Her boot lashed at the crossbow, sending it spin-ning towards the foot of the steps. She continued the motion and came up facing the enemy as he charged her, hands out, ready to grab. Gowan rocked back, taking the arm and twisting, letting the soldier's momentum carry him over her hip.

Shit.

She stopped, staring at the man's back as he lay on the floor, the shock of combat hitting home. Gowan took the moment to think. Breathing heavily, she realised her mistake—that she wasn't strong enough—and panic set in. The soldier groaned, rising, and she lashed out, catching him under the helmet. His head crashed into the metal wall. Now overthinking, her decisions were suddenly swathed in the urge to run rather than attack.

Not the time, there's the other guard.

Disregarding an attempt to smother him, the thought of a dagger in her kidney sending shivers up a sore spine, she headed inwards along the damp cylindrical passage. After four rapid strides she came to another door, and with eyes adjusting to the faint, resid-ual light, recognised the carved versions of the Seven Gods. A silent prayer to Fate slipped unbidden from worried lips. With no handle present, she planted a hand on the door, casting a glance back towards the still prone enemy soldier. Her fingers tingled, Gowan looking to find Fate's eyes now shimmering blue, and the door shifted slowly inwards. Another waft of stale, musty air assailed her nose. With trepidation she stepped through as soon as it was wide enough—no time to waste as boots scraped on metal and slime behind.

She stood a step inside the domed chamber, metal ribs rising from both sides of the door to curve upwards to what she assumed was a single supporting strut somewhere in the darkness overhead. The near edge of the strange, metal walls appeared covered in a decaying mosaic, with absent tiles piled on a stout alter table below it. As her eyes adjusted, it appeared to show what she assumed were the Seven, though they held the objects depicted upon the House sigils, rather than their traditional weapons. Fate carried her spindle, and not the bow. Death an hourglass and not the sickle for reaping souls, while Penance, resplendent in purple, bore an empty plate bearing someone at prayer, the scourge waiting below.

Gowan shook her head, heavy breathing echoing from the near walls, bouncing off to be lost in the void. She scanned the rest of the chamber, desperate for some kind of weapon. The metal floor lay empty except for a few rotting furs, barely held together by the last vestiges of tanned skin. The poor light caught the outline of a few aeons old wooden chairs arranged to look inward. But none of this was helping and she felt a sudden panic, regretting the decision not to strangle the enemy soldier.

Is anything normal going to happen today?

Sensing a change, possibly a shift in the air further across the dome, Gowan struggled to make sense of the proportions in the chamber. Worrying about the impending danger, knowing she didn't have the time nor the desire to go deeper, she glanced towards the altar, catching sight of a spiked pommel under the cracked tiles. With hope resurfacing, she ran over, gripping the bottom of the metal knotwork and yanking out the long metal cylinder underneath.

Now that's what I'm talking about. I am here to serve Justice.

The heavy, spiked weapon bore an indented sigil of Justice at the top of the grip, and taking hold, Gowan spun around to face the door. Checking its heft and balance, she transferred to a two-handed grip, her off-hand nearer the knotted pommel. It was far from her preferred sword though she'd trained with a quarterstaff as all Rangers had—the one weapon always likely to be at hand.

Somehow it felt inert, unready for combat. Perhaps it was the time she spent caring for her own weapons. The contact that enabled her to feel prepared, and that despite the self-doubt plaguing her day in and day out, she could cope. Here and now, the unfamiliarity exaggerated those worries further, stress coursing through her while sweaty palms made the weapon feel greasy and slippery.

Nothing else here, so remember your training.

Gowan's survival instincts screamed at the lack of time she had left, forcing her to lift eyes from the poor weapon to the entrance-way. Four gauntleted fingers wrapped around the door edge, gripping the stone lintel; her nemesis pulling himself through, still groggy but with clear intent, and the recovered handbow cocked and threatening. As the Unbeliever brought the quarrel to bear, Gowan swung the maul, slamming it down on the forearm. It struck a glancing blow, the weapon squirming in her hands, twisting on impact. The armour fractured, almost like glass, the handbow clattering to the floor while the momentum pitched Gowan forward. The man grabbed for something at her side—Gowan's image of a knife in the kidney flashing back into her brain—and she heaved the pommel rearwards. The spike caught between the soldier's hip and thigh plates resulting in a close quarter scream that stunned her ears. Gowan rammed the spike in again, feeling it grind against the bone before pulling it out, only for the point of a dagger to ram into her side. It hit the metal plate sewn into her Ranger's jerkin, sliding off, burying itself into her belt pouch.

Shit, close.

Gowan leaned back, tugging the heavy mace with her as the pained and unbalanced soldier dropped, scrabbling to recover the handbow. Gowan lifted the mace high, but a kick to her ankles sent her careering backwards, stumbling into the table. Dazed for a second, with the soldier in her eyeline, she saw him crawling towards the crossbow, blood pouring from the thigh, the trail thick and viscous along the floor.

It's dark—if this bloody day wasn't weird enough already. Purple in his blood.

Grabbing the edge of the altar, Gowan pulled herself upwards, hands slipping onto a sigil inlaid in the wood that promptly glowed at the touch. Blue light lanced between her fingers soon followed by a tingle similar to that at the door. Gowan started, lifting her hand away to find it wouldn't move.

Come on, Fate. Weave me another path.

Gowan pressed her hand down on the altar table, putting her full strength into arm and elbow as she heaved herself up. When she reached her feet, the table was no longer there and she faced a cobbled road, the streets narrow, blue lights strung up high on both sides. They stretched along the street. Glowworms in the darkness, drawing her forwards.

What in the Seven Hells?

She spun around. Head moving back and forth, looking for the soldier that she knew would not stop until she was dead. Absent, not there. Nor the chamber, the chairs or even the doorway. Just the street ahead and behind, with the line of lights marking her path.

This is madness.

Gowan took a single step, one that stretched inexorably, her spirit pulled and extended in time. She spun along the street, off lanes ranging out ahead, splitting from the path in a maelstrom of swirls and tangents. Initially, she rushed along one radiant street only for it to split into two, three, four ways. Each time a part of her followed a different—and new—path, body and mind unravelling. The weft and weave of her life came apart, each strand pulling taut, stretched thinner and thinner. Disconnected. Her mind began to fade—her understanding of who and what she was so ephemeral only the fear of losing herself kept its cohesion. Amid this turmoil, the sense of being judged pervaded, as if her very spirit was the mere subject of a Meister's curiosity, one of Kinst's test corpses. The sense of loss and emptiness was absolute.

Ahead, the streets unified. Shades of blue merging together as road and lights met. Her unravelled *self* weaving back together as each illuminated tangent wove into the next. She was Gowan again, but Gowan as she was born, as she grew, as she loved, as she cried. Memories flooding through from birth to childhood, from childhood to womanhood. Her first kiss, her first and only kill, laid bare for all to see. Laoch. And amid this, the vein of self-doubt that ran through, colouring each with the purity of failure, questioning each strand Fate chose.

What will be will be.

Gowan's mind slammed back into her body. Time had stood still, fingers still touching the now raised sigil pulsing on the tabletop. Mind reeling, she twisted her palm—where the gleaming, deep, blue-tinged metal sigil of Fate waited for her. Without thinking she reached for the spindle, pulling it from the pile of dust and shattered tiles. Her hand clasped around one side and the sigil of Fate slid into a slot along its edge. Gowan felt a familiar tingle, akin to the doors, and as she stared Fate's bow formed in her hand, growing out from the spindle ends in a haze of Fate's deep blue glow. The weapon came alive. A surge of power running along the entire length with pulses of fluorescent light flowing along the bowstring.

Fate—I can feel her presence.

A cheek caressed a familiar string. Eyes tracked along a known grip. A finger pulled back, feeling a comfort in its strength, while the smell of her favoured bow oil drifted up her nose. A thousand times she had stripped it down and restrung it, oiled the limbs and reinforced the notches. Her bow, her best friend. As Gowan released, the arrow/not arrow slammed home as the soldier turned, striking at point blank range into the lower chest plate as he rose, the handbow coming to bear. The mirrored armour shattered, Fate's blue-flaming arrow driving into the flesh behind. A second arrow was unnecessary, but Gowan found herself redrawing the bow.

After the day I've had, I really want to make sure. It is, after all, Fate.

Gowan blinked, looking down at the flaming arrow she knew she hadn't notched, nor, she realised, expected to. It glowed menacingly. The light of Fate amid the insanity of the last few minutes almost calming her mind.

Almost.

She released, turning away as the man's silent scream ended, his own light leaving those startling white eyes as the burning tip drove home.

Gowan peered at the weapon gripped in her right hand. It was her bow, down to the nicks and scratches it had suffered over the years. The grip worn where it had allied to her hand. The only difference was behind that slightly frayed grip, where a small metal sigil sat, just where her forefinger would be. Gowan raised her eyebrows as she gave the weapon a once-over.

Nothing was ever going to surprise her again after today.

33
NOT ALL LIES IN FRONT

NORTHWEST ERSTEN FOREST

"Well?" asked First Ranger Oisin.

"I saw just one of the mirrored enemy," said Conch, spitting on the floor. "Near the doorway, nervous as a cat in a dog kennel. No more, but there's a definite path through the undergrowth. Recent and rushed, mixed in with some familiar tracks. Want me to look?"

"We wait on Fenecia," Oisin turned to the side, eyeing where she'd sped off at the same time as Conch.

A small twig landed on Oisin's shoulder, the broken end recent and a broad hint as he glanced upwards to Tanka. A hefty man, out of his best condition since the return to the city but he climbed like a Mishkin Python when it meant he could rest. He scanned the canopy, Tanka hard to pick out as he used the tree and its drooping—and soon to drop—pine needle-laden branches to hide. A brown covered hand slipped out, signalling that he had sight of a single target.

But which? And how many more? And the light's bad, so no guarantees.

The tracks were blurred with the Ranger's pursuit, but if pushed, Oisin believed there were three enemy soldiers and right now only one in sight. He sent Tanka the hold signal, receiving a rude response in return. Oisin knew Tanka would be swearing in every language in the Union right now but would be enjoying the rest at least.

Decision time. We know nothing about that armour they wear.

The warning call, soft but familiar, preceded Fenecia slipping through the bushes, bow low but in hand. "One dead enemy—pot bomb I reckon. That armour's strong and light, but there are weak spots, Oisin. There are two Rangers heading this way, one of 'em injured, and an acolyte."

"Rangers?"

The roar tore through his ears, white light crackling through the darkening forest. The pine tree above them shattered, fire erupting as the sap instantly took. Smoke billowed and Tanka's screams tore through it all, cutting off as his smouldering corpse crashed onto the forest floor.

Oisin had thrown himself to the side, shoving Conch to the floor as the air burst into fire, pine needles spurting flames as they cascaded down. Fenecia, heart pounding, rose from the burning branches now surrounding her, dropping in beside Tanka and flinching as she caught sight of his charred clothes and skin. A cry rose, harsh and angered, and the Ranger stared into the forest murk to see an apparition charging her way. It glowed, the huge sword it wielded hacking a way towards them. The mirrored-plate armour pulsed with unreserved power, leaving branches and saplings sizzling in its path. It filled her vision, the drive towards her unrelenting.

A hand grasped Fenecia's upper arm, dragging her back. "Fenecia, Conch, move. Run."

And they ran.

Sweat poured off Laoch's head, the after-effects of the Unbeliever's boot ringing in his ears. He swept a hand over his sodden, shaven scalp, unable to decide if he was in a terrible mood or just a bad one. He shrugged off Sura's helping arm, waving his reassurance that he could move by himself.

Sura's alive and that's all that matters.

And then Laoch felt it, the shift, that moment in a battle when the momentum changes. An eruption of white light swathed the leaves, lighting the canopy as it streaked high and towards the hill.

"Laoch?" whispered Ecne.

But the rest of her words were lost in a few seconds of mayhem. A pine tree erupted, lighting the forest as it burst into angry flame. A choked cry soon following bit at Laoch's soul—a never forgotten scream of pain as someone died wreathed in fire.

A shout cut through the woods to their right, and in the fire's ambient light he made out figures crashing through the trees. They headed towards the hill and the remaining Unbelievers who waited there. Shouts followed, the words indiscernible, but they were his people. Queen's soldiers. Another bolt crashed into a tree, barely missing the rear Ranger lit by its flame.

"Rangers," he said. "That bolt came from behind them, not the hill." Feeling naked without his sword, he kept low, breathing heavy as he looked towards Sura. He realised she had already made a decision, turning back towards the hill. "Aye. No choice."

And then he saw it, the trees' floating embers lighting a large carved snout protruding from the rocks, metallic teeth glinting orange. Laoch swallowed hard as his eyes wandered upwards along it, catching the faint outline of an entrance between the jaws.

"Oh shit."

34
A COWARD'S LAST STAND

NORTHWEST ERSTEN FOREST

The shouts of pain and strange explosions knocked Gowan out of her reverie. She quickly scanned the chamber, eyes scrutinising the huge room lit by the light from her bow for any danger. Dismissing the risk, Gowan moved to the side of the chamber's entrance. Needing to see around the doorway despite a creeping sense someone was waiting for her, she readied herself—after all, she'd trained for this. But that last Unbeliever could be waiting for her, and her gut sprung with acidic turmoil. She spun through the door, quick, lithe, bow drawn back and her face aglow with Fate's blue. No one waited for her, and looking up the ridged steps she caught the faint light from outside. A twang of a crossbow echoed back towards her, and she took the first step.

Perhaps throwing in a pot bomb would be a safer bet.

Gowan reached behind, pulling out the pot secured in her pouch. Smiling, feeling Fate's hand upon her shoulder, she kissed it lightly and hurled it through up the steps. She heard it strike the wall, and a second bounce before it stuck fast in the slime. Sighing to herself, Gowan calmed her breathing and took the next few steps, assessing the passageway above, while noise from outside masked the quiet grind of the stone door closing behind. The enemy guard squatted at the corner of the main entrance with his back to the strangely curved metal inner wall. The reflective armour appeared whole, unmarked. Outside voices echoed with words Gowan knew. Someone was on their way to rescue her, and the guard was aiming towards the woods and about to release a glowing quarrel.

Gowan didn't hesitate, taking the last few steps and pulling back the fire-laden string, loosing a blue arrow into the enemy's back. The man screamed, pitching forwards across the threshold as blue fire bit between the plates. Striding forward, she pulled the bowstring back again, aiming for the same spot. She simply couldn't take the risk—and released.

Cautiously, Gowan moved over to the left side of the doorway, away from the newly flaring corpse. A shaft of white light shone into the canopy dead ahead.

Their leader must still be out there.

Blinking out the sweat and grit from her eyes, she looked up as the last vestiges of the enemy's light flashed across three Rangers retreating in unison towards her door. Each took position to cover the others in turn. Whatever had happened while she was inside, a rescue Spear had arrived, but they were in trouble.

An attack from behind. Another enemy we didn't see. A shadow troop.

Searching outwards, waiting to pull her bowstring back for fear of Fate's light making her a target, Gowan caught sight of the advancing enemy. She could only see one, but they were big, armour sparking with a now familiar light. It ignored combat convention and rushed towards the Rangers with little care for being hit.

Gowan pulled and released. A rapidly taken shot targeting the advancing figure, trying to delay by forcing them to cover. The arrow struck, reflecting off the armour's leg. Its green energy washed back out and away into the forest. The huge sword swung down, striking a retreating Ranger across the back, white fire slicing from shoulder to hip, splitting and charring. The horrendous, agonised cry sent shivers up Gowan's neck.

The last two Rangers turned and ran. Feet pounding across the muddy ground, heading for Gowan's position. She drew the string back, willing Fate's light to fill the arrow, and let loose. The burning bolt seared through the dark, steam forming in its wake, and slammed into the chest of the huge, armoured assailant. Flames erupted. Multi-coloured sparks bouncing back off the chest, leaving a scorch mark and a crack to show where it struck.

Panicking as the figure powered on, Gowan took aim again.

35

THE SPIRIT OF
DEFIANCE

NORTHWEST ERSTEN FOREST

S oil and debris erupted from the rocks, the explosion's boom
pounding over the trees, and Laoch hit the dirt. Ahead, the
lead runner had taken the blast from a detonation. The Ranger
was down, struggling for breath, sparks of light arcing across the
shattered metal plates sewn into her leather armour. Sura ran
past Laoch, grabbing the woman's jerkin to pull her up, pulling
her towards the carved entranceway. Laoch caught up, keeping
low, before gripping the Ranger's arm and shoulder. Unscathed,
Ecne followed behind, picking up the woman's discarded bow and
the single arrow at its side, spinning to face the forest as another
Ranger backed into view. Ecne waited, covering the soldier's retreat, focusing on what needed to be done in the chaos around
her.

A shout echoed through the doorway, bouncing around the
metallic teeth, distorting the sound but causing Laoch to swear
anyway.

Gowan. Of course.

On passing through the rocky entrance Laoch peered at the inscribed door, taking a sharp breath as he recognised the dragon glowing upon it and the Seven by its side. Pushing any concern away, survival his first thought, he took stock of the strangely configured passage as he helped heave the injured Ranger against the metal wall. Gowan remained at the entrance, peering out into the night, a familiar bow in her hand. He tried to ignore the low green light lacing the string and limbs. Somehow it didn't surprise him anymore.

Laoch dropped in beside the First Ranger, drawing his bow. "Surprised you're alive," he said, waiting for the retort.

"No more than me."

Ecne's shout broke through the noise outside, a warning as a panting Ranger sped through the entrance and threw himself against the right wall, bringing his composite bow up to aim back out towards the forest.

"Now girl," shouted the Ranger. Laoch recognised the accent, marking the Ranger as being from the forested foothills near the Unspoken's Lands. A Handren.

Must be Oisin. A fine soldier by all accounts. Elite.

Ecne careered through the doorway, throwing herself to the floor as the Ranger loosed. A splash of white light seared across Laoch's vision. Instinctively his eyes shut, hands covering his face as his primal instincts reminded him of the consequences of the fierce light. When they opened again—relieved to be still alive—Oisin was covered in stone chips and dust. His bowstring drawn back to his eye, sighting into the woods.

But Gowan had gone, Laoch looking round to see her sprawled on her back, the jerkin's metal plate over where her heart lay seething and charred. Then the woman's eyes widened, Laoch recognising the fear that washed through them, and she erupted—the thud of the pot bomb muted by her flesh and blood.

"Oh shit." Laoch stared at the tangled mess on the other side of the strange room, legs skewed, back shattered. Blood pooled underneath, but Laoch knew her heart wasn't pumping, he doubted it was even there anymore. Sura, further back and tending to the wounded Ranger stared—mouth wide, pointing. But not at Gowan's corpse.

"Ouch, that bloody hurt."

Laoch flinched. The voice in his ear all too familiar, turning to find a glowing Gowan peering back at her own corpse. Her body glimmered, laced with blue light. The ethereal appearance threatening to close down his mind.

"Bloody Fate. Not in the least bit funny. That thing is closing in, Ranger." Gowan turned to look back at Laoch, a rueful smile formed by ghostly lips. *"You need to move."*

Laoch felt the paralysis in his limbs, unable to speak let alone move.

"Laoch," shouted Sura, the directive strong and he managed to meet her eyes. "Help Oisin."

He looked back at Gowan who raised an eyebrow in return, flicking her head towards the Elite Ranger. It broke the spell, Laoch shaking his head before dropping in next to Oisin, the soldier releasing an arrow towards an armoured man-mountain pounding through the forest edge. Its boots slammed into the earth, each stride sending mud splashing onto its calves that simply melted away. The plates shone with a white light, marking the figure out against the night. Laoch couldn't miss, drawing and releasing, the arrow streaking towards the hulking armour and ramming into its knee. It ignored the blow and drove on.

Laoch gawped as Sura took position beside him, her brow furrowed as she not only saw the huge armour but registered its sheer power. She pulled an object from her pouch.

"Last pot bomb heading south, move back." She hurled the explosive, knowing her aim was true.

"Laoch, through the next door. Move, Ranger."

"Next door," bellowed Laoch. Grabbing the stricken soldier, he pulled her towards the beckoning doorway with Ecne coming to help. "Please, Sura, move."

Sura, headstrong to the last, followed with the handbow pointing out to the forest. Backing away with all hope of any further survivors lost. An impulse made her look down, grabbing Gowan's bow, heart weighing heavy as she followed Laoch to the door.

"Push the door. Do it, Ranger!"

Laoch slapped his palm against the carved stone, following orders and pushing. An odd tingle lingered over his hand, and fear curdled in his stomach as red light glowed around his fingertips. With a shove it scraped open, Laoch unable to let himself think about how as he strode through, dragging the injured soldier with Ecne's help. Ranger Oisin and Sura followed in, expecting to take high and low guard at the side of the second door when it briefly glowed a deep blue and started to close shut, squeezing them out of the way. Both stared out as the gap narrowed, trying to slow their breathing after the firefight when the huge armour filled the far entrance with a white, angry light. The door sealed with a gentle scrape of stone upon stone. The last thing they saw was the enemy armour's raised and pulsing hand aimed their way.

Ecne blew a huge sigh as she gently helped the wounded Ranger onto the floor, placing their back against the wall. "First Ranger, you want to check on your wounded?"

"I trust your capabilities, Ranger" stated Oisin, standing by the stone door and staring at Laoch's fingers that glowed with the last vestiges of red light. The mountain man shook his head clear, but peering back, he caught the last fade of its glow.

"I'm not a Ranger," stated Ecne, lifting the wounded woman's jerkin to examine the ribs beneath.

"Though she knows anatomy," added Sura, dropping to kneel on the other side of the wounded Ranger, reaching for her pouch. "Especially burns."

Oisin's eyes never wavered off Laoch's hand. "I'm Oisin, Queen's Elite. And that's Ranger Conch. We left Tanks and Fenecia out there, in pieces."

"Ranger Henti. Elven in your language—if you hadn't noticed." Sura bent to tend to Conch, feeling for the cracked ribs she fully expected to find. The wince told her all she needed to know, bringing her belt around and rummaging in the large, right-hand pouch.

"I know who you are. All my people do. Though I thought you might remember me."

Sura turned, eyes narrowing, staring at the Ranger Elite. Her lips parted, and a flush rose. She felt Ecne stir, the acolyte pulling the jerkin back, and asking Sura to lift the Ranger up a little so she could wrap the first part of a cloth bandage around.

"Ecne Perstan, Acolyte to Meister Kinst," said Ecne while she worked, oblivious to Sura's change of mood.

Laoch, backed to the wall, sliding down into a sitting position, oblivious to Sura and Oisin. His breath felt heavy. A headache thrumming at his nerves as he pressed two fingers into the bridge of his nose.

"Ranger Laoch, for my sins," he stated with some bitterness.

"First Ranger Gowan, Spear Leader."

Laoch sat up straight, startled as the voice echoed in his head. That hated sound, one that took great joy in berating him for every failure. Realisation finally hit home about the orders he'd followed. In the moment of battle, you don't question what you're told to do—second guessing a superior when trying to survive means hesitation. Moments lost that could be the difference between living and dying. And whose orders had he followed?

Bloody Gowan's.

His eyes searched the room, frantically looking for any sign of the spirit Gowan. The one he could have sworn he saw in the entranceway; the one he knew Sura had seen too. But he remembered where her body lay, he'd seen the smashed corpse, the shattered bones of her back. Gowan resided in the Veil—likely that of Penance considering the woman's obsessional behaviour.

So, am I seeing and hearing things? First, the bloody ghost owl I dare not mention, then the white explosion that slapped down Conch—and that armour—the bow!

"Laoch." His name reverberated in his head. *"Stay calm. I've had a bloody shit day too."*

Laoch let out a strangled cry, startling Sura. She immediately spoke to Ecne, asking her to tie off the bandage and stood, glancing at Oisin and then peering his way. Laoch saw the change in demeanour and knew Sura would take the outburst as a show of stress and anger—the loss of Gowan perhaps triggering the darkness and memories of his past. He couldn't blame her; he'd kept it together so far, but there was only so much any of them could take. The world had turned completely upside, and he was spiralling with it—hearing a dead woman's voice who he'd spent years ignoring. And he'd not had a drop to drink.

Maybe that's it. Did I imagine it, hallucinating without the rum?

Sura knelt by him—noting the distress in his eyes and clearly looking for signs that he was finally slipping back into the mire. Laoch knew there was a tremble to him, that it had been there since his encounter with the Unbeliever, and the glimpse of an impossible glowing owl at his back. He needed to hold her, make

Sura understand his need to be loved, but realisation hammered home his doubts. In the past she wouldn't have kept her distance, would have chosen a calming touch.

"I think I may be going mad," whispered Laoch.

Sura locked eyes with him, a worried frown appearing. "After all we've been through, I think we may all be a little messed up, Laoch," she spoke with a softness that defied his worries, but the eyes didn't, signalling the emotional wall he'd forced her to build. He'd screwed up, handed her the mortar to seal each brick.

Resigned to his fate, he broke the eye contact, looking to the ground. "I'm hearing things, Sura. How did I know how to close the door? How? And the glow, did you see it?"

"It was Gowan, Laoch. I saw her in spirit too and heard the words. You're not going mad. For some reason she hasn't left for your veil. Our shamans, for all their junip chewing and ridiculous chanting, appear to have been right."

"It was me."

Laoch flinched, the voice he thought again to be only in his mind, setting his heart pounding until he stared across at the others. Each one looked towards Gowan's bow, lying where Sura had left it next to Conch and Ecne, both of whom slid away from the deep blue light emanating from its grip. And the words. They looked from Laoch to the bow and back, shock reflected in their faces at what they'd just heard. It sounded like Gowan; the tone was certainly hers. Ranger Oisin, stationed at the door, glanced behind him for the first time, wary of what lay beyond it but concerned about what was happening behind.

"What's going on, Rangers?"

"Eh, ah. The bow," said Ecne, voice quivering, "did you not hear it?"

"I heard something, but I cannot profess as to what. A bow?"

"No, well yes. It was Gowan," said Sura, eyes still on Laoch.

"Gowan?"

"The dead Ranger smashed against the wall outside." Laoch pointed angrily, desperate to not think about it, but knowing he was trapped. "She's the one we came to rescue."

"Me," said Gowan, a wisp of deep blue light swirling from the bow, forming Gowan's face for a moment before fading away. *"I am Queen's Ranger Gowan, or I was before I died."* With each

word lips formed in the light, giving Laoch a place to look. One he was desperate not to take up.

Loach stiffened, eyes taking in Sura ever so briefly: the curve of her mouth, the eyes that shone with a passion for life. An anchor against whatever this was if nothing more. Maybe he was just shaken up about Gowan's death; the violence and loss had been sudden and shocking. She had been their focus over the last hour or so. Duty to their Ranger overriding the fear of the unknown—and they had failed.

I can't let myself slip into the darkness. I can hold on. This is not real, it can't be.

"Okay," started Oisin, his back straight and holding himself stiff—but his face betrayed him, remaining as perplexed as the rest. "What are you, Ranger Gowan? Report." Oisin coughed, clearly uncomfortable, but refusing to show it.

"I don't know. I remember fighting the enemy in this room—and finding Fate's bow. And then ... and then I died." The light contorted, Gowan's face reappearing, fear and pain inlaid into the complex shades of blue. *"I died. It bloody hurt, and now I'm here."*

"A ghost?" said Laoch.

"A spirit," said Oisin, looking back to the door. "My people believed that ancestors can be conjured, brought back to provide lost knowledge. To me it involved a lot of herb smoking and drinking, very little talking. Funnily enough, only the Elders ever saw them."

"Until now," said Sura. "At least there's something the Handren and the Schenterenta can agree on. Other than the value of horses, and a life."

"I'll let that pass, Ranger. Those were times gone by, a lot has changed since then. And even more today." Oisin turned his attention away from Sura, raising an eyebrow towards the spirit form floating above Fate's bow—his chosen God, Her sigil glowing with yet more light.

"I'm a ghost? A spirit?" Gowan pulsed, her central core coalescing below the head, soon followed by a widening of ethereal eyes. *"It's coming. That thing 'outside' has been gathering power."*

The stone door shook. Its seal holding but dust puffed through with tiny fractures forming along the edge. The white light seeped in, sparking across the stone and diving into the fractures. Another boom resounded, and this time the door slipped forward an inch or two, the cracks widening.

"We have a few minutes while it gathers power again. It may break through next time." Gowan's pulsing stopped, the head and now the upper body fully formed. *"You must arm yourselves. Those weapons will not be strong enough, I—."*

"How do you know?" Ecne stood up from Conch, shoulders and arms clearly shaking. "How do we know we can trust whatever you are? There are no ghosts, no spirits. When we die, whatever we are goes to the Veil. We reside with our God. Not in a hole in the rock, or in a ... in a bloody bow!"

"This day simply can't get any weirder," sighed Sura, the cuts on her shoulder and neck standing out in the room's glow. "The alchemist spouting scripture, of all people. Gowan, what's my favourite human drink?"

"You can't stand our gnat's piss—fermented horse milk is your foul preference. You'll drink cow's milk with potato spirit if I force ye."

"It's Gowan. Or at least it has her memories. We are outmatched and if it gets in, I can't see us surviving this day. I know we all want to live so what do we do? Laoch?"

"Not my call. First Ranger Oisin is in charge," said Laoch, desperate to pass on any responsibility, needing to relieve the pressure of the darkness buzzing at the edge of his mind.

Ghost owls and a spirit Gowan. Which of the Seven did I piss off?

Oisin stood next to a pile of rotten cushions, his boot sole deep in a stringy animal skin he didn't even recognise. Laoch watched him carefully, avoiding having to look at the hovering Gowan spirit. He knew which way the Ranger would choose. He was Handren.

He'll hold here awhile, then let it in, take it down or die. He won't try to brace the door and wait it out.

"What weapons do we have?" Oisin looked at each of the Rangers, pointedly ignoring Gowan, expectant and then disappointed as the lack of pot bombs hit home. Just pointy sticks against something that brushed off their previous attacks.

Laoch faced the spirit, hardly believing what he was doing, but Sura was here, and the acolyte. However hard he tried, or feared the darkness pressing in on his mind, he couldn't avoid the inevitable. And Oisin would make a last stand, he had no doubt. The man's, and his people's, reputation preceded them. Never been conquered and never surrendered. During a previous reign, they had worn the Regent's soldiers down to where both declared an uneasy peace despite the pressing of the Seven Houses. Godless they had been, though that was changing, but they had an honour and a fierceness that belied the Union's wrath.

"Any other weapons, Gowan? Like the bow?" He winced as the ghost-like eyes fell on him.

"Four of the Seven left them here. According to Fate they were old symbols they could no longer allow the people to see. They remain on the altar table."

Laoch turned around, eyeing the tile-laden table with trepidation. Walking over, he felt everyone watching him, especially when he reached out and swept his hand through the tiles. As he searched, Gowan's words made a little more sense, fingers brushing around the circular metal discs each with a sigil, a sign of one of the Seven. Blowing the dust away but refusing to touch the holy items, he drew out the other objects beneath the remaining tiles. He laid out the thick tome and a pair of scales. From the floor, he picked up the maul, the heavy symbol of Justice that he placed beside the other objects. He patently ignored the bow, knowing full well that Fate, Gowan, or both resided there already.

"Weapons, Gowan? I thought you were a little strange when you were alive, but these?"

"They are the decreed manifestation of our Gods, and not to be besmirched by your shitty opinion. When you spoke the code, you spoke for the Queen and the—"

"—Houses. Yes, as have we all except Sura. I know my scripture and my code. But there's a bloody thing at the door, and we are in the shit. So can we get on with it because if it's bullshit, I'd quite like to sharpen my boot knife." Laoch pressed his fingers deep into the edge of his nose, memories of flames and the smell of flesh assailing ears and nose as the pressure built. "Now."

"Touch a sigil and it should rise. Then place it in the appropriate God's symbol. Think of a weapon, and it will form with the light of that God. You will ... you will experience some of your past. At least, I did, but that may be just Fate's weft and weave."

"I do not believe in your Gods, Gowan," cut in Sura.

"No matter. This is not about belief. You may wield what others provide."

Laoch turned back to the table as Sura nodded in agreement, his mind troubled but the rumble outside the door was escalating and time short. He gathered the maul, the sign of Justice upon its lower grip, and reached for the sigil with apprehension.

"Okay, we need to find if this madness works." He admired Sura's response; a woman of conviction, no quarter given. But he didn't want to relive everything he'd been through—the worst of it already haunted his dreams every night. So many days the panic rose its head when life piled on the stress, crippling him at times. The rum and Sura his only solace. Laoch knew the pain of loss and grief that many on the Crusades went through. Lived it daily. But despite Sura's demands that he should begin to open up he'd avoided such things like a deadly plague. His greatest fear was being forced to step back through those burning fires that raged in his mind. What if he never came back out? The priests at the House of Hope had reasoning for him, referring to the balance of life that came from looking forward, that you needed to offset the pain by looking to the future. He'd walked out that day, refusing the tenants of his birth church and knelt before the God of Justice. The pain, in his eyes, was a payment. A debt owed to others. And that's why the dark pressed and the smoke rose. He needed to pay that pain back. But failing to do so led him onto the streets and alleyways of the drinking dens, forever using fists against those he could not remember in the morning. A parody even of Justice—but he still held out *hope.*

Nothing like a bit of contrary behaviour, is there?

Laoch grasped the sigil, the familiar tingle from the door returning. A red glow wrapped his fingertips, the colour of his God providing comfort. A calming. He brought it up to his eye, glancing over the crossed aspects of maul and quill upon the sigil that bathed his face in the scarlet glow. And then he was there, back in the mountain forest. Ahead of him his Spear burned. The horror returned, Laoch moving between his friends and colleagues. Those he'd drunk with, those whose children had sat upon his knee. The revelry and the grind of daily life shared as one. Each face implored, though he never knew what for. Help? Redemption? An end? It was the latter he gave, taking the pain away one by one, releasing their agonised souls to join the Veil. It never left him, however much he drank, fought or railed against the world. Justice and redemption always just out of reach. Alcohol as his crutch and oblivion. Sura a hope that was slipping away.

Laoch stared down at the sigil. Back in the room, yet the sights and sounds of that moment swirled around him. The sigil felt hot, expectant, and he eased it into the maul's handle, the shaft coming alive in his hands. Pulsing under his grip, he felt a fire rush along both arms, searing into his shoulders and swathing his mind. It did not flush away the dark, rather merged with it, drawing it in and absorbing the pain—the veins of the black abyss merging with the pulsing red *need*.

Stone flew. Shards clattering against Laoch's side as the battering restarted. The door gave on the second hit, Laoch raising his arm, the Ranger's cloak and leather bracer absorbing or deflecting the chips flying his way. With mind raging, Justice demanding, he charged forward towards the huge, armoured figure in the doorway. Its hands were outstretched as the final blow broke through, a white energy wreathing the double fists it had clattered into the door. Laoch brought the maul down hard, smashing the heavy metal head into the reaching arms, hearing the crack of plate and bone as they gave under the assault. Overbalanced, he leant back to pull the weapon up, expecting the creature to be howling in agony. Except the white light drew inwards, the plates reforming, joints healing, growing together as if the very metal was alive. Startled, Laoch threw himself forward, choosing to change tack and drove his shoulder into the creature's stomach. Beneath the plate, he heard a sickening puff of gas and dust, as if what lay within was bereft of flesh. He pictured the husked faces of the enemy they'd already seen, but the image he held now was of those left on the battlefield to rot. Two reformed arms struck down, weaker but pummelling at Laoch's back, clashing against his shoulder blades. Pained nerves echoed through his body, quashed by Justice's pulsing energy in his mind. The armour clattered backwards, overbalancing as Laoch's momentum carried them both out the door.

Sura, hands trembling, grabbed a sigil with barely a glance at the image, desperate to help Laoch. The light in her elven eyes briefly flickered and went out, almost imperceptible unless you were gazing into them. Her chest ached, the heat of shame rushing to her cheeks, increasing as her whole skin burned with an orange flame. Her mind lay at the edge of a precipice, mountains glinting in the blue sunlight, feet feeling the bite of the snow beneath bare soles. Reeling, she pushed the memories away, locking them inside an orange edged box she forged in her mind. She reached for the heavy scales with her off-hand. Grasping them, she pulled it towards her while still staring into the distance. The sigil slotted home, and Sura turned towards the door, the short spear forming in her hand the true weapon of her people.

Laoch was already rolling away from the armour, with Oisin beside the door, his face covered in streaming cuts from the shattered stone. He loosed, the arrow driving into the gap between the creature's armoured plate. Sura rushed past, driving the spear tip towards the groin guard, automatically choosing the most vulnerable place. The shaft raged with an orange flame that licked at the tip, and she caught a moment's hesitation from the armoured figure before its legs kicked out, battering the spike. The flame guttered, then sprung back as it made contact with the mirrored boots, raising a high-pitched screech when it scraped along the metalled wall. With her side vulnerable, Sura spun, bringing the spear round in her left hand to parry away a second kick as the armour rolled to its feet. The immense power caused the spear to flare and orange light splashed against the armoured foot, reflecting off as she clattered back into the wall. A huge arm swung towards her face, Sura flinching from the razor-edged spikes on its edge, when the mirrored suit erupted with green energy—a thick, heavy quarrel ramming into the ribs and hurling the armour up and backwards. Laoch dodged to the side, coming up under the flailing arm and swinging the maul, the impact adding to the armour's momentum. The huge armour crashed against the top step, only to rise as another green bolt crashed into its chest, forcing it out of the entranceway. Deep blue light flooded the dragon adorned stone, and the door heaved shut—slamming into place with walls shuddering. Gowan's face hovered next to it, fading in and out, hanging above the floor.

"Well, that went better than expected."

36
A FATED SIGHT

THE HOUSE OF PENANCE, ERSTENBURGH

T he silence fell, ominous and heavy, the people awaiting their
fate as the tap, tap, tap of Lord Penance's cane walked down
the centre aisle. Underneath the practised scowl, he admired the
faithful within Fate's Supplication Chamber. Devout, and stu-
pid—a fine combination to lead the blind away from a painful
future. This Lady Fate had changed little since her rise from a
Priest-in-Waiting, leaving much of the chamber as it was when
Lord Reghon lcd the House. A Lord who held the faithful in thrall
with his pontifications on their futures, and how they were set true
by their adherence to scripture. Reghon could retell and reframe
the impact of their belief in a thousand different ways, blinding the
people to the daily reality. The only part that never changed was
the moment of prayer when they gave to Fate their utter belief.
And Fate took her due, as did all the Houses, draining just enough
spiritfire from each member of their flock to keep them safe and
unaware. Then the gift. Their God returning their faith with a
strength giving morsel—if only they knew its true purpose.

He watched Lady Fate, resplendent in her sapphire cloak, as
she slammed the Book of Scripture closed. The chamber walls

echoing that moment, carrying the sound to the furthest and nearest in equal measure. One of her priests held out their hand, and the Lady stepped down from the pulpit, leaving her faithful with a radiant smile to uplift their spirits before the ritual prayer. Lord Penance let no smile grace his lips. His demeanour a key-stone in his House's interpretation of the scripture, though he let a glimmer of light fill his eyes, letting Lady Fate know of his admiration for her duty. She, however, depended on the flock understanding she accepted her future, and that she faced it with a joy they should all share. Despite keeping the dour Reghon's Supplications the same, her words spoke of the possibilities to come and how the scripture would lift their hearts and minds to welcome it.

Clever, and her flock has continued to grow in return. Both approaches forging a worthy House once again.

They walked side by side as the silence broke, the fervour murmurs of those uplifted by her words.

And ready to give and receive.

She led him into the side chamber, bypassing the many hallways that wove through the building, opening the steel bound oak door and stepping aside. The deference to their High Lord unwanted, it was a title earned by right but wore heavy on his heart. In his eyes, they were all equal, carrying the burden of a faith that was naught but a sham. He eyed the room as he stepped through, sighing as Lord Justice and Lady Honour rose to greet him.

"Sit, in the name of the Seven. We are alone." He leant the cane against the table, choosing not to sit but placed his hands upon the blue veined marble table. Lord penance sucked in a slow breath as he eyed Fate's Wyrding stone, its glare mottled, the pulse haphazard. "Yours the same?" he asked.

"Yes, Lord Penance. Though possibly a little stronger. It still allows the transference, and feeds the Veil, but it appears—"

"—troubled," interjected Lady Honour, the orange fleck to her eye flaring. "Do you think ...?"

"Think?" said Penance, sweeping his black, shrivelled hand towards the stone. "No. I know, as do you. Did you try and *see*?"

Lady Honour bowed her head, "Yes. I had to take the risk, but my servant was ready, and the pain was much less than a full scry."

"And? ... I don't care for your pain and suffering, Lady Honour. This is our duty, our calling. If Penance burns the very skin from my fragile body, I will rejoice in the agony if it means the flock live." He spat the words, nailing each to the Lady's soul. Still young in his eyes, still much to learn about the true burden.

"I saw Honour's Scroll, infused with his light—not that of the flock, but his. And it burned in the hands of a Schenterenta, though I could not see their face. Has he risen?"

"No. The word you are looking for is *awoken*. If his sigil burns, then it has been found. I hate coincidences, in fact I hate even the thought of this being a coincidence. Nothing hidden from us for this long just *happens* to appear after a Soul Tear. Lord Justice?"

"The same. Though with the awakening of my God's symbol, I did not see by whom. Only that it was being wielded as intended. I saw a flash, a reflection, my Lord. I think it alighted upon plated armour, as of old, but one shined to a high polish." Lord Justice was taken aback as Penance's glare fell on him. The sheer terror and anger in the High Lord's eyes draining his self-resolve. Panicked, he held up his hands. "I could be wrong. It was brief."

"No, and I need you to not run from it like a cowering cur. Own it. Like I said, no coincidences. Mirrored, would you say?"

"Aye, I could see two of the maul's heads. What does it mean? Why the importance?"

"Because," said Lady Fate, sliding her hand inside Lord Penance's, gripping his good hand and feeling the tremble. "Lord Penance is thinking of the Constructors. Their armour was designed to reflect spiritfire inward to retain its potency, and outward to ward off attacks. Am I right, my Lord?"

Penance dropped into the chair, pulling his cane over and resting his hands on top as he peered at Fate's mottled Wyrding stone. The burden suddenly felt heavier, the expectation overwhelming.

"Wisdom awaits you at his House, Lord Penance, but he will tell you the same. Only I saw something different, for Fate's Spindle was inhabited by a spirit. Not a Constructor, before I add to your worries, but a recently deceased human. I saw little, except for the pathways Fate led her along. This is not a coincidence, no, but nor have we been found yet. That spirit still retained recent memories of *people* within mirrored armour. Drained, husked, but alive. You and I both know the Deeper Scriptures, and the spirit-dolls were never allowed to wear their Master's spiritfire armour. There is more to this, my Lord. We do not need to reveal all yet."

Lord Penance let his eyes flit over each member of the room, mind chewing over each morsel of information, a knot of dread tied tight in his stomach.

There are no coincidences. None.

37
A RANGER'S BURDEN

NORTHWEST ERSTEN FOREST

"Take it. That's an order." Oisin threw Fate's bow to Laoch. "Fate's bow belongs with you now, Ranger." Laoch stared at the thing nestling in his hands as Oisin moved to check on Conch, the female Ranger covered in blood from several sharp stones that had flown from the inner door.

Why bloody me?

Laoch looked in desperation towards Sura, but Ecne caught his eye. The heavy crossbow in her small hands glowing with a green light, signifying its allegiance to the House of Wisdom. If he had time away from his exasperation, anxiety and frustration, he'd have found it quite funny. But the acolyte had forced the monstrous armoured Unbeliever out of the main door, buying them much needed time.

He stared at the bow, Fate's sigil glowering back, blue shrouded.

Fate? More like my bloody penance.

"Why me, Gowan? Can't you just follow us about? Or annoy Sura?"

"You are in most need of my soldierly advice. And I find it funny that you have to carry me, for once. But in truth, Oisin refused me."

Laoch knew then it was Gowan. A ghost that bore her face he could maybe discount, but not one with the same shit attitude towards him.

"Hah bloody hah." Laoch eased his shoulder back, feeling the bruise that was forming. He used the movement to steal a glance towards Sura who also knelt beside Conch. The spear lay inert at her side—he'd caught her charge towards the massive armour, and the movements that kept her alive as it countered. Impressed and relieved at the same time. He wanted to go over, desperately needing to touch her, to make everything that had happened feel real, grounded.

"I need to go deeper in the chamber, take a quiet look," said Gowan, the whisper in his mind rather than his ear. *"There's a presence at the far end. But weak, distant. Like me, but not."*

"The Gods?" said Laoch far too loudly, heart jumping as his adrenaline flickered. Unready for whatever revelation came next.

"No. Something else. Bestial but intelligent—and weak. A wisp, or a memory if you will."

Laoch didn't know how to answer that, Oisin throwing him a stare as he looked up from checking his backpack. Laoch realised the look was due to yet another outburst.

Nothing like a drinking man talking to himself, is there? Gotta watch that.

"Hey, Ecne," Laoch said, signalling the acolyte over. "How about we check the rest of the chamber for any more of the Gods' mosaics or ... or anything else."

Ecne nodded, heaving the Unbeliever that Gowan had killed against the wall as Sura had asked, and away from her ministrations with Conch. Lifting the heavy crossbow onto her shoulder, she headed across the chamber. Laoch grasped the maul, its red light penetrating the dark beyond. It lit a table set for seven—The Seven—with their symbols etched on rotting chairs and in the mould covered tabletop. In its centre, the light refracted back from a huge gemstone set deep in the wood, scarlet sparkling in eddies against the mosaic covered walls.

Ecne followed, her weapon's shine adding to the mix, heightening the strangeness. Her jaw dropped as she turned to face the images on the surrounding walls, lips moving as curiosity overcame the surprise, and she began to read the many lines of ancient script below.

"Have you read any of it?" asked Ecne. "Deciphered what it means?"

"Can't read."

"*What?*" shouted Gowan, Ecne's glance back letting Laoch know it was out loud.

Ecne, to her credit, ignored the spirit and returned her attention to the wall. "The form is old, but not so far from our own. It says something like: Here lies Lorent, a Dragon of the Veil, a Hunter of Souls." She pointed towards the sagging wall, the tiles all in place but teetering on the brink of a collapse as water seeped down. "I assume that's the dragon, of a form unlike depicted in the Gods' Houses."

Laoch walked over, scanning the mosaic. "No. Ours has leathered wings and bone teeth, and those scales are odd and the proportions, I dunno, twisted. The look is similar, now that's the evil the Houses mastered." He soaked in the clearly metal scales, the jointed legs and stretched wings that matched both. Laoch turned, eyes roaming the ribbed walls. Three more mosaics were mounted up there, each in disrepair, words and depictions missing parts.

"Can you read the others?" Laoch said, his own curiosity raging as he spied Lord Justice amid the chaos, standing tall next to an image that appeared to be a wide, swirling circle.

"Possibly." Ecne peered closer at the first, lips moving as she scanned the archaic lettering, her face stern as she finished, brow furrowed as if in thought.

"We—"

Ecne raised a finger without looking back to the Ranger, Laoch silenced, finding himself accepting the demand as the acolyte moved to the next mosaic.

"I ... This has to be false. Lies," she whispered, lips twisting in disgust. "This cannot be." The silencing finger rose again as Laoch passed her to peer at Lord Justice, running his eyes along the words as if seeking some form of understanding. Glancing up, he took in the depiction. Armour clad soldiers, much like the one outside, swarming the Seven as they stood with weapons in hand while people headed into the strange circle.

"Ecne?"

"Those," she pointed back towards where Loach stood, "are the Constructors. Eaters of souls. The Seven were Magi, according to this, wise people who could ... control spirits, or what spirits are formed from, I think. They, and the people shown, were food for these creatures—they were like locusts. Falling on a town, feeding until sated then ... farming the rest. They named them spirit-dolls." Ecne moved beside him, pointing to the circle. "The Seven call that a spirit gate, a pathway, one the Magi formed to help their people escape." Ecne grimaced, squeezing the bridge of her nose. "I think it's saying our Journey, as written, is a lie. That we didn't cross an ocean to find Brandsholm. Rather, we escaped along—or through—this gate. Not a Landing, but an arrival."

"These are just pictures and words, Ecne."

"In a sealed place, with the Gods' weapons. I can feel Wisdom's sigil, Laoch. I can feel the shame of the lie."

"But." Ecne stopped him with a look, tears in her eyes. A hint of green pulsed amid the white of her eye. Laoch felt a pang, and a warmth spread along his hand, a red glow seemingly trying to ease the maelstrom of his thoughts. "The dragons then?"

"Real and not a depiction of the Unspoken, the evil that followed us. They are the hunters of the soul-eaters, sent to bring us back. And this mosaic," Ecne shifted over, standing in front of the last curved wall. The tiles here mostly upon the floor though the words remained. "See this," she waved her hand, pointing towards dirtied white tiles in a row, a mixture of heads and upper bodies still visible despite the damage. "That's our ancestors leaving, and here the dragons hunting us down, tearing the gate or the path open. I think many fell before we arrived here, and then the Magi fought. Though the rest," Ecne waved to a large section on the ground, tiles crumbled, the remaining words blurred with mold and water ingress, "is lost to me."

"I cannot take all this in," whispered Laoch, spinning, letting the acolyte's words soak in as he married the mosaics with the supposed meaning. Justice pulsed in his hand, almost as if it knew his thoughts and was trying to calm his addled mind.

"The crystal," said Gowan. *"That is what I can feel."*

Laoch looked towards Ecne who shrugged, letting slip a grimace with her mind lost in thought, before walking over to pull back a chair and study the crystal. She set the crossbow down on the table and reached out a hand towards the cut stone reflecting Wisdom's green light.

"No!" shouted Gowan, Laoch wincing as the spirit rushed out from the sigil. *"No, Ecne. Don't touch. No human should go near it, or elf. Anything alive."*

The acolyte drew her hand back, eyes wide at what Gowan was implying.

"What I sense is imprisoned in the crystal, Laoch. Set me down close, touching the crystal."

Laoch dropped Fate's bow beside the stone and then eased it over with his hand. "Near enough? What am I doing? I'm talking to a bloody bow who's afraid of a bit of rock."

Gowan's deep blue head formed, shot through with the light from their weapons and glowering at Laoch. Eyes fixed firmly in the same glare she had used daily in her past life, before looking up to the Veil, a loud tut slipping between ghostly lips.

"I am not 'the bow'," the spirit said as it spun to face the crystal. *"I am Gowan ... or what Gowan was inside. Her spirit ... my spirit. Shaped by Fate. And you'd do well to remember I have her favour."*

"Aye," replied Laoch, dropping the heavy maul within inches of the wavering head. "And I have Justice on my side, and a bloody big maul just the right size for smiting those that are a pain in the arse. Do whatever you're here to do."

Gowan let a snigger slip, and facing the crystal, extended tendrils of light from ghostly fingers. *"Justice in the hands of a drunkard. The Seven do choose strangely."* With that, Gowan was sucked into a facet of the crystal, winking out before her tiny face pressed against the inside, mouth wide, staring outwards. A silent scream vibrated the crystal, and as Laoch blinked, he swore two taloned feet landed on Gowan's shoulders, wrenching the spirit back into the midst of the glowing stone.

38

A DREAM OF DRAGON'S BREATH

LERONT'S HEARTSONE

B ird song, light and sweet, filled her ears. Beneath her booted feet, a deep green grass grew in a carpet full of white and yellow meadow flowers. The smell filled the gentle breeze with a heady scent bringing Gowan's senses a joy she revelled in.

"Oh shit." Gowan looked to the ground, reaching out and pressing a gloved hand deep into the thick grass. Fingers caressed the stems, feeling their rough edges and the earth beneath. She pressed her glove against her nose, letting the aroma waft into her nostrils, trying to understand.

"Oh shit, oh shit." She spun, hand lifting the bow in her right hand that lit with blue fire.

Dragon. There was a bloody dragon with me. I ... crap, I'm dead. What's happening?

She was on the brow of a hill with the stream at its foot meandering past. Along the far banks a forest rose—though not reflective of the surrounding sweetness. It elicited a foreboding, a warning she felt within her bones ...

I have bones?

Mind running through her training, the Ranger's code expecting a calm assessment of her situation, Gowan began to run through the possibilities.

Except the code isn't for a bloody spirit sucked into a bloody stone.

Where in the Seven Hells am I? A Veil. Is this Fate's Veil? Have I ...

The ground shook, vibrations thrumming through Gowan's feet. Dropping, with face towards the noise, she eyed the dark, withered trees as cracks echoed across the stream. It felt like a strange tale of the fae, one her mother used to torment her with if she'd been at her worst. Usually a monster would lurk somewhere, hidden, unexpected in a familiar story. Or when she'd been really naughty, she'd start it dark and just keep going, laying it on thick and fast.

It feels like one of those. I'm in my own nightmare.

Birds flew from the edge of the woods, rushing out over the stream. Twisted wings and toothed beaks rising in a storm of feathers and squawks. On an ordinary day, it might have set her on edge, but the path being cut her way as trees toppled superseded that fear.

I should stay here. I have the high ground, a stream that whatever is coming has to cross and an escape route behind. Almost perfect, as if I chose the field of battle. Did I? Is this my tale to tell?

Three trees back, a fire licked against wood, and the tormented trees erupted in flame. Smoke rose, black, billowing with ash as it filled the sky above the blighted forest. Gowan waited, pulling the glowing bowstring back. Setting herself ready and aware not to give her position, nor firepower, away too early.

The flames spread, rampaging through the tinder-dry trees, the branches alight with their oily smoke and choking the sunlight. Unable to see what was coming, Gowan felt an urgent demand to run. Her mind recounting her mother's tales, knowing the ending was nigh. Some nights she would stop just before the end and let Gowan finish the tale. Let her daughter bring some light and hope to its ending. Those were the days the drink hadn't taken her into the abyss. But when it had, Gowan rarely heard the end. Small fingers squeezed into tiny ears while being berated with a painful death. A mother laying upon a child's shoulders the tatters of her own life.

It's coming.

The gigantic head shot through the blackened smoke, heralded by the flame licking at its maw. Two curved horns rose from the massive, metal enshrouded skull, like a crown of promised pain. Eyes lit with an iridescent fire, a brilliant blue shining back at her. Gowan flinched at this revelation—the glowering eyes shining with Fate's own light.

Or...

She let the string relax, the bow's deep blue energy easing off, and the light died from the dragon's eyes. Clear faceted crystals glared back. The dragon's tongue flicked out, its split end licking each eye in turn as saliva dripped between dagger-long teeth.

Just a reflection. Like in the room ... the room. I'm dead.

The first taloned foot broke through the fire, metal scales shimmering with an oily rainbow as it strode across the stream. The claws tore at the soil and rock, each talon as long as a short sword, ripping the ground as it pushed itself over the stream.

Gowan drew back and loosed in one motion. The glowing arrow crashing into the dragon's snout with a burst of power. Its nostrils flared, fire spouting outwards to wash away the deep blue pulse of energy as it carried inexorably on. She pulled back again, focusing her mind on the arrow itself, willing it to strike the crystal eye and hopefully the brain behind it. The longer she held it, the more it appeared to glow, the bowstring thrumming with an energy she couldn't hold long. She let fly, the dragon flinching as she released, rearing up and preventing it from hitting its target. Instead, the arrowhead burst upon the chest scales, the metal reflecting some—but not all—of the light. Gowan saw scales crack and shatter, pieces tumbling to the ground.

Some success there. But those scales, almost like the Construct we just fought ... how do I know that name?

A dread hit her. The dragon's eyes boring their way into her mind as its forefeet crashed down to earth. The hill shook, but Gowan didn't wait, throwing herself to the side as the beast's chest expanded. The gout of flame tore at the ground, soil and grass charred into a maelstrom of ash, the soot swirling in her wake as she rolled back to her feet. The deep blue power licked at her fingers as Gowan drew the bowstring back, muscles aching. She waited while the head pivoted her way, a screech of metal on metal piercing the smoke as the neck swivelled. The eyes lit upon her, the dragon rearing itself back as Gowan released.

You are in my nightmare, and I want to decide the ending.

The blue arrow sped forwards, and as Lorent pulled away, intending to let its chest take the blow, the dragon's nostrils flared in panic. Gowan's arrow slammed into the maw, driving inwards after she'd aimed higher, letting Fate *decide*. The mighty head wrenched back, a deep blue pulsing from its throat as it tried to roar. Gowan could sense the beast's pain, and didn't wait, pulling back and firing again and again, pouring Fate's power into the dragon's mouth.

The huge, round neck, pulsed. Scales erupted outwards; a thick skin beneath frayed with edges burnt as they spurted out. Underneath, Gowan could see a metal frame, a repeated set of circles attached by multiple long rods that flexed and heaved as the beast slewed from side to side.

Trying to put it all together, her mind a mix of old memories and current agonies, she stopped firing. Changing tactics, she rushed towards the dragon as it toppled forwards. Its horned head crashed down, driving deep into the earth and Gowan fell. The rumble through the ground forcing her to the ground, before she scrambled back up, desperate to get to the scaled beast. Something drove her on, a need—a need to *know*. There was a secret hidden in the battle. An old memory, a key to unlock what was happening. Gowan slapped her hand upon the dagger-long teeth, rewarded by a smell of old death and burnt ash washing over her. She grasped her sword, raising it high, smashing it down into the maw. Its edge clanged, notched, with not a scratch left upon the dragon's tooth.

A tremor ran through the ragged lips, like worms seething under the skin, and a white flame licked the scaled edges. Gowan felt the bow, the sigil within it, pulse in response and instinctively reached out, placing it against the flickering flame.

Why did I do tha—

39
WHEN CERTAINTY FALLS

NORTHWEST ERSTEN FOREST

L aoch swallowed, a dread spreading across his shoulders. If the day hadn't been weird enough already, he could have sworn Gowan—that is the *spirit* Gowan, resurrected from her *corpse* by Fate—had just been pulled into the centre of a crystal by a dragon's taloned feet. His eyes flickered over to Ecne, the acolyte and sceptic who was the Learned among them.

Her startled eyes lay upon the gemstone, lips mouthing nonsense words as far as Laoch could tell until the scripture came through in disconnected sections. He couldn't help the smile, despite the dread. Nothing like a mini crisis to make the disbelievers of this world suddenly pious. On the eve of battle, so many found their God in the flames of a campfire.

He reached across, shaking the young woman, gesturing calm. "I need you, Ecne. You must focus. That armoured bastard is still outside, likely digging his bloody way in. Stay with me."

Ecne blinked, swallowing. Then she sucked in a breath as she leant back, her chest heaving as the acolyte repressed the disquiet coursing through her. The God's light pervading the room highlighted her screwed-up face, yet she dropped a hand onto Laoch's that still rested upon her shoulder. Pulling herself up, she glanced over to the Ranger, squeezing her eyes shut for one last time before nodding.

"I'm here. But ... it's beyond anything ... the weapons, I can almost understand those. You know, like something focusing the power in an alchemical reaction. And that armour, the mirrors ... it reflects the energy away. Reduces the effects. Science. But this—her?"

"Perhaps you shouldn't try to explain it. Just go with it, or you'll end up staring at the bottom of an empty jug like me. Or in it, if Gowan actually comes back."

Ecne nodded, looking back to the crystal as it began to vibrate, attempting to hold herself together. Laoch suspected the acolyte's mind whirled with scripture or science, or both in a turmoil that may well drop her into the abyss Laoch was so familiar with.

Need to keep an eye—and I owe her after she took down whatever dead thing is in that armour.

Blue light flickered in the crystal's centre, and Gowan's image stretched from the same facet she'd been sucked through. Expanding before snapping back into a full, human-shaped ghost. She was wearing her parade uniform, medals proud upon her chest, immaculate. Her hair trimmed to perfection—the way she had it cut every time she returned from whatever mission she'd been supervising. And Laoch was sure the look on her face was the one she saved especially for him—utter disappointment.

Not strange Oh no. Not on this day. But nor do I like the look of this. I expected her not to return, or if she did, to be lesser or wounded in some way. She looks like the Consort after his first victory, all full of himself despite those that fell on the battlefield for his pride.

"*I've never been a spirit before,*" stated an almost apologetic Gowan. "*But we need to pull together and save our people. Duty and the code can get us through this if we have a plan.*"

The uniform, and now the code. Definitely Gowan. Shit.

"What was in there?" blurted Ecne, pointing to the now inert faceted stone. "In there—with you?"

"Lorent," replied the spirit, *"at least part of him, like me. But old and weak, a fragment and he still near ripped me apart. The stone is a dragon's heart, at least Lorent's heart, bearing his spirit. Well, it did, until I ... well I don't know what I did. It felt like a battle, combat, but I'm not sure if it really was. Lorent is inside me now. Merged, perhaps like one of your elixirs, Ecne. I have his spirit contained."*

"And you expect us to trust you now?" said Laoch.

"I have Fate on my side, so yes. I can use this spirit's knowledge, or what remains of it, to help. There is a fading, gaps. But I know that thing outside is a Constructor—Lorent names it 'master', as if he is its slave. A hungry spirit, one that inhabits the armour as if it were alive and seeks us as sustenance. Food."

"Well, that makes me feel a whole lot better," said Oisin, striding over. "A full-formed spirit from a dead bloody corpse, and now armour that walks on its own. And so, tell me *spirit*, how do we fight it?"

"I don't know. I assume with the Gods' Weapons. Fate says they can overwhelm the armour. But there may be a bigger issue."

"What?" Oisin stepped closer, incredulity at talking to a spirit finally framing his face, yet clearly keen to find out what was going on. Laoch gave the Elite Ranger some credit, prepared to accept what Gowan was if it meant any chance to escape and inform the city.

That I can respect.

"There's another like Lorent. A second dragon's heart. Lorent suspects the Constructor is here for one or both of them. Searching for their long-lost dragons. Stolen slaves. I thought it was after the Gods' artefacts, but I was wrong. Before I defeated Lorent ... Fate says he sent out a message."

"A second?" repeated Oisin. "Another place, like this?"

"I don't know. The dragon hearts are linked—like a river flows from one to the other. The connection is old, quiet now. But Fate decrees there was a stir. A responding ripple."

Oisin approached the table, placing his hands on the top, bow still within reach. "Do you think this 'Constructor' will know that?"

"Fate thinks it possible, and Lorent sent the message for a reason. These 'masters' found this place. They knew it was here somehow, and remember I felt Leront's presence."

"Like a lodestone or compass," interjected Ecne, hands clasped in front as she thought. "Something pointing the way. Does that mean you have awakened it, Gowan?"

"And if so, can we assume this dragon's heart is weak like this Leront? What if it's not?" added Laoch

"We hope the Constructor takes the heart and leaves."

Gowan's voice remained steady, without emotion, almost forcing a calm to reduce the strangeness of the words just a little. It wasn't helping Laoch at all. He could feel Justice at his side, a touch that had quickly become a comfort, cutting through the peculiarity to lay a calm on his mind. Yet the logic eluded him, everything he knew of his God's House being slowly eroded.

"You're talking as if dragons are real, not the religious icon of humanity's ills as the scripture says. And the mosaics point to this too." Ecne stood, pushing back the rotting chair, hands still clasped tight. "They showed Leront in defeat but no other. What if it's not just a dragon's heart they are after?"

Oisin sighed, drawing his hands back from the table. "I don't like where your thoughts are going, Learned. Are you saying that the Houses ... that the evil they portray, the Unspoken's beast, is real?"

"She is," said Gowan. *"And I believe it to be true. Leront lies around us in pieces. His memories speak of flying, fighting, feasting. If we accept the Gods' weapons, then ... "*

Oisin held up his hand, a gesture to stop the flow of words and heresy spilling from the spirit. The First Ranger pressed his lids shut, clasping both hands against his cheeks.

"We are on our own. No one but us. I was sent here by Lord Penance with the Queen's agreement. Not to rescue you all, but to this exact spot and report back on what we found." The words were strained, the mountain man clearly struggling to share the maelstrom in his head.

Laoch started, eyes locking on Oisin. Lord Penance was not one to forgive, nor ever forget. If the Elite had been sent, then the House of Penance evidently knew far more about what was happening here or suspected as much. Perhaps the Soul Tear had spurred the order, but why this spot? Too much for a twist of fate.

"I doubt anyone will miss us for a while, for it's likely word will only be reaching the city about now. The Queen needs to know of this Construct and these husked humans—and the Houses of the Gods' artefacts. But above all else, the heresy spoken here. We have a duty to get word out at the very least. Gowan, if anything changes ..."

"I will let you know." Gowan faded away slightly, her ghost form once again expanding and contracting—ripples coursing through the light.

Oisin locked eyes with Laoch, a need there. Laoch felt the man's confidence shift, an Elite First Ranger seeking help, an anchor to set his thoughts. Not sympathy, nor equality.

He needs me to back him, whatever he decides. Certainty. I am not so sure I have any.

By the time he'd collected Fate's bow, the Handren had returned to the inner entrance, Sura standing eye-to-eye with the First Ranger. Laoch recognised the posture, tight, angered. Sura had something to share, he just hoped Oisin had the patience to listen.

"They are tired, with an acolyte and an injured Ranger among them. We've just been through your Seven Hells, Ranger. You need me."

Oisin sighed, cracking a single knuckle with a crossed finger. "I understand your kin's stamina, and your bravery. I do, despite your words earlier. But for this plan to work, we must pull together. I need you to go."

Oisin could see Sura bristling. Laoch glanced across at the Ranger, managing a smirk despite the circumstances.

You haven't seen anything yet, First Ranger. Here it comes.

"Ranger, if you are saying you should go out there with half a Spear and fight that thing so I can run off and tell the Queen, and the mighty Lord Penance, then you can stick your Elite status up your arse." Sura had taken a step towards Oisin, tending Conch lost amid her roiling emotions. This was the Sura he admired, all venom and spite, wrapped in a good heart.

"I am well aware of the difficulties. But this is beyond us. A happening so significant that it endangers our people, maybe yours too. Word must be sent, whether this Construct leaves or not. They wanted this ... this dragon within the stone enough to risk attacking Union soldiers, and therefore the Crown. You have the best chance to get through; I need you to go warn the city."

Laoch caught Sura's flinch, the fire erupting in her eyes. Oisin might need *certainty*, but he didn't understand the firebrand he was dealing with.

"Sura!" Laoch stepped between Oisin and the Elite. Sura's hands were flexing against the spear, its orange glow rising in the enclosed room. "Ranger Henti," Laoch enunciated each word slow and firm.

Sura threw Oisin a look of fury and sparing little shared it with Laoch before spinning and walking away. The atmosphere crackled in her wake. Oisin stared at her back as she strode towards Conch, raising an eyebrow as he looked back to Laoch. He continued, unheeding of the warning Sura had brought, "As I was saying—we need to get word out, even if we die doing so. By the code and the oath we swore."

Laoch knew where this was going, and although he didn't want to trade any more blows with the monstrosity outside, the argument was powerful. He felt anxiety surge from the pit of his stomach—unsure if it was the fight to come or facing Sura's wrath.

"You mean to fight it?" said Ecne, trailing behind, a frown remaining upon her face.

"It may buy us time to get Sura through," replied Oisin, his hand scraping along his jawline. "It's the right thing to do. If it's gone, then some of us can follow, observe. If the Gods' Weapons prove strong enough, then we try to take it down."

"Without Sura?" Ecne peered over Oisin's shoulder. "Folly," she whispered.

Light splashed from behind. Refracted blue motes highlighting metal ribs as they flowed towards the ceiling. Gowan flickered in and out, her smoke-like form flashing. *"I have found a fragment, a memory. The other dragon heart, it was never beaten. Lorent's body was broken up and encased in stone after the Seven took him down in battle. But they could not defeat the other."*

"What do you mean?" asked Ecne.

"Ah, well," The spirit sighed. *"The other is, or more likely was, dormant. More asleep or trapped rather than actually dead. Right now, it's letting Leront know it's very hungry."*

40
WHEN A LAST HOPE CALLS

NORTHWEST ERSTEN FOREST

The Captain knelt upon the muddy floor, his metal poleyns over his kneecaps covered in a mix of mud and white light, straining as Wisdom's energy coursed over his chest plate. He felt it search for an ingress, forcing him to expend much needed spiritfire to quell what remained. As it finally dissipated, he rose to his feet, bastard sword now drawn and resting point down in the ground as he surveyed the newly closed doorway. The dragon depicted on its outside, a familiar sight to his faded eyes. His realm's own tales spoke wonders of the slaved artifice beasts, and how they would track down and consume those souls brave enough, or foolhardy enough, to escape the Constructors. Built for the hunt, nasal systems attuned to the spiritfire, they created their own pathways through the veils humans cast to shroud their worlds. Magi, and their kin, learning to hide. Shielding their spiritfire from the dragon hunters and their masters. Veils that made each realm appear dead, empty, worthless. But veils leak. And with their dragons lost, the hunters use new ways to seek their prey.

I surrendered my life, my family, to this cause. The Wyrm sacrificed its existence after millennia riding the realms, knowing the Constructs hunted them down for their ability to pierce the veils. If a few people must die, so mine shall live, so be it.

We have sacrificed enough.

The thrum of the heartbeat changed in pitch, waves of power wavering, flickering in and out. The Captain stood stock still, helmet cocked towards the stone door, sensing a battle within. The *calling* had directed him here, the steady rhythm sparking recognition in the dark body he inhabited. Its residual spirit recognised that rhythm as—hope? Possibly, if a creature so bitter and twisted could understand such a thing. More akin to *need*, the dragon's drumming a sign of the energy contained within, one the beast was compelled to share with its masters.

It stopped.

No, not ended. The beat has changed, a new, softer rhythm. Absorbed. The Spirit Walker has been taken, like I have been forced to do with this eldritch horror I inhabit. And therefore, likely weak—too feeble to re-inhabit its form. We are lost. Failed.

The Captain walked over to the newly closed outer doorway, spirit eyes running over the depiction of the dragon it contained inside, and recalling the seven heroes that fought it. His own realm's folklore, Mondrein, spoke of the dragons' loss, sent to hunt down their masters' fleeing spirit-dolls. A people lost for a millennium, only for him to have finally found them, and the dragons he sought.

The Captain placed his hand upon the door, mirrored gauntlets reflecting back the power held within it. "The Seven Magi—and these must be their people. Survivors that have lain hidden from the Constructors, and we, on our search, opened their veils. A few falling to our cause is but a drop in humanity's ocean, but a whole realm now exposed? Is that what I am? A Harbinger, predicting their death by exposing their presence to those that hunt. What have I done?"

A heartbeat rose, powerful, hungry. The drumming sending deep ripples through the air, setting each tiny part of the realm's natural spiritfire into whirls and eddies. The inhabited armour shifted, helm turning, sensing the shift—a thrill lined with dread.

The other is here—Nathair. And now awake.

The Captain pushed himself away from the door, lifting his visor high, the bulbous, vaguely human skull within scarred by deep cuts into cheekbone and forehead. Reminders of the rituals the Constructors took to achieve their immortality. White fire shimmered in the crystal encrusted eye sockets, light dancing to Nathair's beat.

"Different, angry, stronger. At least that way lies hope for my people. For Mondrein." His ghost lips slid over a cracked and withered jaw. He flicked down the metal face covering, turning to the north and began his journey to redemption.

41
THAT WHICH IS HIDDEN

THE HOUSE OF PENANCE, ERSTENBURGH

The smell always hit Lord Penance first. A rankness that marked the deepest room within the House. Poison and rot that exuded from the ancient moulds and death that pervaded the dank, prison like corridor his cane tapped along. Every joint screamed its agony, demanding his attention. Their complaints tinged with the fear that they would have to carry this sack of bones and meat back up the same staircase. Penance welcomed the agonies, a distraction from what was to come, and the fetid atmosphere he scraped his leather-shod feet through.

He coughed, the phlegm sticky and green. "Sneed." He reached out, grasping his servant's shoulder as his body reacted, taking a rest while the next cough sent his joints into spasm. "How did you last so long, Sneed? How?"

"For my penance, I did not have to descend those stairs towards the end, my Lord. During the Regent's period I mainly spent time tending my flock as they marched to redeem the deniers, or questioning those that did not." Sneed pulled at the man's hip, feeling the click as it readjusted. His own withered and blackened arm, taking the strain as he held him through the pain.

"I think my time may nearly be done. A last act, before I can give my body a rest from its punishment." The Lord squeezed Sneed's arm, pushing off his shoulder, tapping his way through the slime and murk of the corridor. "Soon, I think."

"A fancy, my Lord. You are needed. Now is not the time to rise up the one who waits. Experience and a firm hand are what's required. Leave the vigorous for when we truly do have to fight ... or run again." The servant's eyes bored into the Lord's back, waiting for the inevitable pause in the tapping of the cane. The moment of self-doubt that would mark the man as reaching the downward slope towards the end. His own servant, Mistress Shan, had done the same for him. Read the moment and provided council. The final penance of an ex-Lord before they too can rest. But there was no misstep, no hitch to the stride or a brief pause for thought. Sneed blew out his cheeks.

The stone doors were thick with growth, old roots entwined with moulds and slime that slithered under Sneed's burning torch. Chitinous tails disappeared beneath furred growths, clicking legs and undulating bodies writhed before seeking cover from the light. The doors rose to twice a human's height, curved at the top in perfect join. They hadn't been opened in a thousand years, sealed the day their God had died. And the Magi, the man who had sacrificed himself, as had the other six fated heroes of a twisted, hidden story, rose to Godhood as his very being formed the outer Veil.

Lord Penance stopped in front of the mighty doors, tapping the cane on the floor before daring to look up towards his future. "The irony, eh, Sneed? I wonder what Fate has in store for me, heh. Or Hope, even. The only certainty is that Death will have her due in the end. It is perhaps the greatest of our achievements, to nurture each of these virtues as symbols for our people to fall upon and devour in their need to *believe*. Yet in reality, we need each and all, intertwined like the roots of a tree if we are to be truly ourselves. And for a thousand years or more, we have been tasked with preventing that, stripping our people into one of the seven strands, needing the purity of those beliefs to feed the mighty Veils that keep us safe."

"And to prevent the seepage, my Lord. At times, the importance of the suppressant gets lost amid the prayer leeching. Our flocks would sing to the Constructors without it, the Hidden Scripture talks long about how the masters and their Dragons hunt by the merest wisp."

Lord Penance balanced his cane against his pained leg, easing the hip joint, before reaching inside his purple robe. The withered, blackened hand emerged with his symbol, the pendant that bore the sigil of Penance. A kneeling human in prayer, the scourge beneath. He squeezed it tight, felt the thrum of power within that had taken its toll on his body, for the Lord of the Highest House bore his burden every day. He rubbed a withered thumb over the glowing metal, a wry smile reaching his lips. The humour of a warm, caring man hidden deep amid the mummery of his role. "Ah, it is time." Looking up, he spied the one spot the creatures and growths of the dark left untouched and slotted the sigil home.

And waited.

It was subtle at first. The sigil's purple glow fracturing into tiny vein-like sparks that spread radially out. Then, a charge of intense violet broke the moment, before rushing along the join, the seal beneath cracking, jolting the doors open a fraction. Sneed eased in beside his Lord, keeping his shoulder close, aware that the burdens to come outweighed everything the man had been through already. The rumble went deep, the corridor shuddering with the weight of time as the doors slid inexorably apart. A blackened palm rose, the purple glow gentle, rhythmic. But as the rot from within washed over them both, Lord Penance parted the wind with a word, a thin veneer of power encompassing them both.

Sneed gave his Lord a glance, and a subtle shake of the head, but Lord Penance ignored him. It was up to him when and where he used that which was forbidden to his people, and he'd had enough stink for one day. "I'll pay for it later, Sneed."

Lord Penance wiggled the cane in front of him, knocking off whatever foul insect crawled its multi-legged way up, before entering the tomb. He'd seen drawings, at least the copies of copies the Priest-in-Waiting painstakingly produced, of what to expect. The stone walled box with its heavy marble plinth came as little surprise. Nor his God's sculpted presence on top, the scourge and the sigil held in crossed hands. He ran his hand along the cold marble, eyes only for the carved representation of a man who'd given his all for his people. The Seven had held the gate, which, in his mind's eye, was formed of mighty pillars of stone, as their people, the spirit-dolls of the Constructors, poured through. Blood covered. Encased in the stolen armour of their masters and wielding weapons forged in secret as the Constructors became complacent, they fought the minions who sought the gate's closure. The dream, for he knew it would be less heroic and more pained than his mind saw, had settled in his mind from endless replays. And where his God stood, his own eyes would peer through the helm. Shot through with purple spiritfire and chin thrust forward, determined that all shall pass.

He harrumphed, feeling a hand touch his shoulder, and he knew then that Sneed had lived the same dream, and likely all the Lords after their Gods' sacrifice. "I am not alone. Do you think if I press the sigil in place, he will arise and take my place, Sneed? Ease my burden. And if I am right, lead us as the Houses' foundations crumble around us?"

"No, my Lord. The Seven's sacrifice was absolute. Their spirits forming the bonds and scaffold around which we sew the spiritfire of our flock. They are no more sapient than the insects that bite at your boots. This is your time, however much I wish we had more opportunity to prepare."

"If ... if it's true, I intend to open the library, Sneed. To the Meisters."

Sneed nodded, gripping his Lord's arm. "Then you must be certain, that way leads to ... ahh. You mean to free their minds ..."

"Yes, they've been shackled too long, and I fear the flock will need *weapons.*" Lord Penance reached forward, sliding the stone sigil from his God's hand, pocketing the intricately carved marble and replacing it with his metal pendant. No prayers or incantations, no rituals that their lies and deceit accused the Unbelievers of. The scourge glowed. Its stone covering crumbling away and strands glistening with intent, the metal tips emanating his God's purple power. He took hold of the whip's handle, pulling it gently free of the stone hand, feeling its weight. Despite the power, it felt dead to the touch, and he reached for the sigil, removing it from the sculpted palm before slotting it home. The thrum vibrated through his hand with the scourge's luminescence spilling into every nook and cranny of the tomb, greeted by squeals and skittering.

Sneed blinked away the last of the light, squeezing his eyelids, before looking for his Lord. He stood a little straighter. The pop of hips and elbows a little less evident as the scourge reformed.

"Here, Sneed. I won't be needing this now," The Lord handed over his old cane, in his withered hand sat a perfect copy, the sigil of Penance gleaming on top.

"And? Do you feel it? Do you know?"

Penance nodded, eyes distant. "Yes. And Death and Hope agree, the three Gods who entrapped Nathair at the end. I can feel them, the connection is strong and the spiritfire must be tuned down lest we bring the Constructors ourselves. But yes, there is an awakening. Though I taste fear on Nathair's spirit. There may be hope yet—and may the Seven help us, I know now where she lies. No coincidences, Sneed. None."

42
WHEN LOVE DEFIES

NORTHWEST ERSTEN FOREST

S ura seethed; and she knew Laoch recognised the tension in her body, that he'd read her and knew to be wary. He stood next to the Gods' Table, searching under the tiles for the missing sigils of Penance, Hope and Death and coming up short. Neither the symbol, nor their icons were present, and Sura could see the tremble set in his shoulders as the pressure fell.

Not the time to say you agree, Laoch, though I expect you do.

Sura turned from her post by the shattered door, a simmering glare giving him no quarter to avoid what was coming.

"So you agree? That I should be coddled, sent to the city while you fight?" It had to come out, and she awaited his response with trepidation. Another rock to seal away the corpse of her feelings.

"No." Laoch turned to lock eyes. Visibly shaking as he kept his own roiling emotions in check. "I have given him my view, that you are needed. But nor do I agree with your sniping at his people. You talk of those who deride your race, yet you did so to his on first meeting."

"Second." She held his gaze, angry at the hurt the words caused her. Truth always did that. Her eyes dropped briefly, only to return. "Though you are correct."

"Second?"

"I was young, but yes. He's one ... one of the Handren who returned my brother's body." Sura began to shake, arms wrapped tightly around herself. "He went without me. Always the reckless one. The Handren had entrapped a wild herd in a valley, corralled them in. Denied their freedom. Our Chieftain was turned away, refused entry to ask for their release, but my brother rarely took no for an answer. A family trait. He went back and released the horses, yet the herd refused to take him. The horses would not let my twin ride despite his actions. They always refused us when we weren't together."

"So they killed him? The Handren?" Laoch turned back, looking towards Oisin as he spoke with Ecne, examining Wisdom's crossbow.

"No. For all their ways, they were horse thieves not murderers. The horses ... from what the Handren said their shouts caused the horses to stampede. He was crushed. They returned his body the next day, and that's where I saw Oisin, though it was some time ago. He has changed, I did not recognise him at first."

"I knew you lost someone, but not that it was your brother. I never sought to pry," Laoch's mind flooded with a beseeching face, his own brother asking for death. "I-I have been unthinking. Selfish. Floundering in my own ills."

"All true."

Laoch grimaced, accepting the barb. "It does not stop Oisin from being correct. You would have most chance of reaching the city—"

"I can't run from this. It is not who I am. You know that." She needed him to feel the sudden heat of her anger, to understand this was who she was, and would always be. Not an apology.

I don't need a protector.

"I know. And I have told him. I spoke of how you fight, the cold fury. And who I would prefer to have at my side, or my back, and why." Laoch reached out—breaking her tribe's taboo set between elf and man, placing his hand gently against her cheek. The warmth of the touch sent her thoughts spiralling, the soft skin along the back of his hand awakening the root she had tried to kill. She knocked it away, casting her eyes to the floor and boring a fire-laden hole to whatever pit lay below. It wasn't a deliberate act of rejection; she had no time for games.

Why now? What am I doing?

Her emotions roiled, tearing at her. Raw after spiralling into the depths the sigil had taken her. She had stood once again by the precipice, the fall to the razor-edged rocks far below calling, asking her to pay the price of grief. Her heart lay broken, torn asunder—the pain bleeding into her torn soul. One step and it would be over. No more pain, just an ending. But one full of dishonour despite the keening for the other half of her soul.

Sura gave in. Slowly reaching out and taking the same, despondent hand, and placing it back against her cheek, glancing up. Cat eyes laced with grief and need.

See me, Laoch. Commit. Because I need to know.

"I have to fight, Laoch. It's who I am. Then ... maybe we can ..."

Laoch moved his hands to her lips. Perhaps to prevent her from saying any more, to stop her from going back on the hope she'd seeded inside him.

"I cannot be left alone again," she whispered, the words bearing a sliver of truth, but unable to voice it all.

For I am so far from perfect. Half a heart.

Sura felt a surge. The spear in her hand pulsing with orange light.

"This sigil—it's Honour, yes? My people honour our ancestors, and our children. The past, the present and the future. I failed them Laoch. I let them down and was cast out. The Rangers gave me a family again and ... and you ... you are forbidden too." Sura pulled herself up, mind filled with the orange energy that rippled along her hand and deep into her mind.

Honour.

My way.

"But the Elders no longer have a say in my life. I choose, not them." Sura locked eyes with Laoch, intertwining her empty fingers with his as she drew his hand away. "Be patient with me. But I fight by your side, not coddled." She let her eyes flare with an inner fire.

Laoch nodded, a smile reaching his lips. "This is going to be some journey," he stated, eyes glistening as he squeezed her fingers. "In all this madness, you now choose me." Laoch glanced over to Oisin who had coughed as he walked through, picking up the end of the conversation.

"I take it you're coming with us, then." The First Ranger strode over, lifting his pack from the metal floor.

"Oisin, I am ... I—"

"Apology accepted. As for the mistakes of my people's past, then mere words won't help. Naru freed your horses, though in truth I think we had met our match in their wildness. Let time heal, Sura. Bitterness has no respite, Fate taught me that."

Oisin made a show of slinging his pack over his shoulder, cinching the straps before picking up his bow, making sure they both had seen him prepare. Sura watched him, the expected argument fading into the air. He strode over to his wounded Ranger's side, sparing no glance for either of them.

Oisin, kneeling next to his Ranger, took the woman's hand. "Conch will go to the city alone if we can get her past this 'Construct.'" The Ranger returned his firm grip and responded with murmured words, accepting the duty that was expected of her. "She has a few sore ribs, but she can walk. We need as many fighters as possible. Conch has Meister Yanpet's map and knows the path back to our horses. You are with us, Ecne, if you please."

"But ... I'm no soldier," blurted the acolyte. "I can help Conch."

"With us." Oisin stared at the glowing heavy crossbow like it was a nest of serpents. "We need your crossbow. I won't be carrying one of our Gods' weapons."

"You should ..." started Ecne, well aware of her position in the room. "Sura is."

Sura flinched. The Gods were not part of her beliefs. A weapon was a weapon, a tool with a purpose she could maximise. Whatever inhabited the spear in her hand made it a stronger, faster tool. And that's all she needed from it.

"I cannot, Ecne. I will not. My soul is Fate's and no others. That is the will of my people. And Fate's sigil now lies entwined with the spirit Gowan. She has already chosen another. It is how I think and in all this madness it brings me peace. That is my choice. But we all saw the power your weapon wields, and it is needed," Oisin set his jaw, clearly not taking questions, nor protests.

Sura spotted Ecne's flinch.

Is her concern Oisin not taking her weapon? Or the battle with her faith?

And what did she see when taking up the sigil?

Ecne suppressed a grim smile, pushing herself up off the floor, seemingly half-pleased and half-fearful of the position she'd been thrust into. She lifted the crossbow, checking the balance and feeling its weight, with her muscles only complaining a little.

"You'll be fine," said Sura. "That thing only has to hit once."

Except, of course, that armour took it and got up again. Lock the worry down.

And if you think your Gods are fickle, you should meet the Schenterenta shaman.

43
WHISPERS OF THE RIGHTEOUS

THE WHITE PALACE, ERSTENBURGH

The Prime watched carefully as the Queen entered the Consultation Chamber, her eyes alive, dancing around the room as she swept past the guards at the door. She assessed him in an instant. Jacka knowing she'd made assumption after assumption about his mood, his day and how their conversation would go. What riled him most was just how accurate those views would be. All based on gossip, supposition and an animal instinct to survive in the political theatre of the Seven Houses and the Union—honed in the bear pit of the Palace Court.

The Council of the Houses had chosen her consort well. A shackle around the Queen's ambition. A burden to prevent her from *ruling*. Unleashed, she'd sway the people to her side, and the ridiculous swathe of Dukes and Barons who claimed Union lands at the outer reaches of Erstenburgh. And he doubted it would take much more than a sabre rattle, or a demonstration of Erin's Wrath, to have them come to heel. But with the Prince Consort at her side, he took the shine from her power, blunting the Court and the human world's wider view of her. At the moment, the Queen had little room for manoeuvre, playing the University against the Houses as her only true means to flex her power. And for that, she needed him. A need he cherished.

"Queen Erin, and Prince Consort Adama," said Jacka, bowing at the head and shoulder as his status allowed. "Err, Queen?" He lifted his eyebrows, the tired smile and glance towards the Consort enough for the Queen to know this was for her and her alone.

"Yes, Jacka. Adama, why don't you check on the Regents' Guard? They do so like your visits and attention to detail?"

The Prince smiled in return, the man's pepper grey beard and balding head nodding in unison as the aged Consort waved towards the guards. Jacka watched as he pulled his uniform down, brushing at imagined lint before following the soldiers out. As old school as it came, the man was half of what he was. Lost to the ravages of a head injury during the retreat from the Crusade, his moods slipping between fury and docility. His decisions more paranoid by the day, yet often forgotten or reformed on the next. The Council had chosen him as the most noble of consorts, honouring his family and Fate's House. But everyone in the Court understood it was a marriage decided by the Seven. And though they knew not why, a continuing symbol of their power *over her*, and therefore the people of Erstenburgh and the Union.

With the Consort gone, the Queen descended the stone steps, ruffling her dress in annoyance before taking her place at the marble table. A few years ago, it had been the place where they had planned the Crusade, though truth be told, the Seven had held sway over much of the wealth and the will of their brethren. Decisions made on a religious platform seemed to make little sense, focused on smiting the heathen with one hand, while the other offered redemption and a return to the fold. It left them with fire and pain as they attempted to burn their way through to Anvil, their capital, while managing thousands of prisoners they could not trust on the other. A debacle that had left the Houses having to raise a Queen to the throne who could provide a steady hand, but who they did not trust.

And here I am in the middle of the maelstrom, hampered by the last Regent's decision to insert his spies into the Seven Houses to find out why they had decreed such madness.

The Queen signalled he could sit, Jacka letting his hands separate having locked them behind his back to curtail the inner anger coursing through him. He gave the sideways nod he'd perfected, taking his place opposite the Queen, hands palm down on the table.

"My Queen, apologies for the need of—err—an introspective conversation, but something has come to my attention."

"Go ahead, Jacka. After the, what did Lord Penance call it? Ah, yes, the Soul Tear, we are all a little on edge." The Queen's eyes flashed as she mentioned the High Lord, enough for the Prime to confirm the urgency for the conversation. His House of self-punishment oversaw much of their decision making from afar, and the Queen's continuing distaste for the man lay evident in that glance.

"Yes. How much candour does my Queen wish?" Jacka let his eyes wander around the room, his own people on watch. Knowing they were free from others listening in, he still wished for his beloved Queen to be in control of their choices. If all went wrong, and the Seven chose to *end* his tenure before the Queen, he would need at least her support to survive what they had in store for him.

"None. Tell me what you have, and I will then repeat Lord Penance's words for you about your web of eyes and ears."

"For me?" The Prime swallowed, brushing his fingers lightly against his throat, trying to ease the knot forming there.

Putting me on the back foot, but I am here for you. Do not take out your ills with the Houses on me, or we will both fall.

Jacka slid his hands off the table, squeezing his fingers together. The Queen gently sighed, indicating his signal they were alone in their conversation had been received. "It is him I wish to speak of. Him, and Meister Yanpet."

"Yanpet? Lord Penance had a conversation just today with the man. A long one, I understand, related to the Soul Tear investigation. Wanted advice on maps, and such like."

Jacka let a pained smile reach his lips, enough for the Queen to see his view on the conversation. "Yanpet has returned and is—err—very rigorous in his views of the Overseer. He has eschewed Wisdom for Penance's House. Whatever happened to him in there has led to a miraculous conversion."

"You mean he's changed Houses? A Meister? It's ..."

"Not happened for some time, however, there's precedent. But rarely to the House of Penance. He has a period of grace and maybe his fervour will cool. Though I doubt it. I think this sudden transformation has been acquired out of necessity." The Prime let that sink in for a second, knowing Queen Erin would pick up the nuance.

"So whatever true purpose Lord Penance had in mind, he wanted it kept silent. And Yanpet does not know the meaning of that word. Jacka, he came here with regard to the Soul Tear, but he was adamant you should widen your web. That I needed to be more informed. It felt like something was afoot out in the Union, though he warned against spies in the Seven Houses."

"No doubt, his especially. And your thoughts on this?"

"The High Lord said it was necessary. That is enough of a mandate, I believe."

Jacka nodded, steepling his fingers. "And my coin for this?" The Queen gave him a tight smile in return, coin always on her mind.

"Double, Jacka. But mind, recruit well and with care. If the Houses take offence to your decisions and choices, our standing with the people will mean nothing."

"Are you aware they have also started increasing the Masses, as a response to this *Soul Tear*, to calm their flocks? The Houses have opened their arms to the people and dampened the rising panic. They act swiftly, quelling the current stress with prayer and community."

"And acting in a way I can't. It feels like the right thing to do, where I can only use words—what actions can I take? Double the city patrols or decree a curfew and the people will be increasingly alarmed. Their thoughts will turn to something they truly should fear. The Unspoken."

Jacka agreed. The Houses held the people—not in thrall—but in their hearts. When they had undertaken the Journey, and the Seven Gods sacrificed themselves to keep their new home safe, the Houses had risen to give the people peace. The scriptures providing tenets to live by; protection in a community that prayed together. Those that had rejected the words of the Seven, turning their backs to choose their own path had been few. Yet, in the last few centuries, those rejecting the Gods had increased, the trickle becoming a stream the Houses refused to tolerate. Hence a religious war, one the heathen had prepared for as they dabbled in their science. "I hear Lady Fate will be visiting you soon to draft the Crown's response?"

"Yes. Tomorrow at noon. I assume the delay is so that they can be seen as the shepherds rather than the master. Pay no heed, it is their usual game playing. You already passed word among the Court and the military that the University Meisters are investigating what happened. It is enough for now. The University is still trusted in the city."

"There will still be some that will look their way, wondering if they are the cause. Many say Kinst's actions, or even Arknold's creations, are against scripture. It will only take a word from the Houses for the mob to point the finger. Some *distance* may be prudent." Jacka pushed himself back from the table. He was unsure of where the Queen would go if the ire of her people did fall upon the Meisters. Respect for learning only went so far, and the Houses, if they wished, could whip up fervour with the people so on edge after the recent event.

"Lord Penance hinted as such and wanted reassurance those two would not cooperate in their endeavours. On that he was adamant. But if the Unbelievers bring their machines here, the Houses will fall just as we will, Jacka. Can they not see it?"

"I believe them blinded by scripture, my Queen. The words that bind us together, allowing us little freedom for ought else. Even you are expected to pray, though it be in your own chamber, and I mine. None of us are truly free, and though you permit me to widen my web, the priests are *everywhere* except the lands of the Eighth. I sometimes wonder if that is what truly rankles with Lord Penance and the other six Lords and Ladies. Not the heresy."

Queen Erin narrowed her eyes, knowing just how the Houses would act on hearing such words. But Jacka had chosen his time well—when she felt at her lowest. Despite the danger, they bit deep.

44
A SPIRIT'S WORTH

NORTH ERSTEN FOREST

L aoch led the way, his head swimming as he replayed Sura's response to his touch. A risk that had overtaken him, an urge he would have suppressed a mere few hours ago. They had clashed, disagreed, and though the time period was short, he felt she had cut any faint hope he held dead. And now, in the midst of madness, she had turned all that on its head.

And she still may do so again, should I fail her.

After Sura had checked over Conch one last time, they had waited a few minutes before opening the main door. Gowan had insisted it was clear, the Construct having left and likely following whatever calling had brought it to Leront in the first place. With silence reigning, Oisin had led them out, declaring the spirit true to her word on the discovery of deep boot prints leading north in the darkness.

Conch had then been sent on her way, Oisin insisting she took Laoch's composite bow and quiver with her for protection. Laoch doubted how effective the injured Ranger would be with such a weapon considering the state of her ribs.

And then there was the problem filtering through his head right now. Gowan.

"Are you listening to me, Laoch, or daydreaming?"

Laoch sighed and tapped at the grip of the well-oiled composite bow. "Does your sigil fit correctly? Any chance it might accidentally drop out any time soon? It's dark, I might not be able to find you."

"Fate will simply glow until you do; We decide when it comes off, and you are supposed to follow Oisin's orders, remember. And you need me, Laoch. We can work together, as long as you follow my direction."

"So why not travel with Sura? You get along, some might even call you friends, if you have them. Why me?"

"Because this is the Gods' work, Fate's. And for all your ills and unruliness, you hold to the Gods, and to scripture."

"Aye, now that I understand. Elven. So, you think she'd have trouble with what you are. Not so sure on that, Gowan. But I'll accept it. How are you doing this, anyway? You're a bloody spirit talking in my head." Laoch glanced around, realising he was talking aloud though more in a whisper.

"It's the God's work. Laoch. I ... err ... inhabit Fate's sigil. On my death, my spirit was drawn into the metal. When I first touched it, Fate knew me, read me—did that happen to you?"

"You could call it that, aye."

"Well, when I died, she wrapped me in her weave. At first, I think it was to use me, like firewood, to keep the flame burning. But that kind of changed—this part of Fate is weak, old. So, instead, she wove herself into me, imbued herself in my ... well I suppose it's my spirit. Made me whole."

"Doesn't explain how you know where we are going."

"I can feel—Fate calls it spiritfire—a power or energy as she calls it. And it's all around us. It's very low, like a glow worm, but always on. It's what the Seven used to open the gate the mosaic showed. And you have it, and Oisin and Ecne."

"Not Sura?"

"Not that I can see. No."

"Well, I can see it. Full of fire and fury," whispered Laoch, glancing behind, catching her eye and getting a nod in return. "Are you going to be in my ear all the time?" Laoch tripped over a branch, boots fighting for grip in the mud before coming to rest against a splintered tree trunk.

"You need me."

"So, I let you do the talking and I just hit things with a heavy, metal weapon."

"Good choice, Ranger. There's something strange happening ahead."

"After today, that's saying something, Gowan. How strange?"

Laoch crouched, arms raised to signal a halt and waited. He was convinced the Construct was rushing, choosing speed in an urgency pounded into the mud as it headed directly for wherever this dragon heart lay.

And where we now go, for whatever folly bloody Gowan has caused.

"I can hear your thoughts," said Gowan.

Laoch baulked, the voice in his head once again for his ears only.

"I'm leaving you in the first pile of boar shit if that's true," he whispered, louder than he meant.

"Every time you use my name, or think of me, I hear. We need to work together, Ranger. With no doubts about my orders."

"Not sure it says anywhere in the code about following a dead Ranger's orders. Especially one who is such an arsehole."

"They'll be writing an extra line just for me. 'Should your second-in-command be a drunken bastard with less tactical understanding than a pig's dick, come back from the dead and provide competent and considered instructions.'"

"Fox shit, I reckon. It's stickier, harder to get off and stinks to the Seven Veils and back. Like your opinions."

"What's happening," whispered Oisin, settling into a crouch next to Laoch. "Gowan making any sense of where we are?"

Laoch snorted. "Sense? You didn't know her, did you? When she was alive, I mean."

"The Construct is close by, unmoving, but I think its power is rising. It's leaking spiritfire all over the bloody place."

"Leaking? You mean ..."

"I mean whatever power it has, the spiritfire inside is seeping out. The body and armour can't contain it all. That plate definitely

deflects its spirit inwards as well as out. And the dragon heart, I can feel its beat. It feels stronger with each pace."

Laoch shook his head, trying to make sense of what was going on, and finding himself trapped into a spiral of disconnected thoughts. They'd started the day with an explosive cart full of Erin's Wrath and finished it with a giant set of armour leaking 'spirit' in front of a dragon's heart. He'd lost another Spear, searing his own heart, only for the last one in the Union he'd have chosen to resurrect to be now talking inside his head. And then there was Sura.

And it's likely not even reached midnight yet.

He relayed to Oisin what Gowan had detailed, adding a few swear words of his own, but as he stared ahead, it seemed obvious the spirit was right. The forest had begun to glow. A pulsing white light rippling through the canopy and setting the trees dancing with shadows.

"See. You should trust my judgement. Leaking like an old bucket."

Laoch rose, sliding in behind the tree where Oisin now stood with spyglass in hand, surveying the hill. Sura, with Ecne following on her orders, moved to cover them both, watching the flanks, so he brought Rakslin's eyeglass up to his own eye. Over the bushes he made out the Construct armour kneeling before another rocky hillock. It had wrenched bushes and trees from a section that curled out from the main rock face—flinging them to the sides as it focused on this one spot. From their recent experience with the Seven's doorway, he guessed the Construct was seeking an entrance, though to Laoch's mind it was more likely back in the main body of the rocks. The armour had its back to him, but from the posture Laoch had a distinct sense the thing was praying, or at least it was the same pose as he had adopted a thousand times in the House of Justice. There he always left cleansed, burdens taken, though often tired from the stress of release.

Is that what the Construct seeks? A release?

I could do that for it—with my sword.

"Look to the left and right, Laoch. What do you see?" whispered Oisin.

"Nothing," Laoch swept the area again. "He's alone, and nothing above either."

"He *must* be with the group who took Gowan, attacked the camp—similar armour."

"And the light, Ranger. It has the same hue as their shafts and quarrels."

"We can't be sure he's alone. The mirror plates are deceptive, and who knows what other tricks they may have. Keep your eyes on it, and your bow ready with Ecne. Sura flanks left; I'll go right. If we birdcall 'clear' then count to five and loose."

"And if not?"

"Use your judgement—but the priority is to stop that thing from doing whatever it plans. Not Sura. Understand?"

Oisin dropped his eye from the spyglass, Laoch feeling the Ranger's gaze fall on him. He waited, settling the rising tide of anger and dread. The darkness pressed in a little, and he smelt a tang of smoke caress his tongue. Mentally counting, he nodded, but felt Oisin wait, unsatisfied. Laoch lowered the small spyglass, turning to face the Elite Ranger eye-to-eye.

"I understand, sir. Crown and the Houses are my guide and code. They come first."

Oisin held his gaze for a second longer, then reached out, squeezing Laoch's shoulder. Without another word, he turned to speak to Sura, relaying the plans.

"I can hear you swearing in your head. He really wouldn't be able to do that with both legs attached."

"I never said they would be. And I didn't use your name."

"I was just checking it wasn't me you were planning on grinding into paste. The leakage is increasing, the air is thick with power."

"Does it know we are here? Can it feel like you?"

"You are mere wisps, like shadows to me. I think I can only see you because I know of you, what form you take, and the Gods' Sigils reinforce that. Oisin is more ill-formed, more smoke in my head than man. The Construct thrums with power. It can't possibly see us amongst all that vitality. But it may expect, as you would, to be followed."

"Aye. Keep watch, Gowan. I want to know what's happening to—"

"—Sura? She's kicked more arse than you've sunk pints. Though what she sees in you ... ah. She can hold her own, Laoch."

"Let's say it'll help me focus. Keep the darkness at bay."

"I've seen that darkness, Laoch. I knew, but ... "

"Keep that to ye'self. Right? It's my pain, not to be shared with every git who thinks they can cut it out." Laoch sucked in a breath. "I'm sorry, Gowan. Too late, I know. But I treated you like shit. More than once."

"I have a tally count if you want to look. Loach, back at the encampment ... I have a conf—"

Laoch felt a tap on the shoulder, glancing around as Sura smiled his way, before slipping into the bushes. She carried Honour's spear in her left hand, the loaded handbow in her right, with a crystal-tipped quarrel in place. He let out a grunt, sensing Oisin disappear behind him towards the left flank.

"You were saying, Gowan?"

"Never mind, another time."

"Okay."

Laoch signalled Ecne up, eyeing a fallen tree branch just ahead. "There, Ecne. Settle in, take aim with that armour-shredder. You loose on my signal, got it? If I fall, then you release and seek Sura."

"It's glowing," Ecne's shoulders shook, the strain in her voice bringing Laoch up short. She was a bloody acolyte, probably not even a good one, and here she was facing something that even the University's library hadn't ever detailed or imagined.

What am I doing? That's the old Laoch talking.

"We need you, Ecne. That weapon gives us a chance, right? Settle in, calm your breathing, keep your eye on that bloody giant. Got me? Count in yer head. Concentrate on each number—draw it in your mind, slowly. Then on to the next. Each one a breath." Laoch grabbed Ecne's forearm, pulling the young woman towards him as she made to move. "And don't hit me, ye?" Laoch left her with a smile, heading to find a position ahead.

"Might make a trainer of you yet. Though that smile might just have made her crap herself."

"Piss off Gowan."

45
WHEN THE TRUE ENEMY STIRS

SMERRAL RANGER ENCAMPMENT

R anger Conch winced as she stumbled over the protruding root, the bandage wrap providing little comfort. Whatever Sura had placed inside lay warm and fuzzy against her skin—but the ribs were having none of it. Every breath pressed against her sore chest. The resultant sharp pain response forced the air back out in short gasps. Conch knew the quick breaths were affecting her pace, and having already suffered during the initial chase, she dreaded the stumble back. But she carried news that the Crown, and the Houses, needed. Her God, Honour, decreed she should act for the good of others whenever possible. Her pains were nothing compared to the needs of the people. She'd seen inside that strange, polished armour, and the withered faces they contained. It wasn't natural, sickening. Whatever had come for them this day suffered from a skin malaise or an inner illness. Or maybe they'd turned from their God, and it was a punishment. Either way, they had killed Queen's soldiers, and struck down whatever else was in their path. And the thing that attacked them inside the House of the Seven, as she saw it, was bigger again. According to Oisin it had sliced through Felecia with one swipe. And through the stone and dust thrown her way when it barged into the inner room, she had seen the light and energy arcing around it.

Whatever it is, it fought in the House of God against those chosen to defend it, and that makes it an evil I need to prevent.

Conch shifted her shoulders, missing the weight of her jerkin armour. Not a choice she enjoyed making with the possibility of Unbelievers being around, but it helped her breath just a little easier. The route back was less demanding to follow than she'd expected, able to use a torch whose flame flickered and guttered with the lessening rain but held its own. It lit the forest with the shadows of ghost trees and rearing monsters. Conch ignored these, having spent most of her adult life in woods or forests, either on the hunt or on a mission. It got you used to the tricks light and shadow could play, and the calls that always seemed to herald your approach. This was her home, and these sights held no fear. But the pulsing light cutting through her torch's range ahead did cause a tingle of dread in her mind. It blinked with each flicker of the flame, a mix of blues and deep green piercing the night.

I need to ignore it and get back to the Erstenburgh. Let the Queen and the Houses know what's happening.

Conch caught movement in the corner of her eye, unsure if it was shadow play from the new light or eye shine from a creature stalking the woods. Wolves were rare this close to the city, and boar too, though sometimes they entered the forest during the night, seeking the delicacies hidden amid the roots. She lowered herself down carefully, trying desperately to calm her pained breathing in the crouch she took. Easing the composite bow into her grip, she kept her gaze ahead, blindly nocking an arrow with an experienced warrior's touch. Now feeling more prepared, she stalked towards the movement for waiting wasn't going to work. She was in too much pain, and a wolf would sense her difficulty, recognising the weakness. It would harry, chase Conch down and wear her out. Whereas boars were less reticent, and if spooked or with young, would simply run her down.

Need to take charge.

She planted the torch, letting it sit under a protective branch, moving slowly out of its range and stalking painfully into the underbrush. Moving sideways, eyes on the last place she saw the eye shine, she flanked right through the damp vegetation. As her night vision adjusted, she made out the flicker of blue light with greater clarity. Trying to keep it out of her eyeline, fearful one eye spot could lead to further injury or death if attacked, she continued to sidestep. Underfoot, the tangle of bushes and ivy snagged at her feet, and with laboured breathing Conch began to worry how long she could keep the movements up that inflamed her chest.

A rustle to the left scraped at her nerves. The sound emanating from the exact spot she focused on. A gentle parting of the vegetation nearby signalling the careful movements of an animal.

Not a boar at least.

She moved into the thicker undergrowth, her ribs sending sharp reminders, but still raising the bow. A snap underfoot sent her heart racing, and the thicket ahead burst with life, something leaping outwards. Reflexes triggered, and she aimed and released, the shaft splitting the air. Conch flinched back, slamming her eyelids shut as the distant blue light shone out, fearing for her night vision. She heard rather than saw the arrow hit something, and blinking away the light spots, pleased to be still standing, she was rewarded with the bark of a pained deer.

Relieved, Conch returned for her torch. The flame lighting the tree canopy, forging shadows while she searched for the injured animal. She traced the broken trail to the wounded deer, its haunches and head bent backwards in a U-shape as it kicked at her arrow.

I wish I could carry you back.

Conch, thanking Honour, slid her boot knife across the animal's throat. Ignoring the spurt of hot blood, she looked around, finally settling on a tree to leave her Ranger's mark.

"You never know," she said, a cough finishing her words.

Another sound dragged her back into the here and now, and then a movement under a tree nearer the flashing blue light. A holler echoed above the crackle of her torch, a panicked hail, and with the light weaving between the branches she made out a hand waving above the bushes. The tone was stressed, and the accent local. Conch, caution still permeating within her, nocked a second arrow before approaching closer. Using the trees as cover, she surveyed the area as she moved in, wary for a poacher's, or more likely a thieves' ambush.

As a woman came into view, her clothing ragged and a sackcloth bag across her back, Conch relaxed a little. The snares and poorly worked dagger slotted into her belt declared her as a poacher, and if this was a trap, then her mummery would earn her a place in the city's theatre. She waved a cloth in her hand, and at her feet lay an older child, somewhere in their early teens. His face was dry and rippled. White light pulsed beneath the skin bathing his face in a ghostly light.

If the day hadn't been so strange already, she'd have backed off, fearing an apparition and checking her rations for Tanka's favourite dream inducing mushrooms. But tonight, it was far too real.

"Don't kill me," said the woman, her heavy accent even clearer now she lowered her voice. "It's Ren. He's sick. He touched that thing ... the shell. He thought it'd be worth a coin or two." Dishevelled and distressed, she pointed over her shoulder, the blue light fading in and out, mirroring the flicker of Conch's torch. The flame was reflecting off a pile of oily-blue metal shards, which lay next to a freshly dug pit in the forest floor.

"Your boy?"

"No, my nephew. We were ... were..."

"Poaching—but no matter." Conch stared down at the lad. His eyes blazed white under eyelids that were slowly shrivelling as she watched. The skin drying out, forming a husk she'd only seen once before. But far too recently.

"Can you help? You've the Queen's Mark." The woman pointed to the insignia on her cloak.

Conch lifted her wrist, Honour's sigil tattooed beneath. "Honour bound. But I need to see that shell first." She threw the woman some string from her belt, admitting to herself she feared touching the boy herself. "Truss his legs and feet, find a couple of branches." With the poacher immediately understanding, Conch, took a short, sharp breath as her ribs sent a reminder, before walking towards the pit. Hairs on her arms and legs rose as she closed; the air full of the static charge that often accompanied thunderstorms. Each piece of metal was razor edged, its inner oily, reflecting a rainbow glow from the remains of the torch's light. The outer displayed an all too familiar mirror shine, setting Conch's nerves on edge, forcing her to glance around even though whatever had been in there was long gone.

Who am I fooling? I know what was in there, and I've left others to deal with it. I must fulfil my mission, make Fenecia and Tanka's deaths worth it.

Looking back, Conch spied a sack at the tree's base, half-empty with a spot of dried blood on the outside. She walked back, claiming the bag as the woman finished tying the moaning boy's legs. She let the rabbits inside drop, pulling out a squirrel before returning to the shards. With the point of her short sword, she pushed several of the metal pieces inside, trying to ignore the spark when they scraped together.

Like flint, but with a blue flame.

Conch tied the top, returning to find the boy now ready beneath the two poles. On any other day, she'd leave them both behind, Honour bound or not, to speed up her return. But the boy was evidence, proof of what she'd witnessed and of the power of the metal in the bag she tied to the branches.

This is going to hurt.

Taking the lead, but with the lighter end, she shifted the two branches onto her shoulders, her muffled swearing echoing among the trees.

46

A PENANCE ACCEPTED

THE HOUSE OF WISDOM (ADJOINING THE UNIVERSITY), ERSTENBURGH

Jacka quailed, staring at the empty wooden pews that seemed to go on forever around him. The wooden seats worn. Smoothed by the thousands who had sat squirming through sermon after sermon about how science was bad, and the future only lay in the scripture and the knowledge it espoused. Before each of the soothed spots, a cushion lay on the floor, two worn patches where the wise would fall to bow their heads when the Lord, or his Priests-in Waiting, would anoint each on the head with Wisdom's Words—water that they had read the scripture over. It was, in Jacka's mind, a way of physically reinforcing their God's word, to ensure the academic sheep stay in line.

Baah. Some of the most righteous and pious have knelt in those places, cowed into rehashing what is already known for fear of angering their God, or worse, Lord Wisdom and the High Lord Penance. Emotional blackmail to keep the most errant in line.

The cane's tap behind brought him up short, his panicked mind telling him to keep looking ahead, not back. He was here at Lord Wisdom's insistence, something of such import it had to be now. And here he was, the Queen's Prime, a man of standing with a great future as long as he kept the Houses sweet, and avoided the potential of ex-communication, or worse, should he fall foul of ...

"Lord Penance," he squeaked, coughing into his hand, turning his head only for a cane to land on his shoulder, keeping him facing forward.

"Let's keep this," Penance sucked in a slow, rasping breath, "informal, Jacka."

"I... the Queen informed me I was to keep my people out of the Houses, Lord Penance. She was adamant that I should follow your word."

"That is good, Jacka. And as it should be, and should that ... change... then you and I would *talk* again, yes? Though in my House, not in the holiness of Wisdom's."

Jacka felt the sweat form at the base of his neck, a prickled heat rising as the Lord's stained, sweet breath fell upon it.

Oh crap.

"I need to know a price, Jacka. And you... well you have the Queen's ear."

The cane tapped on the Prime's shoulder before caressing his ear.

"Lord, I would not betray my Queen, I—"

"You have me wrong, and I would warn you against vocalising such leaps in thought without careful consideration, Prime Vardrin. I am not here to talk of treason, or blasphemy for that matter. No, I need to you to delay something for me, with the Queen's agreement of course. I just need to know the consequences of that request."

"Delay?"

"The signal arrow that the City Guard are preparing to pursue. That needs quashing, Jacka. I want nobody to go into the forest until I or my House agrees it. We already have the Elite Rangers that way, sent by mutual agreement for another role. I want this kept quiet, for now."

Jacka made to turn and speak, the cane lightly tapping his ear as a reminder.

"The guard won't like this, the code ..."

"Tell them the Elite are already out there. Just make sure you intercept them on their return and not let them speak until they report to me, yes?"

"It can be done, Lord Penance. As for the Queen, the Rangers mean much to her, and especially the Consort." Jacka winced, but the cane lifted.

"Ah. That's a high price, for such a little favour. I will bring things forward, Prime. It is politically delicate, but inform the Queen I will ensure it occurs." Lord Penance drew in a breath, the next words sitting heavy. "Jacka." The cane rested gently on his shoulder. "Should Sneed approach you both, you must listen, understand? If he wishes an audience with the Queen, it is by my order. For all your dislike of the Houses, and especially mine, do not delay my emissary. Now leave by the back, and remember, none of your people are to venture into my Houses. I like you, Jacka, and would not want anything unfortunate to happen to you."

Jacka heard the scrape of cloth on wood, followed by the tapping of a cane that matched the beating of his heart.

47

A GHOST'S LIGHT

NORTH ERSTEN FOREST

S ura took each step with care, splitting her glances between finding a near silent trail through the undergrowth, while watching the rippling glow to her left as she got closer. Her world had been turned upside down inside a day. From the pain of closing her heart when Laoch had pushed too far, to releasing her own cherished grief as she opened back up to him. The Elders would formalise their banishment if they knew. Their oral history was bitter, full of the sorrow associated with the arrival of humanity. Claiming that the spirits were angry, that allowing the humans sway upon their lands had led them to abandoning the Schenterenta. Just as she had abandoned her people the day she leapt from the cliff. A brief second of falling, only to wake in shame and bitterness on the same spot, an Elder above her, horror upon the old woman's face. She knew what Sura had come to do, had failed to do. The ultimate taboo of her kind.

Were their stories true? Did we once dance with the spirits of our ancestors as the shamans said? And what of those spirits? Where did they go?

Sura glanced back towards the kneeling Construct, about forty yards away, its size masked by the shimmering light around it. Spiritfire, as Gowan called it. Like that running through Honour's spear she held.

Have you got them? Is that what you are? A creature that took our ancestors?

It's nonsense. It cannot be.

She stopped, turning to survey the surrounding trees, and satisfied, checked again on the Construct only for her heart to leap. She took a double take, raising the handbow in her other hand as she did so. A ghostly armour charged down upon her, a replica of that still praying before the rocks. It shimmered, sparks flying, and as she loosed the quarrel, the apparition faded in and out with each ripple of light. One moment corporeal, the next a mist that crackled with white fire. The quarrel flew true, piercing the shadow Construct's heart, driving on through for the crystal tip to erupt somewhere in the distant forest.

No.

Sura took a step back, rising from her crouch, knowing the area behind her was more open, less tangled. The spear now gripped in both hands, she bore it before her, eyes locked on the onrushing armour as it emerged from the bushes. No branch or leaf responded when it cut through. An ethereal form that stopped, legs astride, sword in hand with arcs of white lightning crackling around it. One gauntleted hand reached up, raising the helm's visor, baring the scarred skull within to her elven eyes.

The urge to scream rose from the pit of her stomach, driven by the acid boiling away. Sura bit it down, seeking to use the adrenaline rather than expend it. She adjusted her stance, swinging the spear into a defensive position, ready for whatever was to come.

—✦—

Oisin threw himself to the floor discarding the bow as he pulled at his sword's hilt. With his shoulder taking the brunt of the impact, he rolled to his feet, sword swaying in front. He waited, expecting a downward blow from the huge hand-and-a-half sword the ghost-like armour held ready to strike. His eyes strayed upwards, catching the rising of the visor, the exposing of the pierced skull beneath. Thoughts swirling, he stepped in, unable to contain the need to strike out at the horror. The short sword cut through the light, glinting as it sliced into the shadow Construct, striking the bush behind. Oisin overbalanced. The lack of a strike or parry unexpected, and he toppled to land within the creature's legs. A heat, dry, like the desert's sun, sucked at the moisture of his skin. Terror washed over him, images of the husked humans assailing his mind's eye. The Elite Ranger hurried backwards, feeling the heat recede as he brought his sword up to fend off the expected attack. Still none came and the monstrous skull clattered, teeth against teeth. Misty lips moving as it tried to speak, crystalline eyes boring into him.

Oisin felt his stomach flip, fear cramping his body. He'd faced the worst of the Crusades, locking the death away. The Construct, with a mere look, plucked at those memories, bringing them to the surface. Playing them out like a theatre in the Ranger's mind. The sword wavered in his hands, slipping from his grip as the scream finally released.

Ecne's finger twitched. The Construct hadn't moved. The glow, if anything, had flickered briefly and shadows had played across the clearing—but no more. The agonised scream beseeching from her right triggered a dread that shivered down her spine. The finger pulled in response. The heavy quarrel surging from the crossbow, lit by Wisdom's green that washed Laoch's shoulder and face as it rushed by. Ecne could only watch as it slammed into the armour's left shoulder, the surface erupting with the green fire, the plate crumpling inwards as the bolt hammered home. Shaking, she dipped down behind the stump, searching for another quarrel, a tremble to her hand. Sweat-stained fingers grasped a bolt, and she rose, gripping the crossbow and sliding it onto the rail. In the Sevens' Dragon House she'd not loaded the weapon. Instinct, or the sigil possibly, driving her to release without thought. It seemed logical that the weapon needed loading, but when placing the second quarrel, with eyes on Laoch's back as he drew Fate's bow, she began to wonder.

No time.

The quarrel slipped from the weapon, flipping out as her uncertain fingers fumbled it towards the rail. Ecne swore, glancing towards Laoch as she reached for the quarrel stuck in the muddy ground. Laoch had risen, bow string on fire, the arrow absent and a deep blue bolt of light in its place.

Managing to grasp the quarrel, Ecne brushed off the mud. A glow emanated from the crossbow, and there, in the rail, an expectant bolt of green pulsed. Its tip sparkled with arcs of tiny lightning whose impossibility addled the acolyte's mind. A thump brought her back into the world, eyes flicking up as Laoch ran towards her. Behind an armoured, mist-like figure charged their way. Ecne dropped behind her weapon, finger squeezing the trigger, and the flash of her bolt rushed to break against the armour's chest. The lightning swathed the creature, tracing forked pathways across the armour, crackling the air with ozone and the smell of charred meat and bone. The shadow Construct staggered, brought to a standstill while Wisdom's energy raged.

Laoch slid in beside her, spinning and drawing his bow. Fate's blue light splashed over Ecne's wide eyes, but she only saw it in the corner as her attention remained on the Construct rippling in and out of existence. She could see through it. Her mind filling in the gaps when it reappeared, knowing that behind it, still on their knees, the Construct prayed.

This cannot be. What ... what's happening?

The arrow slammed into the shadow's chest, Fate's blue spreading, wrapping the entire form and squeezing inwards. The ghost-like armour fractured, then tore apart, a ragged skeleton beneath briefly appearing before it too shattered. A waft of ancient air brushed their senses, a horror that plucked at their minds with promises of pain and death that washed away in the breeze and rain.

"There's two more. Oisin and Sura are both under attack," said Laoch, tapping his head until he realised the shaking acolyte was in enough of a mess without mentioning Gowan.

The Captain let out a heavy sigh, his focus lost. The ethereal mind drawn back inwards from its search for the dragon's heart. He was more than certain it was in there, but he could not find the exact spot, the encasement so different to Lorent. A creeping sensation flowered in him. Fear that it had gone, the *call* in his head a feint or trick of his own spirit. Perhaps tainted by the residue of the Construct whose body he inhabited. Was it still there, hidden somewhere, overshadowed by his own agonised soul?

Behind him, he felt a shadow fall. One of the guardians his armour had sent in response to the perceived danger of the pursuing humans. Beneath him, the grass and bracken withered and died. The worms drying husks, beetles empty of life where the hated armour had drawn upon them. The Constructors took, it was their way. Their path to immortality that left nothing but death in its wake. Unlike these lesser creatures, humans and some larger, intelligent beasts, regenerated the spiritfire. Yet the Captain knew the armour could kill. Thirst driving a draining so rapid, death was certain. And the need, the hunger he felt within it, was ever increasing. He remembered the tales of the spirit-dolls. Those the Constructs fed off regularly and harboured in their menageries to ensure their futures. It was from these that the Seven had led them to freedom, only to be lost on the way.

The Captain pushed himself up, turning towards the left, surveying the creature that stood against his shadow. A Schenterenta and found in every realm, each tribe so different from the last. Everywhere he and the Wyrm Ship explored had smatterings of her race. Weavers of spirits, speakers to the dead, shamans. Call them what you would, they were among the few that could truly see the spiritfire within their realm. Deeply connected to the land and its beasts, Spirit Walkers who waded in the beauty of life. Prized by the Constructors and twisted into their hunters. It was their spirits, merged and forged with spite and hate, who were spewed into the heart of their greatest creations—the Dragons of the Veil.

Lorent and Nathair.
And Nathair is mine—please do not make me kill you.

48
WHEN THAT WHICH IS HIDDEN RISES

NORTH ERSTEN FOREST

S ura heard the clack of teeth, the ghostly lips moving, words slipping out that her mind could not hold. They were non-sensical, a mix of guttural rasps and clicks that she immediately blanked out. Imprisoning her thoughts behind a wall, she rocked back. Feinting to run left, before dropping and sweeping her leg round to strike at the armour's right ankle. A sudden heat swept her calf, a prickle of sweat beading upon its skin, drawn towards the apparition. Sura kept the movement going, bringing the spear round to thrust up into the upper thigh. The shadow reacted, the first movement its body had made, flinching as the spear pierced the air and slashing downwards with the now opaque sword. Sura felt the weapon strike her spear, muscles resisting as she would an ordinary sword. It crackled and sparked, white lightning rushing towards her grip. Honour's sigil pulsed, the orange energy swathing and negating the white, before rushing upwards and through the tip brushing the shadow Construct's thigh. There, the orange lightning forked and spread like veins, before seething beneath the armoured plate. Sura withdrew the tip, bringing the shaft up as the huge arms powered a double-handed blow down.

Sura threw herself forwards, and on through the shadow, heat drawing her skin upwards as the moisture rose to the surface. The spear followed behind, scraping against the Construct's leg, staggering it as the sword swept down to bite into the muddy ground. The grass shrivelled, with a mist forming in the air around the blade where it struck. Sura paid no mind but noted the sparking orange energy writhing along the armoured knee, and rose to her feet, driving the spear deep into the join between the shoulder plates. The tip sang, orange power spitting down into the heart of the shadow creature. Sura felt the shaft jolt in her hand, energy surging into the Construct. The Patterning demanded she withdraw the spear, spin downwards, sweep the creature from its feet and drive the tip deep into its heart. But she resisted, feeling the weapon's call, allowing it to boil inside the ghost-like armour. Orange light spilt out between the plates that fractured and split in turn, before rupturing as the armour exploded. Sura ducked, hitting the ground, arms up—expecting metal shards and bone to thud into her body. But none came. Just the breeze of its passing and the smell of old death and charred meat.

Laoch crashed through the bushes, the branches and twigs underfoot ignored as he charged towards Sura's orange light. The air alive with flashes of power, his heart thumping as he broke into the small clearing to witness the Construct explode. Sura was on her knees with spear held high. Getting swiftly to her feet, the spear twirled his way, point out, threatening.

"Woah," he said, "it's Laoch."

Sura blinked out the light spots. Her elven eyes narrowing, focusing and a smile met her lips before she spun back towards the true Construct that stared her way. This one solid and obviously marking her and Laoch as the Ranger dropped in by her side. He drew Fate's bow, the one Gowan inhabited, gripped in his hands with the God's arrow pulsing to the rhythm of his breath. He held it, and Sura felt the power within the bow thrum, setting her hair on end as the static grew. His release came almost as a relief, and the arrow's light swirled through the air. Only for an armoured arm to rise, the mirrored plate taking the strike, shattering but dissipating the energy into the air. Sura briefly spied bone and dried skin beneath before the arm dropped. And then the Construct flew sideways, a bolt of green energy slamming into its lower ribs sending the monstrous armour spinning to crash into the rocks.

The whoop from Ecne let them know what she thought of the strike, the acolyte rising, cocking the crossbow again. Sura placed her hand on Laoch's arm, concern in her eyes. "Your skin, Laoch," she said, reaching to touch his rough face, flakes falling into her hand like snow.

"Fate is draining you, Laoch. The sigil is near empty of spiritfire, the energy it uses. You must be careful, as it will continue to draw on you. You need to let Sura and Ecne know this."

"Could have told me that before," growled Laoch.

"I didn't know."

"Will you be leeching me too, Gowan?"

"Erm, possibly. Not yet."

"See that you tell me before you do, so a cow's arse can wear you instead, bloodsucker."

"You say the nicest things. It's getting back up."

Laoch eyed the armour as it extracted itself from the rocks. The back plates were dented and cracked, Ecne's green energy draining away into the ground. Another bolt crashed into its chest, but the armour hardly flinched, the light washing away as Ecne cried out to their right. The strangled voice soon followed by a sob.

"Gowan's saying the sigils can drain us too if they run dry. Be careful." Laoch glanced down at the bow, his hand flaking dried skin as he flexed his fingers. "Might be Ecne's found that out the hard way."

"Oisin?" asked Sura. "Any word?"

"No, none. It's ... ah shit." Laoch strode out, raising but not drawing the bow as the Construct headed Ecne's way. It began to pick up pace, the bastard sword in its hand slicing through the air as it broke into a jog towards the stricken acolyte. Laoch passed the tree edge, catching sight of the acolyte, her eyes wide, staring at her owns hands as she turned them over again and again. With no time to think—the Construct almost upon Ecne—Laoch pulled and held the string for a second, letting fly before the armour reached the tearful acolyte. The burning arrow struck the armoured leg just behind the knee, the lightning arcing out, rushing towards the thigh. The Construct crashed to the ground, its sword striking Ecne's stump and finally bringing the woman out of her stupor.

"Laoch."

"Not now." Laoch took a step forward, trying to decide whether to risk a draining bow shot or prepare Justice's maul.

"Laoch, you need to turn around."

"Piss off, Gowan," With his hands flaking badly, Laoch moved to shoulder the bow, his other hand reaching for the maul as he approached the stricken armour.

"Turn bloody around, Ranger," bellowed Gowan, the shout reverberating around Laoch's skull, forcing a scowl as he turned away from the danger threatening his charge.

As he spun, an impossibility towered over Sura. A dragon's head, the metal-scaled neck shedding rocks as it reared up, forked tongue tasting the air. Crystal encrusted eyes flared red, the dual horns sparkling with the refracted light as its maw distended wide, sword-like teeth bared.

"Oh shit."

—

Bloody ribs are killing me.

Conch eased the branch from her shoulder, lifting it aside and flinching at the pain in her chest as she rolled the shoulder joint. A squeal behind her let her know the poacher was still annoyed at the need for respite, despite her own exhaustion.

"I'll be no use if my bloody ribs give out, so stop your moaning," Conch spat over her aching shoulder. "Besides, we're nearly at the Queen's Road. Not long now."

With her shoulder still complaining, caused, she assumed, by favouring it due to her pained ribs, she sighed heavily. Conch took another few steps before the forest widened out. The undergrowth appeared trampled by recent deer tracks, and older boot prints lay deep in the mud. She renewed her efforts. Despite the darkness, she could sense the road was not far ahead. Another fifty yards of pained walking brought her within sight, and she upped the pace. Shouting over her shoulder to the poacher, she caught the white glow from the young lad in the corner of her eye, his flaking skin fluttering in the sway of their movement. Swallowing down the fear, she reached the road and firm ground—its mix of crushed stone and rock enabling heavy goods travel to the city despite the wet winter. A Queen's fancy, according to many, though Conch knew well enough how easy it made the movement of troops as well as commodities.

And night travel because you can trust the road.

She felt the poacher stumble as they walked up the road's banked sides. Taking a little more of the strain, Conch reached the top and dropped the boy onto the roadside. An eerie glow burst through his eyelids, his skin thin and dry. Mottled lips spouted rumbling, harsh words and clicks that set her teeth on edge. She grabbed the bag and untied it, placing it away from the litter. All the while, wondering if its presence had made things worse. Slowly, his glow faded, returning to the deathly radiance Conch had first seen back in the woods.

This is beyond my reckoning. May Lady Honour keep us safe in the times that are coming.

The roar tore over the top of the trees, ruffling branches, tearing wet leaves that flew towards Conch and the road. Cries from bird and deer broke as the noise passed, and then the forest suddenly seemed to pause. Conch spun, chest aching, eyes searching the forest edge as everything came to a complete standstill. A scream cracked the potent silence, laced with pain and longing. The poacher's nephew fought the ropes, struggling to be released as his skin and face lit pure white. The rope strands flared. The burnt ends tainting the air with a sharp tang as the poacher dropped onto the lad, forcing him back down to the road. Conch stared in horror, the woman's pressing hand streaking with the white light that sparked and raced along her forearms. Leaning back, eyes wide, the woman made to scream as the veined light split and split again, smothering arms and shoulders, driving upwards from her neck. No sound came, the throat constricted, tight, dry.

The pulsing energy reached her eyes. Fierce, wild, and blazing towards Conch as the woman rose only to be met by the Ranger's blade hacking down into her neck.

49
A DRAGON UNVEILED

NORTH ERSTEN FOREST

H ot air flashed against Sura's back. A furnace that singed the
ends of her hair and scorched the tips of her ears. Her
instincts were on fire too, shouting at her to run, that there was
something rearing up behind, its breath rasping against her body
as it prepared to feed. The rest of her body betrayed her. Joints
turning to jelly, muscles pulsing and a rash of goose-pimples
rushing across her front.

Take control. Let the Patterning in.

She spurted into movement, driving forwards towards Laoch
whose raised bow crackled with a deep blue flame. Three strides
in she feinted right, then spun left, tucking herself in, before
twisting and rising with her spear out front, eyes now on whatever
enemy waited for her. Sura's stomach lurched; the massive, split
tongue lolled from a metal-filled mouth. Red heat growled within
the maw, the light flickering between razor-edged teeth as long
as her arm. As she looked past the metal-scaled snout, to the red
crystalline eyes, dread slammed into her chest. A fear that fought

her resolve for supremacy. Standing before her a dragon of human myth—its gaze demanding her subservience.

Laoch's arrow slammed into the snout. The blue spiritfire flaring, spreading tendrils that arced into the dragon's nostrils as it sucked in the air. A roar shattered the clearing. Pain and defiance in a combination that stripped leaves from the surrounding bushes. The wash full of ancient, searing dust that battered Sura. It broke the spell. The elf twirling the spear into both hands, point forward and her mind set.

I will not fall without a fight; however big you are. Can you hear me, brother? I will join you soon.

A second, green-laden bolt crashed into the dragon. The spiritfire driving into the beast's open mouth accompanied by a yell of pain and despair from behind. Metal teeth lit with the explosion, highlighting the tongue swirling in agony—each tendril curling and pulsing as the pain seared into the beast. Sura brought the spear up, assessing the throw that would leave her defenceless. Instinct called for her to press home the advantage, but that was against natural enemies, and she hesitated. The dragon's chest billowed out, warping impossibly forwards. Its interlocking plates extending, though not enough for gaps to appear or expose the skin beneath. The head whipped back, only to surge forward—Sura's elven eyes barely registering the movement as red flame spewed from the hellish mouth.

No.

A rush of movement behind was lost amid the torrent of fire gushing her way, her feet frozen as fear overcame any instinct to survive—for where was there to go? For the last few years, she had awaited this moment. A release from the grief—the death of her twin borne upon her soul. The tear never healing, a wound that seeped the poisons of self-doubt and loneliness that Laoch had begun to fill.

Do I welcome this?

A force drove into her back. Mirrored arms wrapped around, momentum carrying both of them into the flames. The metalled chest filled her vision, glimmering plates alive with the reflection of red flame that poured into the ground. She braced, expectant of a thousand cuts as they both whirled towards the dragon's scales, but the agony never came. A white energy wreathed her body, spreading from the mirrored arms that encased her torso. The power intoxicating as it slid over her skin in a wave of ecstasy that plucked at her mind. The spiritfire surged into her brain, firing her thoughts into a strange mix of pleasure and timeless agony. A calling, a duty to help. Tinged with an agonised resistance to the need to feed and devour, to live. Two spirits fighting for precedence, and Sura ducked her head, waiting for the blow and recoil as her cheeks met the dragon's razor-edged scales. And nothing, less than nothing—an emptiness filled with only the strange, ethereal light that swathed her. Out in the abyss, nothing moved. Silence and age pervading the blackness while they tumbled on in their strange embrace.

Sura crashed into the floor, rolling—its metal cold, and bleak—and the embrace broke. She clattered onwards, off balance and disorientated. Bones and muscles protesting as they finally slammed to the ground. Where there had been a lightness as they spun through the void, a weight hit. Polished armour smashing into her back, pinning her down. Sura bellowed in frustration, scrabbling at the metal floor, hands seeking grip to rip away from the monstrosity pressing against her back. A lace of eldritch white light crept along her shoulder, flickering in and out, snake-like as it rose. It whispered with an evil she recognised, the second spirit, the one desperate to feed. It speared towards her ear. A gauntleted hand snapped out, catching the arc of foul energy that wriggled, fighting the grasping fingers before the gauntlet drew the foul light back and out of her eyeline. She screamed, pouring adrenaline into her body, demanding muscles and mind work together to pull herself free.

The armour clattered against the floor, with Sura scrambling forwards, dragging the spear from where it lay against the odd-ribbed walls. The Construct had one knee planted on the floor, a hand braced against it before pushing itself unsteadily up. The visor leaked power, the armoured plate fractured and pierced where Laoch and Ecne had struck the creature. At its feet lay the bastard sword—inert, flat and lifeless—and the Construct kicked it aside, glancing down as Sura brought the spear directly into its path. The helm turned, an internal glow falling upon her. The Schenterenta felt like her very soul was being examined.

"Look," came the hoarse whisper from deep within the helm. Sura froze, staring back, realising she understood the clattering speech.

It reached out a hand, palm up, gently pushing its gauntlet through the ethereal spear tip before striding on past. Sura baulked, the Patterning taking over and coming to her feet, stance set. Yet not attacking as her mind replayed what the gauntlet had done. The Constructor walked on, the door ahead of it carved with the very dragon that had just tried to cook her whole. An armoured hand reached out, wisps of white lacing the carving, igniting in a flare of cold fire. She heard the groan of ancient stone, and the door shifted, before opening wide. Air rushed out, filling the metal corridor with an ancient, damp smell mixed with a growing heat. Crimson light rippled through the entrance, pulsing with hatred and anger, and the Construct strode through.

"Look." It repeated, and Sura looked. And there, at her ghostly feet, lay her own charred body, gripping Honour's spear.

—

Fate's bow lay loose in Laoch's hand, the right rubbing his eyes before drawing Justice, holding the maul high as fear pounded in his heart. Flame roared, tearing the soil, searing the grass and bracken. Smoke and steam mixed, filling the clearing as the moisture boiled. In there, amid the maelstrom of heat and dragon's fire, was Sura and the monstrosity that had torn past him to pin her within the flame. Hatred spilled out. Laoch's own roar masking that of the dragon flame, arms wide as his hate and fear erupted into the rain-filled night.

With his mind swirling in grief, he charged. Justice's scarlet light glowing as the maul warped and reshaped. His usual sword now in hand, he powered towards the metal-scaled dragon that pulled its head upwards. Laoch ignored the heat, the char of the hole seared into the ground. His rage manifested in madness, leaping, smashing the weapon against the dragon's jaw. The edge bit into the scales, sparking. The surrounding air laced with power and the dragon reared back, twisting its neck, pulling the sword with it. Laoch, muscles flexing, slid the weapon free as the dragon's head whipped out to his left. Expecting the beast to slam it back towards him, he ducked, tucking close to the ground to be rewarded by a rush of air and heat sailing overhead. Rising, he drove the sword upwards, attempting to pierce the jaw from beneath. The tip scraped against the metal, sliding across and under an overlapping scale. The dragon roared, but where Laoch expected blood, a viscous crimson substance flowed over the blade. Its inner light matched the dragon's flame, a lava that tainted the air with a chemical tang. The dragon's growling head pulled back, releasing the sword, before a huge taloned foot erupted from the rock face, swinging towards its assailant.

Laoch raised Justice. His whole world spiralling, watching death wing its way as marked by the claws slicing through the air. A blur crossed his vision, lost in the haze of battle—a clash of short sword and dagger as Oisin deflected the swinging foot. The blades scraped across the talons, the Elite Ranger ducking beneath, then driving sword and knife against the armoured limb as it swung past. Laoch, finding the darkness goading him—decreeing his failure to protect those most precious to him—spurred forwards. But with all reason lost, his anger tore into the dragon. The sword's blade—a conduit for his grief—pulsing Justice's red.

—

Ecne staggered to her feet. The stock of the spent crossbow remained entwined in her frail, husked fingers. Her very spirit felt tired—worn and raw—and as she pushed upwards from the tree stump, she felt a sickness rise as her thin, wasted fingers pressed against the rotten wood. In her addled mind she knew fear. An understanding that the God's weapon she bore had drained her, used what it could to power itself. Science and learning spiralling amid the sheer impossibility of what was happening. The dragon, a metallic, almost mechanical beast, reminiscent of Arknold's mad plans that shouted of its very wrongness. One that bore down upon Laoch and Oisin as they struck at the curved claws. In her befuddled state, she knew they were dead, that one strike would slice through leather and flesh. Expose the meat beneath to the world before it feasted. Wisdom's sigil demanded she gave her last for a final strike. To give herself up to those that fought for hope. It was the logical thing to do, the final act of a lowly acolyte. To end her life so that those more able, more worthy than her, could live. A sacrifice.

Yet Ecne could not, would not, let herself fall. She had lifted herself from despair with a determination born from derision. A resolute spine encased in sheer will. However far she was belittled or ridiculed, she rose above it, or waded on through. Reaching down, she grasped the handbow discarded amid the fight. Its crystal tip inert but reflecting the myriad of light in the clearing. She took aim, feet spread apart, eyes only for the dragon's head. And Wisdom's kiss caressed her mind.

50
A TWIST OF FATE

NATHAIR, NORTH ERSTEN FOREST

Mirrored plates glinted with the crimson light, the Captain's eyes drinking in the beating crystal heart inlaid in the centre of a marbled table. Within it, he could feel Nathair's anger. Frustration as it fought the rocks weighing down upon her, while human gnats buzzed and bit. Food that was just out of reach. Sustenance that would drive her motors, allow the mechanical muscles to pull her from the Seven's trap.

You are to be mine, Nathair. No quarter given. In this fight, you either supplicate or die.

The Captain slid the polished gauntlets from his bone-white fingers, dropping them to the table and grasping the dragon's heart with both husked, near skeletal hands. With head back, a scream echoed through the metal-lined chamber, freezing the Schenterenta spirit who crept up behind him. Not a threat, for she was in anguish at this time, wrenched from her body in his attempts to save her. Though should he fall, he had no doubt the Magi's weapon she now inhabited would end the Construct within which he resided. The one whose voracious spirit had near taken her a few seconds before.

No matter, for I will not be re-entering this cesspit.
The Captain forced his spirit to detach. Tendrils of his *self,* his
very *being,* separating from the remnant of evil that leeched at his
soul. He felt the Construct's ancient, dead body relax; its power
too weak to hold itself up. Only the hands gracing the stone, the
elbows braced on the table, held it in place. Wondering if the
female warrior spirit would notice him leave, he felt Nathair baulk.
The twisted Spirit Walker suddenly realising that this Construct
was about to enter her heartstone—an act of a Master looking to
dominate a slave.

*And I am not weak, Dragon of the Veil. For I have wondered the
pathways for a hundred years, and I am not meat for the beast. I
will be your master.*

—————

Oisin slashed downwards. The weighted sword biting into the
dragon's foot—the edge parting the first layer, digging into its
glittering sole that flexed like a snake's skin. A crimson glow the
reward, with a lava like substance seeping from the cut. The First
Ranger drove his small dagger into the gash, ripping upwards and
out, before whipping down another blow. With Laoch two steps
behind, flame washed over the mountain man, swathing his body
in red heat—searing hair and boiling the leather jerkin. Laoch
threw himself back as the flames licked at his eyes and face—instincts demanding he survive and overriding his hate and anger.
Falling to the floor, his mind filled with horror, an image of Oisin
aflame boring in. An imagined howl released from peeled back
lips as the fire engulfed the Ranger's head. The Handren driving
the falchion in again and again, while jaws full of sword-like teeth
wrapped themselves around his torso, clamping down, shearing
the Ranger in half. Eyes beseeching an arrow to end the pain.
    Face down, the horror pressed in on Laoch's mind. Flame,
smoke and cooked flesh assailing his walls, demanding he acqui-
esce. Sura had been the barrier he'd built around the loss of his
soldiers. Getting him through grief-stricken days that the Seven
Hells would have baulked at as a punishment too harsh. Now a
man he barely knew had given his life freely for his own. Dying

with the honour he aspired to. Forsaking his life—a gift he could not just throw into his personal pit of despair.

Laoch rebuilt the wall with blood and Justice.

He rolled to the side, instincts screaming for him to move as a lick of flame flowed over the soil. Heat scorched his legs, ignored as he raised the sword, willing Justice to take what he needed with the dragon's maw bearing down upon him. To his surprise, Oisin's Falchion lashed out, slashing the Dragon's lower jaw as it widened to engulf Laoch. Smoke rose from the First Ranger's cracked armour. His face red, hair ash, yet alive. The dragon reared back again.

"She's alive, Laoch," shouted Gowan, filling his mind as he willed Justice to take the last of his spirit.

A quarrel smashed into the dragon's eye. Fire erupting as the spiritfire contained within the crystal tip flared, half-blinding the beast seeking its prey. Pain pierced the metal skull, forcing the dragon to rear the huge head backwards, metal-skinned lids blinking in pain and desperation. Flame poured from its mouth—but weaker—forcing moisture from the air with mist forming around the snout. Laoch reeled back, feeling Justice's sigil continue to drain him, to take the sacrifice he'd offered up.

"She's inside. The dragon's heartstone hides much from me. More than you can imagine, yet Leront can taste her spirit."

"But the Construct, the flame ... how?" Laoch staggered back, eyes upwards. The dragon roaring its defiance against the pain.

"Get me close and press my sigil against the chest. I'll ... shit I'll go and help—wherever 'inside' is. If it's a bloody stomach full of old meat, then we're going to have words."

Laoch grasped the bow, mindful of the level of madness Gowan was spouting. Sura must have been cooked and eaten or torn apart by the Construct wherever it may be. He felt the loss in his chest—deep, and riven.

Hope? Among all this fire and flame?

With Oisin swaying at his side, Laoch pressed Fate's sigil against a heaving metal scale. The deep blue light pulsing once, merging into the oily metal. A sudden thought cut through as the dragon shook its neck and head, and he allowed his eyes to wander over to the clearing's edge where Ecne lay sprawled on the ground.

Laoch, torn, havered a second before Oisin shoved him away, towards the stricken acolyte.

"Run," was all he said. The words dry and cracked.

Laoch, compelled by duty, ran across. His beleaguered body arguing against every step and instincts screaming that the dragon was upon him.

Nothing came. No breath nor lick of flame, and he leapt over Ecne's prone body, turning to face the dragon. Its freed foot dragged at the wounded eye, Oisin backing away with smoke and steam streaming from his jerkin. Laoch glanced down. In his charge's hand lay Sura's handbow, and underneath her the sigil of Wisdom glowed with a faint light. The acolyte looked sallow. Her skin crumpled and dry, the eyes open but unseeing. Laoch placed his hand upon the Learned's neck, feeling for a pulse, praying to the Seven that the young woman's heart still beat. Under the rough skin, his fingers sensed a slow, shallow rhythm. It was barely there, and he reached over to feel a weak breath exude from Ecne's mouth.

Alive, though for how long I don't know.

A roar emanated from the raging dragon; its front foot now pressed against the earth. The neck and head pressed down beside it. A ripple heaved under the scales along the left flank, and rocks crumbled, shearing away. Stone and moss rolled down into the bracken. Another wave spilled more debris onto the ground and Laoch felt his heart lurch when a second taloned leg emerged from the escarpment.

Shit.

51
A DREAM OF
INNEALTÓIR.

NATHAIR'S HEARTSTONE.

T he Captain sat on the metal ledge, the wind whipping against the woollen scarf wrapped around his chin and neck. It smelt of the sea, and of home. Its weft and weave familiar against his stubbled skin. Knitted by his daughter with the holes unpicked by time, and rarely washed for fear it would not survive. It set his heart pounding. A life forsaken. Sailing the seas of Mondrein, skimming the waves in search of the kelp islands his people harvested and stored for winter feed. A life he had loved and sacrificed for the people that sat in his heart, touching his soul every day with kisses of love and remembrance.

The storm had been unpredictable, one of those that occurred every few years or so. A tumult of air and spiritfire that exuded from the sea life below. It had torn through his small fleet as they cut and prepared the seaweed. They were ready as always; the ships moored, with just enough slack, sails and spars stowed, and the smaller ships' masts dropped. The crews, as was best, rode the kelp field. Its tangled platform much stronger and flexible than the ships, and they endured. But on that day, his brother's family were torn asunder. The island wrenched apart. They'd cut too deep—roots sheared—and the Captain's wife pleading for him to help, to save those tumbling in the storm. Folly. But family is all, and he'd gone in frustration and pain, only to witness their deaths as their bodies smashed upon the waves.

Lives lost, smiles forsaken. And a family he could no longer enjoy as he watched another die in his dreams night after night. First it was the drink, then the days and weeks spent searching for the furthest, the richest islands. But it was all an excuse. A time apart, away from the pleading that had torn his life asunder. In the end she set him free, his wife cutting the bonds of handfast. One last kiss full of love to cast him upon the seas. And the Captain had withered, for he had been blind to the real pain. The fear he would lose his family as his brother had—only to find it needed no sea storm, just a man and his own personal maelstrom.

Pain, loss and anguish, muffled by the smell of old wool, salt and kelp beds. Love.

When the first glyph fired, and fear crept across their realm, he had stood, throwing the bottle aside. The pleading tight in his mind. Dead eyes of his nieces and nephews rolling in the froth of the storm. The seeker of the kelp, and later of his own pain, gave his life for a second time. His spirit torn asunder. Ripped from an already dead heart and bound to the Wyrm to sail the void's pathways searching for hope. The Constructors had found them, though weaker than before, but hungrier. And they would not stop until the last glyph fired and Mondrein's veils broke, and the humanity beneath subjugated. Forever spirit-dolls until the frenzy took over, or the *will* died. Families lost in the storm of their need.

So he left, chasing a myth. The Dragons of the Veil that had pursed the Seven. For if they could be turned as their realm's Schenterenta claimed, the fabled hunters would become the Constructors' own nemesis. So here he was—a spirit lost on the sea of his own despair—ready to do battle for those he'd forsaken. Though he knew, in his heart and the smell of old wool, that he now fought for their grandchildren—and those dead eyes bobbing in the sea.

The Captain stirred. The scarf ripped from his chin once again as the wind rose in fury, heralding the approach of Nathair and the battle to come. Below, the vista spread like a nightmare of twisted metal and stone. A horror of a city—devoid of a soul. Steam rose, forced between pistons, and flames flared, spiralling oily black smoke into the darkened sky. A choking mass hovered just above him. A fog that clawed at his chest, the taste of metal and sulphur seeping into his soul. Far below the twisted spires, metal-legged beasts clattered along arrow straight streets. Their spider-like legs rising and heaving the brass machines step by step towards whatever fatuous goal the Constructor within had in mind. Ordered, regimented madness, as engineered monstrosities fought for space while spewing their foul smoke into the air. Somehow, the Captain knew, for all the strangeness below, that the brimstone and fire were affectations. Creations of insane minds that saw beauty in the twisted and macabre. The Constructors had lost their sense of beauty in the hunger to live, and when fed, had little to do but make their nightmares become real.

"Madness," he said, letting slip the words between fleshed lips. But it wasn't real. This dream he sat within was not his. And the screeching roar tearing through the dirtied air was the confirmation. This was Nathair's world—at least as she remembered it—the greatest of all nightmares. Built to hunt those that kept her masters alive. A mighty metallic dragon, constructed from alloy and hate, and powered by spiritfire like its makers. But the beating heart, the soul within, now that was not a construction. More a tortured spirit. A Schenterenta Spirit Walker—a female elven shaman corrupted and merged with the artifice Nathair. Existing within the drumming, crystal heart and forever hungry.

This is their world, as was, and somewhere down there may be the answer to their demise.

But it is a dream, and dreams are where I've wandered for years.

Keran rose, spinning the Sea Axe. The mighty tool his people used to cut a swathe through the tough kelp of his home realm. The blade glistened in the weak sunlight battling through the smog. The Captain peered down to the mighty metallic dragon beating its wings below.

"If you're going to go out, may as well go out in style." And he leapt. Once more Keran, the Captain of his own destiny.

52

ACCEPTANCE

NORTH ERSTEN FOREST

L aoch wrapped both arms around Ecne's chest, dragging
the acolyte over to the nearest group of trees. Feeling the
woman's dead weight, his own tired limbs protested only for a
gentle warmth to flood through his limbs. The sword, still within
his grip pulsed. The scarlet creeping along his forearm and up
through his body. Glad of any respite, he dropped Ecne behind a
lump of moss-covered rock, sliding her feet up. He hoped a combination of tree and stone would give the acolyte some protection.
Snatching the quiver, he ran with one eye on the dragon as its
scaled spine quivered. Rock, soil and plants sliding away from the
raised vertebrae, each sporting a gleaming spike. Oisin knelt by
the stump, a sag to the man's shoulders, with his falchion stabbed
into the earth before him. A lump formed in Laoch's throat. A
fear dispelled when the Handren finally sucked in a huge breath
between swollen lips, raising his head again.

Pure bloody-minded will.

Laoch grabbed the large crossbow. Its green light weak, barely
perceptible despite the darkness. This he threw across Ecne,

ensuring it landed away from her body, mindful it may drain the remainder of her energy otherwise.

She has no more to give.

Taking the mini crossbow in hand, he rifled through the quarrels, the three remaining all tipped with an inert crystal. He'd seen the impact of Ecne's strike to the dragon's eye and he wasn't going to discount the effect of the handbow's power. Loading a bolt, he turned, the dragon's roar almost lifting him from his feet as one last surge of mechanised muscle cleared the second half of its body. Laoch knelt, finding himself amazed at the distance from which Ecne had hit the beast's eye—a weapon designed for close quarter release and forget.

Did Wisdom help?

Maybe it's not all about power.

With Justice's sword resting against his arm, Laoch took aim. The huge dragon's efforts to free the remainder of itself focused on the tail, and what he took to be the beast's wings lying under a secondary layer of stone. The sword pulsed and a strange memory slid into Laoch's mind, as if seeing something from another's eyes. Wings—the great dragon being pinned. A trap for a creature the Seven couldn't kill. And here they were—two battered warriors—as the beast rose from its slumber, furious at its plight.

Laoch focused his mind, taking aim when a second memory awoke, one from only a few nights before. The child he had killed.

Perhaps I deserve this death.

The scarlet warmth wrapped his elbow and hand, steadying the tired tremor. Laoch smoothly depressed the trigger, the bolt tip flaring as it released from the crossbow. Its flame whirled in the air before striking home just below the dragon's eye. White fire washed over the metallic scales, causing the beast to flinch back, but little else. Laoch swore. The impact less powerful than whatever Ecne had used to save their lives, though admittedly she'd struck the eye. He quickly reloaded as the dragon rolled slightly to the left, pulling the right wing clear. The limb lifted into the air, the metallic skin spread like a mighty torn sail—damaged, yet still moving.

Laoch released again. The bolt searing through the smoke to slam into the corner of the bejewelled eye. Crimson flared bright as the bolt erupted. The dragon's pained roar tore into the sky, and Laoch saw its great eyelids drop over the flame, blinking the pain away. He loaded the final quarrel, then looped the weapon around his belt and grasped Justice, raising the sword.

I hope the Seven are with me, and this damn thing doesn't shoot into my bloody foot.

Crimson fire charred the ground. A spout of angry flame pouring across the floor as Nathair released its pain towards the source. Earth and grass erupted, ash dropping in the fire's wake, searing heat preceding it as the air itself burned. Death knocked at Laoch's door with the raging gout of dragon fire washing towards him far swifter than a man could react. Fear froze him solid, and the last grain of sand spilled from the hourglass. And Justice flared.

———

Sharp, jagged rocks beckoned her to step out, to find her ending. But dread dragged Sura away from the precipice. Loss was prominent in her mind—pained grief a constant. And, despite the refusals, her need for Laoch threatened that wrench again. Easier, perhaps, to drop—to accept death's embrace. But Honour held her. A snake of power that wrapped itself about her spirit, enveloping her heart. Not just a chain to hold her fast, but an expectation that went beyond the Schenterenta in her. A need to see Honour done and thus maintain a link to the physical world.

Cat-like eyes opened, and Sura stepped away from her smoking corpse, accepting. In many ways, she had already died once, only for it to refuse her. And now, death's embrace gave her another chance—one filled with Honour.

She strode back through the doorway, her spirit sight taking in the armour now frozen in paralysis as its inhabitant melded with the crimson crystal. She caught a glimpse of the spirit—no more than a flicker of light—that slid into the stone. She had expected something twisted and evil, seeking control. But instead, there had been a sense of warmth, though tinged with loneliness and loss. A depth to the soul with her eyes and mind filling in the spectral gaps. To Sura, the spirit had been ... complete.

Tantalisingly close to knowing it. A connection in death, maybe.

Dread rode a breath of wind, raising hairs on her ethereal neck and goosebumps appeared upon her imagined skin. Friendship reached out, touching upon her heart.

Laoch? No, someone else.

A second presence flowed in, familiar—and then she knew. Gowan slid through the walls behind her, the dead Ranger's spirit laid bare. If she wanted, she could rifle through the woman's memories, explore her emotions. Strip them apart to find the true Gowan beneath.

But I have no right.

Sura pressed her spirit hands together—the spear somehow between—trying to regain herself as her mind expanded into the space. It was making connections, as if her mind had broken out of a prison and *needed* to know. To explore the wonders around her. But it reeled back, sensing the true evil that lay in the room. Not the tainted spirit of a Construct, but the heart of a dragon dipped in the blood of millions. From the outside, looking in, death rode upon scaled wings, but she could not bring herself to look upon its face—for there lay the ultimate source of her dread.

"*Sura,*" whispered Gowan, her spirit sliding from the metalled walls. "*I knew you lived. I need to help, Nathair is too strong, she is trying to free herself from the rock.*"

"Live? Look closer, Gowan."

"*I—*" Gowan whirled, the blue fading out before returning, eyes back to the corridor and upon the charred corpse. "*No.*"

"Gowan, it has happened. As to you, it has happened to me. Accept it. Laoch and Ecne, do they still live?"

"*Yes, though I know nothing of Oisin. He suffered. And it will not be long before the dragon is free. The Construct? It killed you?*"

"No. I think it tried to save me, or at least my spirit. Nathair would have consumed all of me if it had not."

"*Then where is its spirit? The armour lies empty.*"

"In there," said Sura, pointing. "But I do not think it is a Construct. I saw it, felt it. I believe the spirit is inherently good, and that Nathair railed as he entered. As if the twisted spirit wasn't seeing what it expected. Or at least feared what it saw."

"*That doesn't mean they will help,*" said Gowan, her smoke-like form rippling with a gentle blue light. "*Though it is my fate to find out.*" Gowan probed at the crystal, trying to slide between its bonds as she had Leront. But they were bound fast, hard, resistant, and her energy was low. Laoch having expended Fate's spiritfire, and in truth much of hers, in the fight with Nathair. Frustration rose, and she battered at the crimson jewel.

"Stop, Gowan," said Sura, reaching out and gently caressing the outside of the crystal, her hand immersed in the spirit's blue glow. She sensed the thrum of the stone, its power shielded after the Construct's spirit had entered. Nathair had blocked the pathway, fearing what would come next.

How do I know this?

A pulse rode her arm, and she peered down at her other hand—the one wrapped around the grip of the Schenterenta's spear.

How can this be?

Honour's sigil lay under her thumb with its orange glow encasing her spirit hand. Outside Laoch fought for all of them, and now Sura stood at another precipice—with a choice to make. And Honour demanded, filling her mind.

Were the shamans right? Did we truly dance with spirits?

"Can you lead me, Gowan? Show Honour the way, so I can follow?" Gowan wrapped around her, curiosity woven into the spirit's form. The gentleness of her touch tentative as she alighted upon Honour's spear. She let herself entwine with the raw energy of the sigil—immerse within it—parting her *self* from this world. Not a tear, more a disconnect.

"Guard Laoch, Gowan. Do not let Nathair have him. Please." Sura let Honour's power fully in. The energy washing through her, immersing her spirit and lifting it away. She suddenly felt stretched, narrowed and needle sharp—driving into the crystal to pierce Nathair's barrier. Sura leapt off a precipice and rode Honour into the heart of a dragon.

53
TO UNVEIL THE FORBIDDEN

THE HOUSE OF WISDOM (ADJOINING
THE UNIVERSITY), ERSTENBURGH

S need rippled his fingers along the chair arm. His eyes staring
ahead, mind in so many places at once he could hardly think.
Beside him sat Lord Wisdom, his emerald robes adorned with
sequined quill and books. Sulking as was his wont, the moaning
loud and vociferous. Sneed had been his High Lord for only a
year, and still wondered if the man had done more to hasten his
retirement than the crippling burden Penance asked of his Lords.

But it says much that I am here, and not the Priests-in-Waiting.
What does it portent for our future when he cannot choose one to
follow? Does he avoid the jealousy that such a choice would lead
to? I am too old and frail. My time has passed.

He glanced at the white-washed walls; the hallway covered
with the portraits of past University Chancellors. People that had
sequestered themselves in the written word. Exploring, seeking
answers where only the stifling Houses allowed. The scripture
had prevented much. Limiting human ingenuity, the memories of

the destruction caused by such creations at the forefront of the Seven's thoughts when they laid the word of The Seven down. It had been necessary, he supposed. The pained memories of humanity's slavery to a new race that saw them as much as an experiment as the machines they so loved. He had read those diaries forbidden to many. The few remaining in Penance's House which told of the fire and steam, the coal and the heat. How the realm they fled held horrors over and above the spirit-dolls they were. Where the menageries were used to feed their machinations, to power their nightmarish designs. As a Priest-in-Waiting he had only heard the whispers. Glimpses of the knowledge the High Lord held. When he had risen to that seat, those books forged the resolve needed to carry the burden of the House. That, and the pictures of the flailed, and the tortured. The twisted and the maimed, and the foul Constructor's themselves. The abhorrence sat heavy in his heart.

And now I must stand by my Lord's wishes, to once again take on some of the mantle.

Footsteps echoed down the polished stone corridor. Bejewelled shoes ringing out the Queen's approach through the House of Wisdom, the only church where those of the University Learned were allowed to worship. It loomed next to the palace, side by side with the University building. A constant reminder to refrain from taking science too far.

Lord Wisdom rose. Lifting his heft from the cushioned chair with a sigh, his back a pained symptom of his tenure. Sneed had little sympathy with his body a temple of sufferance to his God. Joining Lord Wisdom, he bowed low, taking in the dainty feet that belied the powerhouse they bore. Queen Erin was formidable, and he loved her like no other. She had been his choice for the throne and a last act before he relinquished the cloak. The other paired feet belonged to Jacka, a man he'd not yet made his mind up about. But the Queen was here, so at least the Prime had followed through on Lord Penance's request.

"Arise, Lord Wisdom and ... err."

"Just Sneed, Your Majesty. It is all I am now." He stood, eyes gracing hers, allowing the flicker of a smile he was never permitted as High Lord. It was returned with warmth, his heart flickering a little.

Is that pride?

"Lord Wisdom, it is early morning. Why could this not wait? What is so important, that I must forsake breaking my fast? Your House rarely acts with urgency."

"Well, eh, Lord Penance, well ..." Wisdom looked over to Penance's servant, nerves as normal tying his thick tongue. It wasn't as if his lips were out of practice, having moaned constantly for the last ten minutes in Sneed's ear. "Sneed, would you be so kind to explain?"

Sneed bowed his head to the Lord, before turning to the Queen and her Prime. "It is early because time is short, and you need to consider what I am about to show you before Lord Penance returns from the Forest." Sneed noted the Prime's wince, keeping the smile internal. Knowing well the games Lord Penance had played to put the man in his place. But the Houses had ears everywhere, and this was not the place for talk. "An urgent need I am afraid, a soul in need of my Lord's ministrations. I will explain in a second, my Queen. Lord Wisdom, if you would."

The Lord turned to the bookcase behind him. The shelves dust free, but the aged books and scrolls stacked high. Easing his hand between two of the piles, he felt the catch give, and then repeated this lower down before shoving the shelf over to the side on unseen runners. A plain door lay behind. Unremarkable except for the trio of well-worn locks.

"What games are you playing, Lord Wisdom? It is but a door. I have given up my ham and eggs for a bit of theatre?" The Queen's hands landed on her hips, raising a second smile from Sneed, and a look of worry upon Jacka. Both for the same reason—the fire reaching Erin's eyes.

Erin's Wrath—such a well-named elixir.

"No, my Queen. This is more than mere theatre. This is my burden. As Penance takes on the sins of our people, I take on the knowledge."

"Surely, that is the University, Lord Wisdom," cut in Jacka, trying to intercept the Queen's ire. "The Meisters' library and written works are unsurpassed across the Union."

"If you say so," replied the Lord, the last lock clicking open, and the key bearing Wisdom's sigil slipped back under his cloak. "In the Union, you would be right. But in the Houses, it is but a mere scrap of what is known." He pushed the door wide, lifting the lamp he'd left near the chairs and entering the mighty room first to light the way. The Prime went next, the Queen holding back to ensure all was safe before accepting Sneed's proffered hand to enter herself. As she stepped through, the flickering lamp lit a wide floor, row upon row of tables and aged chairs readied, each with a book mount in place.

"What?" said the Queen, spinning around, eyes roaming over layer upon layer of books and scrolls that rose from the floor. Yet only the front row of the three-tiered room was highlighted by the low light of the lamp. "Why do I not know of this place, Lord Wisdom? Why have you kept this from the Crown?"

"As I said, my Queen, it is my burden. The agony of knowing the forbidden. Watching those you respect, even admire, flailing to discover that which is already known. This is the Forbidden Library. Decreed by the Gods to be unseen by humanity's eyes. Yet, the Houses, the Lords, could not see its destruction through."

"You went against the word of the Gods? Against your own scripture? What are you saying?"

"That," said Sneed, "the Gods were not always right. Their actions were heroic, their sacrifice unparalleled. And much of what followed kept us safe after the Landing. But they were short-sighted emotional beings, as all humankind is. Our curse. The First Lords could not burn all knowledge, but nor could they go against scripture and let what is stored here be remembered. The Houses would collapse, and with it, humanity enslaved. We closed the people's minds, discounted truth as myth. Let our past fade, so we could live."

If only you knew it all. But there are some secrets we cannot tell.

"The Gods' Council has decreed this knowledge to be shared with you both, as we face a great peril. The dragon in our scripture was not metaphorical, my Queen, but real. And the Gods laid down their lives not so we would hear their words, but so they could hide us and entrap the beast that threatened our kind. Lord Penance believes it has arisen, and he goes to find out more. If the dragon rises, then more of our enemies will come in its wake. We must prepare."

"Prepare?"

"Yes," said Lord Wisdom. "We must rally the Union. Ready our soldiers and explore the potential of Meisters Arknold and Kinst. To do that, you must believe, as must Prime Vardrin. We have just shattered everything you knew to be true. Knowledge we cannot share with our flocks as panic would rise. But you—if you believe, then they would follow your lead with the word of the Houses as its foundation. Perhaps masked as preparing for a second crusade to the Unspoken's lands or sew a fear that the Unbelievers are rising again. But what we share here can go no further until the High Lord decrees it."

"If he lives," said Sneed.

"I cannot believe what you are sorely hinting at, Lord Wisdom. You have brought me here to-to explain that your scripture, the word of the Seven we have followed for a thousand years, is built on a lie?" The Queen shook, her hands squeezed tight against her hips, before she noticed and placed them behind her, gripped tight.

"Half-a-lie, Your Majesty. A myth built around a truth to keep the people safe. Here," Lord Wisdom pointed to a table. The lamp flickered under his movement, bringing him up short momentarily. Sneed saw the decision made in the man's eyes, and likely a step too far at this moment. He stepped in, forgetting himself as he gently shook his head.

"I will send for a second lamp, Queen Erin, and will bring your eggs and ham personally so you will not be disturbed." He reached over, black hand dousing the Lord's green glow he was about to release, while flipping open the huge book propped at the table. "This is Wisdom's diary. A succinct précis of the events around the ensnaring of Nathair, and the threat she may pose if she arises. You'll find the art plate on the next page quite terrifying."

Accepting the Lord's curt nod as an apology, Sneed headed for the door when Jacka called his name, hurrying over as the man tended to do when his mind was sparking. Sneed wondered just how long he'd survive, if and when the Lord returned.

"Ah, Sneed. A word?" he asked, Sneed letting a slow blink show his consideration. The temptation to walk away burning in his mind. Three years ago, with the Lord's cloak around his shoulders, he may well have done.

"A brief one, if may. I am under Death's hourglass, Prime Vardrin. The sand never ceases to flow."

"Eh? Well, the Lord Penance. I assume you are aware of what he asked of me? To keep the City Guard away from the forest? Is this dragon that close? Should we not be calling out the guard, mobilising the militia?"

"And if the Queen agrees, Prime Vardrin. Under what pretence?"

"Well, we have the Prince Consort's moods ..."

Sneed stopped, berating his old mind.

Ah. Clever. Maybe Lord Penance had better keep a much closer eye on this one.

54
THE SPIRIT OF
REDEMPTION

NORTH ERSTEN FOREST

H eat poured into the ground, booted feet sweltering under
the onslaught. Laoch, shoulder braced against Justice's newly formed shield, protected Oisin from its effects. The crimson
flame licked at the shield's edge, singeing hair and cracking leather
armour. Laoch pulsed inside, as if his soul were being dragged out,
pulled to the surface and drawn to the dragon's flame. The flame's
odour a reminder of pot bombs, but stronger. Infused with ash
and charred flesh, as if the beast cooked whatever still lay within
its mouth.

Overwhelmed by the gout of fire whirling around his and Oisin's
body, the scarlet light of Justice faltered against the bestial force
of the dragon's need. With shoulders shuddering under the weight
of flame, knees braced, Laoch knew Justice's power was waning.
The sigil's glow within the shield's grip flickering, guttering. That
moment of hope Justice provided as the sword transformed, lost
amid the sheer terror of the dragon's relentless flame. Laoch

swore, risking a glance behind at the unconscious Oisin, seeking a way to at least save one.

A blue light arose amid the heat. Streaking outwards, wrapping itself about the shield and forming an additional barrier along its edges as a huge gout erupted from the metalled beast. The scarlet fire wreathed the shield, expanding. Only to be met by Fate's avatar, Gowan, holding fast under the onslaught. And then that too slowed. The flame's intensity dropping, its width narrowing. Laoch stepped back, his body awash with the residual heat. His hood set alight as he knelt to the ground, tucking behind the shield to prod at Oisin. With the flame rising along the cloak's edge, a wisp of power arose from the shield. A last vestige that quenched the flame. Then the glow dimmed—leaving with a soft caress along his cheek and a touch upon his mind.

Gowan.

Laoch felt her sorrow. The grief, before it faded away.

Sura.

Nathair lay with neck and head upon the ground, metal scales rising and falling as if the great dragon panted for breath. Yet one eye gleamed, the corner singed, the beast's regard locked on to Laoch. The other wept, lava spilling from beneath it and a film of white lay across the clustered crystals. With one wing still trapped beneath stone and rock, Laoch could make out the creature's tail rising from behind. Its edges adorned with hardened crystal, shaped like Justice's maul, spiked and heavy. It struck out, lashing at the rock, beating a rhythm against the stone as Nathair rested.

Once the wing was freed, the dragon would be able to crash through the forest and hunt him, or Ecne, down. However, Laoch began to wonder how tired the beast truly was. Gowan had mentioned its hunger, and right now it was struggling to emerge from under the weight of the final rocks. The dragon must have spent vast energy with the gouts of flame, more perhaps than it wanted, spurred on by anger and pain. Though should he be in range of those taloned feet, or the mighty head—even the lash of its tail—Laoch doubted he'd last long. And then there was Ecne and Oisin to protect. Vulnerable where they lay, and finally Sura. The pain squeezed at his heart, chest pounding. The very idea that she may be alive hurting near as much as the moment he thought her dead.

But Gowan's grief? Was it for herself?
And Justice glows weakly. Near spent. Unless I give my last
onto my God. But where is that best spent? Attempt a rescue or
protecting those that fought by our side.

⊢━

The Captain slammed onto Nathair's back. The mechanised dragon barely flinching as it wheeled through the tall, twisted towers
and flaming chimneys. That was until the axe bit. The two-handed
tool Keran's people wielded to cut through the mighty branches
and roots of the kelp islands. Fibrous seaweed—resistant to the
small teeth of a saw—the great axes honed to bite deep with
each blow. The strength of a worker's shoulders complemented
by powerful core muscles and bull-like thighs. Of course, Keran understood the axe wasn't real. An embodiment of his will
as he stood astride Nathair. He hooked his plated boots under
the metallic back plates, their soles vibrating with the thrum of
its mighty mechanical engine thudding away, feeding the beast's
wings with reserves of refined spiritfire.

He swung his axe—the symbol of his will—using all those remembered muscles. The weapon's edge crashing down into the
metallic, oily plate. The second blow slid off, catching against the
plate edges. To the outsider, it would appear little had happened,
but the Captain felt the beast flinch. A missed beat in the machin-
ery, a taste of fear at the unknown. The axe rose again, but as it
lifted, Nathair twisted her neck, pouring hate and anger through
a river of flame bathing the Captain. In this embodiment—this
realm within a realm—he'd still chosen the armour of his enemy
for this very reason. The polished, mirrored surface—bonded and
resistant to spiritfire—reflected much of the flame, the dragon's
will made real. Wreathed in dragon's fire, his mind and spirit
body still acted on instinct as he dropped beneath the torrent.
Nathair's glowing red eyes watched, and she chose that moment
to turn and bank. Raw power heaving her to the side, the sail like
wings beating against the heat from the chimneys. They drove
the beast towards the strange city streets and their collection of
scuttling, rolling and striding nightmares the Constructors built.

Wing tips cut through those slow to react. Slicing mechanical limbs and strange protrusions, scattering those that walked and rolled in equal measure. Keran found himself reeling, sliding along the smooth scales, feet losing purchase as he scrabbled to grab Nathair's spikes. The sea axe spun away, whirling downwards to crash into a multi-legged creation scrabbling its way across the street. Keran's forearm strap went taut. The rig brace designed to keep the axe close should an island split, or the kelp heave. So often a saviour in the days when he still lived.

Keran's gauntlet began to separate. The razor-edged spike he'd grasped slicing through the plates. Sawing through to his hand beneath as the vibration of the dragon's wingbeat shook its body. He felt it slip, slick with blood.

My time is done.

Taking a glance down to the street below, Keran said a final farewell to those he left behind, and a welcome to the family he was about to join. His grip gave, the pain too much, when a hand reached out to grasp his forearm. Dappled Schenterenta skin shone in the orange half-light of the city flames. The Schenterenta spirit standing astride the dragon—feet planted—no slip or movement impairing her as she heaved him upwards.

A Spirit Walker indeed. One who has found their way.

Sura compensated as Nathair flattened out, bringing her mechanical body level. Swooping down an arrow straight passage towards a monstrous building, its black, tortuous structure screaming of internal pain. Fluted columns gushed flame and black smoke. The windows irregular and strangely shaped, writhing in the mind's eye as the heat haze flickered. Sura saw the portent but remained focused on her purpose. Leaving the Captain safe she strode across the metallic scales. Each placement of her feet attaching like glue, lifting them more of an effort than forcing her mind to ignore such impossibilities. On reaching Nathair's neck, she dropped to straddle the scales, sliding her way until the dragon's head flinched, the mighty artifice realising she was there. The head bent back, a roar tearing through the city. The smoky black tower glass beating against their window frames as she flew by. Sura dragged Honour's spear off her back, marking her spot. Her mind sensed the pulse of Nathair's spirit driven body and the place where the inner glow shone through. A weak spot that lay behind the join of neck and metal-forged skull. Two-handed, she drove the spear deep into the join, feeling the spear tip pierce the metal-cum-flesh beneath. Honour's orange glow drained into the huge machine and Sura screamed, her mind assailed. Pure, twisted evil pouring its filth inwards towards her spirit. Tendrils of ancient, ancestral pain hooked into her brain, seeking the will and spirit that was her *self* to corrupt and consume.

Keran leapt. The axe swinging, both hands wrapping the grip in mid-air as he crashed down into the back of Nathair's skull. The axe's edge split the plates like kelp, splicing vertebrae as the axe bit deep. And the Captain tumbled into this split between realm and time. Screaming as his spirit drove into the pure hate that was Nathair.

—

Lord Penance felt the pain in his heart. The fear racing through his once stricken body. God's power sang within him, but as with all of Penance's gifts, there would be a price to pay. Someone would suffer, and though it would inevitably be his time in the end, he feared for those that cut and sliced their way through the forest ahead of him. They were his flock. The lower priests, and all thinking that Lord Penance had once again chosen a mighty punishment for their lack of strength and belief. Though he had to admit, a penitent soul would surely suffer at the pace he expected. He feared more for what he may have to do afterwards. For if—as he dreaded—they needed to be silenced to stop fear and panic spreading, could he bring himself to do it? Had they not, as the Seven Houses, caused enough pain and grief over the centuries?

But should we arrive too late, what then? All humankind would suffer. Be they devout or devoid of belief. They would be exposed to the Constructors, and the Houses draining and stunting of their spiritfire would pale in comparison to their feeding. Though I doubt any of us will ever be thanked by the people for our actions. Especially when they understand the choices made.

A roar swept through the trees, accompanied by a ripple of wind that caused the tangle of bushes ahead to part. A worn pathway lay exposed, perhaps a deer path, though this was far from the panicked priests' minds as the roar's echo bounced from tree to tree. Penance felt their fear. Muddy and torn cloaks swaying as they turned to gawp at each other, and then at him.

"Hah, see—I can set fear amidst your belief with a simple sound. The truly penitent would turn that aside, swallow their fear, and stand by the side of their Lord and God." The shame shone from the twenty men and women, as he knew it would. A second roar ripped through the path, sending birds squawking into the night air. And met with a little less trepidation. Lord Penance sneered, spitting on the floor in defiance of their fear, before pulling the purple-liveried horse around to face the deer trail. The cane strapped to his saddle pulsed against his inner thigh, the sigil barely masked as it glowed. Behind, he felt Lady Death stiffen on her horse, and the fear within Lord Hope as he waited alongside her. They couldn't wait. The dragon's roar called to their Gods' sigils, demanding their attention. All three had worked to entrap Nathair, with the Forbidden Books talking of how close the Construct's hunter had been to escaping. Stunned but unable to kill it, the three Magi had buried it beneath rock and stone, awaiting the day when they would have the power. But forced into sacrifice, the last of the Seven to give their lives to the Veils, it had lain forgotten. The knowledge either stricken or hidden within the Forbidden Library.

The Seven were just people, far from perfect. Yet they were Magi, strong with spiritfire and purpose.

"Follow on," he bellowed, spurring his horse onto the exposed trail and praying to his false God that it would take them where needed. "Double speed, my flock."

Lady Death sucked in a breath. A plume rising from her exhale in the cold damp air while her gloved hand traced a line along the scythe strapped to her saddle. Trained from the day she first entered the priesthood to accept the souls of those passing, she had always known her ending would be shrouded in spirit. Her fate to provide solace and warmth, comfort to others. An adherence to the passage of time. Not the evil of death, but the welcoming arms of a God who understood both the fear, and the memories frozen in time. Her heels urged the black stallion forward, with Lord Hope following. His sword's glow barely contained by the scabbard across his back.

55
WHEN RANGER'S
FALL

QUEEN'S ROAD, WESTERN GATE,
ERSTENBURGH

C onch's feet dragged against the Queen's Road. Mud-laden
boots leaving a wet trail of soil as she walked inexorably on.
Hooded, she had passed through the city gate. The Ranger's sigil
recognised from afar as her cloak billowed in the rain-sodden
breeze. With the hood wrapped tight and gloved hands gripping
the front to prevent the sodden night from entering, she had not
registered the city guards, or hailed them in the night. The guards
smiled as she passed through, joking about the weather from their
guard station. The wooden hut a welcome relief from the wet
and cold, with little to spur them to challenge a Ranger clearly
tired and in need of a bed. They let Conch past, and now her
feet trod the steps of the House of Honour. On reaching the huge
doors, husked fingers encased in damp leather pressed against the
stone, their oiled hinges opening for her. She spared no glance
for the carving of her God, nor the mighty dragon beneath their
feet. Ignoring Honour's sword held high and ready to strike down.

Conch pulled the cloak in tighter, as if the chamber were as cold as death's night, where the warmth of her God had spluttered out.

With her feet still dragging, the trail of debris continued to wind along the stone floor behind her. Each pebble or splash glowing with a faint white light amid the dark of the chamber. On reaching the plinth, Conch cast aside the cloak and unfurled the scarf encasing her chin. Exposed, her cheeks burst aflame with white fire. The skin flaked and rose into the chamber's cold air, fluttering on an unseen breeze. She fell to her knees, feeling the stone beneath. The pulse of the prayer crystal calling her spirit, but Conch's soul did not answer. It lay torn. Consumed bite by bite as the last wisp of a Constructor's spirit regained its strength, and with that *a purpose*. Having escaped from the Captain's ancient armour, it had waited in the shattered shell for one chance to resurrect. A passing life to consume and a chance at revenge. White eyes flared. Light searing into the darkness as her clothing burned upon the plinth. What was once Conch shrivelled, bones consumed by the heat. A memory lost, with nothing but ash in its wake. And Honour's plinth welcomed the spiritfire, ready to feed the Veil.

＋

Laoch stooped, keeping his body balanced and the sword in his hand. At his feet, just behind the rock, lay Ecne. Her pulse weak but chest still moving. Oisin was by her side. His face blistered and covered with ash but breathing still. Laoch made his decision, knowing well enough that Sura would both hate and love him for the choice made. Nathair's wing ripped clear. The metalled skin holed but spread out behind the huge beast and flapping in the wind. The dragon screamed defiance at the rock and stone, and with tail whirling, Nathair's gaze fell upon Laoch. A spittle of loathing dripped from between metal teeth. Wrenching itself clear and dragging hind legs out, the beast quivered, shaking the last of the rock from its body. The great beast beat its wings, head rising above the trees to trumpet freedom.

Heart swelling as Justice flooded him with his light, Laoch readied the sword. Nathair rose, wings beating. Lifting the mighty dragon only for it to crash down upon him with talons extended, ripping.

And Lady Death released. The black arrow scything through the hot air with the hooked tip striking the dragon's snout. The scream tore through the rain, swiftly followed by a searing flame washing towards the black stallion that reared in fear. Another blackened arrow lashed out—piercing the fire—crashing against the dragon's forehead between crystalline eyes. The arrow flared. Nathair's scales reflecting much of Death's spiritfire, with only the armoured plates left cracked and sizzled.

Lord Hope charged in. His mighty sword extending—growing as he drove onwards—his horse lathered with fear. The Lord sent his grace to calm the animal's mind, desperate to take the chance Lady Death had provided. He galloped towards a distracted Nathair swinging his blade, slicing under the scaled armour. The glowing edge cleaved into the metal-skin beneath, lava spurting from the rupture. An acidic hiss rose from the horse's neck and the animal reared—the pain too much for the Lord to quell though he was thrown clear. Landing with a crunch on his shoulder, he rolled to his feet, swinging his blade as the dragon's rear foot swatted him away—sending the Lord twirling into the rocks.

Penance strode out on foot. His mighty whip lashing, cracking in the air before Nathair's snout. The whip it well remembered, and hated, the one that had bound the mighty beast in the past. Dragging the weakened dragon from the air and binding it while the Gods buried it beneath rock and stone. Nathair flinched. A memory, Penance assumed, rising to the forefront of her mind. He strode forward, striking out. The purple energy lashed against the metal scales, scorching as it sought to wind around Nathair's neck. Lord Penance flicked the tip backwards, cracking the whip. Purple lightning arced before he lashed out once again towards the beast's head. And Nathair had waited for just that moment, the dragon's barbed tail slamming into the Lord's hip, cracking bone, smashing limbs.

Nathair shouted defiance to the forest. Bellowing her joy to the veil when her eyes flickered. The crimson within pulsing once, fading out—their colour drained. The head twitched before dropping, crashing into the trees beside Penance's limp body.

Laoch felt the talons tighten, the muscles, or whatever Nathair had beneath the skin, pulsing as its forefoot wrapped about his body. The squeeze choked the air from his lungs. His pelvis feeling the pressure, legs screaming. Beside him, wrapped in the taloned rear foot, Ecne lolled. Her eyes wild and laced with green. Laoch feared that Wisdom was taking its last, when Nathair's head twitched. The mighty skull turning his way and eyes shining a brilliant white. Lady Death screamed. The scythe sweeping down, slicing into the dragon's side, spilling lava-hot metal onto the ground. Nathair's mechanised muscles rippled, and Laoch sensed a sudden shift in the beast's purpose. Pressure beat downwards as the dragon's wings flapped once again with one limb striking Lady Death on the downward stroke, throwing her to the forest floor. The dragon heaved upwards—the slow, rhythmic beat rising in tempo as Nathair, Seeker of the Constructs, a Dragon of the Veil, rose above the forest.

Penance's priests threw themselves to the ground. Muddied and wet, exhausted by their labour, they watched. Fearful as the huge embodiment of their faith rose above the trees. Water and hot, molten metal dripped from wings and torso. White eyes seared into the darkness and, with another beat of the huge wings, Nathair passed from sight.

Rising from the mud, the priests searched for their stricken Lord. They soon found him wrapped around a rock with his hip smashed and eyes glazed with pain. Penance's hand was reaching out, fingertips within a hair's breadth of the glowing purple whip. The first priest to arrive listened to the whispered pleas of their Lord, lifting and placing the weapon of their God in his hands. Then fear finally gripped him, bowels releasing, as his Lord's hip and bone reformed. Blood rushed back in, skin resealed, and Penance rose with a cry of agony rooted deep within his soul. The priests dropped onto their knees; heads bowed. Waiting for the scourge as Lord Penance shone before them.

56
WHEN A HEART
SHOULD HURT

NATHAIR, NORTH ERSTEN FOREST

O *range. An orange light. Honour's calling.*
Laoch's eyes flickered. A voice within his head beseeching, demanding he awaken. Wind and rain lashed at his face, with memories flashing by of rock and soil and a dragon's claw ripping him from the earth. Laoch's lids sprang open, eyes fearful as he gazed over to the mighty dragon's chest riven with hardening metal as its blood cooled upon the wind. The heavy rhythm of the wings beat at his mind, though strangely he felt little fear.

How many times has death knocked at the last grain of sand today? Yet I still live.
The orange glow seeped into his eyes. The light infusing the dragon's scales and splashing across Ecne and Oisin who lay within the rear talons. A lump formed in Laoch's throat, one of fear and gratitude. A sense of togetherness in what was still to come. While he pondered those who fought and possibly died at his side,

a warmth spread across his chest. Enshrouding his heart, though with a caress, not a squeeze.

Sura?

The breath of her mind touched upon his. A presence, one of joy and hope. The glow extended, forming welcoming arms that pulled him inwards. And Laoch found himself lying upon a metalled floor, eyes drinking in the elven warrior who had taken his heart. Sura's hand cupped his chin and cheek, her thumb playing at the corner of his mouth. Fierce eyes drank him in, and Laoch rose, trying to pull her into his arms. And Sura stepped back, eyes locked on his, waiting without words. The Ranger stared, suddenly seeing beyond his need. The doorway behind stark and clear, seen through his love's spirit form.

He choked, acid rising, until the softness of her touch played across his mind.

"By my side, Laoch. It is all I asked for."

"I—"

A spirit finger touched upon his lips. He'd not seen her move. "You live, as does Oisin and Ecne. It is all that matters for now, to me. The Construct pulled me through. Saved my spirit from Nathair, but not my body. I would ask you not to grieve for this *is* me. I remember all I was and see much more. But the rest, the future, I cannot perceive. Except I remain here, with you, until Honour releases me."

Ecne coughed beside them, her eyes opening, the green lacing now gone. Sura reached out a calming hand, applying a touch upon the acolyte's forearm, sharing her relief with the young woman. Oisin lay curled by her side, wrapped around his weapons, a slow rise and fall to his chest. A whiff of flame ensconced his body, ash on the floor around him.

"Come on," she whispered into Laoch's ear. "We are needed. Let Oisin rest, he sleeps and heals."

Sura backed away. Laoch unable to do more than simply follow, his mind whirling. A glance to Ecne saw her push her top half up from the bronzed floor, but the effort was too much, and her attempt quickly faded away. Sura sent a wisp of Honour's light to fall upon the acolyte's shoulders. The energy enthused Ecne's body, allowing her to rise to her feet.

"How?" asked Laoch, watching as the link broke. "I don't understand."

"The sigil holds me here, no more, no less. Though I find I have control. Ecne, the crossbow. Don't leave it behind or Wisdom will rage at the ignorance."

The young woman grasped the heavy bow—the metal sigil still aglow with a faint, green light—and placed it upon her shoulder. She looked around the apparent corridor and realisation struck when she took in Sura's new form. Sadness wrapped itself around the acolyte's body, and she began to shake. Sura again reached out but this time to quell the woman's mind, sending a gentle warmth to wrap her thoughts and calm the emotions.

"How? Where? I can feel the beat—are we inside Nathair? I ...?" Ecne spun slowly around, the metal-ribbed hallway so similar to that of the Seven's Dragon House.

"I don't understand it, but yes. We are within Nathair, but not. Like a pocket inside a pocket, but we move with the dragon. It is how the Constructors first travelled under a veil because they never trusted their slaves to tell them true. At least, that's what Keran tells me."

"Keran? Who?"

"The spirit. The Captain who was within the Constructor's armour. We ... well we worked together to overcome Nathair, in the dragon's heart. He waits in the next room, though he is much pained by Nathair's evil. It is not an easy relationship."

Sura stepped through the doorway and entered a room awash with white light from the pulsating crystal. Laoch could make out the face within it, pressed against the façade. A man, maybe in his forties, eyes ablaze with shimmering skin. His hair replaced by metal scales and braided with razor spines. Two spirits intertwined—layered over the top of each other—much like the Seven's door where Leront's heart lay.

After today, it seems the lesser of the things I should worry about.

Sura let the fire enter her eyes. Honour's orange light aglow within the elven orbs that fell upon Laoch, thrumming with power. Laoch stepped back briefly, before fortifying his mind.

By your side.

"Keran, the Captain, controls Nathair. Yes? But his agenda is far from ours. He intends on using the dragon to raid the Constructors' home realm, Innealtóir. The realm from where humans fled—your people—before the Veils were formed."

"Raid? Where is this Innealtóir? Over the ocean to the west?"

"No," said the Captain, the crystal pulsating with the words, his voice rasping. *"Another place, another world. We will slide through the veils and fall upon the Constructors. Find a way to fight back. For they have come for my people and when they are done, they will come for you. They will enslave you. Feed upon you, as they did in the past, before the Seven freed us all. We must go."*

"And if we choose otherwise," said Laoch, hand touching the pommel of Justice's sword.

"No matter. I am a spirit, so the sword is of little use, Ranger Laoch. And the decision has been made. Besides, I think you will find the Seven's residual spirits bound in the sigils agree. My arrival here may well have led to the Constructors' eyes falling upon your people, and therefore I must make reparation for both. This is something we should do together."

Sura grimaced, and then drew Laoch's attention, locking eyes. "I have seen their world, though in its past. I experienced Nathair's memory from a thousand years ago. She came here on the hunt for humans, only for three of your Seven Magi to entrap her. It was a twisted, evil place, and I saw enslaved life everywhere. If this is what is coming for us, then we must take the chance."

"Us?"

Sura glanced to the floor, then towards Ecne and finally Laoch. Narrowing her eyes, a flair of orange flecking the edges. "Nathair is a ... well a Spirit Walker. Corrupted by the Constructors. One of my kind, though from another realm. A shaman warped by their madness and lost to us. She is now a seeker of humans for her masters, so they both may feed. They drink your very souls, Laoch, bit by bit, or farm you like animals. My people, they either corrupt or feed upon—if they can walk with spirits they have a purpose. Otherwise, we are just in the way."

"There is so much to take in, Sura. After what we've been through, we need time to rest, to recuperate. And to think."

"That time has passed," said Keran, his form swirling about the crystal before settling again. *"We approach the first veil now. There is no going back, Laoch. Not yet. I ride Nathair but do not yet have full control. I nudged the dragon's spirit to return home, to inform her masters, and on that she is set."*

"Inform? Then you'll be opening us up to these creatures whatever happens."

"I hope to prevent that. There will be a little time before we arrive on Innealtóir. Time to wrestle with her spirit."

Laoch ran a hand over his sweat-stained and soot covered face, looking down upon the fingers. The ash remained pungent. Sparking memories of the flame that had taken Sura from him. The Captain had saved her spirit, he knew that. Brought her through into this 'pocket' when it could have chosen to ignore her. It meant something.

I just don't know what.

A warmth spread from his hip, and Laoch spared a side-eyed glance down to his sword. The God's weapon having remained in the form of his favoured blade. There was a comfort there, a connection, and a responding pulse from Fate's bow washed across his back. The gentle combination, as far as he could tell on this mad day, soothed his aches and pains. Easing the encroaching grief addling his mind. Laoch had always retained a natural distrust of anyone forcing him in one direction, borne from his own personal pain, but there seemed a consensus among the living and the dead.

One minute I'm close to decommission, the next I'm in the fierce but gentle arms of someone I love. Only for a great big bastard not-so-symbolic dragon to take her from me. Yet I-I am not grieving. Not yet. I sense the pain, but distant. Locked away. Is this Justice's touch? Or Fate's weave? Am I just a tool, more useful if the pain is hidden?

"Okay, Captain. I see we have little choice. But cross me, or any of my people, and I set Sura on yer. Understand?"

57
AS FOUNDATIONS CRUMBLE

FORBIDDEN LIBRARY, THE HOUSE OF
WISDOM, ERSTENBURGH

Queen Erin pushed the ham and eggs aside, barely touched. The cold and gelatinous meal as unappetising as the thoughts streaming through her head. Her mind struggled to make sense of what she read. The words had begun to merge into one as she scanned from page to page. The picture template had set her heart racing—an imaginative rendition of a gate in the ether that trailed into the sky like a river of rainbow light. At the side, the Seven stood, though not the Seven as depicted upon the House ceilings or doorways. These were muddied, weary. Cloaks torn and mirrored armour, pierced. Around them gathered a glowing horde—metal armoured as the Seven were—that hammered away with light and weapons at the heroes who held them back while others fled. In the orange, smoke racked sky, two dragons swooped. Again, these were not the near lizard like creatures that flew from tree to tree in the foothills of the southern reaches. Or the Unspoken's evil symbolised upon the House ceilings. These appeared almost as if they were built by Meister Arknold. Joints and metal struts. Eyes aglow, but crystalline and faceted like some of the windows in the Houses or the rings she wore. It struck far more fear than the drily written words of a Meister, and she guessed even these were interpretations rather than the fear-filled flow a witness would produce. Either way, they heralded the lies of the Houses. That the church of the Seven had deliberately veiled humankind's eyes to the truth, and if she wasn't mistaken, by the order of the Gods themselves. To hide here, away from the Constructors who fed upon them, and to keep the Dragons of the Veil—those beasts that had broken the gate in their pursuit—from rising again.

Yet there were hints. Subtleties in the text alluding to some-thing deeper, hidden. She had always seen the Veils as the Gods' heavens where they awaited their flocks. But the book hinted at more—a deeper, physical existence. That the dragon was real, and not an allegory for evil and the refusing of scripture, had pulled the keystone from her belief. But the revelation the Veils were more than just their specific heavens ensured her faith crumbled.

A hand reached across; the Prime's ring and seal of office prominent on one finger. Jacka had been reading a copy. Its pages surely less old, but not by much—a painstaking recreation. Briefly she wondered if they had copied out the subtleties of the original text to keep the faithful in deeper ignorance.

The hand broke with decorum, landing on her forearm, and she looked to the Prime with wide eyes, unsure of what it meant. But the fear in his eyes spoke for him, and he proffered a handkerchief with the other. Blinking, she realised that tears were flowing. The salt-filled pain of lost belief streaming down her cheek and one drip away from the precious book. Queen Erin took the cloth, wiping away at her cheeks and dabbing her eyes. The agony welled, stifling her breath. The air refusing to release from her lungs as her choking sob broke the near silence.

A dread crept up Jacka's spine. A fear for what to do with the steel-willed Queen wracked with the same sorrow the book had placed in his own heart. He wanted to hold her, whisper the pain away. Bring hope where her Consort would simply feed paranoia and religious fury. A forbidden need that gnawed at him.

A movement in the air, barely perceptible, marked the purple cloaked servant's passing. He brushed by, gathering the woman in his arms, letting her free the pain. Sneed's eyes fell upon the Prime—not with admonishment at his indecision, but with the look he always wore. For years, Jacka had put the Lords of Penance down as overacting purveyors of mummery. Drumming up business for their House by preaching self-disgust. But the look Sneed bore, and his Lord, now spoke of the burden of *knowing*. That the pain was real, just not how they wanted the world to perceive it. For if the people knew that a constant shadow lay over their future, that the dragons and their masters awaited a chance to fall upon them, to feed, he suspected the outcome would be very different. Not an ordered world with lives being led in ignorance, babies being born, laughter upon their lips. More likely a disordered, in-fighting world, where stress and constant fear would draw the worst out of humanity. The Union would crash. Fear reigning and the umbrella of the Queen and the Seven Houses broken.

I can see the purpose of their secrecy. But there is something more to this. Hidden deeper.

And angry, jealous eyes fell upon the Lord's servant who held his Queen.

58
BE IT EVIL OF SPIRIT

House of Honour, Erstenburgh

H onour's Priest-in-Waiting brushed the stone walkway between the pews. Eyes scanning side to side, tutting at the
younger priests who busied themselves cleaning and preparing
for the first Mass. It was early, and this morn the outlying farmers
would come for the huge weekly market. Many would be brim-
ming with excitement. Ready to pray and then spend the day
selling their wares. Perhaps buying a few themselves before an
evening spent in the drinking dens and a night on the wagon.
Nesca blushed briefly. Memories of her own time bringing the
fattened lambs to the market, and the night spent with whoever
had taken her fancy that day. Never frowned upon, for the world
was young, wide and the joy of life needed celebrating. For all the
rules of scripture: how to pray, when to pray, even the words to
use—the God's offering and what books to read by the fire—none
of it sought to bar the people from a good life. Only the House
of Penance preached punishment, and often for the temptation
of turning away from the Seven. His flock garnering the deepest
faith as he drew them back in.

No, this was a good time, with only the spectre of the Unbelievers shadowing the Union. And, after serving her God for the three years expected of all children, she could read and write. Spout scripture and feel truly at home in the world. Yet here she was, overseeing her own acolytes, her time as Honour's Priest-in-Waiting now five years passed. A choice taken with joy and belonging.

Nesca shooed her acolytes away. The chamber spick and span, the prayer stone swept and ready for the first worshippers of the day. Only one more job left to do. Checking the acolytes had left, she pulled the fist-sized crystal from her robes. Placing the orange stone upon the plinth, she covered it with a thick, black cloth. The warmth rippled up her hand, as it always did, and she felt the love for Lady Honour pour into the jewel. A daily duty, and on the best days the faithful could pour their love into three or four of Honour's crystals. The power held within of great import, and her privilege to stand at her Lady's side as she gave up the prayers to Honour's Veil. A curtain of power to keep the evil of the dragon at bay and fortify their God in the fight to keep them safe.

She felt the ripple fade, and on the last, gentle pulse, gathered the stone within the blackened material. Nesca slipped it inside her robe. Glancing up, she signalled she was finished, and walked to Lady Honour's chambers. She knew the suffering that would take place. The pain of transference a burden the Lady shared with all the leaders of the Houses. The withered and blackened arm a result of so much love and faith given to Honour's Veil. A burden of office, and though she had not witnessed it yet, one the Priests-in Waiting knew would be one of their fates as Death's sand poured. Nesca would gladly take on the obligation, if, as seemed likely, she was chosen. Not the reason she shared the occasional night with Lady Honour, but the whispered words of encouragement meant much.

Her rap on the door was met with a voiced response, and Nesca opened it to find Lady Honour already resplendent in her orange robes. At her side, Pintar, the Lady's servant. Unlike for the House of Penance, most House leaders stayed until deemed unfit of mind by the Council or had passed under Death's hourglass. Pintar had been a Priest-in-Waiting. One passed over, who had left in a fit of pique before life took him along a path to the Unbelievers. He had returned, heart sore, with Lady Honour lifting the man and bestowing his new role. A salve, some say as a repentance for his fallen honour. Others that the Lady was simply kind. Either way, Pintar served with as much love as the rest, and he waited with the siphon and the black elixir the Lady would need after the Wyrding.

Nesca handed over the wrapped crystal, bowing her head as the Lady smiled her way, taking the bundle with a thank you. She witnessed the transference. A flock's prayers pouring into the Wyrding stone, its facets shimmering, dancing upon the white walls. The Priest-in-Waiting then took her leave. Turning and exiting through the door, mind full of the wonders she may see in the future if she were ever to be the Lady. To see Honour's Veil, to touch heaven itself.

Before the door closed, a man's deathly scream rattled the frame. A white light breaking through, bathing Nesca's back and washing the corridor. She turned to help, the brightness blinding her in the desperation to help Lady Honour. The scream doubled in intensity. Building towards an agony Nesca's mind fought to blank out, eventually choosing the void as a sanctuary. With her mind spiralling into the unconsciousness, the wail faded into a long, painful wall of white fire.

59
A BEACON OF HATE

NORTH ERSTEN FOREST

Lord Penance knelt before the dying horse with hands upon its neck, feeling the pain inside. He could do nothing but choose the method of the animal's death—either by sword stroke or over a long, agonised wait as the injuries took their toll. He rose, sweeping the scourge back. The weapon transforming as he brought it down, a sword's keen edge biting into the horse's neck. Blood pooled on the ground with a last breath steaming the air.

He stepped back and held his hands out, letting a silent prayer slip between his lips. Lord Hope stood beside him, a branch he'd cut easing the pain in his legs while the last of his power healed his broken body. Lady Death's burns were also slowly receding. Blisters on her face and hands draining as Penance's priests stared, emotions spinning as they watched fearfully on. A shiver far beyond that caused by cold and damp, quivered through them all.

A brilliance washed across the forest canopy. Pure white, penetrating deep below the trees and bathing the High Lord and his people in its power. Lord Penance's shoulders drooped; the weight of his burden doubled by the power thrumming around him. Dread took hold of him then. His expectation that the dragon was the source dashed by the pillar of light driving upwards above the trees.

Towards the Veils and for all to see.

And I am so new to these powers.

He let an odd smile cross his lips, watching as the priests' eyes rose to the column of light piercing the clouds above. It meant so many things, not least that the Houses of the Seven may well fall in the next few hours. A wave of lost faith would surely follow. One they needed to twist so the flocks turned again to the Houses in search of hope.

But at least I don't have to kill my servants to keep the secret. A flicker of light in the dark.

A tug at his skeleton was the first sign. Then a lifting, a pull of his spirit as the Soul Tear rippled through the realm. It was brief, and he pressed his power inwards, holding on to that which he was while observing the priests' struggle. Their spirits sliding away from their core centre. He reached out a hand, letting the purple light flow and wreath his people. Protecting them from the fear that would no doubt be running through the people of the city. It passed, far more quickly than the last. Likely a sign the penetration was outward and therefore most likely the column of light. A beacon he knew would call the Constructors, rather than the Dragon of the Veil that roared above them with the same intent.

How long to prepare? A thousand years we hid, only to be exposed by that same mechanism. Hiding the truth—veiling it under scripture, and now unprepared for what is to come. My penance. Is the burden too heavy?

———

Sneed felt the disconnect. The moment the Soul Tear threatened to pull his *self* from his body. He gathered his power, meek though it was with the suppressant he took along with the faithful. Using the skills honed during his time as High Lord, he contained his spirit. But he let the sobbing Queen feel it all, and her Prime. It wouldn't have taken much. Just the caress of his touch. A soft purple light to encase her spirit, holding it in place until the Tear healed, or the Veils collapsed. Yet their burden was necessary, a sign of what was to come. And as it passed, he probed outwards, sensing that both their spirits still held tight. With heartfelt relief, he let his power touch their spirits and eased them back within their bodies. He could have calmed their minds, brought some peace.

But we may need that dread, a conduit to ready them both for the trials ahead. And maybe that fear will help us if ... if the High Lord takes the ultimate step and reveals our greatest deceit. It may well come to pass that we have to reach out to ... to her.

And was that Nathair? I think not. The books state she gated through the Veils, or at the very least hid her presence, sliding between the ripples of spiritfire. That was a force, like a punch. And brief. Outward, maybe?

Sneed let the Queen go. Easing himself back and looking across to the doorway where Lord Wisdom stood, his skin sallow, tears streaming down his cheeks. Two of his Priests-in-Waiting stood behind him with one hand under their cloaks, their fingers on the Gods' weapons all priests carried as a sign of their status. Sneed let a grim smile pass. The Queen's eyes whirring as he looked down upon her and then towards Jacka. The recovery would be quick, but he doubted the emotional effects would pass so easily. The first rupture had disturbed the people, and though calmed swiftly by the Houses, they had increased the frequency of their services. Here, the Houses had talked of the Heavens' Veils need for their prayers, and in turn the suppressant calmed their minds. As true as that need was, he doubted the faithful would respond so positively this time. Fear bred upon incidence, and they needed a focus for it that wasn't the Houses. His eyes alighted across Jacka, the memory of his recent words alighting in his mind.

60

WARRIORS OF SPIRIT AND BONE

NATHAIR, ABOVE ERSTEN FOREST

Nathair's will pressed against the Captain's. The spirit surging, rushing from side to side, battering against the spiritfire sphere he had wrapped around the beast. Though Keran understood what he contained was not a dragon, it was how the Spirit Walker perceived itself—as the embodiment of its mechanical casing. When the wings beat, Nathair's spirit drummed to the same rhythm. Where the scaled legs trailed, the spirit, in its mind, commanded every twitch and flinch of the curled talons. It was Nathair—a synergy between machine and spirit. But to the Captain, accepting that was the first step towards losing his control. He needed to separate the Schenterenta shaman, a Spirit Walker, from the mechanised dragon. Otherwise, the size and scope of the task would be overwhelming. Currently it raged inside the spirit-containment. Forming and reforming itself between the image of the metal-scaled dragon and the twisted, sick, elf from which it had been torn. It was in those moments the Captain pressed, surging through the sphere in an attempt to dominate the spirit. Hoping to bend it fully to his will—combining whispered soothings with the demands of a master to a slave. During those encounters, he hoped to glimpse memories of the shaman's past. Of a life spent in ritual and communion with the spirits, helping her tribe. But nothing came. Whether these had been torn from the elf during her entrapment and subjugation, or the memories were so bitter she'd burned them away, he could not tell. What remained was a shell forged by slavery. A fragile jar which it filled with its perception of what Nathair should be. And that fragility was the danger. The moment that layer cracked and fell, and the spirit was released, the mighty dragon would cease to function. And he had only grazed the surface of *how* the enslaved Schenterenta controlled and manipulated the mechanisms driving the artifice dragon. So yes, he was riding the dragon, not controlling it. Whispering in the ear of Nathair's spirit rather than directing the wings to beat, and it was dangerous.

"Nathair, we approach the first veil." The whisper was low, informative. "We need to slip through quietly, not disturb those below, give them less time to prepare for our return."

'Yesss, Master'

Keran sensed the surge of power within Nathair's horns, realising the glittering metal spines were more than just a Constructor affectation. Nathair's energy surged upwards, filling the space between. White light that spiralled in on itself, building with each sweep and curve. The moment it released, Keran experienced a moment of panic as it roiled towards the spirit curtain. His fear for the veil, however, was built on his ignorance of the beast. The spiritfire thinned, focused into a single blade, slicing the curtain across the veil with precision. The mighty dragon slipped through the envelope with one delicate wingbeat and the veil's light immersed the scales in an orange glow.

The Dragon of the Veil slid through the curtain, and despite remembering the impact of the glyphs on entry, Keran was unconcerned. The veil's spiritfire remained passive, inert, and whatever façade the Constructor's hunter used left it unaware. He sensed the dragon's temptation to drink of the power, to feast and replenish its reserves after the enforced slumber. He quelled that thought, worried it would weaken the veil to the eyes of the Constructors, and allow what was below to be seen. The inner veil was the Seven's last defence, and if he was to allow the dragon to feed, it would be on the outer veil. The vast and thinly spread outer layer where it would have least detriment to the realm.

Inside Nathair, his new companions stirred. They all required sleep, healing and recuperation, even a little food. All things he had long since left behind. The latter had the Captain stumped with both he, and the Constructors, not partaking of physical nutrients to sustain themselves. And nor the dragon, though he surmised there had to be some form of mechanical degradation that required repair. So, he'd settled for the alternative and gently let the bodies slip into a hibernation he named sleep, including the newly severed spirit who faded into Honour's spear. Reducing their needs down to a bare minimum allowed the Gods' sigils to draw from Nathair's meagre stores, and in turn enrich their wielders. The Gods' spiritfire healed wounds, soothed pained minds, and allowed his companions to recover as they broke through the veils, seeking a pathway to Innealtóir. Laoch had been the last to fall into an unconscious state, determined he would keep watch over Oisin, and only succumbing once both Fate and Justice leant a hand easing his turbulent mind. The Captain admired the grim determination, sensing the duty coursing through Laoch, and the inner pain of his loss besides. It tugged at his own past. Memories that would never cease reminding him of the sorrow. Yet his success in raising Nathair was a balm, calming those thoughts. Not redemption, not yet, but a second step on that path.

The object of Laoch's love and grief rested the least easy, her spirit mind opened by the contact with himself. An innate Spirit Walker, a grieving twin, shielded from her ability by the might of the Sevens' Veils. He assumed they drew from whatever spiritfire they could find, and though Keran had not yet discovered the main source of their sheer power, he could sense the angry spirits of the Schenterenta swimming amid Honour's Veil. The elves' shamans had not lost their ability to summon their ancestors—the spirts were simply locked away behind the veil curtain. The Captain let his spirit mind slide over the restless elven spirit. Touching upon the love she returned for the Ranger, finding his own comfort in its strength. Though a sad tale. One still to be fully played out, a tinge of guilt running through him as he thought of the prolonging of grief he had likely caused.

Ecne lay curled upon the floor with Wisdom pulsing a gentle rhythm to calm the acolyte's mind. Keran sensed her discomfort. The discoveries piled on top of each other, fracturing her certainty about the world. But she was young, still flexible. Her belief and knowledge would heal and form a truce as necessity played its part. Somewhere in the maelstrom the Learned would find a firm foundation to rebuild and would be stronger for it. At least, that was the path he foresaw, but Fate forever played a mean hand.

Keran felt Nathair open the next curtain, slicing through and gently sweeping into the ensuing veil. He waited, counting time, accepting they were safe as Nathair's wingbeat drove them on. Foreboding fell upon him then—the spirit turning to find Fate's bow pulsing nearby. The spirit weapon an enigma, and he was unsure of how it came to pass. There was an absence, perhaps a lack of personality that spoke of a recent change. The flicker of Fate was so weak she lay buried in a deep slumber, though still the sigil drew upon Nathair. Something had come to pass beyond what he was party to, and a need to know sat heavy upon his mind.

A conduit perhaps. One that drained heavily of the Magi they named Fate. Was it their doing? Forming a connection between herself and the human world that I cannot see? An avatar, perhaps. So many questions.

Four of the Seven were within Nathair. An element of each rooted in the sigil, though all far from the great Magi they had once been. A sliver of their soul and deeply connected. And if Fate had made such a link that had been severed, then what became of that avatar? Had it dissipated on death?

Looking at Sura, you would think not.

Without any care for privacy, he analysed her exposed spirit. Finding the bond with Honour absolute. A pact between Magi and spirit. An avatar, sealed in their souls even if Honour denied it.

Perhaps that is what happened to Fate, her embodiment lost in the battle.

I just wonder if she chose wisely?

Keran let a ghost of a smile pass across fated lips.

———

The weak blue glow seeped through the doorway, keeping low along the ground and past the purple-robed Priests-in-Waiting guarding the dragon carved door. With hardly a glimmer, Gowan flowed unnoticed, letting the energy maintain the last vestige of her spirit form as the dragon's heart called. Wrapping herself around the table leg, she spiralled up. Edging over the dark table-top to alight next to the waiting heart.

She wreathed a facet before sliding through the crystal. The solidity of its embrace welcome as she merged with the bonded stone and began drawing what she could from the room. Leront railed, but they were entwined. He as much a part of her as she him, yet still dominated, weak. For now.

Memories. Images of the battle with Nathair flickered across those bonds—Gowan using these to reinforce her control—ensuring Leront knew of the fight with his sister, and the lives she'd helped save. Without Fate, she needed all her will and guile if she was to remain in control of the dragon spirit, to be of use against what was coming. Fate had shown her the weft and the weave, the possible futures now the Veils had been penetrated. That fear had kept Gowan from dispersing despite giving her near all to save Laoch at Sura's behest. And it drove her now.

According to Leront, they are both Dragons of the Veil. What would become of Brandshold should more arrive? And their masters.

61

THE STRENGTH OF A QUEEN'S WILL

THE WHITE PALACE, ERSTENBURGH

L ord Penance sucked in a pained breath, his ribs sore and hips twinging as if his God were reminding him of the penance he bore. Though, if he were honest, the Captain of the City Guard was far more of a punishment than anything his God could have contrived. The moustached man, his helm shining in the sunlight that finally broke through the clouds, could achieve a perturbed and vexed stance with a mere shift of his head and body.

Truly, if I were to choose a fate for our Prince, nothing would compare to spending an hour in a cell with this man.

"Lord Penance, this is a matter of State. The Prince should be chained in our deepest darkest jail, or the highest tower of our city prison. Merely forcing him into one of your House's cells seems rather a ... a light response for treason."

The High Lord let his eyebrow shift up, one eye drooping while his purple toothed scowl completed the mummery. The man's flinch brought a little glee to his pained soul. The captain's eyes downcast in response.

"The Queen has spoken, Captain Mordant, and the Prince Consort is to remain with us until the case is fully heard. Though his connection with the Unbelievers appears proven, he still has the right under the scripture to plead his case. Honour and Fate would not see it any other way. You do *know* your scripture, Captain?"

"Yes, Lord Penance. But this is ..."

"Special? I agree," cut in Prime Vardrin, eyes darting to the Queen who appeared unsteady and pale upon the throne above them. "But your time would be better spent organising the local militia and preparing for whatever the horde has in store for us. Is that not right, my Queen?"

Queen Erin winced, her heart pounding as Jacka brought her back from the brink. Her mind still spinning as the layers of the Houses' deception peeled back like a rotten onion. She glanced down at the collection of dignitaries below. Each here to hear her words as they prepared for yet another sham. She sat up, feeling the expectation fall upon her.

"It is, Prime Vardrin," she squeezed the errant thoughts away, needing to act so the Union did not split at its precarious seams. The last thing she needed was for the Houses to be seen as holding her realm together. They had enough tendrils woven into her country, and her court, and she needed to take some control. Otherwise, she would simply be their puppet, and having seen their theatre already, she wanted to rewrite some of the script they had in mind. "We do need to ensure we have a plan, Captain. The City Guard will be responsible for much, and Lord Penance has offered to take the burden of the Prince Consort's treason for now. The dragon appears to have left. Perhaps the destruction of the Erin's Wrath was the Unspoken's main goal. Once we have our army recalled, and our borders set, then we can look again." She waved her hand, dismissing Captain Mordant. He bowed stiffly and, keeping his eyes averted from Lord Penance, turned to leave. As he did, he gave Prime Vardrin a stare full of anger and frustration. The Prime took note; Mordant was a trusted servant, one they needed to build the defence of the city around. Any whiff of future trouble was an issue, and perhaps he needed to draw him back into the fold before that happened.

"Now Grand Meister Arknold and Meister Kinst," Queen Erin glanced over to Lord Penance, positive she caught the briefest of smiles as the Meisters stepped forward. "The Gods' Council has reviewed your requests about scripture." Both Meisters looked awkwardly to each other, and then Lord Penance, who bared his purple teeth in a grimace full of remorse.

"What review?" asked Kinst, a lump forming in her chest as she spoke. "I was asked to ..."

"Withdraw it?" jumped in Jacka. "Yes, but I requested the Council look again on the Queen's behalf. It was some time ago, but the Council's workings can be slow. Am I right, Lord Penance?"

"At times, yes. Though we can be hasty when required. You have permission to 'dabble' Grand Meister, though the Seven only knows where it will lead. Lord Wisdom is to oversee and may have some insight for you. Should you cross the word of our Gods, he will make the judgements necessary. Please do not vex him as he brings it all to me if you do."

"Do we have ... boundaries?" asked Arknold, looking to the Lord and then the Queen.

"See the safety of the realm as vital. Lord Wisdom will corral your thoughts, keep you within the confines of what we regard as appropriate."

The Queen gave a smile that spoke of dismissal, and both Meisters bowed and turned away. A spark of excitement barely held in as they headed for the doors.

Lord Penance eased himself into the wooden chair, his hip once again complaining as he adjusted. The remaining collection of local village mayors and councillors of no interest to him right now. He let the time wash over him, mind cast over the beat of a dragon's wings and how long they would have to prepare. They were Seven. Yet of lesser stature than the Magi who brought them to the realm, their spiritfire weapons providing a spark of hope when they were discovered by Lorent. The second dragon of the slave hunters. The one whose great mechanism was all but destroyed, the heart locked away. And inside its corpse, four of the Gods' Weapons had been stored. The first of the Seven to lay their lives for their people, giving of themselves to build the inner Veils. That was until Nathair broke through, seeking them out. The remaining three Magi were too weak on their own—unable to bring it down, nor kill the mighty dragon. Only for luck to intervene.

Leront's location had been lost amid the same purge of Nathair's whereabouts, and with it the four weapons. And now they were lost again. Taken, he assumed, by the defenders who had fought the pseudo-Constructs left dead around Leront's resting place. Weapons that awoke the mighty Nathair and subsequently fell to the beast as it fled to seek its masters. There was no greater loss than those weapons of Honour, Fate, Justice and Wisdom—with them gone, even faith fades.

The High Lord shifted in his chair once again. This time due to the despair that lay upon his shoulders, and no penance would ever relieve that pain. A thousand years of guile and suppression shattered in one night.

It is time to speak to our last vestige of hope. If she will listen.

A revelation that will break our faith, I fear. And the Houses may fall.

But what other choice is there?

"Lord Penance?" The Queen's voice cut through his thoughts, dragging him away from the gloom settling around his heart.

"Sorry, my Queen." He looked around, the Queen's open-air Audience Chamber empty for all but him, Jacka and the Queen. "Apologies, a momentary wandering of my mind."

"You have been through much, Lord Penance. I understand. But we need to look ahead, to define just how much we reveal to the masses about the Gods' Houses and their purpose."

"I agree, and the Council will meet to pro—"

"No, Lord Penance. This is not a matter for the Houses on their own. Counsel needs to be sought from the Crown. I represent the people of Brandshold and to a degree the Union, and these decisions cannot be left to those who chose deception, however well meant. Strength will only come from the Houses, my Lord, if there is certainty in tandem with the Crown. My will is to be heard."

A purple grin washed over him; the High Lord unable to maintain his usual grim façade.

Ah, perhaps there is more hope than I thought.

62

WHEN UNSPOKEN HOPE RIDES A DRAGON'S WINGS

ANVIL, THE UNSPOKEN LANDS, HANDREN MOUNTAINS

A porcelain hand rested against the silver-laced marble. The delicate fingers gently caressed the cold stone, tracing the metal with what many would mistake for awe. Ice-blue eyes followed the lines, breathing in the icy air and holding that breath for a fraction longer than most, before exhaling. The billow of warmed air rippled in on itself, dancing in the sunlight that rode the mountain top, dust motes glinting. The orange, flame edged sleeve swished against the smooth marble as the fingers continued to kiss the stone, exposing the white arm beneath to the cold—though little notice was taken. Hairs did not rise, nor dimples form.

Mmmm. A glamour wasted when there is no one here to see. One of my best.

The blood-red lips curved into a thoughtful smile; lips pursed. A metallic dust powdered the high cheekbones and across the flickering eyelids, its shade matched to the flame red hair crowning the porcelain face. A moment of joy graced those eyes as a warmth tingled along her fingertips, and the Unspoken stepped back from the intricate doors, admiring their beauty.

"An Chéad," the red lips whispered, before kissing delicate fingers and placing them back on the cold stone. "It is time. I think your rest has come to an end."

The doors swung inwards. The hinges smooth. A series of cogs and pulleys near silent as they whirred behind the stone. The Unspoken waited, admiring the simple beauty of the mechanism as the ten-yard-high doors eased inwards.

"Some things I miss," she breathed, the words hanging in the frozen air as she stepped through. One side of the chamber lay exposed to the valley. The balcony huge and windowless, greeting the morning sun as it pierced each new day. Curled upon the grey stone floor, the scarlet dragon lay wrapped around the marbled steps leading up to her throne. Its snout nuzzling the west side. The razor-edged tail wrapped once around the steps and the crimson-scaled body before coming to rest on the throne's east side, arrow straight, menacing those that oft waited below. The eyes, usually dulled, burnt orange in the morning light, shimmering against the marble walls, lighting the Unspoken as she approached the mighty dragon.

"A symbol no longer, An Chéad. You are needed, my time may have come to an end, unless you have finally weakened.

Ignoring the crystalline, ice-like throne—its semi-circular form akin to a cogged wheel—she ran her hand along the tail. Fingers traced against the base of the spines until she reached the dragon's torso where they stood proud, equalling the size of a short sword, but twice as sharp. Her smile wavered from joy to uncertainty. Placing both hands against the ribs, before sighing as the scales pulsed. She pushed on through, forearms and finally shoulders sliding impossibly inwards as no door had opened.

The room smelt of oil and grease, triggering memories of a flight long past. The dive through the newly formed veils. The already fired glyphs mere wisps on the onrushing wind as An Chéad broke through the final curtain. Piercing the cloud, he had seen

Nathair rear back, the dragon's huge jaws wide and sword-like teeth glistening with human blood and gore. All this had poured from An Chéad's heart crystal, washing this very room. The Inhibitors within caught up in the adrenaline—for Nathair fought her Emperor's favourite pets, three of the Seven. They had been found.

All but one Inhibitor had sung with the joy. One whose eyes drank in the blue-grey mountains, the sun that capped the highest, the air clear of smog and dust. One whose heart broke for her own loss in that moment. Another layer of distant memories rippling through her spirit. Naked feet pressed into sweet, emerald grass. The air cold and clean, yet a warm sun on her neck. The tinkle of a stream splashing upon the rocks, brown eyes looking upon her with unfettered love and devotion. Ghosts she could not reach, and the joy flipped to anger. Her Inhibitor's sword, a soulreaver, driven deep into the back of the Controller, draining the life from one of her own. The other looked on in shock. Lidless eyes accusing, raising hands to strike her down with white fire. The engorged blade whipped out, slicing the hands, sending them spinning to spurt dust upon the dragon's heart. White fire then crackled from the swords tip, lashing the open-mouthed Inhibitor, draining the last of his life.

And the Unspoken had fallen to her knees. Spirit mind wreathed in her own treachery, yet somehow freed. Sucking in a dust-filled breath, she had pushed herself up, white eyes falling upon the pulsing crystal. With the soulreaver in hand, she had laid her gauntlets upon one facet. And sensing the twisted life within, poured the furious spirits of her now dead brothers into the crystal, quelling the slaved Spirit Walker. Subjugating its mind to hers while the power lasted.

An Chéad had quivered. His mighty scaled wings pounding the sky, motors and cogs straining in unison as the blood-red dragon tore down towards Nathair. Talons extended, he slammed onto the huge machine's back. The squeal of metal upon metal tearing through the air until the talons gripped hold. With her wings held fast, Nathair plummeted to the rock floor, head smashing against stone and the body crumpling behind. It had been sudden. The Unspoken almost in shock at her own actions, stunned as Nathair let out a roar that shook the ground.

"Ah, so many years ago, An Chéad. Time has passed so slowly. Yet it only feels like a moment of freedom amid my mountains. I do not want it to end." The delicate, porcelain hand stroked the crystal, the glamour shattering with a silvered gauntlet pressed on the stone in its place. "But Lord Penance is right, we must prepare. No more charades, and no more shall I be the *false enemy* of his kind. He declares the Crusades will be at an end, and the true enemy of humanity will soon be announced. But not yet. The Houses of the Seven built on the charade of my *Unspoken evil* will fall if they move too fast. But he says they have muted that threat to focus on their own. And we must do the same, my Dragon of the Veil."

Ancient lungs drew in a pointless breath. White eyes sunk deep into aged, leathered skin focused into the depths of the pulsing crystal. Behind her the pocket slid open. A tendril of her spirit reaching towards the ice-spiked throne. The marble beneath it thrummed with power, the metal-laced throughout the walls and doors joining the cacophony. A thousand years of sipping upon her flock, the Unbelievers that saw enlightenment under the Unspoken's wing, streamed into the Inhibitor. An Chéad screamed, writhing within the stone. Awoken and subjugated in one stroke of pure spiritfire.

"And now we are one."

The bearded head rose first from the floor. The scrape of forged metal upon stone reverberating around the throne room. Crystalline eyes flickered, the orange glow increasing as the Unspoken awoke the enthused and twisted Spirit Walker within. She felt the pulse ripple through the pistons, and the sinuous, scaled body lift from the marble. The screech of age-old joints and connections were soon smoothed as An Chéad spread himself amid the machinations of the dragon form. Reading the needs of each, sending the spiritfire to ease and lubricate.

A shiver ran through the Unspoken. A pleasure unrivalled even in the days of unbridled feeding. The dragon matched her response, scales lifting, popping and realigning. The jaw agape though no sound slipped out. Four great legs pressed into the marbled floor, the claws sparkling with white spiritfire as they leeched the stone. Awkward at first, the forelegs creaked forward until the Unspoken—bound with An Chéad—sent out spiritfire to wreath the knees and ankles, smoothing each movement. The scarlet dragon padded towards the open gallery, eyes flashing as the sun poured inwards, heated breath billowing as it drew itself out along the balcony to overlook the green valley below.

The Unspoken commanded An Chéad and the dragon's crystalline eyes responded, focusing upon her valley below, sharing the vision of the home she had created. Fluted columns towered straight and true, rising from the valley floor amid the myriad of trees and square blocked buildings. Each conveyed the beauty of simplicity, functionality. Layers of precisely cut stone that rose from the surrounding flora, with each storey slightly smaller than the last. No smoke rose, nor chimneys churning fire and ash. The people, her people, revelled in the beauty as they walked under the canopy of a multitude of trees.

"This is our home, An Chéad. One of my creating. I do not want to return to the choking ash and smoke. Nor the death and fire. Here, that which is me, my spirit, remains free and I am Queen. This is what you protect now, for the Constructors will come. We are drawn to life like a moth to a flame—to enslave and feed, burn and suppress. It has become our nature. But do not fret, you will need to eat, I know this. The hunt ... must return."

The flash of scarlet scales rippled across the mountainside as An Chéad unfurled his wings, tips caressing the silver-laced marble ceiling, and dropped into the valley below.

**The End of
A Dragon of the Veil,
Book One of the
Warriors of Spirit and Bone**

THE WARRIORS OF SPIRIT AND BONE SERIES

T hank you for reading the first book in this series of three novels. I was asked at the beginning of my writing career why I didn't choose fantasy. In truth, I spent much of my late teens and early twenties exploring the worlds of the Eternal Champion with Michael Moorcock, one of my early literary heroes, along with Ursula K. Le Guin, and it seemed the logical thing to do. However, I needed to cut my authorship teeth on something a little less layered, hence my sci-fi series, Weapons of Choice. However, I found there was so much within those books that I could take and develop further, and it was that temptation that led to the writing of 'A Dragon of the Veil'. So, yes, this story is, in a way, a reimagining of elements of the first book. The Weapons of Choice, for instance, change via nanobots—whereas in this novel, the weapons transform through the sigil of the Gods. And also, some of the characters, it could be argued, retain a few traits. However, the storyline is richer as fantasy should be, and the world within which they reside complex as humanity runs from their past and tries to survive what is coming. And there, after all, mechanical dragons!

Book 2 will follow Laoch and Sura as they arrive on Innealtóir, the Constructor's realm, in search of weapons to fight the coming invasion. In Brandsholm, the Houses and the Queen vie to keep the people on their side while preparing for the war to come, and the Unspoken and An Chéad become more prevalent. We learn more about the Schenterenta and their religion, as well as the Dragons of the Veils themselves.

We also, of course, meet the Constructors and their death-dealing, soul-eating ways. They have their own rich history, where arcanepunk meets steampunk in a clash of magic and steel that causes dread upon the realms they descend upon. You will get to understand their motivations, and as we move in to Book 3, just how far they will go to retrieve their escaped slaves and spirit-dolls. I hope you like your fantasy a little dark!

Book 3 has been planned to build towards a final battle — it is, after all, fantasy. But the twists and turns along the way are going to be real fun to write and those who've read my work before will know there is little guarantee who will come out on top — if anyone.

ABOUT THE AUTHOR

If you have read my previous books, you will know that most of my work has been in the action/military science fiction genre with the Weapons of Choice series. This is not your usual action series as it delves into aspects of the human condition and has a reputation of being surprisingly thoughtful in its emotional depth and social conscience.

However, I have also released the first in The Scorching science fiction/climate fiction series with two more books to follow. This is a daring take on the mystery thriller from a first-person point of view. It was a real joy to write, and though full of humour, it retains a dark undertone that will surprise. The next two books will also be standalone novels exploring the Drathken who arrive to help as the Earth dies, and humans who leave the planet to seek new worlds but have a dark, secret history of their own.

You can view my other books, sign up for a newsletter and receive a free novel related to the Weapons of Choice Series at my website below:

www.nicksnape.com

AUTHOR BIO

Nick Snape has been steeped in Science Fiction and Fantasy since his friends first dragged him from his schoolwork and stuck a book under his nose. Lost to the world of imagination, he became a teacher by accident, though he thoroughly enjoyed developing the joy of reading and writing in his pupils. Having retired after thirty years, he thought it was high time to practise what he preached.

BOOKS BY NICK SNAPE

Weapons of Choice Series
(Amazon Only)
Hostile Contact
Return Protocol
Zuri's War
Finn's War
Alien Rebirth
Invasive Species
Legion Earth
Nemesis Earth
Weapons of Choice Box Set Vol.1 Bks 1-4

The Scorching
Just Press Play

Warriors of Spirit and Bone
A Dragon of the Veil

ACKNOWLEDGEMENTS

As with all authors, this book and my other series would never have existed without the dedicated friends and family who were there by my side throughout the entire process. The least I can do is give them a mention for their patience with my obsession! My Beta readers, supporters and fiercest critics have been Pak, Paul and Mark. Amazing friends who put that aside to make sure whatever I put out there was something they wanted to read. I have also had great support from Martin Lejeune—an author who has given generously of their time during my trials and tribulations.

Very much appreciated, and the book would not be where it is without you all.

Julie, my wife, needs a special mention. Over the past years, she has kept me going, being there at every step through the dark and joyful times. I can't believe how lucky I am. Finally, the New Year and Pub Night Crews. Wouldn't be here without you.

Thank you all.

PRAISE FOR THE AUTHOR